West of Wawa is a funny, moving exploration of a surprising journey towards self-realization — and Benny, its pill-popping, wise-cracking heroine, is a treat. De Nikolits's book will ring true for anyone who has ever had even a moment of self doubt.
—*Chatelaine Magazine*

West of Wawa bursts with a sense of immediacy and freshness. Full of humour and tragi-comedic elements, in a style that is smooth and fast paced, *West of Wawa* is a delight to read. The characters, particularly Benny, are so idiosyncratic and unique that they prick at, then fully permeate the heart. I couldn't put it down.
—Danila Botha, author of *Got No Secrets*

Vibrant characters and intriguing plot make *West of Wawa* an engaging and rewarding read. Travelling from city to city, traumatized Benny tries to put the torn pieces of her soul back together. Readers will experience awe as they follow the main character's travelling therapy, which will surprise and then haunt them.
—Ava Homa, author of *Echoes from The Other Land*

Lisa de Nikolits is an amazing writer. She has a gift of being able to pull the reader into the story, and keep them turning the page. *West of Wawa* shows how a life can turn from emptiness to one of fulfillment. *West of Wawa* is a great read.
—Nikki Rosen, author of *In the Eye of Deception*

West of Wawa is a story readers can easily connect with. Benny flees the known for the unknown by adventuring north with her bags full of narcotics to help numb the pains of her past. On her travels she seeks anonymity, but can't help engaging with various characters that add to her personal trip of self-discovery, new friendships, and new found identity. Once you start the journey with Benny, you can't stop reading until you follow her through destruction to destiny!
—Amy Lance, Wondrous Women Worldwide

WEST of WAWA

A NOVEL
LISA DE NIKOLITS

Inanna poetry & fiction series

INANNA PUBLICATIONS AND EDUCATION INC.
TORONTO, CANADA

Canada Council **Conseil des Arts**
for the Arts du Canada

ONTARIO ARTS COUNCIL
CONSEIL DES ARTS DE L'ONTARIO

We gratefully acknowledge the support of the Canada Council for the Arts and the Ontario Arts Council for our publishing program.

We are also grateful for the support received from an Anonymous Fund at The Calgary Foundation.

This book is a work of fiction. Names, characters and incidents either are the product of the author's imagination or are used fictitiously, and any resemblance to actual persons living or dead or events is entirely coincidental.

Cover art: Bradford Dunlop
Cover design: Val Fullard

Library and Archives Canada Cataloguing in Publication

de Nikolits, Lisa, 1966-
    West of Wawa : a novel / Lisa de Nikolits.

(Inanna poetry & fiction series)
ISBN 978-1-926708-24-9

    I. Title. II. Series: Inanna poetry and fiction series

PS8607.E63W38 2011   C813'.6   C2011-905506-6

Printed and bound in Canada

Inanna Publications and Education Inc.
210 Founders College, York University
4700 Keele Street, Toronto, Ontario, Canada M3J 1P3
Telephone: (416) 736-5356 Fax: (416) 736-5765
Email: inanna@yorku.ca Website: www.yorku.ca/inanna

To Bradford, Snowflake and Mom

TULIP TOWN

AT THE PINNACLE OF THEIR DISGRACE, HER HUSBAND TURNED to Benny and said, "I just didn't think it would feel like this." He was referring not to the disgrace, but to their marriage, which Benny had thought was perfectly fine, thank you very much.

She bought the cheapest ticket she could find and flew from her hometown – Sydney, Australia to Hawaii, Los Angeles, Minneapolis, Vancouver, and finally to Toronto on consecutive flights. Benny traveled hardcore, fuelled by vicious intent.

The tulips were in full bloom when she landed and from this she took Canada to be a land of perpetual sunshine – not that she cared about the weather one way or the other. She needed a place to run and Canada worked just fine.

She dropped her bags off in a downtown furnished apartment and immediately set out to look for work. She had enough money to last a month.

Benny had the sinking feeling imminent failure was once again headed her way, that she might not pull this one off, despite her determination and her respectable résumé. Lack of success would just be too much to bear; she had to make this work. To make matters worse, her throat felt scratchy and raw and she felt exhausted, foggy. She wasn't sure if it was stress or a bug she'd picked up on the plane but she couldn't afford to get sick; she was her only asset. She dismissed jetlag, telling her body she was too busy to indulge in luxuries of that nature. Well-trained in matters naturopathic by her ex-husband, she found a health store and stocked up on Echinacea and garlic. Expensive, yes, but this was an emergency. She also asked the skinny New Ager behind the counter for codeine; the request was met with disapproval and directions to the nearest pharmacy.

Clutching her bag of naturopathic anti-cold remedies, Benny ventured into the vastness of a Shopper's Drug Mart and got the pharmacist to sell her a bottle of codeine headache meds, even though she had a good stash in her luggage. It never hurt to stockpile. She didn't pick up prescription sleeping meds or quality tranquillizers, she had enough of those to put an entire army into a state of soporific splendor, courtesy of her family doctor who was sympathetic to the Titanic disaster of Benny's life. Her doctor had made sure Benny could avoid having feelings of any kind for the rest of her natural life, if she so desired.

Benny picked up copies of *The Toronto Star, The Globe and Mail,* and all the free weeklies she could find and went back to the apartment. Her head was aching, her body screaming for a nap, but she scanned the newspapers with desperate certainty and found one post with potential:

> Trendy downtown boutique agency looking for a talented, creative multi-tasker: a graphic designer who can produce websites, brochures and flyers, act as personal assistant to the CEO, and assume duties of office manager if needed. Some overtime may be required.

Benny thought it unlikely any reputable high-end agency would be looking for this particular combination of person but she needed a job and couldn't afford to be choosy.

She summoned the fading reserves of her energy and picked up the phone, promising herself the reward of a lie-down on the sofa bed as soon as she was done. To her astonishment, given her recent lack of good fortune, the conversation was a success.

"Come and see me tomorrow morning," the creative director/publisher/agency owner said. He had a thick Scottish accent and Benny imagined a short, stocky, red-haired fellow with bristling whiskers and a countryside of freckles.

Her job prospects sorted, she crunched a couple of codeine and swallowed half a sleeping pill, then added a generous handful of Echinacea and garlic capsules to her regular nighttime meds, and washed it all down with a large glass of water. She allowed herself to collapse on the thin mattress that was a poor excuse for a bed and quickly fell asleep.

The next day, she arrived for the meeting feeling infinitely healthier than she had the previous day, and found herself greeted by a lanky John Cleese, mournful and watery-eyed. He shook her hand, introduced himself as Colin, CEO, and led her through the tiny reception area to a meticulous corner office. He waved her to sit and she sank down into a sagging sofa, wondering how she'd get back up with any kind of dignity.

Colin pulled up a chair and sat across from her, elbows on his knees. Benny, positioned two feet lower than him, had to stare up at a sharp angle and her head began to throb.

"I just canna understand it a' all." He shook his head. "I mean how hard it is for people to follow a few rules? Come in on time, on time, no later, on time. Read and follow the Employee Manual and get the job done?"

He reached for a thick, bound volume and waved it at Benny.

His eyelids were red-rimmed, his bulging pale blue eyes imploring. Benny noticed that his sparse ginger eyelashes sported a generous sprinkling of dandruff and she tried to look elsewhere, agreeing it shouldn't be too hard.

"And deadlines, what's with these people that they canna make a single deadline?" he asked. Then, to Benny's astonishment, he picked up a saxophone and played a gloomy moan. A few minutes later, he put it down carefully and read the entire Employee Manual to her.

"All clear then?" he asked her, two hours later.

"As a bell," she told him, thinking more like bats in the belfry, mate.

"Any questions?" he asked.

"I don't have a work visa," Benny blurted out. "But I do have the qualifications."

He waved a hand at her. "Na' worry 'bout that. Come with me."

He led her out into the general office area to meet a group of five who made up the rest of his staff.

"This is Benny, your new lead graphic designer," he said. "She works for me and you all report to her. Okay then?"

Benny stared at the motley gang scattered between pyramids of abandoned computer hard-drives and defunct monitors. Colin, confused by his staff, got their names mixed up and appeared to have no idea who did what. Benny felt panic rise in her throat and she tried to pretend she was amused instead of dismayed by the level of chaos.

Colin gave her a list: a plethora of flyers and posters, brochures and websites – all needing to be done yesterday. Benny sighed.

"But which one's needed first?" she asked the air in general.

"All of them now, all of them now," the mournful Scot said and he slouched back to his office, hands deep in the pockets of his shapeless oatmeal cardigan.

"Right then," Benny said to the assembled group. "First off, which one's my computer? And, second, who are you all, and what do you do? Come on, people, let's get cracking."

AN UNEXPECTED ANGEL PLAYS GUITAR

At the end of the first day, Colin's assistant came to find Benny. "Colin says I'm to start proceedings for your permanent residency," she said sounding bored, smoothing her blonde hair around her face, her pale eyes blank. Benny's heart leapt. It seemed her luck had finally changed. Okay, so, Colin's setup was the worst kind of disorganized nightmare but for her residency, so what, she could take anything.

She reached for her passport, always on hand. "Give me the forms," she said to the assistant. "I'll fill them in right now."

"I'm not a personal assistant," the girl said, picking at something under her nail. "Colin got confused after he hired me. I'm actually an illustrator, I studied at OCAD."

Benny had no idea what she was talking about.

The assistant smoothed back a strand of her hair. "Ontario College of Art and Design. Can I show you my work?" Her gaze was now fixed on Benny.

"Sure," Benny said, but Colin, eavesdropping, strode around the corner and reminded Benny of the section of the Employee Manual in which Employees were never supposed to attempt to acquire new duties without the consent and signed approval of the Agency Owner. He took the assistant by the arm and led her away, she protesting loudly it was all a mistake, that Colin had in fact hired her to be an illustrator and designer; that he'd got the two of them confused the day she and the real personal assistant started.

"Ask the designer why she can't design," the assistant said with a defeated whine. "Ask her. It's because she's the personal assistant, and I'm the designer."

"I'm no' interested in asking anybody anything," Benny heard Colin say, his Scottish accent thick as Mulligatawny soup. "I just want you all to do your jobs. Is that too much to ask? Is that really too much to ask?" He picked up his sax and mourned his life while the designer/assistant went back to her desk, hissing with anger and twirling a piece of her long hair furiously around one finger.

Benny worked late into that night, and all the nights following. She watched the automatic night lights rotate in the office blocks next to her and she watched the sun rise and set through her tinted window. In the weeks that followed, she watched assistants and designers come and go, production managers fail and leave, and all the while, Colin wandered in and out, lamenting his fate, his sax by his side. Benny survived by taking on more and more work herself. It was a far cry from the high profile agency she'd come from but it was her way into Canada and she told herself that as soon as she got her papers, she'd be free. Free to find the success she knew the universe owed her.

In the meantime, she was happy, sort of, in a grim, stoical way. The kind of happy that was more numb than anything.

Then, in May, she met Eli and everything changed.

It began as a glance, a mutually voyeuristic relationship, and it was perfect for what she could take, and what she could give.

The first time she saw him, it was midnight. She was just back from work, another "urgent" website, this one for a cheap Chinese takeout, the food photography so bad Benny couldn't imagine anybody ever wanting to eat there.

She was so tired it was an effort to undress. She glanced vaguely across at the building opposite and saw a boy – not really a boy, more like a youngish/younger man – on the balcony directly in line with her window. He was surprisingly close to her, playing a guitar. Watching him, Benny felt a surprising tug of hot lust. Before she could stop to consider how long it had been since she'd felt that way, he looked up, their eyes met and he stopped playing. His eyes were amber brown and she felt as if he was looking right inside her. He had a sensual mouth, with full lips and he gave her a half smile which she, frozen, did not return. They stared at each other for a moment, neither of them moving. Benny was the first to look away. When she looked up again the boy was once more bent over his guitar, his cigarette end glowing a pinprick of red.

Benny, without so much as a flicker of romance since the demise of her marriage, was shocked by the intensity of her reaction, and she fled to the cool sanctuary of her tiny green bathroom to gather her scattered emotions.

She felt weird, alarmed and confused by the flash of intimacy and long-forgotten desire. And what would she do with the boy/man if she got him? Even if he fell into her lap, this juicy fuzzy peach of a young man, what would she do then? She'd married Kenny for a reason; he was safe, although of course he hadn't been, not really, not in the end.

She ran a hot bath and climbed in, shaken by a recollection buried so deep that she'd almost forgotten it was there. She had been young, thirteen, and the late evening sun was hot on her skin, while the boy, a rough lad, a stable hand with strange eyes and alcohol breath, pulled her close and slipped his hand inside her shirt, his tongue insistent against hers. She was wearing her training bra, the one with pretty blue daisies patterned onto the small cups and she thought he'd laugh if he saw it. She'd felt his erection digging at her through his trousers, hot and hard, and she was aroused by the feeling of excitement, and danger.

They'd been meeting at the yard every evening for a week, the intensity of their touch escalating daily. Benny, crushing big time on the boy, thought he was how a drug would feel; she could think of nothing else at school, and she couldn't wait to see him.

But then he'd gone too far too fast and he'd frightened her, although it wasn't him that alarmed her so much as her own desire.

"No," she'd said, when he tried to unbutton her shirt. "No, Dad'll have you for brekkie. He'll kill you."

The boy laughed. "As if I care," he said. "I could take your dad on any day."

Benny pulled away, straightening her shirt. "You shouldn't have said that," she'd replied and she'd left the barn without a backward glance, running, Dad her excuse.

The boy was fired soon after and Benny was sure Dad watched for her reaction when he told her, but she didn't move a muscle, nary a twitch.

And that was the only time she'd felt this kind of hot longing lick her groin – shaken by her brush with the boy, she hadn't let her passion see the light of day again, and certainly never with her now ex-husband, Kenny. Her reaction to the boy on the balcony had her completely unnerved.

Several weeks passed and it seemed she didn't have to worry about what she'd do with the boy if she met him, because the most contact she ever got was him watching her, watching him. And watch each other they did; he could be relied on to be on his balcony, no matter what time she staggered in, home from one more day of Colin's oddities and nearly impossible demands.

One night, after a particularly grueling day, Benny dragged her bed across the room of the tiny apartment so it was under the window and closer to the boy. He returned the gesture by tipping his hat, a Burberry fedora, and releasing an explosion of dreadlocks.

While Benny came to rely on his presence, she pretended careless disregard of his male bird struts. She avoided his gaze, peering into her fridge instead and searching her cupboards. Or she lay on her bed and stared at the ceiling. She kept her window closed. She could have opened it and called out to him but that would have destroyed it because after all, what did she have to offer?

"I'm broken," she said to the ceiling, as if he could hear her instead. "I'm too damaged. I have to work harder, build a new life, be stronger. Get back to the top of my game, go back and show them all. Go back high on fame and fortune, put them all to shame."

What this success would be, she had no idea. But she was confident that if she did the work, her reward would follow. All she had to do was work harder.

"But this loneliness hurts like a knife in my heart," she said out loud, sure he'd know what she was saying, even if he couldn't hear her. "It's nearly unbearable, being so alone."

Outside the boy, playing songs she couldn't hear, stood silent guard.

THE FIRST KISS

One Sunday in the middle of June, Benny was home, Colin-free and restless. She was exhausted, wide-awake. She pondered her options: buy a book, see a movie, read a newspaper, have a nap. Nothing appealed. She pulled on a pair of jeans and dragged herself outside, thinking she'd go for a walk at least. She turned into the small park next to her building. She walked down the asphalt path, spotted the familiar Burberry hat and stopped. Even from the back, she knew it was him. She was afraid to continue walking down the path. What if he recognized her? What if he didn't? She was about to walk away when he turned around. He looked at her for a moment, then got up and sauntered toward her.

"Hey," he said, and his voice was easy and kind. "You're the girl from the seventh floor."

She nodded. "You're the boy from the balcony," she said. There was a quaver to her voice she hoped he didn't hear. She tried to smile but ended up folding her arms quickly across her chest instead. Then she felt foolish and dangled her hands at her side, trying to look relaxed, casual.

"Ah, now, I just turned 21 yesterday," he said, and she was right; he was a juicy Georgia peach – freckle-faced and grinning, with a scraggly, sandy goatee.

"So, listen," he said, "you want to come celebrate that with me? How about we go and get a coffee or something?"

"Sounds good. I'm 26, by the way," Benny said, lying quickly about her age as she always did. None of her felt casual at all – her heart was pumping like a giant frog in her throat. Up close, he was even sexier than she'd thought and a part of her wanted to wrestle him to the ground and kiss his beautiful mouth, taste his tongue. She felt like a complete idiot for feeling this way. She had difficulty even looking at him so she stared at the ground and scuffed at the grass, wondering where all this desire had come from.

"Let's go to Yorkville," the boy said, saving the moment from awkwardness. We'll find a Starbucks. So, could you hear me playing guitar for you? By the way, I'm Eli."

"I'm Benny," she said, walking next to him, her hands shoved in her pockets. "No, I couldn't hear anything you were playing. What kind of music?"

Eli shrugged. "Well, I wasn't sure what you liked, so I played a lot of stuff. But what a waste, man, since you couldn't hear it anyway." He was long and lanky and wearing a woolly shirt, a whimsical combination of homemade and designer.

"It wasn't a waste," Benny said. "It was great to see you even if I couldn't hear you. I liked seeing you there."

He laughed, happy. "I thought one day you'd open your window and talk to me but you never did. You work some crazy hours, you know that? What do you do?"

"What I'm doing," she said, "is time, until I get my papers."

"And then?"

"Who knows? I don't. I'm just making my way to that. It'll take about a year, I think. Maybe less."

"Where in Australia are you from? Cool accent."

"Sydney."

"And why are you here, so far away?"

"Because it's so far away," Benny said. "And what do you do, Eli?"

"I blow glass. Down at the Harbourfront Centre. They have a course there and I'm doing that. I'm also learning jewelry making. I'm lucky I guess, my dad's stinking rich, so I don't have to do much of anything."

"What does he want you do to?" Benny was curious. "Most fathers want their sons to follow in their footsteps, don't they?"

"He knows I cannot be controlled," Eli grinned, and he seemed proud of the fact. "He's just glad I'm not into heavy drugs anymore; he's just glad about that. So am I. I nearly fried my brain. Not healthy, man. Now I only smoke pot, that's it."

They reached Starbucks and Eli held the door open for Benny.

Eli smiled when she ordered a venti green tea.

"I figured you for a health nut, straight-up tea, no sugar, no milk, no nothing. Me, I like the works." He got a caramel latte with whipped cream.

They sat outside in the sun, chatting about the philosophies of entrepreneurs like his father and their ethos of never-ending greed.

"I like working hard," Benny said. "I work because I like working, not because I like the money."

"You work to escape life," Eli said, latte foam on his upper lip. "You work like I took drugs, to numb out."

"I love the creative process," Benny objected. She was alarmed by his observation; surely that wasn't the truth?

He laughed. "Yeah, right, like on Mister Chow Chow's website for bad takeout." She'd told him about her various clients.

"I don't care what I'm working on," she said. "I'm not an elitist designer." She pointed to a few street posters. "Even those needed to be designed. Design's everywhere. I go where I'm needed." What she didn't say was that art and design were worlds apart and art was the only thing that mattered to her; design was nothing more than bread and butter. And who was he anyway to say she was escaping anything.

Eli shrugged. "Hey, I heard *The Exorcist's* playing at a theatre downtown, a one-off. You wanna go and see it?"

"I've never seen it," Benny admitted.

Eli jumped to his feet. "Well, then you must! Come on. Hey, you'd like my sister. She's studying fashion design out in B.C. She made this shirt for me, cool eh? It's a mix of alpaca and tie-dyed cheesecloth; everything she does is totally organic. I might go and join her in Vancouver when I finish my glass course."

"When's that?" They weren't even into an hour of their real-time relationship and Benny felt a tug at the thought of him leaving. There it was again, that inexplicable longing for him. She felt impatient with herself, angry even, but she couldn't seem to stop herself from wanting him.

"'Bout six months, give or take," Eli was airy. "So, listen, our differences in age ... does that bug you?"

"No," Benny said, but she felt like she was lying because she had no idea what this thing was between them, so how could she know what impact the difference in their ages would be?

Eli stopped and peered into the window of a cheap fashion accessory store. "I have to tell you though, I kinda have a girlfriend."

"Kinda?" Benny was relieved. She wanted him, she did, but in amounts she could handle. A girlfriend made him safe – ultimately inaccessible.

"Yeah." He swung his head forward and captured his dreads in his hat. "She's Russian. She's crazy, man. She tells me she's pregnant, so I get her this huge ring, big expensive freakin' thing. My dad nearly had a heart attack when he saw how much I spent." He laughed. "We're all set to get married then she loses the baby. Ah, well. Now I don't believe her when she says she's on the pill; I use condoms all the way. Once bitten, twice shy."

"Why do you stay with her?" Benny asked, wondering what happened to the ring.

He shrugged. "Who knows? Too hard to leave, I guess. Hey, you don't mind, do you? About her, I mean? It doesn't mean there can't be meaning between me and you."

"I don't mind at all," Benny said. "And I like that you told me upfront. That's cool. What I don't like, what I cannot stand, is when people hide things. Like when you're together for years and next thing this huge elephant comes forcing its way out of the closet and that's what I don't like. That's what makes me crazy."

Eli looked at her curiously and held up his hands. "No elephants in my closet," he said, his smile wide, his eyes kind. "Peace out. Let's smoke some pot before we see the movie, okay?"

"Okay," Benny said, and Eli led her down an alleyway. He rolled a joint and was about to light it when he stopped.

"Hang on," he said. "What's the matter with me? It's only like I've been dreaming about this very moment for weeks. What kind of a dumbwit moron am I?"

He put his hands on her shoulders and kissed her softly, his straggly facial hair brushing her upper lip lightly. His tongue was gentle and he tasted sweet. She leaned into his narrow chest, and put her arms around his waist.

They kissed for a long time in the cool shade of the alleyway and Benny liked the way his T-shirt smelled fresh and clean.

They drew apart and Eli fired up the joint, inhaling deeply. Benny took a cautious hit and was immediately awash in surreality. She had no idea what pot did to other people, but she never got the giggles or the munchies, she never got silly. She always felt as if she'd taken a sidestep into an alternate reality, one just outside of normal, with a strong twist of weird. She learned to smoke pot in art school in order to blend, deliver the expected; she smoked pot like she did her homework – as part of her curriculum.

They went to see *The Exorcist* and Eli held her hand and fed her Reese's Pieces. Stoned, and blissed-out by the nearness of Eli, Benny couldn't concentrate on the movie. Eli walked her home in the electric blue light of the evening and kept her entertained with boyish antics.

"You want to come and hear me play guitar for real?" he asked as they neared their apartment buildings. She looked at her watch.

"Can't now," she said, "I've got to get ready for work tomorrow. But we'll hook up again, yeah?"

He seemed disappointed, then relieved. "Well, I'm supposed to be meeting Krysta anyway," he said. "Krysta Alexandra Baryshnikov, just like the dancer. Isn't that the coolest name?"

Benny agreed it was lovely and quickly changed the subject. She, of all people wasn't about to discuss the coolness of names.

Eli walked her to her apartment door and kissed her again. He was taller than her by a head and she hugged him, thinking that touch could be the greatest gift after a span of dry loneliness.

"So, listen," he said. "When you get home tomorrow night, come to the window. Either wave me over or shake your head if you're too tired and don't want company, okay?"

"Perfect. Have fun with your Russian princess," she said and he kissed her neck.

"I will. She thinks she's genuine Russian royalty. You know, I'm so glad me and you hooked up. I thought we were never going to get to meet, but fate intervened." He turned to go. "Hey, you remember that hallway in *The Shining*, where the twins appear at the end on their bikes? Well, this corridor is like that, man, look. It's totally creepy. Look at this wallpaper, it's like from the '50s."

"They're good to me here." Benny said defensively and he laughed.

"It's like a retirement home, man," he said, "but whatever works for you." He strolled wolfishly down the passage and Benny, looking around the hallway, realized for the first time that the furnishings were old-fashioned – brocade-paneled walls, faded paisley-regal carpets. She also realized she didn't care. It was home as much as anywhere could be.

She watched him leave and snuck back out of the apartment. She went down the street to the seedy Internet café filled with gamers and gangsters and logged on to her email. Yeah, there it was, just like always, a message from her sister.

AT HOME ACROSS THE WORLD

Reliable old Shandra. Not like unreliable old Benny. But somewhere along the way, life had just been easier for Shandra, that's all there was to it. Starting of course with her name. Shandra. Nice, feminine, with a touch of a baroque swirl. Not fair at all. And then there was Shandra's softly rounded femininity. Again, not fair. Shandra was a sensual girl – she brought to mind richly-decorated birthday cakes, resplendent with cream and sugar. Shandra was fresh and luscious and Benny was confident that Shandra would mother a whole soccer team of babies, given time. Meanwhile, Benny considered herself the opposite of her sister: she was a small twig of a girl – dry, brittle, barren. Dusty.

Shandra, two years older than Benny, wanted nothing more than to have babies and cocoon them in her love, wrap them in her soft sugar embrace. She'd been married for four months and was trying hard to conceive but no luck.

It had been a tough pill for Benny to swallow, having to be Shandra's matron of honour when her own marriage was failing so spectacularly and so publicly. But Benny was stoic. She'd swallowed her pride and a handful of Valiums and stood by Shandra's side while she'd said "I do" – Benny, wearing the lavender meringue dress she ordinarily wouldn't be seen dead in.

The email message from Shandra was the usual:

> Mum's fine, her business is doing good. Dad's okay but his leg's acting up. I'm ovulating again but Jeremy's away on a business conference, go figure. Sometimes I wonder if he plans it. Hope you're doing good there, and it's not too cold. Why you must be in such a cold part of the world is beyond me. Love you lots and lots of smartie pops. Shandy.

Benny never understood why Shandra chose to butcher her name to Shandy. Shay was okay, Shandy unacceptable.

"A shandy's a poor man's drink. Lemonade and beer," she told Shay but Shay just laughed and shrugged her creamy shoulders.

Benny read the email and looked around the darkened café at the boys shouting and swearing. Regardless of day or time, it seemed the same crew habituated the sticky neon-lit darkness, all shouting the same profanities, playing the same computer games.

She wondered if she should tell Shandra about Eli but thought not. She'd wanted to mention him before, her boy who guarded her from his window, standing between her and the loneliness that was too much to bear.

She knew Shandra wouldn't judge. Shandra was her biggest fan, the most loyal of her supporters, the one who cried all the tears Benny couldn't. And it was she who had stalwartly insisted to the world that Benny be called Benny if that's what Benny wanted.

Sisters.

In the end, Benny sent her the standard note:

Hey Shay, sorry about Dad's leg. Is he off work? It's hot here and summer only started! I'm fine, waiting for my papers, working hard, so what else is new!? My job sucks but hey, having my papers will be worth it. Why? I dunno. Just because. I miss you. I'm sorry Jerry's missing the egg appearance. You and the Egg go and visit him maybe? Love you too.

They didn't talk about it anymore, Benny's fall from grace.

She signed off and walked back to her tiny apartment. Her home was sparse as a nun's cell – pristine and blanched and Benny worked hard to keep it that way. Not a single knickknack, and certainly nothing to remind her of who she'd been.

Benny, a poor girl graduate of an expensive all-girls' school, liked her world neat and tidy, her edges sharp.

She looked over at Eli's window. It was dark.

Time for a shower. The tiny soapbox-green washroom tried for art deco, missed by a mile. After her shower, Benny got into her nightie, an old-fashioned affair with an embroidered lace neckline. She'd found it at a store near the St Lawrence Market and loved it for its purity, its virgin crispness. She climbed into bed and flicked on the TV. She lay there, cosy, thinking about Eli, how he smelt so clean, with a spicy pot aroma like the faintest cologne, and how his dreadlocks felt so soft to the touch. She thought about his strong beaked nose, his high cheekbones with a smattering of freckles and his amber brown eyes. She thought about the Russian princess and probed for jealousy, finding only a wary dislike for the girl's power.

She took her sleeping pills, crunched on two codeine, and waited. She finally fell asleep, woke early, and went to work.

And so the weeks passed. Benny, waiting for her permanent residency, saw Eli regularly and somehow managed to endure Colin's constant depressive lows. She endured his rigid working conditions and his increasingly bizarre Employee Manual restrictions. A couple of her colleagues tried to befriend her but they backed off in the face of her resolute work ethic, preferring to gather on patios to talk about her, while she worked all hours of the day and night on flyers and websites that no one would ever see.

"Take a break. Come for a drink with us this evening," one of the copy editors had urged. "We're going to a new club, it'll be wild. Let your hair down for once."

"Ta, thanks anyway, mate, I'm good," Benny had said. She wondered if she was afraid she'd drink like she worked – to excess. She drank a lot with Eli but he never seemed to notice or mind, given that his own inebriation levels were high.

Benny knew that her ex-husband, Kenny, wouldn't approve of her drinking. He was a firm believer in the ethos "your body is your temple," and he only ate food of organic and "high vibratory content," and drank organic juices, water or herbal teas.

Benny had her own reasons for buying into his elitist nutritional phi-losophies and the non-drinking aspect of it had worked – up until now. But then again a whole lot of things had worked up until now. She was disconcerted to find she liked the buzz alcohol gave her, she liked the warmth as it hit her belly, the harsh rawness of drinking neat Southern Comfort – Eli's favourite beverage – although he mixed his with a variety of different sodas. She couldn't fault anything Eli did.

COTTAGE COUNTRY; FIREFLIES DANCE NEAR

At the height of summer, Eli came to collect her from work in a big rented truck. It was the Civic holiday of the August long weekend, and he had the whole trip planned.

He'd gathered her toothbrush, her nightie, and a change of clothes, and he'd brought along his guitar. He took her up north with his shy grin and the air of child about to share a precious gift, stopping at Wasaga beach where they waded into the pebble-lined waters and floated side by side. The sky was bright blue and Benny watched a single cloud intersect with a child's lost balloon. Yellow balloon. Blue sky. Hot sand. Being so in love that her stomach ached and it was hard to breathe.

She had given up trying to understand her feelings for Eli. She craved him and even when she was near him, a claw of wanting something more clutched at her heart. But what that something was, she couldn't say.

She photographed him constantly, insatiable in her desire to hold onto him, and at night in the motel, she sat him naked in an easy chair, his dreadlocks falling across his eye, one eyebrow raised in that quizzical grin.

"These won't go on the Internet, will they?" he said, covering his balls.

"No worries, for my viewing pleasure only."

Eli liked being photographed. He lay down on his stomach, his head turned to one side. "I find it arousing," he said, "being photographed by you."

The next day they went back to the beach and reclined in long chairs, watching the lazy hazy day glide by. Eli napped, his expressions changing without guile like a baby. Benny wondered if this was what obsession felt like.

"What does Ms. Nostrovia think of you being here with me like this?" she asked, sunburned and happy.

He laughed. "You mean Princess Krysta. Don't you worry about her. Hey, I want to give you something." He sat up, tugged a large silver ring off his little finger and handed it to her. "Most likely be way too big for you but I want you to have it."

For a moment Benny thought of the diamond ring he'd given the Russian princess and she felt slightly resentful but then a wave of joy washed over her. He was giving her something far more meaningful; he was giving her a ring she'd seen him wear since the day they met – he was giving her a part of himself. She could hardly speak. She took the ring and threaded it through her necklace.

"Cool," she said, "thanks."

Sunday night they stayed in a log cabin and toasted marshmallows over a fire pit. Fireflies danced and Benny knew he could never leave her.

HE LEAVES WITH RUSSIAN ROYALTY

Back in Toronto, the time passed to October and the trees turned fiery red and vivid gold. When she wasn't working or sleeping, Benny hung out with Eli who remained content to see if he'd be given the welcoming nod by Benny; if not, he headed out to Krysta.

On the nights Benny wanted to see him, she waved. He came to get her and they went back to his bachelor apartment where he played guitar and they smoked joints and drank Southern Comfort. They sat on twisted rag rugs on the floor, with incense burning, candles everywhere and lava lamps bubbling up and down. The walls were covered with posters of Jimi Hendrix, Che Guevara, and Bob Marley. And all the while, Benny watched Eli with a kind of wonder. Sometimes she'd stay the night, set her alarm clock for early, and go back across for a shower. Go back to change her clothes and her persona.

With Eli, she was on holiday. Holiday from herself. She could be the girl she'd never been, in a place where life was a party and she was with the cool guy. He was gentle with her, made love to her sweetly with his generous cock, and that was Eli: generous, warm and kind.

And they talked for hours, Benny listening.

"I never meant to be a dealer," he said, stroking her hair. "It was just that I knew people who knew people and I always had what anyone needed and it seemed so … impolite I guess you could say, to tell somebody no when everybody knew I was connected. Anyways, so then I fully got into it. I was making a shitload of money and I got to party twenty-four-seven. But then I did too many drugs myself, I dyed my hair bright pink and had more piercings than the human body should take. Hang on a second, I need a refreshing beverage. Can I get you anything?"

She loved the way he talked. It was like poetry. "No, thanks," she said, "I'm good."

"So, what then?" she asked when he came back.

"Where was I?"

"You were pierced beyond human recognition and drugged out of your skull."

He laughed. "Yeah, well, that's a fact, Jack. My dad put me into rehab for like three months and they cleaned me up. Got myself all straightened out, got this nice little apartment and a new career in glass. Now, I won't do more than pot and alcohol and cigarettes. No acid, no meth, no nothing."

She pulled him down and stroked his chest. "Do you think lesser of me for doing that stuff?" he asked and she was surprised that he seemed to want her approval.

She shook her head. "No way. I'm just glad you got out alive. But are you serious about going to British Columbia, come New Year?" She couldn't help it, she had to ask.

She was hoping he'd changed his mind.

At the mention of B.C., his face lit up like a Christmas tree while her spirit went cold and dark, extinguished.

He sat up, talking excitedly about the spirit of the west and the life that awaited him. And about Krysta, who was going with him – of course she was, the bitch.

"Don't be sad," he said, noticing her mood. "Maybe you'll come out and see me? And anytime you feel sad, think about our weekend up north, okay? That was incredible. It was one of the best times of my life."

She realized their trip to the country had been his farewell gift to her and she was grateful they'd gone, although she'd gladly have foregone the trip if it meant he stayed instead.

On the other side of the world, Shandra was three months pregnant. She had gone to see Jeremy like Benny had suggested and it had worked. Benny felt guilty for missing out on the whole miracle of her sister's gestation but she couldn't bring herself to go back to Australia, not even with Christmas rolling round. Colin had said he'd give her ten days off to go home if she wanted but she couldn't go back, and she lied to her family, saying she had to work.

She made sure her apartment remained untouched by the festive season and she worked even harder, with her self-medication levels rising as Eli's departure date neared.

"Come watch me blow some glass," he said, during his final week in Toronto. They went down to the Harbourfront Centre where Benny met his teacher who was also from B.C. The teacher made glass crustaceans and mollusks and layered them like ancient volcanic rock.

"This guy's got real talent," the teacher told Benny who was too choked up to talk. All she could think was that she was losing him.

She watched him work the liquid glass, twisting, pulling, and turning it like taffy.

The glass cooled, and he packed up his apartment and got ready for the drive across the country. Benny bought him a gift – *The Places You Will Go*, by Dr. Seuss, and he loved it, turning the pages back and forth and exclaiming in delight.

"You totally get me," he said, "the bedrock me, man. You get the bone-bed of who I am, man."

Benny beamed. That he felt understood was of far more importance to her than being understood in return. She'd been careful to keep so much of herself hidden from him that she knew there was no way he could have any real inkling of who she was—and she liked it that way.

"So, anyways, Krysta says she's pregnant again. Who knows, man, maybe she's lying but I did get kind of slack about the condoms. Too much bother. And a kid, that's a rush. It'd be good for me, make me grow up. Be a man, take responsibility. I gotta tell you Benny, I cannot wait to get my first taste of that most excellent weed they have out there. I was born to live in B.C., I'm telling you now."

Benny, dismayed by Krysta's wiles, was silent.

Eli hugged her. "Thanks for the book. Thanks for being so totally you, man. Now, hey, you know I don't do Twitting or Arsebook or any of that crap but I'll always think about you, okay? This was truly one of my greatest adventures, being with you."

She was glad she rated as an adventure. "Well, here's my email address anyway," she said, handing him a piece of paper. "You never know, you might want to drop me a line or send me a picture of your kid."

He pocketed the paper and pulled out a CD, *Porno for Pyros*. "And this is for you," he said. "I made you a copy. I know you liked it."

"I wish you'd made me a necklace," she said. "A glass necklace. I thought maybe you would." It was as close as she could come to telling him she loved him.

"I'll send you one from B.C.," he offered.

"Maybe I won't be here," she said. "Maybe I'll be gone."

He shrugged and leaned down to kiss her. She kissed him politely, holding back her passion. He stepped away, raised a hand goodbye, and walked away.

Benny lay on the bed and listened to him leaving her – the door closing, his footsteps padding down the hallway, the ping of the elevator, the metal whoosh of the doors closing, the whine of descent.

She went to work the next morning, overwhelmed by loss and longing. In the days that followed, she marked her desk calendar with thick black crosses. She lay in bed on New Year's day, watching Eli's window, willing him to reappear.

SHE BEGINS TO PLAN

Benny discovered she liked the wintry cold and she went for long walks with her hands jammed deep into the vintage fur coat she picked up at a Goodwill. She avoided talking to anybody unless she had to. She went to movies late at night, bundled up like a cocoon. Waiting. Waiting for spring, waiting for her papers, waiting to leave. Waiting. Working. And waiting. Waiting for Eli to come back. She missed him. His companionship, his kindness, the way he smelled, and the way he talked. His enthusiasm for the smallest things. She missed holding his hand. He'd been her only friend, her lover, her unexpected Prince Charming.

She doubled up on her sleeping meds and wondered if the Russian princess had held onto the baby. For the first time, she hated the Russian princess. She looked out her window at the falling snow, at the beautiful thick flakes swirling in the cone of the streetlight. It was an alien world, a quiet world, and she was so alone.

She flicked the TV on in her stark apartment, turned it off, flicked it on again. She thought she'd known pain when her world fell apart but not even that hurt like this. Her time with Eli had left ghosts behind. Ghosts to join the other mocking ghosts, and there were too many of them. She'd come to Canada to leave her ghosts behind, but she'd mistakenly gathered more. Benny hated the ghosts. She wished she could hit them, punch them, and fly at them in anger. She wished she could cry and release the abscess of pain, but it was pushed down too deep. She crunched codeine and Valium and washed them down with Southern Comfort, somehow, getting through the empty corridors of her days.

She was waiting to run as fast as she could, as far as she could and who knew, maybe she'd find herself in B.C. in the arms of Eli – "How did that happen?" she would say.

Slushy gray February arrived and with it came her permanent residency. Colin drove her across the Peace Bridge to Buffalo to get signed in. She felt bad about wanting to leave him but she'd been with him ten months, way longer than most.

"So, I take it you'll be going then," he said mournfully on their way back to the office.

"Ah, Colin," she said, smothered by guilt and the blast of hot air from the car heater, "don't say that. You're not easy, you know, and no one could have worked harder for you, or produced more work. You'll have to hire five people to replace me. You kept promising I could hire people to help, then I come in and you've gone and hired a whole bunch who are hopeless and I've got to fire them. You constantly threatened to fire me unless I made your impossible deadlines and then, after I worked my arse off, you'd change the deadline. You changed direction more often than I change my underwear. It's an impossible situation and you couldn't blame me for leaving, if I did."

"Aye, you're so very right lassie. And for that, I'm most abjectly, apologetically, and sorrowfully sorry," Colin said, hunching over the steering wheel and hanging on with both hands. "I really am sorry, Benny, trust me. You're the best designer I've ever had. In future, when I say the decisions are up to you, believe me, they are, scout's honour." He tapped two fingers to his forehead.

Benny laughed. "Colin, what you know about scouts couldn't fill a teaspoon but okay, we'll try for a bit longer."

He promised her a salary increase and a better title with the word "Senior" in it. He told her she could move her desk to face the direction she wanted and that he was sorry he hadn't let her do it before. In fact, he said, she could even buy a new desk. He told her not to come in at all that weekend. He said everything was going to be different and it was, for about a day.

Despite the hardship, Benny stayed with Colin. Mainly, selfishly, because she wasn't ready to leave. She began to plan her journey, figuring she could afford to do a three-month trip, starting in June.

And, come the second week of June she was ready. Newfoundland to Vancouver – she was going to travel the weather map of Canada. She wasn't sure if it was the lure of Eli (from whom she had heard exactly nothing) or simply the need to run as fast and as far as she could.

"My door's always open for you, girlie," Colin said, his watery eyes more bloodhound than ever, his tired suit loose on his melancholy frame. "You ever want to come back, you just tell me."

Benny hoped to never see that cluttered graveyard of old computers again.

She walked out with nothing but a jar of old face cream that Colin gave her as a farewell gift; he'd been given it as a sample at a trade show. Benny passed it on to a homeless man who was sitting on the sidewalk.

"Moisturize," she said. "For God's sake, don't eat it."

She grabbed her backpack and her camera bag from her apartment and that was it. There wasn't much to leave behind. She stood for a moment and closed her eyes. The hot sunshine had resurrected the gritty carpet deodorizer and Benny, inhaling the chemical potpourri, thought her heart must weigh at least a thousand pounds.

LEAVING ON A JET PLANE

And so it came to be that Benny sat waiting for the St John's-bound plane to take her to the easternmost point of her journey, from which she would begin her travels into the great western unknown.

Benny was prepared for any eventuality. Her hair was freshly dyed jet black. She was manicured, pedicured, exfoliated, and medicated, confident she could take on whatever lay ahead. Sitting at Pearson International, she pictured her meticulously-packed traveling pharmacy and felt comforted—she wasn't going on this trip alone. She had a carefully accumulated wealth of guaranteed serenity: bottles of bitter blue prescription sleeping pills, tangy orange Xanax, and tiny crumbly bricks of white lorazepam, as well as a reassuringly solid stash of codeine.

Benny was a judicious daytime dabbler of tranquilizers, dissolving half a tab under her tongue whenever the office shenanigans became too much for her to bear, or she felt the uncontrollable urge to tell Colin to take his job and shove it. Xanax and Valium, kindly companions that made the blows of life feel a little softer.

She had an hour to wait before her plane left. She was always early, even when she tried so hard to be late. The A.C. was on super max and Benny was glad for the warmth of her fleecy hoodie. She'd even planned a new travel wardrobe, buying a hoodie with the front emblazoned "Come to Papa" in Goth rock script; splurging on four-inch black leather boots, and accessorizing it all with a careful selection of biker-style silver jewelry.

And, of course, she had Eli's ring, held safely in place by not one but two silver wedding bands even though she'd paid a small fortune to have his ring correctly resized.

She'd had fun shopping for the trip and she wondered what Shay would say about her new style. Maybe she'd say Benny finally looked like an artist. Benny had always worn black but it had been a faceless uniform. This street-cred, mean-girl look came from a place of her anger and it felt good.

Her flight eventually boarded. They were scheduled to leave at 7:30 p.m. and arrive at midnight. Benny stared out the window and thought about Eli. Then she wondered whether she should she take a Xanax and why was she doing this trip anyway? Which was exactly what Shay had asked.

"I'm worried, Bee," Shay had written. "I'm worried about you. You seem lost, if you ask me. You don't need to find yourself out there, you know who you are."

"I know I know who I am," Benny wrote back. "I'll be safe, don't worry. I don't know, Shay, I've just got to do this."

She'd never told Shandra about Eli. He was her secret, her private self-gift.

Shandra had given birth to a baby boy – Harold Arthur – named after his two granddads. Benny thought they'd have learned their lesson after her naming disaster but apparently not. Little Harry was two weeks old, a bundle of mewling energy. He was a tiny brown berry with a shock of black hair. Shandra emailed Benny, typing with one hand, expressing milk with the other.

Benny's random thoughts were interrupted by the dramatic and late boarding of her doppelgänger, who was draped in black cashmere and clutching a Mac Air.

Benny suddenly felt horribly invisible to the world. What had she done by leaving her desk? She had no home, no sense of belonging, no computer to call her own.

She had come to Canada with a clear goal: get a job, work hard, succeed. Sabbaticals were excuses for losers who couldn't hack it, so what did that make her now? She reminded herself that she was going to claw her way to the spotlight – to that moment of glory she knew to be hers. She would stand on the podium with the whole world cheering. She just had to figure out the specifics.

She sighed and adjusted her seatbelt while the woman next to her listened carefully to the safety instructions. Benny shrugged, as if you'd really remember all that if the plane went down. She wished she could sleep and thought about having a tiny bottle of Southern Comfort and a codeine pill to generate a nap, but it was too much effort to retrieve them from the luggage under the seat in front of her.

She wondered what Newfoundland would bring. She'd thought the plane would be empty on a Friday night but it was jam-packed. The air was long-dead and Benny felt her sinuses closing in. They waited on the runway while Benny kept an eye on her look-alike who fell asleep with her mouth open. A baby was crying with full force and the noise was piercing and unspeakable. Benny, dehydrating by the moment, felt her skin turning to parchment.

They finally cabin-checked and cross-checked and the flight to St John's prepared for takeoff. Benny wondered whether it would be impolite to offer crushed codeine to the mother of the distressed howling baby.

The two teenage girls behind Benny were, *like,* on their first flight, *like,* ever.

"Look at the cars. They're getting tiny, like ants and the houses are like so small. Do you think people are watching us? I bet they're like watching us. Where's the CN Tower? Look, there's the moon."

Twenty minutes into the flight, the plane began to bob and jerk in an unusual way. Benny began to pray to any and all possible gods.

The woman in the middle seat craned to look out Benny's window, her breath hot on Benny's shoulder. Benny wished the woman had her own window. She could smell the woman's Big Red cinnamon breath and she willed herself to stare directly ahead.

Hell, the flight was hell.

She closed her eyes and traced the planned route of her journey. Except for the Newfoundland and Halifax flights, and a possible train up to Churchill, the entire trip would be on Greyhound buses.

Benny had tapped into the bus netherworld one work-free May weekend a couple of weeks before she and Eli had met in the park. The trip had been Colin's idea after he'd nearly driven her batty enough to quit.

"Sorry, lassie," he'd said. "A wee bit frayed around the edges I am. Give yourself a holiday. Go to Montreal for the weekend. Take the bus, it's cheaper. Tell you what, I'll even pay half as a bonus."

Benny followed Colin's advice and took the trip for no real reason except for the satisfaction of forcing the dour penny-pincher to make good on his offer. To her surprise, she bonded instantly with bus travel and the freedom it gave.

While the bus droned through the countryside, Benny had day-dreamed about tearing Eli's clothes off. In her fantasy they were bride and groom and he wore a suit held together by press studs. She tore it off and straddled him in her rose-cloud wedding dress – she, a creamy bloom perched astride his thick upstanding stamen. She had blushed at the clichéd romance novel nature of her desires and broke out in a sweat at the memory of her real wedding night. She quickly chose to leave thoughts of that fumbling night behind and returned to her fairytale love story with Prince Charming, the standup stamen and the press-stud suit. She'd never told Eli about her fantasy but she did savour the memory of that bus ride – that zen out-of-time, out-of-touch sense of isolation. And Montreal had been great. She'd taken a city tour, dined in the historic district, and allowed herself the extravagance of purchasing a bold umbrella with a carved parrot head for a handle.

The success of that small journey had led to her decision to do this bolder excursion primarily by bus, and she was particularly grateful for this choice, if all the flights were going to be this tiring. The plane continued to list awkwardly from side to side until the wheels screeched on the tarmac of St John's. Benny's restless depression vanished and she was filled with a rush of excitement.

It was time to have some fun! There was no doubt in her mind that Eli, at least, had found himself some excellent times in B.C. So good, in fact, that he hadn't even written. So, she was owed a party big time; the universe of all partying was in her debt and it was time to deliver.

Benny had heard that the Newfoundlanders could party hard and well, without judgment or reserve, and she was suddenly optimistic that it would work out well. She was going to party like a Newfoundlander and show the world that she, too, could have a good time.

She grabbed her backpack off the carousel and hailed a cab to her B&B.

PARTYING LIKE A NEWFOUNDLANDER

Benny punched the pillow, lay back on the unremarkable bed and realized two things. The first was that she was furious with Eli for not calling, for not writing, for not coming back. She wondered if she should take off his ring but she knew she wouldn't.

The second realization was the dismal acknowledgement that she was locked out of her own life with no visitation rights in the foreseeable future either. The entire world was getting on just fine without her.

Benny was used to her life being a drama. Even before she found herself in the centre of a media circus, she loved being in demand. At work in the agency, at home. Even with Colin, she had a daily dose of theatrics and drama. She was constantly saving the day or being uniquely remarkable.

But now, alone and far away, she was adrift on the sea of sleeplessness with no mapped-out role for the forthcoming day.

Benny felt panic rise like bile.

It wasn't even two days ago that she'd been pulling that one last rabbit out the hat for Colin and now she was here with no plan in sight. How could Colin have let her leave? She was angry with him too. He should have made her stay.

Why did no one try to keep her? They all let her leave. Or, they had left her. She sighed, looked at her watch. It was 1:37 a.m.

There really was only one course of action left to take. Medicate to the gills and pass out. Deal with this holiday in the morning.

When morning came, she got up early. She was ready for her party, no doubt about it. She rushed out into the quiet unstirred morning and was disappointed by the immediate lack of apparent partying.

Patience. It was early yet. Really, really early: 6:40 a.m. She wandered the silent hilly streets of St John's, camera in hand. She spotted a boarded-up old hospital and found a way to crawl inside.

The ruined and the destroyed had always held a fascination for her, even before the devastation of her own world. She liked to stand among the decay and pick through the aftermath of vanished lives, searching for clues to uncover what had made it all go wrong. And finding the perfect images to capture her imaginings, well, those were moments when she felt close to serene.

She inched her way down the thick dark of the old hospital corridor to a junction of doctors' rooms, waiting areas, and small wards. The paint was peeling off the walls in tired swathes, bubbling as if diseased. Glass crunched underfoot as she made her way between upturned chairs and rotting mildewed mattresses. She searched for treasure and found none apart from long-exposure photographs of sunlit dust motes land-sliding down through coarse-grain mustard curtains.

Hours later, done exploring, she brushed the grime off her leather trousers and headed downtown to see if her party had arrived.

She tried to tell herself she was having fun, wishing she didn't feel so angry all the time.

She walked along Water Street down to the harbour and poked around – still not finding any semblance of a party even although it was nearly 11:00 a.m. She was disappointed. So much for the legendary party-animal Newfoundlanders. She was panning scenery through her viewfinder when she was drawn up short by a camera focused directly on her.

She lowered her camera and scowled at her voyeur who immediately rushed over and introduced himself. He excused his Peeping Tom antics by saying that people on holiday so rarely got photographs of themselves and she looked like a model, so he thought he'd take some pics of her. Did she mind? Benny glared at him, secretly delighted to be appreciated.

"Yeah, all right then," she said, "I'll stand here, by this yellow wall. I love the colours you all paint your houses and things."

Twenty minutes later, she'd had enough. "Well, that's it then, it's been fun. Here's my email address so you can send them to me. And send them to me you'd better, mate, or I'll hunt you down." She smiled to show she was joking, sort of.

"Just a few more, if you don't mind," he said. "There's a boat that goes out and takes tours. Let's go ask the captain if we can take pics of you on it. Hey, I'm Jackson. This'll be great, okay? Let's go."

Benny agreed, having nothing better to do, and she trotted in tow, arriving slightly breathless to find her photographer friend explaining his story to the boat captain.

Benny realized she'd found her party. *Eat your heart out, Eli. Eat your heart out, world.*

"Hi, I'm Benny," she said, with outstretched hand.

"Chris," said the captain, surly.

Benny struck a pose as instructed by Jackson, much to the amusement of Chris who leaned back and watched with a half-smile. They were about to wrap it up and Benny thought she might be leaving disappointed, since Chris didn't appear to be making a move of any kind. But, with departure imminent, Chris finally said, "Hey, just because I like your style, I'll take you on the tour for free. Be back here for noon, no later." Oh, the killer accent he had.

Jackson, deflated, told Benny he'd email her and he walked off.

Benny hung around the boat, waiting for noon and then she climbed back onboard to go and see the humpback whales and such.

St. John's scenery was great for sure, particularly when the wind was blowing through Chris's thick blonde hair. Later they cruised back into the harbour and dropped anchor.

"Well, that was awesome," she said, exhilarated by immensity of the raw landscape and the salty fresh air coming off the Atlantic Ocean. "I liked the birds flying around the whales. The whales were cool too. Thanks for that."

"Not so fast then," he said. "If you're keen, I'll take you to a party. All's we need is to get us a bottle of Scotch."

"I won't say no to a party," Benny said. "I'll get the scotch, be back in a flash."

She walked up the hill to the liquor store, stopping at a Shopper's Drug Mart for condoms, just in case.

Chris finished up with the boat and he directed her into a weather-beaten old car that belonged to his parents. Benny buckled up and they set off for the party that Benny had known was in her future.

Take that, Eli.

They drove about two hours inland. Chris was hilarious as well as gorgeous. He kept Benny entertained with tales of how he nearly – purely by mistake mind you – smuggled a canoe-load of pot into the States for some hippies who he thought were just keen sailors.

"So I says, 'Roight officer, dese here are my friends here asleep in da back o'da carh officer, we're just passing dru … it's ull elright, really.'"

Benny was having the time of her life and they hadn't even arrived at the party yet.

They pulled up to a mansion and Benny turned shy. She hadn't been expecting opulence. Turned out Benny had been invited to a dinner party of note. This one was right out of the pages of *Vogue Entertaining and Travel*, right down to the silver candlestick holders, the polished crystal glassware, and the family silver cutlery.

The house was filled with children who might easily have been borrowed from a Martha Stewart shoot. In fact, the whole house was totally Martha. Benny was introduced to the adult contingent – intelligentsia hailing from Memorial University. They loved Benny immediately and she was quietly grateful for having purchased a good bottle of Scotch and not some cheap rotgut variety.

The children were put to bed and the big folk got down to the partying aspects of the equation. Benny had stumbled in on a feast. A four-course dinner. Moët champagne in silver buckets, followed by countless bottles of wine, followed by cigars and liqueurs. At 1:00 a.m., they moved outside to the fire pit where the party raged on. At 3:00 a.m., they moved to the trampoline, jumping up and down and rolling on each other. Benny marveled that no one was injured. At 5:00 a.m., they called it a night.

At 10:00 a.m., they began to rise. It was a slow process, not an easy one. The children, feeling no pain, tugged them to come out to play.

Benny, hidden behind dark sunglasses, staggered up from the sofa in the basement and out into the light. She had not so much as brought an overnight bag or a toothbrush. Martha's perfect house was savagely ravaged like the aftermath of a protest riot. Chris's beautiful brother, an artist himself – Benny having gone silent at this dinner table mention – was facedown on the polished wooden floor where he'd settled some hours earlier. He remained an immovable leaden weight despite efforts to hoist him up onto the sofa.

"You know we'd stay to help tidy up," Chris said, scratching at his stubble, "but I've got to get the boat ready to go out at noon, so we're a bit pushed for time already."

They thanked their generous and fragile hosts, who were more than a tad shaken by the consequences of the festivities, and drove away. Chris stopped for coffee at the closest stop.

"So, what was the party for, anyway?" Benny asked when they were back on the road. "Someone's birthday, or anniversary or what? It was incredible. I've never eaten food like that in my entire life. Jenny's husband, the chef, he's British?"

"Yeah, well, he's a Brit and you know the Brits. They just have those shindigs every now and then. I think this one was a farewell for my brother. He's supposed to be going to Toronto to make his way as an artist. Some gallery's interested in him but the money's on him staying put."

At the mention of a gallery, an ice-cold fist clutched Benny's belly. "When's he leaving?"

"Ah, well, he might not go. He's not sure. Supposed to leave on Monday, tomorrow. I guess he'll see. Me, I'm stuck here. Me and the sea, we're all we've got, each other, that way. So now, where can I drop you?"

Benny had no desire to return to the B&B. She had yet to see another living soul, having picked up her key on a Postit note inside the hallway when she arrived. The B&B reminded her of a deserted out-of-season holiday apartment even though it was high tourist season.

"Um, do you know any abandoned old buildings I could check out? I had a fine old time at the hospital. Anything like that maybe?"

"Yeah, for sure," he said, "I know a place you'll like, nursing home, burned down a while back."

He dropped her off at the blackened wreckage of her dreams and they made plans for dinner later that night. Benny explored the charred wreckage and took her photographs. Then she went for a walk up Signal Hill where she bought a fridge magnet with sayings from Newfoundland: *she's gone bye she's gone; rain, drizzle and fog; crooked as sin; ya foolish gommel; long may your big jib draw; cookin' up a scoff and a fine mug up.*

She sat in the sunshine, watching Chris far below, sailing his boatload of tourists out to the whales. The wind whipped her hair and she looked out at the whales and the swooping birds and admired the rocky harbour and purity of the vast blue sky. The day had that scrubbed-clean look to it and she imagined the locals had their laundry out on clotheslines, with sheets and pillowcases snapping in the breeze. She wondered if she could live in Newfoundland. Didn't seem like the weather was that bad but then again, it was summer.

"I love the sea and I hate the sea," Chris said later, over an Indian dinner that Benny didn't think her ex-husband would approve of at all. "I wish I could leave it. Leave here. Go to Toronto. Do something different. Live a different life. Who knows? Maybe if my brother goes, I'll go too. But what would I do there? This is my life, the sea. This is my love. This is my hate."

She looked at him, his beauty was fading, his post-dinner party surliness boring, his discontent tedious.

"I've no idea where I'll end up," she said, tearing a tiny piece of nan.

"What about ma and pa kettle?" he asked.

She was confused. "Who?"

"Your parents?" he said.

"Ah. They're back in Oz," she said, subject closed. "So I fly out tomorrow and start heading west. You want to come with me?" She didn't really mean it.

"Ah, no, not me. Not now," he said and she was glad. She'd had enough of him and wanted to be alone in the B&B, its isolation now welcome.

"Great party last night," she said, signaling for the bill. "It was awesome of you to invite me along. And thanks for the boat tour yesterday, and everything."

It was time to leave. He dropped her off and she had a long shower and packed. So much for the condoms that never got used.

The next day, Monday, she took a cab to the airport.

"You'll be lucky to fly at all," the cabbie told her. "Bad weather's on the way. They say a big storm's coming tonight, going to hit Halifax hard. Last big one in June was in 1959. The Escuminac it was called, and it was a doozy. Lost twenty boats in that one and a bunch of people died. Don't think this one will be that bad – hope not, anyways."

The wind lashed at the cab even as they drove, the rain coming down in buckets. The cabbie was right. All flights had been canceled. Irritated by her plans being thwarted, she decided to make the best of it. She picked up a bestseller from the newsstand café at the airport and went to the Holiday Inn, relieved to score a room. She spent the day dipping into the mini bar and reading, idly watching the weather channel on TV. She thought she should be maybe email Shandra, but the idea of a computer seemed remote and alien. She congratulated herself on accommodating the disruption to her plans, telling herself that whoever thought she couldn't take a change of plans in her stride was wrong. So what if she arrived in Halifax a day or so later than planned? She just hoped she wouldn't end up losing the room she'd booked, due to any kind of hurricane emergency. She decided to focus on her book and she tried not to worry.

LIFE, A SUNKEN BOAT

If it was Tuesday, it was Halifax. Halifax, the unremarkable. Benny chastised herself for her snap judgment, no city looked good from the air. Except perhaps Paris, or New York. Or Sydney, glittering like a marcasite brooch.

She grabbed her luggage off the carousel at the airport and settled down to wait for the next bus into town. She was impatient and restless, wanting to get on with it. She tried to do some yoga breathing and be all nice and zen but crawling black ants of anxiety were gnawing at her psyche and her chest felt tight. She swallowed half a Xanax thinking it never hurt to give zen a helping hand.

She took a good look around. Halifax had been rudely battered by the storm. Entire billboards had been ripped out of the ground.

"Pretty bad, eh?" a man near her said, noticing her reaction to the destruction. "Came through last night, ripped the place to pieces."

"You could say that," Benny said. "Wow. Crikey Moses. You here to help with the clean up?" she asked.

He nodded. "Sorry for their misfortune and all that," he said, "but I got a family to feed, gotta make a buck. A buddy of mine called me up, said come on over. So, here I am."

Benny nodded, plugged in her iPod and waited for the bus, grabbing a window seat when it arrived, and marveling at the surrounding chaos.

She got to the YWCA and was relieved to find her room still available. She was also relieved to find that her room was pretty – blue and white, fresh and clean. She had no idea what she'd been expecting. She'd always had prison-type associations with the Y, imagining scowling women in the corridors and foot fungus in the grouting, but everyone was friendly and the washroom was spotless.

She went for a walk and immediately loved Halifax, admonishing herself never to judge a city from an oval-windowed airplane again.

Hours later, in the evening, her feet were aching. She sat down on the boardwalk beside the remains of a sunken boat, the mast of which protruded bravely, bearing a plucky Canadian flag.

The sunset was brilliant with vibrant cathedral-rays fanning behind whipped-cream clouds in a gold stained-glass sky. The water was mirror-still and calm. It was hard to imagine the fury of the recent blasting gale-force wind.

Benny wondered if the sunken boat was symbolic of her life. Was she a sunken ship? She took in her surrounds, a large office building loomed to her right and Benny wished she had a job there with a desk and a computer to call her own.

She told herself she was doing fine, that this trip was a scary thing to do, like bungee jumping after the instructor said you should be fine.

Should? Her panic was held at bay by the easy action of a couple of painkillers she'd downed with a Southern Comfort in a pub she'd passed along the way. All this travel was stressful for a beginner and she'd figured she deserved a bit of help.

"Embrace the freedom," a voice had whispered to her, late into her last night in St John's, when she'd woken up to replenish her sleeping meds.

Easy for you to say, she thought, remembering. *Me, I like being at work, in front of my computer. And I used to love being in front of a canvas, but those days are long gone. This is scary for me. I'm out on a limb here.*

She thought about the voice. Benny didn't believe in God, but the voice did have an omnipotent authority to it, and it seemed as if the all-seeing *He She They It* of the universe had taken an interest in Benny's life. She tried to tap into it, wanting to ask it if she was destined for a bright shiny future or if she was doomed, but now the voice was nowhere to be found.

She looked at the boat again and the feeling of panic increased its grip, like a fist pushing hard at her chest bone. She reached for a Valium but stopped, worried it might see her ending up like Heath Ledger. Heath was dead. You don't come back from dead.

She got to her feet, gazed down at the boat and decided it was time for supper. She had noted, tropical storm chaos not withstanding, that Halifax smelled deliciously, mouth-wateringly of fried fish. But Benny didn't do fried. And since grilled didn't seem to be an option, she got an extra-large house salad instead, no dressing, hold the cheese – all within strict Kenny-standards.

She walked back to the Y, holding her pale excuse for a dinner, passing pizza joints and fast-food takeouts galore and contemplating the pros and cons of her unwavering commitment to the junk-free, "high-vibratory" version of herself.

"Sometimes, Kenny," she said out loud, "I swear you're a food snob. What about the rest of the planet who eats normally? What about them?" She continued the debate silently, arguing back and forth, peering at her salad dispassionately.

BETTY BOOP'S SPITTING MAD

The dawn of her second day in Halifax saw Benny wide-awake and in a funk. It was 6:00 a.m. on Wednesday, Day Five of her trip.

Is it time to leave yet?

She had thought of taking in a play later that night, "I Love You, You're Perfect, Now Change," and going to Peggy's Cove for a look-see during the day, but she wasn't sure if she had the energy.

She got up to switch on the ceiling fan and lay back on the bed, thinking maybe she'd fallen down the rabbit hole into *Apocalypse Now*.

This is the end, the end, my only friend, the end.

Inertia lay heavy across her chest, so bad that the mere thought of brushing her teeth was too much to contemplate. Her body felt punished and tired, a dead weight on the bed.

She'd dreamt weird things about shooting rubber balls at the stars and she wondered what it meant but decided it was more important to tackle tying her shoelaces than to figure it out.

She felt lost and alone. She had vanished off the grid and no one cared. She wondered again at the lunacy of the trip, and quietly cursed her compulsion to do it.

She got herself dressed and walked down to the harbour, thinking she'd grab a large tea, sit next to the sunken boat, and think about what to do.

En route to the harbour, tea in hand, she walked past the glass building and couldn't help but notice a short woman pacing across the courtyard outside the entrance, raging loudly into a cell phone. She was hard to miss. The woman was blonde and very Betty Boop – Betty Boop in a gray pinstripe suit and bright aqua silk shirt. A very angry Betty.

Benny, amused by the wrath, stopped close to the woman to eavesdrop.

"They want me to do a frickin' commemorative high gloss supplement in three frickin' days, man, three days and do I have a designer? No, I do not. A whole supplement, to the printer, in like three frickin' days? They send me here and they give me no one, man, no one. And I will NOT fail, I will NOT fail but I'm telling you, man, it's ridiculous. I've got a frickin' boatload of images, every frickin' newspaper in the area sent images and I don't have a designer."

Benny was impressed by the woman's fury. It raged unabated.

"They send me here because I'm east coast, yeah, right. I don't even know anyone here anymore! I live in Toronto, for frick's sake, like how'm

I supposed to know people here? No, don't tell me to calm down, don't tell me it will be fine. It's bullshit, I tell you."

Benny walked up to the woman and tapped her on the shoulder.

The woman spun around and nearly spat at Benny. "What the frick do you want?" she sputtered, her face an inch from Benny's, her huge brown eyes wide-set, her pink lipstick perfect. "Can't you see I'm busy? For frick's sake, go and earn yourself a living. It's not so hard, you've got two legs, two arms, all working by the looks of it."

Something about the woman's anger made Benny feel cheerful.

"I'm the best graphic designer you'll ever find," Benny said. "Ask BBDO, Sydney, Australia. I'll do your supplement for you. I'm on holiday, I've got nothing better to do. It'll be fun. I heard you, three days. Let me do it."

The woman looked at her, mouth agape. "Gotta go," she barked into the phone. "You'd better be telling me the truth," she said to Benny, her eyes wide, her nostrils flaring. The woman was bouncing on the tips of her toes, like a boxer psyched to dish out punishment. "Come with me."

"You'll see," Benny was calm. She felt exhilarated, powerful.

She followed the woman to the glass door and into the building. "She's with me," the woman barked at the security officer. "Let her in, now!"

The security guard paled and buzzed them in.

The woman led Benny to a bank of elevators.

"I'm Teenie, by the way," the woman said, sticking out her hand. Odd name, Benny thought.

"So, here's the lowdown," Teenie said, glowering at the elevator's slow descent. "We're doing a feature on the storm, on how the various regions in the Atlantic were affected, how the locals all rose to the occasion, brotherly love, battening down the hatches and all that jazz. The supplement's being sponsored by the oil guys responsible for global warming in the first place. This is their way of saying sorry, who knows. We're looking at Halifax, Moncton, Saint John, Fredericton, Truro, New Glasgow and Bathurst because they were hardest hit. I've got their images; well, they're on the FTP, ready to be downloaded. I've got a couple of computers set up in Peter's office. You'll meet him now. He's okay but can't make a decision to save his frickin' life."

The elevator arrived and Teenie stabbed a button to the top floor, continuing her explanation. "Peter was supposed to have everything set up and ready for me but all he did was dump two computers in his office and *voilá*, that was it. Don't tell him I told you any of this. So, he does nothing but stand there looking confused and I'm supposed to make the whole bangshoot happen. I'm glad you came along but you'd better be as hot as you say although right now I can't exactly be choosy, can I?"

They stepped out of the elevator and Teenie led Benny hurriedly through a maze of gray cubicles. Benny felt her heart soar. This was home. They ended up in a corner office, with floor-to-ceiling glass and the sunken boat in clear view.

Teenie introduced Benny to Peter. A tall man in his early sixties, he was white-haired with a large handlebar moustache and Benny thought he was more amused by Teenie than intimidated. His only reaction to Benny was a raised eyebrow and a bemused smile.

Benny headed over to the conference desk at the end of Peter's office and turned on the Mac, sorting through a stack of disks while she waited for the startup screen. She was glad to see the computer was one of the newest iMacs. She could hear Teenie rattling on behind her with Peter making agreeing noises.

Fifteen minutes later, Benny interrupted them. "I need to see your I.T. department now," she said. "There are no fonts on this computer."

"I'll take you." Peter looked relieved to have an excuse to leave Teenie, who was still sounding off like a Duracell bunny on uppers.

"I'll phone Toronto in the meantime," Teenie said. "God knows what's happening there, I mean I have my job there too. They dragged me away in the middle of a shoot with ten babies for our *Toronto Living* section cover. The publisher had some half-assed idea about a gatefold of babies, who the frick knows why and now my art director and associate editor are going instead of me and God knows what's going to happen. I tell you if the VP hadn't wanted me here – "

Benny and Peter left her in mid-rant and wove through the cubicles outside Peter's door. Peter's office took up about two acres of real estate, while the cubicles were about two feet by two feet.

"You on holiday?" Peter pushed the elevator button.

"Yes." Benny didn't elaborate.

Peter smiled. "Glad you can help out. I thought Teenie was going to implode. But our newspaper's a daily, so we couldn't just pull someone off it. Some guy from Truro's coming over but apparently that isn't fast enough for Teenie."

"This guy from Truro, I'll have to share the project?" Benny wasn't amused. "I mean, I can do this thing but I'll need to do it my way, alone. It'll take too long to share, to bring someone up to speed."

Peter looked at her and smiled. "You know, I get the feeling you and Teenie will get on just fine. Don't worry. I won't let the boy get in your way. He can work on the paper and then if you need him for any production or retouching, he's yours."

Benny felt relieved. "Thanks," she said, wondering if she should apologize for being brusque but then they'd reached the I.T. department and she fired off a list of her font needs.

Half an hour later, she was up and running, her eye on the clock. It wasn't even 10:30.

While Benny sat hunched over her computer, immersed in her world, Teenie continued to yell into the phone. It seemed it was what she did best.

Benny waved off Teenie's suggestions of stopping for lunch, but she did grunt approval at Peter's offer of a mid-afternoon tea and she finally sat up, red-eyed, at 7:00 p.m., to see Peter and Teenie chatting quietly on the sofa.

Benny looked at them. "Okay, so the basic design's done on the basis of what I showed you earlier," she said, yawning. "The template's in place. I've sorted out the regions, done a pagination, and filed half the images that are high-enough resolution. We can go through them tomorrow, Teenie, and you can see which ones you want and then you can get going on the copy while I'll finish sorting the other half."

"I frickin' love you!" Teenie jumped to her feet, drummed her feet on the floor and squealed.

"Impressive," Peter said, smoothing his moustache.

"I'll need to be at work at 6:00 a.m. tomorrow," Benny said.

Teenie blanched. "But I only get up at 7:00 a.m., and I have to do my run first," she objected.

Benny shrugged. "Guess I'll meet you here then," she said.

"I'll get you cleared with security," Peter told Benny. "I'll arrange it on our way out. Where are you staying?"

"At the Y," Benny said.

"Oh no, you don't," Teenie said, taking Benny's arm. "You're sharing my room. I'm at the Marriott, two huge beds. You need a bubble bath and room service, my dear."

Benny's heart sank. Of all the things she hated in life, girly-bonding sleepovers were perhaps highest on her list. But, looking at Teenie, her glossy pink lipstick still perfect and her grin wide, Benny knew she had no choice.

"Okay, fine," she said, with obvious reluctance. "But I'm getting up at sparrow. Peter, can I have a cab chit for the morning?"

THAT CRAP FRIES YOUR BRAIN, MAN

On the way to the Y to pick up Benny's clothes, Teenie tapped the cab driver on shoulder. "Driver," she said, "do you know any five-star restaurants around here?"

Benny had never heard anyone call a cabbie "driver" before.

"Teenie," she said, "it's already like 8:00 p.m. All I want to do is have a bath and go to bed. And we still have to get my stuff and anyway, as a rule, I don't eat a big supper. It's not healthy for your digestive system." According to Kenny, the oracle.

Benny was disconcerted by the number of Kenny-thoughts she was having. She'd been so busy – coming to Canada, dealing with Colin, falling in love with Eli – that she hadn't even really thought about her ex-husband but like a nasty weed, or crabgrass encroaching, he was crawling toward her consciousness in a most unsettling way.

"You don't eat much at all by the look of it," Teeny said. "Okay, let's go and get your stuff first and then we'll see."

At the Y, Benny left Teenie still trying to track down a five-star restaurant but when she returned she found she'd been right, the high-end restaurants were closed due to the storm damage.

This did not put Teenie in a good mood. "Frickin' excellent example of when they should rise to the occasion," she complained. "But no, they all just fall apart. No wonder I left here. As a matter of fact though, I do plan to come back one day, start a yoga sanctuary or something."

Benny thought Teenie was one of the least yoga-like people she'd ever met but she kept quiet.

After what seemed like an age getting to the hotel, Benny was finally soaking in the tub. She added more hot water, and planned how she'd do the designs the next morning, only half listening to Teenie ranting in the bedroom. Teenie was shouting at someone on the phone, someone she was clearly displeased with.

Teenie slammed down the phone, opened the bathroom door and wandered in, reading the room service menu aloud. She was in bright pink Lululemon sweats and Benny looked at her warily. Second highest on Benny's list of most-hateds were women who wanted to bond while Benny was enjoying a relaxing bath. Even Shay knew to leave Benny alone when she was in the tub.

Teenie examined her teeth in the mirror and sat down on the toilet.

"So what you up for, eh? I'm having the fish and chips, bottle of red wine, Caesar salad, extra croutons and cheese."

"I'll have the house salad, dressing on the side, Perrier, and vegetarian soup of the day, as long as there's no MSG or animal stock in it," Benny said, wishing Teenie would leave so she could get out of the bath.

"Jeez Louise, you're no fun," Teenie complained and she went to order the food. Before Benny had the chance to get out of the bath, she came back and sat down on the toilet again.

"So, I've been married nearly a year," Teenie said conversationally, "and Ed, my husband, he's such a frickin' loser. He drinks, right, and we broke up years ago and I went out west, Vancouver. Then I came back, he looked me up, persuaded me he'd changed and asked, on bended knee and all that crap, would I marry him? I should've realized he was lying about getting sober because he was drunk when he proposed. 'Course then he said he'd stop drinking after we got married but he didn't. He also said he wouldn't drink on our wedding night but what do you know, he drank. Should have had my head examined for believing him."

Benny silently agreed with her and lay very still in the water, hoping the lack of movement would discourage Teenie from asking Benny about her own relationship history. No way was she going there. But Teenie seemed happy to chat about her own situation.

"So, for sure it's not going to last but it's okay for now, I guess. He spends his nights drunk as anything, sitting at home in the basement, playing games, drinking beer." She examined her nails. "Thing is, I really did believe him. When he's sober, he's such a great guy."

Benny didn't say anything, she just watched Teenie and wondered how she was ever going to get out of the bath.

Next thing, Teenie was crying, fat tears running down her cheeks. Benny, dismayed, backed up against the tub and searched for the right thing to say but Teenie blew her nose loudly and wiped her eyes.

"Ah, sod it." She sighed. "So, what did you think of Peter? Useless as shit, if you ask me, but a nice guy. I could move out here in a nano-second – I know for a fact he'd make me editor-in-chief of their living section and I could have a good life. But God knows I'm not ready. Not yet anyways."

"I'm getting out of the bath now," Benny announced, hoping this would make Teenie leave but she merely reached over and handed Benny a towel.

Benny climbed out and dried herself.

"Frickin' excellent body, man," Teeny said. "Look at you. How old are you, girl?"

"Twenty-five," Benny lied. It seemed she was going backwards in time.

"Well, wait till you hit thirty, man, it all frickin goes south from there and I do mean literally. Which reminds me I must do my sit-ups. I do a hundred every night."

She left the bathroom and Benny soon heard counting and grunting noises. Benny scrubbed her face and cleaned her teeth. She knew she had the order wrong – eat first, then floss – but she was nearing exhaustion.

In the next room, Teenie continued to grunt and count.

There was a knock at the door and Teenie leapt to her feet. She signed for the food and called out to Benny.

"I'm starved, man, let's eat."

Benny examined her salad and watched Teenie attack a large plate of batter-fried fish.

"Teenie," Benny commented, picking at her salad, "unusual name."

Teenie gave a grunt of derision. "My real name's Moira Kathleen. Who the frick names their child that? Catholics, that's who. I come from a big family, there are ten of us kids. Ma and pa are good old-fashioned east-coast drinkers who don't believe in contraception but do believe in divorce. My big sister called me Teenie because I was so little, and it stuck. Not that the family held. My dad's had a bunch of girlfriends, while my ma's killing herself with the bottle."

"Ah," Benny said. "I like the name Moira Kathleen." Then she added, "But I know what it feels like when a name doesn't fit."

"Your name fits you," Teenie said, "Smooth polished exotic Benny. You're like a cat, man, all sleek." She yawned. "You got any kids?"

Benny was startled. "No," she said, "you?"

"Yeah, a boy. Got pregnant when I was sixteen. So I went out to B.C., to have him and what do you know, he got a hold of me up a couple of days before this gig landed on my desk. Been quite the time, I tell you. Soon as I get back to Toronto, he's coming to stay. 'Course Ed's over the frickin' moon about that. Unless of course the boy turns out to be a Wii expert and a drinking buddy. In which case, man, I'm leaving. No wait, it's my house, I'll make them leave."

"Must be exciting," Benny said, searching for what it would be. "Meeting your son."

Teenie shrugged. "Yeah, maybe. I'll mainly be working anyways."

Benny nodded and ate the last of her lettuce.

"I'm shattered," she said to Teenie. "Time for bed."

She pulled the bedcovers free, lined up her sleeping meds and got a drink of water.

"What are those?" Teenie studied Benny's neat lineup of pills.

"Blue one's a sleeping pill, the other two are codeine and acetaminophen," Benny said. "I don't sleep very well."

"I would never take crap like that. It fries your brain, man," Teenie said self-righteously and then she quickly looked around. "Hey, do you think they have the rooms bugged for smoke detectors? This is a non-smoking room right? Frickin' hate those smoke-infested rooms, disgusting, man. But I gotta have my late-night fattie or I won't sleep."

"See if you can open the window," Benny swallowed her meds and wished Teenie would shut up.

"Good plan, man," Teenie said, cranking the window open an inch and lighting a joint. "Want some?"

"Nah, I'm good, thanks. Stuff wakes me up, makes me super neurotic."

"Never heard that before, eh. I can't sleep without it."

"Different strokes, I guess," Benny said, setting the alarm.

"Are you seriously setting that for 5:30 a.m.? Are you crazy, man? Relax, the work will all get done."

"It'll get done alright – because I'm getting up at 5:30," Benny said, and she settled the pillow under her head and turned her back to Teenie.

"Well, do you want me to bring you a latte or a chai or something to eat when I get in? I guestimate I'll be there around 8:00 a.m. I'm gonna use the hotel gym, go for a run, make some calls to the office, then I'll be right in."

"You going to Starbucks or Tim's on the way?" Benny asked, knowing the answer.

"Starbucks."

"Okay, then I'll have venti green tea, a fruit cup, fat-free yoghurt, any flavour."

"My friend, you're too disciplined for your own good. I will not start my day without a muffin, and a good one at that."

Benny muttered something and next thing she knew, the alarm was screeching into the silence of the room.

TEENIE GETS PERKY

At the sound of the alarm, Benny shot up in bed. She was disoriented with no idea where she was. Then she remembered she had work to do and a shot of joy pierced her heart. She leapt out of bed and got dressed, looking over at Teenie who was dead to the world, a pink eye mask with silver sequins covering her face.

Benny grinned, brushed her teeth, went downstairs and hailed a cab. By 6:15 a.m., she was at her desk.

She looked down at the sunken boat and across at the brilliant sunrise that was slowly burning back the blanket of rolling fog. She watched a brightly-coloured tugboat chug across the water with seagulls swooping and diving. Benny knew she was was in her rightful place. Then she got to work.

Peter arrived at 9:00. "Interested in a Tim's?" he asked.

"Extra large green tea, no milk, thanks."

"You got it," he left and a few minutes later Teenie sauntered in, swearing under her breath.

"Here's your breakfast," she handed a large green tea to Benny who accepted gratefully.

Benny pointed at the pile of printouts on Teenie's side of the desk. "Ready for you. I've opened up the files on your computer. All we need is your copy."

"Super duper, mate. Hey, I'm starting to talk like you. Have I told you how much I love your accent, man? I wish I had an accent."

Peter arrived back, laden. He greeted Teenie and told her he'd brought her a coffee.

"Never do caffeine," she said. "Well, not Tim's. I got a latte from Starbucks. But thanks, man. Have you seen what our girl's done here? She's frickin' fabulous."

Benny blocked them both out and carried on working. Around her people came and went and Peter and Teenie pondered headlines and copy. Benny carried on, oblivious, until she sensed a change of energy in the room.

"And this is Benny, our vunderwoman," Peter said, "Benny, this is Todd, your support guy should you need him."

Todd was a lanky hippie-looking fellow with dark eyes and a hooked nose. He had long curly brown hair and small gold pirate-hoop earrings. He smiled shyly at Benny. For a moment, he reminded her of Eli and she scowled at him. She noticed Teenie getting all perky, sticking her breasts out one way, buttocks the other.

"I do have some stuff for you," Benny said sharply, "but we'll need to get you another computer. That one's Teenie's and she's busy." She looked pointedly at Teenie who laughed.

"Oh, it'll get done," she said airily. "We'll all work late, won't we, you sweet boy? We can share my computer." She smiled at Todd who seemed unaware of the undercurrents in the room.

"I'll go and get him a computer," Peter said.

"With the same fonts as mine," Benny shouted after him.

"And you, sweet boy, come and tell me about yourself," Teenie patted the sofa.

"Why don't you tell him about our project?" Benny said. "And show him the pages we've done so far? Todd, Peter said you're a retoucher."

Todd held up beautiful hands. "Magic fingers," he said and even Benny had thoughts other than retouching.

"I'm sure," Teenie purred, and she moved close to Todd who looked nervous.

"Magic retoucher," he said, pointedly, finally catching Teenie's drift.

"So, Teenie," Benny said again, "Show him the pages, bring him up to speed. Todd, your mission, should you choose to accept, is to take a look at all the images, pump up the colours, make them vibrant, clean up the crap. And also, make a file for whatever images you think will work for the cover. We've got to finish this entire book by tomorrow afternoon."

Todd looked nervous and chewed a thumbnail.

Benny focused on her layout while Peter returned with the I.T. guy and a computer.

"Getting kinda tight in here," the I.T. guy said. "You want me to move you guys to a boardroom?"

"No thanks." Benny was quick to reply. "We don't have time." She didn't want to lose her view of the sunken boat.

"It's like one big happy family," Teenie said, happily eyeing Todd. "All of us together here like this, creates good energy, man."

Several hours later, they were all silent, engrossed. Even Teenie was quiet, studying her copy, getting up every now and then to confer with Peter.

The sun set and Peter said he'd order in; Teenie and Todd voted for pizza. "Fine, whatever," Benny said. "Peter, can you get me a large house salad, no dressing, extra large green tea?"

"Anything you like, madam," Peter said with a bow.

At 10:00 p.m., amid the rubble of the day, it was clear no more could be achieved.

"Come on laddie, you're staying with me," Peter said and he led Todd out. "See you girlies tomorrow."

Teenie and Benny were too tired to talk. Back at the hotel, Benny had a quick shower while Teenie smoked her joint and then Benny fell into bed while Teenie had a bath.

"Frickin' exhausted, man," Teenie was muttering as Benny fell asleep. "Crazy to expect us to do this in such a short time…"

SHUT UP … & WORK … & SPEND … & DIE

Then Benny was awake again. It was 5:30 a.m., Friday morning. She lay in bed, wondering if she dare steal another half an hour. But she was concerned that if she did, she'd end up sleeping until noon. They had to get everything done by the end of the day. She still had to find an image for the front cover. She had to check Todd's images and get all the pages ready for production. And she hadn't even begun the ac-knowledgement pages yet.

She groaned her way out of bed and hailed a cab. She signed the cab chit and turned to enter the building when she noticed a scrawl of graffiti on the pillar beside the glass front door – *shut up and work, shut up and spend, shut up and die.* Benny stared at the writing for a moment, then waved her security clearance at the guard and pushed her way inside.

Todd, Peter and Teenie straggled in later, carrying a variety of fast foods.

"I'm just not a morning person," Todd muttered, while Peter looked haggard.

Benny was alert and cheerful, firing out directives.

"We may have to kill her and bury the pieces," Teenie groaned. "Benny, girlfriend, are you an alien or something?"

Benny laughed. "Bury me with that boat down there," she pointed. "That's our cover. I'm super excited. I found the image by pure chance. And look," she held up a printout, "there's a seagull in the shot too, posing nicely!"

The others grunted, agreeing it looked good. Peter said he'd celebrate her find with a small lie-down on his sofa.

The day seemed endless and finally, at 11:00 p.m. that night they were done. Benny sat back and looked around.

Peter's formerly pristine office looked like it too had been subject to a storm; there was a blizzard of paper and mess everywhere. Layouts were tacked to the walls and the floor was covered in trash.

"The printer got everything off the FTP," Peter called out, the phone to his ear. "They'll start running it tomorrow as soon as I get there to press check."

Teenie gave a whoop of delight. "Ordinarily I would say let's go dancing," she said, "but all I want to do is have a long, hot bath and crawl into bed."

"In agreement," Peter said. "Once the press check is done, I'm going to sleep for a week. Hey, Benny, I calculated an hourly rate for you, $60 an hour, plus a bonus. This should take care of you." He handed her an envelope.

"Wow, cool, Peter," Benny was embarrassed and pleased. "Thank you."

"No, thank *you*," Peter and Teenie both chorused.

"Now you can carry on with your big trip," Teenie said, packing her briefcase. "But I gotta tell you, I worry about you, man. Lots of whack-jobs out there, trust me, I know."

"I worry too," Peter said. "And for the record, if you ever want a job here, just say so. We'd be lucky to have you."

Then he surprised Benny by hugging her and patting her gently on the back. She stiffened and hoped he didn't notice her discomfort. "Come back one day, safe and sound," he said, handing her a business card. "And if you get into any trouble on your journey, you call me, okay? Any time of the day or night."

Benny thanked him, embarrassed again, not sure what to say.

"Arggh, I've still got to check how the shoot went back in the old T dot Oh," Teenie groaned, stretching. "I got a whole bunch more work tonight, back at the hotel. Come on Benny, let's blow this pop stand."

They said goodbye to Todd and Peter, got a cab, and crawled into their hotel room.

"I thought Todd was going to be sexier than he turned out to be," Teenie said, yawning ever wider, splayed out on the bed in canary yellow shorts and a T-shirt. "He's only a baby really. So, will you wake me up tomorrow at 6:00, when you get up? I'm on an early morning flight."

"Sure," Benny said. "I'll wake you up, but is it okay if I sleep in for a bit after? I'm going to take the bus out but it leaves later in the day, so no need for me to get up at sparrow."

"Hey, man, you can stay 'til 11:00 a.m, I checked. Max it out. Take a whole bunch of stuff from the bar fridge too, I'll cover it. And listen, you'd better email me, okay? And if you want a job when you get back to the G.T.A., you let me know, girl, I'll find you one for sure." She looked glum. "Hey, frick it, man, this isn't a funeral. But shit, I feel so sad. It's not like we won't ever see each other again. We will. You sure as heck saved our bacon. I don't know what we would have done without you. Can you imagine it, just us, with Todd?"

She and Benny burst out laughing. "Poor boy, he would have chewed his fingers right off, never mind his nails," Benny said.

"Never mind fingers, man, he'd have gnawed up to his frickin' elbow,"

Teenie said. She sat up and turned on her laptop with an obvious lack of enthusiasm. "Hey, I know you're tired as shit and all that, but will you look at this photoshoot with me? I can hardly see straight and I've got to choose the images."

"Sure," Benny said, "Sure, I'd love to. And hey, Teenie … thanks."

When Benny woke the next morning, Teenie was gone. Benny stretched out under the covers, rolled over and looked at the alarm clock. She hadn't even heard it go off. 9:00 a.m. She saw that Teenie had stuck a note on the mirror and she got up to take a look.

> Thanks a bunch girl! You saved my ass! Email me across the country and look after yourself! P.S.: I put breakfast for you on my credit card, so eat up a storm! Or pick like an organic friggin' bird or whatever the hell you feel like! P.S.2: Take anything you like from the mini bar, I covered it! Muah baby, muah!

There was a big pink lipstick kiss on the note. Benny smiled and climbed back into bed. She lay back, looking at the ceiling, thinking about the past few days. A different world, from Tuesday to Friday. Her world. And now, here she was, alone again, back on her holiday. She reached into her backpack for the envelope Peter had given her. A cheque for four thousand dollars. *Wow.*

She hopped out of bed and decided to make the most of the bathroom – steam it up, fling those towels, scrub from head to toe. Then eat some expensive fruit on Teenie's account, do some sightseeing and be on the bus for 12:45 p.m.

SHE CHANGES HER MIND

It was while she was in the shower that Benny was struck by a flash of genius. She paused mid-shampoo, her hands buried in fragrant thick lather. She was going to email Colin and tell him she was coming back. That she was sorry she'd resigned, this whole lark had been a foolish idea and she'd get back on the bus to Toronto and come home. Get her sparse nun's cell back and resume her life.

Almost giddy with relief, she showered quickly and packed even faster, taking a moment to empty the contents of the mini-bar into her backpack. She skipped breakfast and checked out, leaving her bags with the concierge. With a song in her heart and a spring in her step, she strode to the nearest Internet café and logged onto her email. Her hands were poised to type, the message to Colin ready in her mind.

But hang on, what the – ? She peered at her inbox. Clearly she'd been spammed by amandag@cdagency.ca ... but wait, cdagency.ca was Colin's agency's email address.

Benny stared at the emails. There were ten in total from Amanda G. with one small hiya from Shay in between.

Benny started from the bottom. Seemed Amanda G. was her replacement. Her very panicked replacement. Colin, that lying scumbag, had said he was too broken-hearted to even think of anyone else sitting in her chair and Benny very much doubted he'd splurged on a new chair. Hell, he'd never even bought her the new desk he'd promised her.

Amanda G.'s ratio of politeness dwindled in direct proportion to her increasing panic and urgency. Her final message, however, had regained some measure of calm and Amanda apologized for the emails in which she may have appeared somewhat rude. She was fine now, she said, she just hadn't expected Colin's agency to be so cavalier. Apparently Colin had given her Benny's email address, saying he knew Benny would help out, get her on track. Amanda signed off with a smiley face, and told Benny to have a great trip.

Benny pushed the chair away from the computer and buried her face in hands. She rubbed her eyes. Then she pulled the chair back up to the computer.

> Hi Amanda, sorry to only get back to you now, been having a blast, loving my holiday, it's awesome! Glad you're all sorted. Good luck and tell Colin I say hi.

Lying bastard.
She opened up Shay's email:

Baby Harry's fine. Dad's fine. Mum's working hard. Remember to stay warm. Lots
of Love, keep us posted.

Benny, numb from Colin's betrayal and reeling from the cancellation
of the option of returning to him, nevertheless smiled at Shay's refusal
to believe Canada was anything except snowy and icebound. She dug
deep for something positive to write back to Shay. She knew it was
foolish but she hadn't thought Colin would replace her. In a way, she'd
been expecting him to email her, begging her to come back, telling her
he needed her, but not this.

She wrote a quick note to her sister:

Hi Shay! Not much news from me either. Sorry I didn't email before now, I got tied
up doing a freelance job. Killer hours, good money. But I'm back on track now,
getting on the bus this afternoon. It'll be a long stretch before you hear from me
again, okay? So don't worry and tell Mum and Dad not to worry too. Kisses to
Harry the Lad. P.S.: It's lovely and warm here!

She sighed and drummed her fingers on the table. She looked at
her watch. It was 10:30 a.m. The bus was set to leave at 12:45 p.m.,
enough time to do some tourist stuff. She left the café and set off, map
in hand. Although the locals had made great strides with the cleanup,
the destructive force of the storm was still clearly in evidence. Benny
was ashamed to think that while she'd been scrutinizing the images with
an eye for what would work best on the page, people's lives had been
affected, by no small degree. She stopped for a moment, hoping that
she'd contributed in some meaningful way. She trekked up the citadel,
then she learned about the buried dead of the Titanic and visited three
churches of note, relieved to arrive back at the bus station.

She was suddenly desperately, achingly tired. She wanted to be neatly
settled in her Greyhound seat-with-a-view, dozing and watching the
scenery go by. She was now officially on holiday, like it or not. She dug
into her backpack for a mini-bottle of bar-fridge vodka, and emptied
it into her cooling green tea. It made for quite a refreshing drink really.
Then she sat at the bus station and waited.

One thing was for sure. Halifax certainly had turned out to be more interesting than she'd initially thought.

THE BUS SETS SAIL FOR THE WEST

Co-coordinating the bus ride from Halifax to Winnipeg was more complicated than Benny had anticipated. Apparently it would take her one day, 18 hours and 43 minutes just to travel the 785 miles from Halifax to Toronto and she'd have to plot the Winnipeg leg from there. En route, she'd stop at Moncton, change there for Ottawa and again at Ottawa, change for Toronto, as well as do a bunch of other stops along the way. Benny decided to look on the bright side and see these transfers as a good thing. Otherwise she might become attached to her seat by way of a permanent fixture.

The bus was filling up at an alarming rate. Benny closed her eyes and willed the seat next to her to remain empty. She had fallen into a strangely timeless zone. In a manner of hours, the days of the week had ceased to have relevancy; she'd already lost all sense of Teenie and office life.

The day was clouded and hazy, and Benny thought her brain felt much the same. She tried to read a trashy gossip magazine she'd picked up, but she had difficulty focusing.

Questions about the meaning of life and the meaning of her trip kept crawling across the page. She tried to meditate and shepherd the disorder of her restless mind but she quickly fell asleep. She slept deeply and dreamlessly and woke with a start. She had everywhere and nowhere to go. She had too many options in life, too much to choose from and yet no place to hang her hat.

She crunched a codeine and downed another mini of vodka, swigging it neat and soon falling asleep again.

When she woke, she was dying of thirst. She sat up and looked around. Flanking her right was a studious German couple, *National Geographic* wannabes with their camouflage lightweight quilt tucked neatly across their knees. Every available inch of their luggage was covered with the

German flag. They were eating whole-grain sandwiches and staring at her with equally frank curiosity. Benny's mirrored aviator sunglasses were in place; she was inscrutable. Also, her earbuds were plugged in; she was a locked down, a transportable fortress.

A signpost outside said: "Lobster: $15.99. Scallops: $10.99. Diesel: $4.99." Then she read: *bridges freeze before roads*. Later, *road heaves* and *soft shoulder*. Benny's southern hemisphere sensibilities found these anthropomorphic designations unique and entertaining.

She looked over and saw Mr. Nat Geo was eating dog kibbles.

The landscape outside her window was distractingly gorgeous – spruce and fir trees; railroad tracks and narrow dirt roads vanishing enticingly into shady woodlands; quaint gabled postcard houses with shingled roofs; white-painted porches and children's swings dangling from ancient trees. It was quintessentially Canadian, picturesque and perfect in the summer.

Benny turned the volume of her iPod off and eavesdropped shamelessly. Benny could tell that Mrs. Nat Geo was very into him while he found her boring. Benny watched him eat more dog food.

SERVING CUMBERLAND COUNTY SINCE 1893

The bus stopped in Amherst and Benny, thirsty as desert camel, wondered if she could take a chance on a Seven Up Light but she did the responsible thing and got bottled water instead. She also loaded up on a stash of diet gum, the one edible synthetic she allowed herself from time to time. Part of Benny's health food fanaticism came from having acne as a teenager. Her complexion had been so bad her mother had dragged her off to a Hungarian cosmetician – trading treatments for house cleaning. The cosmetician was short, stern, and in her sixties, and she'd poked the pustules with a needle, neutralizing infection by zapping Benny's face with a purple electric current that she'd applied with a buzzing glass cylinder. The cosmetician had banned chocolate, candy, cheese, tomatoes, carbonated drinks, caffeine, orange juice, and bread from Benny's diet. All that acid had to go. Benny, her cheeks pitted, her forehead mottled and her chin greasy, would have agreed to anything, so she stuck to the rigid diet and endured the acrid buzzing of the electric current and the bitter pain of the cosmetician's fingers digging deep into her tender facial tissue.

So, it was far too risky to go down the road of carbonated beverages, although Benny's complexion had been flawless for some time and she had, some years back, re-introduced tiny pieces of chocolate into her diet without dire consequence.

The stopover in Amherst was an hour and Benny walked off to explore. She found the door to the clock tower building open and she ventured inside.

"Can I help you?" A solid young girl in a print frock appeared. "This is private property, you know."

"Oh, I'm sorry, I thought this was the city hall or something."

"It was. But they didn't use it anymore and they were letting it fall apart, so I bought it and I'm going to restore it. I'm waiting for the editor of *The Amherst Daily News* to come and do a story on me, that's why the door's open."

Benny wondered how the girl could have afforded to buy the place, never mind restore it.

"There's a real old clock in the tower," the girl said. "Want to see it?"

"I'd love to," Benny said and she followed the girl inside, eager to look up the old iron staircase that led to the bell tower.

"You can go up if you like," the girl said, "but watch yourself, I don't know how safe the rungs are. *The Amherst Daily News* guy said he wanted to go up and take a picture of the tower from there."

Benny climbed the ladder, gingerly testing each step before putting her weight on it. She got to the top and poked her head out, climbing cautiously onto the roof. The view was spectacular – idyllic as a children's picture book, with emerald and jade green fields surrounding the village of Amherst, a small toy train chugging through the patchwork country-side. A breeze brushed Benny's face, bringing with it the cool freshness of a languid summer day, carrying the promise of freshly-peeled oranges, swimsuits drying in the sun, and melting ice cream cones.

She looked down on the main road at the pedestrian-crossing sign and she saw the Nat Geo couple standing outside a family diner and pointing up at her.

Benny felt a sense of wonder. She closed her eyes remembering Mum, no, it couldn't have been Mum, it must have been a babysitter, telling her and Shay tales of the far north, where thick snowflakes fluttered and fell like goose-down scattered from a pillowcase shaken from up high. Benny looked up, thinking it would be quite possible to touch the sky – touch the curve of the pale blue dome and stroke the scudding cotton clouds. Her reverie was interrupted by the girl calling her down.

"Hello up there, the newspaper editor's here. You must come down."

Benny climbed down slowly. She reached the bottom, brushed her hands on her trousers and grinned at the girl.

"Wow," she said. "Thank you."

The girl nodded politely, wanting her to leave. This was her day to tell her story. There was no place for an upstart intruder.

The newspaper editor was wheezing mightily as if he'd run a half a dozen kilometers, and it wasn't like he was in great shape to begin with. Half of his checked shirt was hanging loose and he sported a large coffee stain on the front of his creased beige trousers.

"Rob Thomas," he said. "Like the singer, only not, of course." He chuckled at his own joke and offered Benny a sweaty hand. "I'm the editor of the newspaper. Serving Cumberland County since 1893. Would you like a tour of our offices? I can come back to see old Beth here any time. I mean I know where you live," he said to Beth and he snorted with laughter, his shoulders jiggling. Benny noticed Beth stiffen.

"Nah, thanks mate, I've got to get on the bus soon anyway. Beth here was good enough to let me climb up. That's treat enough for one day, I reckon."

She saw Beth relax while Rob looked disappointed. He pushed his small round glasses up his nose, leaving a large fingerprint on the smudged lenses. "Yeah, well, not much to show you anyways," he said. "They moved us over into the strip mall for God's sake. Well, they had to, I guess. The old place, that building just down from here, well, it was condemned because of all the toxic crap they'd dumped in the backyard, all the shit from the printing presses. They used to print in the basement, right? Anyways, great old building but no way to save it. So our new offices are boring, not much to show you, you're quite right."

At the mention of a toxic zone in need of exploration, Benny had to get going. "Yeah, well ta to both of you," she said, giving her hand a quick wipe on her trousers and shaking Beth's hand. "That was quite fantastic. Good luck with the restoration. Hey, Rob, do a good story on Beth here, right?" Then she shot out of the old city hall and found the historic former home of *The Amherst Daily News*, which was, as Rob had said, a couple of buildings down.

Benny checked her watch. Twenty minutes tops. She climbed through a broken window, breathing in dusty old paper, layers of ancient paint, moth-infested fabric and rotting wood. She wished she had hours to do the place justice. An ornate wooden railing dangled from the gigantic staircase in the centre of the main foyer, while the rooms off to the side were cluttered with desks, broken bookcases, and ancient computers. The walls were hung with cheap, framed prints of yachts in a harbor, the backing buckling out of the frames. There was a plethora of desk calendars and a bunch of Selectric typewriters piled on the floor. Six inches of dust covered everything. Benny inched her way down into the basement, wishing she had a flashlight. She crept down the rickety steps and saw that archives had once been stored there, with only a few remnants remaining. Benny picked up a fragment dated 1916.

She made her way back up into the main building, stopping to explore one last room. She imagined it must have been the main newsroom; it was filled with every manner of journalistic paraphernalia: rulers, staplers, used illegible notebooks, photocopies of old legal documents, and water-stained manila files. Benny spotted an old photograph under a desk. She glanced at her watch; she was running out of time. She pulled the picture out carefully, blew the dust off the print and found herself facing a very stern bunch of ladies, all glaring stiffly at the photographer. She tucked her find under her T-shirt, climbed out the window and ran from the old place, reaching the bus out of breath. She got to her seat with a minute to spare.

As the bus rolled out of town, Benny settled down and studied her prize. The women – prim and Victorian – stared back at her. Benny inspected their expressions closely. Were they ambitious worker bees like her or were they part of some women's collective? Maybe they ran an orphanage, or organized the tea and biscuits for church on a Sunday. Not one of them smiled but Benny did suspect a coquettish glint to the one woman's eyes – she had her arms crossed and the tip of her pointed boot peeked out from under her long skirt. Benny wrapped her treasure carefully between the pages of her trashy magazine and packed it away.

It may have been the excitement of rushing around Amherst, or the fumes from the toxic old newspaper press, but she felt a headache building. She probed it for clues. Was it sinus, tension, migraine, muscle spasm, allergy or all of the above? She decided she would have to wait until the signals were clear and then she'd overdose appropriately.

She scrolled through her iPod, treated herself to a tangy stick of peach apricot gum, and then got lost in the immense forests and open skies. The bus rolled into Moncton. "Goodbye, Nova Scotia," she said softly. "I'm in New Brunswick now."

KENNY – AND SATAN, THE SUGAR DEMON

Benny had to change buses at Moncton and the new ride was jam-packed. She ended up next to an eight-year-old boy with a fiery mop of orange hair and while she got settled, she watched a large girl haul her way up into the bus. The girl was clutching a dirty pillow under one arm and hanging onto an aromatic brown-paper sack of fragrant fast-food with the other, and Benny's mouth watered. It wasn't that she didn't want junk food, she just never allowed herself any. She realized that her supplies were running low; all she had left was one slightly crushed Ferrero Rocher chocolate, a couple of sticks of diet gum, and a few mini bottles of alcohol. This meager larder was intended to last her right up to Quebec City where they would arrive at dawn.

According to the map, they were scheduled to travel through the Appalachian Mountains, which sounded positively beyond romantic but she figured they'd be doing that stretch in the middle of the night and be privy to no more than blackness.

Benny was suddenly aware that her stomach was growlingly empty. She looked over at the fast-food girl who was eating coleslaw, biscuits, mashed potatoes and gravy with her KFC feast. Benny badly wanted mashed potatoes and gravy. But her food envy vanished quickly when the girl's sharp teeth tugged at a gray-white cord of elasticized chicken ligaments. Nauseated, Benny averted her gaze, and, without thinking, she turned to chat to Kenny, to discourse at length on one of their favourite topics – how the fast food industry was killing the western world, how more people were dying of obesity than starvation, and how it was death by the cruel hand of the food courts and the McDonald's marketing demons. She opened her mouth, ready to talk when she realized, of course, that he wasn't there. There was only some orange-haired kid sitting next to her. Shocked and confused, she stared into space until she was jolted by the kid behind her who was kicking her seat. She turned around to give him a full-wattage quell'em glare but good old mom next to him looked like a pit bull terrier just looking for an excuse to attack. Benny nodded respectfully in mom's direction – mom, who sported a military brush-cut and a tattoo of a snake on her neck.

The bus pulled onwards to Edmunston, signalling it was time to change the soundtrack, get some New Age water crashing on rocks, Peruvian flutes accompanying.

The orange-headed kid dozed quietly next to Benny until mom started poking him, peppering him with sharp questions. Benny, still cowed by mom, sat quiet as a mouse, waiting for the pit bull matriarch to run out of steam. She passed the time by watching Miss Fried Food Fest chug down a real Coke which once again reminded her of Kenny.

"Satan the Sugar Demon's alive and well," he liked to say, "and he goes by the name Coca-Cola."

Benny was disconcerted to be thinking about Kenny again but she couldn't seem to escape him. Without wanting to, her mind flashed back to the first time they'd met. She'd been standing around at an art school social, her back against a corner wall, a first year student, sick with shyness, watching the easily-mingling crowd and wishing the floor would indeed swallow her up.

"No one puts kitty in a corner," she'd heard a deep voice say next to her.

"I beg your pardon, what did you say?" She'd turned to see a good-looking skinny Asian boy slouching next to her, his expression quizzical, his hair thick and unruly.

"No one puts kitty in a corner," he'd repeated. "I've come to take you away from this madness, waltz you to another world." He'd swept his hand around the room in a grandiose gesture and hit another student soundly on the back. "Sorry, man," he said, laughing, and that's when Benny knew art school was going to be just fine.

"I think you mean 'no one puts Baby in a corner,' " she'd said, smiling at him, "and they didn't waltz, it was dirty dancing. Pleased to meet you, I'm Benny, abstract fine art."

He'd held out his hand. "Kenny, caricaturist, geekaturist, cartoonist, buffoonist."

Thoughtful partner, less-than-thrilling lover, unforgiveable adulterer. They were married after Benny's 24th birthday and lived in muted wedded bliss for three and a half years. That it was muted never occurred to Benny; she'd just thought that was the way marriage was, and anyway, they were both so busy working, who had time for great heights of passion?

But, she thought now, filled with fury, even if ours wasn't the most vivid colour in the paint box, that's still no excuse for you to do what you did. *Oh, Kenny, you're the last thing I want to think about.*

In an effort to avoid oncoming gloom, she turned to admire the scenery: the delicate yellow and purple wildflowers that bordered the asphalt; the sloping lawns surrounding grey and red barns; elegant young forests, raw, pure and clean; and the seashell pastel translucence of the sky.

Several hours later, saturated with natural beauty, she got so hungry that she drank a mini of brandy and downed a codeine headache pill. This served to dampen her hunger, get a nice buzz on, and warp her hearing. Surely pit bull mom had not made the loud pronouncement that she "…masturbates comfortably"?

Great sunset, superb. She decided she loved Canada and that she really loved New Brunswick. She considered taking more codeine to enhance her feeling of wellbeing but she was reluctant to try out for the role of a corpse on a bus. Kenny forgotten, she was suddenly overwhelmed by a longing for Eli.

Being with Chris in St John's, Teenie in Halifax, and not to mention the odd reappearances of the absent Kenny, had pushed Eli to the back of her mind, but she twisted her ring now, wishing she could see him. Then, distracted by the beauty of the ice blue sky spread thin with tissue-paper clouds aflame with gold, she quite forgot the perplexities of love.

A FULL MOON OVER QUEBEC

A full moon hung low over Quebec. And beneath it, Benny needed a little help from her friends to get her through the night. Another mini bottle, this time a god-awful liqueur. Add to that half a Valium and half a sleeping pill, followed by another half a sleeping pill. But the loaded assault generated no more than a meager two-hour catnap. The pills weren't to blame for the dismal lack of their success; that fault lay with the bus driver.

Benny was convinced the bus ride was some kind of test, a survivor reality show or torture research on how to transform semi-normal people into wildly crazed, sleep-deprived psychotic half-wits.

It started off well, as most disasters do. Nighttime pills were popped, the cabin lights turned off, and the bus was in motion with the human cargo asleep. Then, sometime around midnight, the bus stopped and the cabin lights snapped on. The driver stood up, stretched and announced at the top of his voice that this was a ten-minute stop, no one was to leave the bus, repeat, no one was to leave the bus.

Twenty-five minutes later, the bus was still lit up like a football field, with the passengers blinking like confused owls. Fifteen minutes after that, the lights were switched off and the bus once again hit the road. Zero explanation from the bus driver.

Just as the bewildered travellers were once again sinking into a slumber of sorts, the bus stopped at a diner in the middle of nowhere. "Everyone get off the bus. Everyone has to get off the bus, now. Go into the diner, use the washroom and order food at the counter in the dining area. And no one is to go into the lounge area, okay? Clear? No one goes into the lounge area. Everyone off the bus now."

Benny was filled with fury. What was this? She wanted to march up to the driver and ask him if he'd like them to form a single line and hold hands like preschoolers but she bit her tongue. They all trooped in, as directed, looked at the menu and recited, one after the other:

Cheeseburger with fries and a Coke;
Cheeseburger with fries and a Coke;
Cheeseburgers, fries with gravy and a Coke;
Tossed salad with no dressing, bottle of mineral water.

The last, of course, was Benny. No way, José, not even in the middle of a drug-addled night, not even half-starved in the middle of nowhere, was she going deep-fried with cheese. There were certain areas of her life that were simply not open to suggestion.

She was the only person who got her off-the-menu order through. Behind her, others tried and failed.

Benny ate her salad quickly in the uncomfortable area outside of the off-limits lounge, and realized she was still ravenous, still craving those fries with gravy. Back on the bus, the rest of the gang fell into a deeply contented protein-carb-grease-inspired sleep while Benny took another pill to no avail.

3:00 a.m. The bus stopped. The cabin lights flashed on. Another diner. "Half an hour. Everybody off the bus."

What was with this driver? Benny indulged in fantasies involving him and her fists. She walked into the new diner as instructed. Used the washroom. Emerged foggily to study the menu. *But it's all in French. Are we in Quebec already? Jambon? Ham? Mais, non.*

She got to the front of the line and was stared down by a very non-Anglais-speaking person behind the counter. Trapped, she pointed to a grilled *fromage* sandwich. Got back on the bus only to discover she couldn't eat any of it because the entire sandwich was deep-fried and doused in butter. She chewed two codeine instead and washed them down with another liqueur.

Half an hour later, in her haze and her hunger, she sampled the sandwich and it was so delicious she nearly melted, much like the *fromage* in the sandwich she was eating. Without further hesitation, she bit into it again, nearly moaning aloud as her taste buds exploded with delighted fireworks of joy. She sank into the heaven of a grilled cheese sandwich and its unexpected crashing waves of pleasure.

Then the shock of having eaten the preserved-within-an-inch-of-its-life cheese sandwich made any kind of sleep impossible. She was drugged, sleepless, acne-bound and trapped, with no escape but to dive into the depths of very loud music.

She leaned against the window, heavy metal pulsating, while the clouds dissolved to free up a clear black sky with a full moon hanging low. Benny was convinced the moon was staring directly at her, and it might have been unnerving except that it was staring in a well-intentioned, kindly sort of way, as if telling her everything was fine and she was doing the right thing.

Hey Moon, are you the voice that spoke to me in St John's, about embracing the freedom? Was that you? Tell me, how I'm doing in life in general? Why'd it all go so wrong? What did I do to deserve that?

The moon just looked at her.

Benny decided not to go onto Toronto, but to get off the bus in Quebec City. She needed to rest up, not to mention round up her unruly cheese-eating actions and lasso them to the ground. Besides, it was time to test-drive the bona fide hostel environment. Did she have what it took, to be a real backpacker? Only time, and Quebec, would tell.

JUST LIKE A LITTLE PARIS

Benny loved Quebec City nearly more than she loved New Brunswick, Nova Scotia, and Newfoundland. *Oh, beautiful Parisian city of cobblestones and daydreams.*

She fared well with the hostelling aspect of things and was feeling quite proud of herself. The only calamity had occurred post-shower when a newly purchased dollar store black towel shed fluff all over her damp body, transforming her into a mangy Godzilla carnival attraction. She tried to brush the sticky damp stuff off with a facecloth, but it stuck to her.

The shower had been delicious: hot, steamy, soapy, a cleansing fest of her dreams. She'd lathered to the max, exfoliated with apricot scrub and enjoyed every blissful second.

Her success with dealing with her first ever hostel environment was helped by the fact that her current abode was more like a hotel than a hostel. Benny realized that, at twenty-nine, her real age, she was a bit old – older than the average young traveller – to be starting her backpacking adventures, but that was in keeping with the way she'd lived her entire life. She'd always been a late bloomer to the social antics she knew other teenagers fell into naturally and found so important.

"I'm a geek, sue me," she'd say to Shay when her sister had teased her. While other girls, with Shandra as their ringleader, had climbed out of bedroom windows to go pubbing and clubbing, Benny was tucked up in bed or planning her next art project or doing homework for extra credits. She'd been driven by a desire to succeed – to work harder, play less. To shed the lower-class, humble beginnings of her poor, endlessly hardworking parents.

Benny had been a quiet child, watchful, analytical. She wasn't going to end up with money a constant worry, and debt a regular companion at the dinner table. She'd observed her parents with careful savvy and had vowed to work not harder in life, but smarter.

Benny had been surprised in her late teens when her mother did quite the about-turn and proved a noteworthy entrepreneur. Mum took her cleaning skills and expanded, hired women to do the work for her, securing contracts for offices and big businesses. Although, since Shandra had given birth to the bouncing baby Harry, Benny's mum's foremost passion was fast becoming her grandson.

Benny wondered how her family was doing as she logged onto the free computer in the hostel lobby. Not exactly state of the art, the computer took ten minutes to find the Internet, making humming and clicking noises. Benny drummed her fingers loudly and sighed. She finally accessed her emails and saw a whole list of messages lined up to greet her. Her chest filled with happiness and she leaned forward to see who had written to her.

Shandra, even Dad, Teenie, Todd, Chris and oh, dear god above ... *Eli. Eli.* After all this time.

Benny's heart nearly stopped beating. With careful precision, afraid any sudden movement would cause the email to vanish, she aimed the cursor right over Eli's name and clicked gently.

Hey Benny! I was walking along the beach in the early wakeful hours of morning, considering options of delightful things to think about 'n I thought of u – one of my fav memories – 'n I thought I must phone u now, immediately, even tho' its only 5 am. But you're gone. U left, u didn't tell me. Where are u? They told me u were traveling. R u headed my way? Eli.

Benny couldn't type back fast enough. But, fingers shaking, she wasn't sure what to say. He'd been silent for so long. Why hadn't he emailed before? And what of the Russian princess? And the baby?

Hiya! Yeah, I'm traveling. Am in Quebec City. Love it. I do seem to be heading west, have no idea how long it will take me to get there. Sure, I'd love to look you up, if I get to B.C. How are things? Hope all is good.

She thought her message sent the right tone of casual interest. Her heart felt like a big ripe plum, bursting out of its skin. She was one of his favourite memories! She twisted the ring on her finger. She wondered if she had worded the message just right, and if should she send a P.S., but what would she say if she did? No, it was better to leave it like that.

She clicked on Shandra's message, which was mostly about baby Harry, with some pics of an intense baby with watchful eyes and a Mohawk hairdo. Mum was fine, working less and less, besotted. Dad was fine. How was Benny?

Benny sent back a message: everything was fine, she was thoroughly enjoying Quebec, no worries, love to everyone. P.S.: Harry's fantastic, thanks for the pics.

Next was Teenie's email.

> Hey girlfriend! I miss you! Come and work for me, I'll fire my art director, she's driving me crazy with her passive aggressive antics, frickin' irritating. Our supplement's spectacular, doll! Do you know they even reprinted? Peter's acting like it only happened 'cuz he's such a genius! As if! Todd emailed me. I think the boy's got a bad case of puppy love! But I can't be bothered, Ed's enough of a kid for me. He and the boy get on like a house on fire, the boy's even got Ed out of the basement! Taken him golfing. Ed's been sober for two days, fingers crossed. Not sure how long the boy's planning to stay but if he's good for Ed, he can frickin' well move in! Anyways, gotta go, meetings, meetings, meetings! Are you having fun? I wish I was with you! We'd paint the town red, eh?

Benny smiled. She read Todd's email before replying to Teenie. His was a sweet generic hello. Benny was sure his email to Teenie had been the same but Teenie was convinced he had a thing for her. Benny sent him a how-do, and then she sent Teenie a cheery message. She realized that she missed Teenie, her feist and her warrior gung-ho aggression.

She saved her message from her father for last. Benny always found emails from Dad endearing. Such an incongruous image – her jockey-sized leathery father with his coke-bottle glasses, tapping one-fingered at the keyboard. Dad didn't believe in punctuation – he wrote one long paragraph with a couple of spaces separating his thoughts.

> How's my best girl? We are fine   hurt my leg again, but its better now   blimmin' horses   yard is fine   saw Kenny the other day he said to tell you he is very sorry he hurt you   try to forgive him luv, he's not a bad fella, we all just want you to be happy Benny girl   Write to your old dad okay? Do you need a few bob? Mum and me got a bit to spare if you need.   Be safe   love Dad

Benny's eyes filled with tears but she swallowed them down.

> Hi Dad! I'm pukka for money but thanks for the offer. I scored some extra work

along the way, got some nice cash from it. Glad your leg is better. I miss you a lot. I wish I was there for one of your super-deluxe extra special hugs! I promise I wouldn't wriggle out of it this time! Tell everyone at the yard I say hi. Any new horses? There are always new horses! Any good ones? Not much news from me. Canada is incredible, Dad. You'd love it. I feel so high up in the world. Somehow you feel closer to the sky, on the top of the world. I never understood why they call ours Down Under but now that I'm On Top, I do! It's like how you used to tell me you felt when you rode a winner, on top of the world! I'll email more, okay? You email me too. I love you, Dad.

She was careful to avoid any mention of Kenny. Even seeing his name had sent shock waves through her body. He could never, ever, be sorry enough. Never. And how come Dad had seen him? Benny never understood why her family didn't hate Kenny the way she did and she felt betrayed by their lack of fury at what he'd done. They hadn't even really seemed surprised when it happened, and their reaction to him was kind, while Benny was sure she would never forgive him.

She logged off and slumped down in the cheap plastic chair.

Whoa. Eli. Kenny. Dad. Emotional overload. Time to go for a long walk, a quick trip to the washroom first.

She bounded up the wide old wooden staircase of the hostel, bubbling with thoughts and images of her family.

Not a great looking bunch by any means. There was tall, wide Shandra, a lot like Mum, quite mannish really, except that Shay was a bottle blonde while Mum was gingery. Dad was a tiny man, a jockey as a lad, head groom later, never heard of sunscreen, smoked hand-rolls like a chimney, hacked like pro. He was a tough little walnut, indestructible, incorrigible.

There was a time when Benny had worried that she'd inherit her mother's propensity for a generous girth, along with Dad's lack of stature. She figured herself no natural born beauty queen either – her hair was thin and mousy; she grew it shoulder-length, dyed it raven and bolstered it with product. A cruel taunt would call her features ferrety, while a friend might call her elfin. She wore Cleopatra eyeliner and double-thick mascara and wouldn't be seen dead without her makeup.

Her skin tone came to her via her maternal grandmother – mottled, with a hide thick as a rhinoceros. But Benny made the best of what she had. She exfoliated her skin to polished and smooth and smothered herself in Factor 60 sunscreen to keep a lid on her rambunctious propensity for sunspots.

"You're a bit vain there, Benny luv," Mum had often said. "Life isn't about how you look. Sometimes I think it was a bad thing, us sending you to that posh school. All those girls, their mouths full of silver spoons. It wasn't good for you."

"You didn't send me, Dad's boss did. His way of getting rid of his guilt."

"Your Dad never blamed him for what happened and it was very nice of him to send you. You know he never had kids of his own. Why must you read an alternative motive into everything?"

"It's an 'ulterior' motive, Mum, not an alternative motive. And you make it sound like I'm looking for things to be negative about. I'm not. I just see life more realistically than you do."

Her mother had watched her pack her bags for Canada. "You can't run away forever, dear," she had said. "Here give me that, you can't fold to save your life."

"I'm not running away, Mum," Benny had replied, her shoulders stiff. "I'm going to explore the world. Big difference. All I've ever done is work, work, work, and I just want something new, okay? Don't make such a big deal about it. Lots of people travel the world."

"But after everything that happened, your Dad and me, well, we'd love you to stay with us for a bit, let it all settle, luv. You don't always have to be doing something or achieving something. You could take some time here, to do nothing, be with Shandy and me and Dad. You know, relax for once, take it easy."

Benny had wanted to hit her mother. Instead she snapped the suitcase shut and swung it off the bed.

"Don't you get it? That's the last bloody thing I need to do okay? It never ceases to amaze me how my own family doesn't understand the first thing about me."

Her mother had made a move to hug her but Benny had dodged

and grabbed a hairbrush instead, pulling the bristles across her scalp, digging deep.

Her mother had taken the brush from her, sat Benny down, and slowly and gently combed her hair. Benny, head down, hadn't moved – she'd sat still as a statue.

"Ah, Benny." Her mother had been sad. "You make life so tough for yourself, luv. It's tough enough by itself, doesn't need any help from you, girlie. But you are the way you are. I just wish you could be kinder to yourself. I worry you push yourself too hard, that one day it will be too much. Everybody has a breaking point."

Benny had remained stubbornly silent, thinking she'd die before she broke. She sighed. "Ah, Mum, don't worry so much, okay?"

Alone in the old-fashioned white-tiled washroom of the Quebec hostel, Benny looked at herself in the mirror.

I miss you, Mum. I miss everything, all of it. I miss that life I took for granted, the one I thought would last forever, the one I thought was concrete but wasn't.

She bent over the basin and ran cold water over her wrists until she felt in control.

No point in feeling sorry for myself. Time to go for a walk. This is a holiday. Anyway, Eli emailed me. I can think about that.

She stepped out into a day fit only for mad dogs, Englishmen and traveling Australians. Benny walked slowly thinking it would be wise to spend most of her day inside air conditioned stores which in turn led to the retail therapy of a large pair of Celtic cross earrings.

She wandered the Terrasse Dufferin with the St. Lawrence and St. Charles Rivers meandering alongside. She was surrounded by beauty: manicured green lawns, the long boardwalk with cheerful ice-cream stands, and banks of picnic benches waiting to give visitors a rest. Colourful flags fluttered high in the cool breeze that lifted the heat for a small, relieved moment. Benny vowed to return one day on the arm of her true love; she'd wear a black sequined cocktail dress and real pearl earrings and they'd waltz on the boardwalk, under a full Quebec moon.

She surprised herself by staying in Quebec City for five long days. She slept well at night on the narrow lower bunk bed – her pill intake minimal. She walked for hours, photographing and exploring, finding no end of treasures: an art display under a highway bridge, accompanied by graffiti extraordinaire and she lay on the high, hilly, green grass near the Citadel and daydreamed about nothing much at all. But she realized that lazing in Quebec City was no way to get red ink on her map and it was with reluctance that she dragged herself back to the bus. Onwards, to Montreal.

FEAR AND LOATHING IN ONTARIO

Benny knew Montreal fairly well, having gone at Colin's suggestion. Restless and lonely, she'd taken the bus out of Toronto, daydreaming endlessly about Eli, who she had seen from her window but had not yet met.

So she'd thought she'd stop in Montreal en route, why not? She'd loved it then and Toronto was going to be strictly drive-through.

The bus arrived in Montreal at 9:45 a.m. Benny immediately hit her old haunt, the Hotel Rue Herbert, but there were no rooms available. Rather than searching blindly for other accommodation, she headed back to the bus station, and attended to basic ablutions in the washroom, thinking it was better she forge on anyway. She had the uneasy feeling that the Toronto leg of the journey was going to be tough though she wasn't sure why.

She climbed aboard the bus at noon, clutching a hot apple-and-cinnamon tea, glad she didn't end up getting a room in Montreal. She was keen to see what Ottawa was like, but decided to keep moving through there too, wanting to get over the hurdle of Toronto. Although she had loved the east coast, she felt her trip would start for real once she left the G.T.A. in her wake.

The bus was eerily quiet while outside the passing scenery was flat farmland, pretty in a manicured way. Benny pulled out her map and inked in her route.

A motley crew of unwashed folk got on at Ottawa. Ponderation en route to Toronto. Realistically a change of clothes would be necessary and in short order too. Benny was sure it would be horribly bizarre, after living in Toronto for a year and getting to know it intimately, to be dressing in a bus station like an indigent person. But the fact of the matter was that Toronto knew too much about her.

Benny thought it was like meeting a stranger at a party, or a business function, or on a plane – you exchanged too much information and then, at the end, you thought to yourself, who was that person anyway? And why did you say so much? And then you parted ways, hoping if you ever saw each other again, that neither would remember what the other had said, or at least have the decency to pretend to forget.

And that, from her bus-seated perspective, was how she felt about Toronto. An uncomfortable reunion preferably avoided.

She dipped into her personal pharmacy, having stocked up on codeine and tiny bottles of Southern Comfort before leaving Quebec City. The weather mirrored her mood – dirty grey clouds, no sun, and blustery outside. Benny had the sinking feeling that she was failing to deliver, but she wasn't sure exactly what it was she was supposed to be delivering. She realized she was hungry yet again. Or maybe that was *still*.

The old guy next to her was scaly like a reptile and snoring in his sleep. His flaking scalp was badly in need of medicated shampoo. Benny climbed over him carefully and navigated down to the washroom. She opened the door to the tiny toilet and the hot stench of urine-marinated feces hit her like a stinky wet dishtowel. Traveling by bus certainly had its tougher aspects. She levitated over the toilet seat, careful not to touch anything. Back in her seat, she sterilized her hands repeatedly.

She dug a fleece throw out of her carry-on and wrapped it tightly around her. The buses were refrigerated ice wagons, always freezing. On the bright side, perhaps the steady seven-below-zero temperature kept the passengers fresher and youthful for longer – the cold was an anti-aging bonus. Benny, hating the imbalance between her age and the success she should have achieved but had not, would do anything to turn back the hands of time, even suffer frostbite on a bus.

She took stock of her life, and tried to get in touch with her former good cheer but it seemed to have slipped like a carnival mask with a cheap elastic strap stretched too thin. There was no escaping the sordid pathetic truth – life wasn't fair. She should, at this juncture of her life, be enjoying a stable, solid marriage and a successful and fêted career in fine art. She felt her chest tighten.

She swallowed a Valium and nodded off to sleep. Woke to witness the drop-off of a zillion people in a nameless, faceless location.

The bus was the coldest yet. Am I in Alaska already? So soon?

She added a knee rug and layered her *Come to Papa* sweatshirt over *Wisconsin Death Trip*. She crunched on another codeine pill and tried to look on the brighter side of things; the dandruff old fellow had left, and her peach apricot chewing gum was delicious and working well to alleviate the furry sensation from her teeth.

Floating on her high, Benny noted that it was indeed the little things in life that counted. The little pills, the little bottles…

She told herself she was sick and tired of waiting for *when*. *When* she got here, or there, or *when* she fell in love, or *when* she got a new job. The whole myth of the happy-*when*-ever-after. Well, no more, she was going to live in the here and now, with immediate effect.

She fell asleep.

She awoke an hour later with the sneaking suspicion that being too now-orientated could have its drawbacks and she was certain that it was the horror of finding herself inescapably in the now that brought on a severe attack of Fear and Loathing in Ontario. The bus had come to a complete stop, but she couldn't help but notice the blacktop moving by. Fast. Really fast.

Had she taken some heavy-duty drugs and not noticed? But that wasn't her style and this was plain freaky, not fun.

No, it was the *now* thing filling her with panic. She finally had proof of that which she had long suspected – that facing reality was far from pleasant and highly overrated. She closed her eyes, which made it even worse, like being drunk on a rollercoaster, and trying to pretend the ride was over while knowing you were inching up a steep incline.

Before she'd left Colin's, a curious coworker had stopped by for a chat, disregarding exploding bomb graphics stuck to the side of the monitor and the yellow-and-black crime scene tape wrapped around the back of

Benny's chair. All flying in the face of the Employee Manual's section on *Keeping Your Work Station Professional and Neat at All Times.*

"So, what will you do if you fall flat on your face?" the perky editor had enquired, nearly dislodging a pile of printouts.

Benny had pointedly rearranged the layouts. "I never fall flat on my face," she'd said.

Which of course, was the opposite of true. The truth was, she'd make a plan, hide the evidence, and tell a good story.

But right now, at 4:12 p.m., as the clock ticked by, oblivious to her anguish, she felt horribly and inescapably flat on her face – a piece of bumper flotsam, dragging along behind the bus, her visage being grazed in extremis.

She wondered – thoughts of Fear and Loathing momentarily cast aside – if asphalt face-down grazing could, in any sense, be considered a successful exfoliation technique.

"Chin up, chickadee," Benny said, self-talking into the depths of her fleecy throw that she had wrapped tightly around her shoulders, but not caring if anyone heard. "C'mon, now, get that chin up off the tar, revolutionary exfoliation technique or not. Best you don't take any more chemicals for say the next year or so and I tell you what, have a field day with *when*-thoughts. You go, girl. You *when* to the max. Get outta the long, dark, fast-moving night of the now and get yourself into the *when*. It'll be okay, it always is. *When* you get through Toronto, it'll all be fine. Just hang onto that *when* and it'll all be good."

Never mind *Fear and Loathing.* This was worse than that. This was *The Place of the Dead Roads. The Naked Lunch.* She'd moved from the sanctuary of Hunter S. Thompson into the crazy obscenity that was William S. Burroughs. It was hard to breathe; her vision was distorted, a fish-eye lens swinging crazily with a finger pressed on fast-forward.

Think about something nice. Like chocolate. How nice life will be when you have a chocolate. When you are warm again. When you have a nice fresh T-shirt and new socks. When you can brush your teeth. Get a lovely big healthy salad. Maybe even some tomatoes, who cares about the acid? After this, when you arrive, you can have anything you want, okay?

The escape into when-thinking proved successful therapy and she dwelled in that land until the world was nice, shiny and friendly again.

Coming out of the killer stretch of highway and flatland that was Ottawa to Toronto on a bus, she told herself she wouldn't do that particular stretch of road again in a hurry.

PAWNING THE GREATER TORONTO AREA

Toronto. They arrived at 6:28 a.m. Benny staggered into the bus station washroom and stared in the mirror.

"You took a fine time to leave me, Left Wheel," she hummed under her breath à la Kenny Roger's *Lucille.* She set about having her basin sponge bath, noticing she was not alone and that there was a camaraderie among the girls with their soap and face cloths and economical movements.

Sweet-smelling and deliciously clean, Benny stashed her gear into a locker and wondered what to do with the five hours of waiting time until the bus left for Winnipeg. She wandered outside, stopping to read a headline – *The Toronto Sun* was denouncing someone for being a wanker. She turned onto Yonge to kill some time at an Internet café. She logged on to find one lonesome email from Shay – Shay who was righteously pissed at her – Benny had forgotten Dad's birthday.

Benny stared at the screen, a tidal wave of shame and guilt washing over her. She sighed. Anybody but Dad and it would have been more forgivable. She was irrationally furious with Kenny. If they'd still been together, he would have told her it was Dad's birthday. He always did; him with the fridge magnet calendar she used to mock. She started typing, wanting to blame the time difference, the discombobulation that came with bus travel, the alienness of her entire journey; she, who had never so much as taken an afternoon off in her life, was now carried along by a force that had chosen her, more than she having chosen it.

Dad, Shay, Mum, I'm SO sorry I missed emailing you on Dad's birthday, I really am, I've been on the bus for like two straight days, we only stopped now. Dad, I'm so sorry but I did get you a present and I'm going to post it today, right now, that's what I planned all along.

She knew they would know she was lying, that she'd forgotten about Dad's birthday, but *mea culpa* apologies weren't Benny's style. Her grudging acknowledgements of wrongdoings always came with a letter of caveats and Mum was fond of telling Benny she should have been a lawyer, she was that wily.

Honestly, the buses only seem to stop in the middle of the night when it would be hard for me to have a coherent conversation at all. Did you have a good birthday Dad? I hope so! So watch for the postie okay? I'm about to get back on the bus, am in for a long stretch; it's one day, seven hours, and forty-nine minutes from here to Winnipeg, covering a distance of 1,317 miles, so don't worry if you don't hear from me for a bit, okay? P.S.: I've covered 3,423 miles so far, which is 5,508 kilometres, but I did do 2,161 miles of that by air, which was cheating in a way. I think it only counts for real if you're on the ground. Love to all, Benny.

She signed off and tried to figure out what to buy her father. She suddenly didn't seem to have that much time before the bus left. Think, think. She walked down Yonge to Queen and, on a whim, turned east. She remembered seeing a whole bunch of pawn-shops and had the idea she could find something unique there, not too expensive either. A fob watch! The perfect thing. She walked quickly, reached the first pawn store and stared inside the window before going inside. The owner regarded her and dismissed her in the same moment.

"Excuse me?" Benny spoke loudly. "I'm interested in the fob watches in the window."

"Fob watches? What is a fob watch?" The man had a thick European accent and was polishing a silver candelabra.

Benny was irritated. "Those big round watches that don't come on a strap. Those ones," she pointed. "You've got about five of them."

"Those are not for sale."

Benny wanted to hit the man. "Why not? Why aren't they for sale? They're in this shop, aren't they?"

"Because people own them." The man smiled, extremely satisfied, and carried on polishing. Benny walked over to him and put her hands on the counter.

"What's the matter with you?" she asked. "I'm here to buy something and you won't even show me anything."

"Nothing is the matter with me, I don't have to sell you anything if I don't want to."

"But why don't you want to?" Benny was baffled. Even hurt. She had no idea how to deal with this situation.

The man didn't answer. He just shrugged.

"How about that?" Benny pointed to an old camera. "Can I take a look at that?"

"But that is not a watch. And anyway, it's not for sale either."

Benny lost her temper. "You're an idiot, mate. Well, screw you!"

"I think you must be leaving now," the man said, but Benny was already halfway out the door, making sure she slammed it as hard as she could. Which wasn't easy since it was on a weighted hinged arm. She stood outside the shop, and glared at the man through the window. He ignored her and carried on rubbing the candlestick holder.

Benny, beginning to worry about time, tried the next pawn shop. This one was much bigger, almost a department store, and not a fob watch in sight. Benny was confused by her lack of immediate success; she was used to having ideas that bore fruit quickly.

She turned back onto Queen and went into the dustiest, most filthy shop, under a dilapidated yellow-and-red awning. Her rationale was that this guy would have to take any kind of offer she'd make and be grateful for her business. The dark store was piled high with old stereos and TVs. Two men watched her, not exactly welcoming, even irritated at being disturbed.

"May I look at your fob watches?" Benny pointed to a few inside the dirty glass counter. Neither man said a word; they just looked at her as if they hadn't understood the question. Benny sighed. She pulled up an old bar stool, dusted it off and sat down.

"I'm here to buy a watch, mate, and I'm not going to leave until you sell me one, okay?"

The old guy behind the counter lit a cigarette. "Why you want a watch?"

What was with these people? You had to write a dissertation before you could beg them to sell you something? Benny decided to play along. Or try to. "It's for my Dad's birthday," she said.

"So your dad likes old watches, does he?"

Benny pointed to a watch. "I'd like to see that one, please."

The old guy had a thick shock of grey hair, most of it sprouting from his ears. He looked over at the younger, sleazy-looking man who was wearing a lot of bad gold jewelry. They exchanged some kind of silent conversation, and the old man looked at Benny. "You got cash money?"

"What other kind is there?" Benny asked.

"Show me."

"Oh, for God's sake, mate. This is ridiculous." Benny got up off the chair and turned to leave.

"Ah, now, such a temper on such a young girl. Come back, I'll show you the watch."

Benny sighed and turned back. But she didn't sit down. "So, show me then," she said.

"I need a drink first. You are making me need a drink." The old guy pulled out a bottle of unopened Crown Royal. "Tell you what. Have a drink with me, and I'll sell you the watch."

Benny thought this was the strangest wormhole she'd ever fallen through. Not that she even knew what a wormhole was but this fruitcake situation seemed to fit the bill.

"I'm not drinking out of the bottle," she said.

The old guy was affronted. "What kind of person do you think I am? That I would ask a lady to drink out of the bottle?" He reached under the counter and pulled out two plastic glasses. He put them on the counter. Benny held hers up to the light. It was grimy but she was getting desperate.

"Fine," she said and the man cracked the bottle open and poured two inches into her glass. She waited until he had filled his two-thirds full.

"Cheers," she said, taking a cautious sip. "So, now that I'm drinking with you, can I see the watch?"

The man looked at her and cackled. He was missing most of his teeth and the ones he had left were graveyard tilted and ashy gray.

Benny, tired of the game, looked around the shop. She decided she'd finish the drink, what the hell, and then get the heck out of there, buy Dad some chocolates. Maple stuff, sugary, that'd do just fine. The shop was filled with junk, all of it covered in a good few inches of grime.

"You married?" the old guy asked.

"No. Why, you want to marry me?"

This cracked the old guy up. The sleazy oily man just sat there, watching. The old guy was snorting so hard Benny thought he was going to choke. "She's got a sense of humour, this one," the old guy said. "Tell you what, I'm going to show you the watch just because I like you."

Benny shrugged. She didn't think he was ever going to part with any of his junk. He surprised her by laboriously opening up the glass cabinet and pulling out a beautiful fob watch. He pushed it across the glass countertop to Benny who took it.

"Does it work?" she asked.

The old guy was offended. "Everything I sell here works. Here, give it back if you don't think it works." He reached for it, but Benny swiped it away. The doorbell chimed and a big guy, a rapper gangsta in shiny blue sweatpants and matching long hanging shirt, strolled into the store.

"You take stuff from me, give me money, right, then I can come back, pay you back with a bit of interest and get my stuff back? That's how it works?" He was carrying a big plastic bag.

"What you think this is? A loan department? Get outta here." The old guy shouted, shooing the rapper out the store. The gangsta looked as confused as Benny felt.

"But I also thought that's what you did here," she said to the old guy, but he just shrugged, topped up his glass, and lit another cigarette.

"So, you want the watch or what?" He seemed to have lost his good humour, such as it had been.

Benny examined it. She had wound it and it worked. It was quite a spectacular piece.

"Twenty dollars?" she asked.

"Forty," the old guy said.

"Thirty?"

The old guy nodded. Benny hopped down off her chair and realized she was tipsy. She steadied herself, counted out the money and pushed it across to the old guy. He and the oily fellow had forgotten she was there. They were back in whatever world they inhabited. Benny realized there was no point in even saying goodbye. She left the store and stood in the harsh sunshine of the day, clutching her prize carefully and looking around for the nearest Canada Post. She wondered why she'd thought of the pawnshops instead of going into Sears or The Bay. She told herself it was because she'd wanted to buy Dad something special and unique but she knew it wasn't as simple as that. Something about this trip was igniting her desire to go places she'd never been – and she knew that didn't just mean new cities and towns.

SALAD DAYS AND GOLDEN BOYS

Two hours later, Benny was onboard the bus, ready to embrace the freedom of the open road. She was armed with supplies: an assortment of tiny, individually wrapped chocolates, two litres of Evian water, and a salad to die for – three kinds of lettuce, a sprinkling of chopped tomato, loads of cucumber, artichoke hearts, red peppers, olives, Asian noodles, a careful portion of feta cheese as well as marinated tofu, sunflower seeds and red onions. She also had a supply of yogurt and apples for breakfast for the following morning. She was ready to face the fast-food highway going west. She knew Kenny wouldn't have approved of the yoghurt, calling it a synthetic dessert, but it was hard to stick to Kenny's rules on the road.

Benny was excited, filled with anticipation. Her real trip was going to start now. The party in Newfoundland with Chris, the hard work in Halifax with Teenie, the mini-Paris vacation in Quebec – all seemed like distant memories from another life. She was ready to start afresh. She knew her sense of exhilaration and anticipation was shared by her fellow passengers who were storing bags overhead, testing seats, and getting settled. They were all buoyed up, while out west, the Prairies awaited. Snug in her window seat, Benny watched people give last minute hugs and climb up clutching pillows.

She watched a pigeon walk in a circle, stop, turn and circle again. She thought she understood how it felt.

Her thoughts were interrupted by the arrival of a sunshine-surfer blond boy. He eyed the seat next to Benny, but she had it filled with her supplies. She looked away. *No way, mate. Find yourself some other friend.*

He took the seat across the aisle from her, pointedly staring in her direction. He was dressed all in white – white jeans and a white linen shirt that was open to his navel, showing his hairless buffed chest.

To avoid his gaze, Benny closed her eyes to meditate, and fell asleep, waking as the bus finally pulled away. *Goodbye Toronto, you biggest, flattest, small-town-city in the whole world.*

She immediately dove into her salad, wishing she'd added more cheese.

"Wow, that looks great!" the blond boy said. "Hi, I'm Jack. Where did you manage to get that?" He was eating a huge bag of chips.

Benny looked at him. He was a post-teenage GAP poster boy sliding into plumpness. She gazed at him vacuously, and shrugged.

They drove by a clinic offering colonic irrigation. Benny thought that sounded wonderful. She decided to treat herself to a spa cleanse in Winnipeg, thinking she'd certainly would have earned it by then.

She finished her salad and studied her map, admiring the advancing red ink. She could see Jack was still trying to elbow his way into her life but she ignored him.

The bus stopped and more people shoveled themselves in. A cute girl with a bare midriff and pierced belly settled down next to Jack. Jack, shuffling his possessions to the side, seemed grumpy, and he looked over at Benny as if to blame her.

The girl in front of Benny was reading *A Preliminary Analysis.* Benny wondered what was being analyzed and she craned her neck, making out the words, "Federal" and "Accountability."

Then she wondered if her hair was falling out. It seemed thinner than ever which was worrying. Surely it was too soon for scurvy? She hoped it wasn't due to travel stress, because if that were the case, she'd be completely bald by the end of the trip. She noticed that the super-cute navel-ringed girl's entire sum of cabin luggage was a tiny handbag and a diet Coke. Benny was filled with envy.

Now that's a free spirit.

WEST OF WAWA AND WHY EVE ATE THE APPLE

8:00 p.m. The night was young, but Benny was already swollen from inertia and from that darn mother of all swelling – gravity. The trip was not a peaceful one. The girl behind Benny was doing her best to cough out a lung. Benny directed a meaningful stare behind, hoping to stare the girl down into quiet submission, but this girl was clearly a few sandwiches short of a picnic. She did, however, have the coughing skills of an Olympian. Benny wondered if anyone else on the bus was offended by the noise or if she was just oversensitive to things. The hacking was interrupted by the *Analysis* girl blowing her nose for six minutes. Benny timed her.

Jeez Louise, what's with all this mucous?

But despite the challenges, Benny was enjoying herself. She was on the bus, heading west. Freedom. She loved the way the bus touched the land; she could feel every lump and bump on the face of Canada and she wanted to run her hands over every pit and pockmark until she knew it with her eyes closed. Something in her heart belonged here; it was as if she were revisiting a land she'd not yet seen.

She looked out at the endless sunset, the clouds haloed by the sun, at the mysterious backlit darkening swamps. She didn't want to look away in case she missed a single detail. Pink and blue dusk, the clouds outlined in magenta. She was mesmerized, watching until night fell and then she drifted into a deep sleep.

They arrived in Wawa the following morning at 5:15 a.m.

The bus pulled up outside a Tim Horton's and the morning was thick with a fog that seemed to be lifting slowly.

It was the start of another long day on the bus. Benny spotted new male talent boarding. He had deep dimples and was definitely more her kind of guy than Jack who continued to eye her while the cute girl slept. This new guy was sexy, distressed, and world-weary – disheveled, a rock star in need of a helping hand. Benny hoped he would be onboard all the way to Winnipeg. She twisted Eli's ring; he'd think her crazy to miss an opportunity for a good time. Or would he? She felt his voice was fading in her heart, although the joy of his emailed message stayed close.

A personal-image check informed her that she needed to refresh her makeup as soon as possible; she was fraying around her eyelinered edges. Being on a bus overnight was not exactly a room at the Four Seasons. Her hair was greasy and spiky, her scalp tender. She checked overnight hair loss and was reassured to find it nonexistent; that, in itself, was reason for good cheer.

Benny had vague travel nausea, the kind of sick sensation from having woken too early at the wrong, ungodly hour and her body was making its protests felt. She was still swollen, and a colonic irrigation in Winnipeg was no longer a luxury but a necessity.

She was struck by a craving for a doughnut, the worst of all hydrogenated deep-fried fatty sins. Kenny had repeatedly told her that doughnuts weren't even neutral bad junk foods; they were the enemy, they refused to metabolize, definitely caused cancer – do not collect $200, go straight to dead. And Kenny knew his health foods. She realized, not for the first time, that he'd been quite tiring, him with his endless search for uber-organic, unprocessed, high-vibratory food.

She ordered an extra-large green tea and decided to take a chance on one tiny timbit – her first conscious statement of defiance against Kenny and his strict regime.

The timbit was surely a morsel from heaven, soft, doughy, sugary. She pictured Kenny's horror and laughed to herself while she drank her hot tea in the early morning of foggy Wawa and savoured the taste of that tiny baked good.

She saw a big statue of a Canadian goose and a sign that said: Truckers, free shower with breakfast. Lots of motels, all neat and tidy. They looked very inviting. The tea was going down well – a real treat.

Benny liked Wawa. Cool name, yes, but she liked it more for its early-morning forest-incense fragrance and welcoming nature. She went back to get another tea for the road, feeling content and holidayish. She wondered what lay west of Wawa and knew one thing was certain – a new T-shirt. T-shirts died quickly on this bus trip.

Perhaps in Thunder Bay. Thunder Bay, she tasted the name. The name reminded her of Apollo Bay in Australia, and traveling on The Great Ocean Road from Melbourne with Kenny on their honeymoon. Apollo Bay boasted a park filled with outlandishly bad statues and the weather was gray with a sharp wind. That trip had been green tea and organic whole-grain biscuits all the way. The memory of all that tea made her stomach turn and she wished she hadn't bought a second one for the bus. She'd rather think about Wawa and what lay out west than dwell on the rocky road she had left behind.

Back on the bus, the sun rose and the fog lifted while Benny day-dreamed. She thought she'd never tire of the Ontario landscape, with the communion-wafer half-moon high in the now-clear blue sky. She wished her mind was a camera, so she could have private and instant rescreenings of the places she'd passed through – secret lakes and rivers glittering in quiet forests, the electric red neon of a single railway signal in the middle of nowhere.

Later, while the bus was being cleaned, Benny painted her nails black. When they reboarded, the coach operator informed them there was a strictly no alcohol onboard policy. Benny noticed that bus drivers no longer existed – they'd been replaced by coach operators. She tucked the mini Southern Comfort back down into her bag until his beady eye was averted.

In general, things had settled down. Jack was lying on his back, sprawled across two seats, his legs spread out into the aisle, his shirt riding high. The cute girl was gone. Benny thought that Jack's belly was a bit flabby for someone so young. Kenny would definitely not have approved. She wished her ex-husband's voice would stop haranguing her.

She adjusted her position again. Her bottom had gone to sleep, and her entire body was voicing protests.

She was booked into a hostel in Winnipeg, but she was also thinking of doing one five-star night in a luxury hotel – one delicious, sinfully expensive night to get back some balanced perspective.

Benny was torn between two worlds: the poor scrimping world of her parents and the rich, want-for-nothing lives of her schoolgirl friends. She had the capacity and longing for the one while lack of funds dictated the other.

She shifted in her seat and wished for the hundredth time that the bus would stop at more than just Tim's – like a Longos or Loblaws perhaps. Delicious as the timbit had been, she was ready to kill for an apple or sell her soul, should that be necessary. Selling one's soul for a piece of fruit was old news, it had been done long before. Perhaps Eve had simply been doing the health-conscious thing when all of that evil went down.

Benny could just hear Eve saying to God: "Give me a break. I was only trying to get my hands on some high-vibratory raw food, surely you get that, God? All those baked goods on the heavenly banquet might be most people's idea of bliss but all I wanted was an apple."

Benny could well imagine the stress of being the sole health-food diner at the endless heavenly fast-food buffet laid out in the sky. It was much like her life now on the bus, with doughnuts lining the way and nary a piece of fresh fruit in sight.

Lost in musings of nutritional dilemmas and Biblical downfalls, Benny was startled to see they had arrived in White River. She was aching to stretch her legs.

ACID TRIP MEMORIES STING

She bought a fresh sweet-smelling T-shirt in the gift store. Black, with *Bad to the Bone* in a vampire old-style typeface, and a fish skeleton beneath. Benny was amazed by how much happiness twenty dollars could buy.

Back to the cuisine conundrum though. The menu at White River listed fried burgers, fried chips, and deep-fried grease-over-easy with ketchup on the side. She ordered a large green tea, bought a pack of chewing gum, got back on the bus, downed a small Southern Comfort chaser and crunched a codeine pill.

Chemicals taken in lieu of food, she fell fast asleep, only to be shunted back to the acid trip distortion of newspaper print, words coming at her magnified and bloated, sucker-punching her big-time: *this young new artist brazenly flaunts a confused use of mixed media. Her message is trite, banal, her abundant childish abstracts are unfinished and imbued with immature insensitivity...*

Benny woke, no idea where she was. Looked around for the screeching gallery owner who had cried that it was all a travesty, that the reporter had it in for her and was looking for vengeance.

"Don't take it personally," the gallery owner had implored, tugging at Benny's arm.

Don't take it personally? They're my paintings. A decade of work cut to shreds in a moment. Me, humiliated. And that was only the start of it.

Benny reached into her carry-on and grabbed a fistful of codeine and another Southern Comfort. She looked around wildly, noticing that the distressed rock star fellow was gone; she must have lost him in the fog of Wawa.

Cruel words whipped around her skull, crashing into each other and banging into bone as they fought to take the lead.

Passion would be the magical ingredient to Benny Harton Chau's artistic debut ... if she had any magic, that is.

And the review had gone on from there, gone on for hours. As if the reporter had nothing better to do than spew reams of venom in Benny's direction. Benny, sick to her stomach, had watched her family mouth platitudes of "it doesn't matter," "what does she know anyway," "it's only one review." She'd looked around for Kenny who was over in the corner being seduced by the "Andy Warhol" of the new art scene – a tall, gangly creature who wore a cream suit two sizes too big for him, bleached his hair to platinum ice and sported black Buddy Holly glasses. Benny had known the glasses didn't even have real lenses in them; it was all for show. That's what a fake that guy was. And there was Kenny, licking up every word, every utterance. Some support he'd turned out to be. She'd looked around at her desecrated art.

"Take it all down, now," she'd said to the gallery owner, a tiny bird-like woman who'd once been a national ballerina. The woman had blinked bulging sparrow eyes and nodded. Benny had left with Shay at her side, Mum and Dad trailing. Kenny, oblivious, had stayed to chat with Andy.

In the weeks that followed, Benny had tried to work through the infinite stages of grief. When it was clear she was making no progress, Kenny had whisked her off to Fiji, thinking a change of scenery might help. Benny had lain numbly on the beach, watching Kenny's skinny body parasailing high above. She was sure she could see his grin from where she lay on the deckchair, splayed out like a depressed sardine. She couldn't eat a thing, she couldn't sleep, nor could she cry.

Reliving the horror was too much. The bus stopped and Benny staggered out. She bought a pack of cigarettes and a lighter, not having smoked since she and Shay tried a few of Dad's when they were young and bored senseless. She lit up inexpertly and gulped in too much smoke. She coughed, it was disgusting, and she felt sick and dizzy. Which was better than having to relive the memory of her shot-down art show. She sucked the cigarette down to the filter, and lit up a second, inhaling better this time, and slowing down.

She had always believed she was no great artist. But she had hoped that enough work on her technique, a bit of creative "borrowing," and a sense of her own voice would see her through. It had to. She and Kenny were headed for the upper echelons of artistic Sydney society – she would finally fit in with the girls at school – her fame making up for lack of money.

Benny wondered if she had time for a third cigarette before the bus left. She studied her nails; her black manicure was chipped around the edges. She gnawed at the paint of her forefinger to even things out.

Back on the bus, her mouth tasted furry and horrible, but her nerves had settled. She pulled on her *Wisconsin Death Trip* sweatshirt and huddled in the soft fleecy warmth.

Benny looked around the bus and couldn't see Jack. She realized she wasn't paying enough attention to what was going on around her. Maybe this was the Stephen King bus from hell where they all got taken out one at a time, murdered horribly by a demon-possessed driver.

By now the regular long-haulers were treating the bus like a trailer park home, strolling around, chatting, lying with one leg thrown across the aisle, hanging over the back of a chair talking to the people behind and moving from seat to seat to nap and doze at whim. And Benny had assumed the grungy dude was simply elsewhere but no, he was gone for sure. Benny was left with Jack, who had moved to the back of the bus and was snoozing on his back again, displaying that wobbling belly action.

The cough-champion girl was still there. Her companion, a pale boy with a delicate bone-structure, guided her on and off the bus, his hand under her elbow while he made cooing noises. The girl was drinking cough syrup, and Benny thought of grabbing it out of her hands and downing it. Anything to get rid of the assault of memory.

The bus pulled over for another leg stretch and a few of the travellers sat at a picnic bench, chatting idly. Jack was enraptured by Benny's map and the growing line of red ink. The bus operator said she was crazy to be doing the trip, that from Manitoba onwards it was grain silos and flat land forever. He said she was going to get Prairie Madness.

"Well, I'm good with madness," Benny said. "In fact, I do it well."

The bus driver picked at a splinter on the bench. "Well, for sure you'll come out a better person on the other side."

Benny laughed. "I'm that bad now, am I?"

"You're gorgeous," Jack blurted out and then he blushed.

"So, what's your story, boyo?" the driver asked Jack.

"Going to Vancouver, looking to work in radio," Jack said.

"You figure there's much call for that out there?"

Jack shrugged. "If not, I'll do something else." He turned to Benny but she was untangling herself from the picnic table. She lit a cigarette.

"I didn't know you smoked," Jack said, disappointed.

"Neither did I," Benny said. "I'm going to absorb more lake scenery," she told the driver, "to store it in my hump like a camel, so I have reserves when I get to the insanity-inducing prairie madlands."

The driver laughed. "Get it while you can," he said.

THUNDER BAY UNDERWHELMS

Much like Apollo Bay, Thunder Bay had little more going for it than its name. It was true that Benny only really met up with the bus station and nearby terminal surrounds, but she was nevertheless depressed by the expanse of muffler workshops, tire suppliers, and short-print-run shops. Thunder Bay, another faceless grey town grown big, with the intention of encroaching on the ever-increasing industrial business perimeter.

She went for a long walk while they cleaned the bus, chain-smoking cigarettes. She found a shopping mall and bought a large salad for the upcoming bus ride – lots of onion and extra cucumber please. The fashion stores were stocked with middle-aged floral and small-town office worker apparel. She walked back to the bus and stood in line, panicking along with the rest of the regular gang because a bunch of newbies were trying to force their way onboard. To Benny's relief, the men in grey suits let the regulars on first and decanted the rest of the new folk to another bus. This was a long haul; the dynamic was fragile, not to be disturbed and the moving trailer park family were not in the mood for newcomers.

In fact, Benny thought, looking around, no one seemed to be in a good mood since getting back on at Thunder Bay. The air felt tense and restless. Even good-natured Jack was glum. Benny fell asleep. Woke and changed her music. Her jaw was aching. She couldn't fathom why Thunder Bay had disturbed her; it was just another town, no more, no less. She decided to think happy when-thoughts and wondered if she might be able to go on a dog sled ride… Would she be able to get to the Arctic Circle? Would she see whales? She was once again excited by endless possible wonders.

She scratched her head thinking that if she didn't wash her hair soon, it would leave her head in a fit of self-loathing. Well, Winnipeg awaited, hopefully with a lot of hot water. She couldn't wait to peel off her disgusting socks and incinerate her underwear.

She thought she might stay in Winnipeg for a week, do some tours, relax, visit museums. Anything except art galleries. Maybe she'd even see a movie. Now that'd be a real treat, but she wasn't sure if that sort of frivolity was allowed on the backpacker to-do list. Was there an unspoken rule that you were only supposed to do unique, place-specific activities that you'd definitely never find anywhere else ever again? Regardless of any traveling code, she thought she might treat herself to the pleasure of sitting in the dark, and being immersed in someone else's life.

Jack came over for a chat and commented that she must really be hungry. "Because I noticed," he said, "that when we stop at Timmie's, all us guys load it up while you buy zero, nada, not a thing."

"Well, I bought a couple of liters of bottled water," she said. Both of which she had consumed in quick succession, an action she realized she'd no doubt shortly be regretting as she would have to visit the very dubious washroom at the back of the bus.

"I'm burning my socks in Winnipeg," she said, and Jack laughed.

"This trip is something," he said. "I'm not saying it's good. I am just saying, it's something."

KENORA: STILL WATERS AND ROCKING CHAIR LIFE

They arrived in Kenora at 8:30 p.m. The bus passed a retirement village on the way in and Benny saw a bird-like elderly woman in a green dress standing by her window. Benny felt a psychic connection, as if the woman's life had flashed before her eyes. For a split second she felt sorry for the elegant old woman and her quiet loneliness, but then she thought that grandma actually had it pretty good. Not everybody ended up in a rocking chair beside a lake in lovely Kenora, watching buses go by.

Benny thought back to a conversation she had with Shay, shortly after the art show disaster. Back from Fiji, Benny had steadfastly refused to come out of her funk, and Kenny had called in Shay.

Shay, before her pregnancy, had been a nurse, working in the home care business in Australia. She flew around the various states and territories and advised solutions for the elderly.

"You should stop feeling so sorry for yourself," Shay had said. "You've no idea how hard life is out there. And anyway, Benny, in the end, life is simply nappies from one end to the other, so you may as well enjoy it in between. Nappies to nappies. That's what life is. Remember that. We're born into nappies and we die in nappies. The only difference is that when you're a baby you have the intuitive knowledge that you'll grow out of them, they're temporary. You'll move forward to better things. But when you're old and in nappies, you know the only thing waiting for you is death. Imagine being an adult and having to wear nappies. Do you know," she continued "that the yearly nappy sales in Australia for adults outsells those for babies? How terrible is that?"

Benny wondered if Kenny had known what the slant of the conversation was going to be. She'd wished he'd stuck around to listen but he was off with his new best friend, Andy Warhol, who was teaching him to golf, which Benny thought was just too weird. Benny had thought golf would be the furthest thing on Andy's radar, but there it was, and Kenny was following his lead. Andy, whose real name was Malcolm Rockwood, didn't much like Benny and the feeling was mutual.

"His mouth reminds me of a small wrinkled anus," she'd said to Kenny who'd asked her how many she'd seen, to make her such an expert.

"You're both artists, you should get along," he'd said. "Malc said they were totally unfair to you in the press. He said he liked some of the show. He said if you weren't so self-conscious and blocked by wanting success so badly, you could be really good."

"You and the Rocky Horrible discuss me?" Benny had been affronted. "Self-conscious? Who does he think he is? If anyone's self-conscious, it's him. Screw him."

"Honestly, Benny," Kenny had said, "I have to tell you, you're behaving like such a bitch."

Benny had been startled. Kenny could usually take her rants in spades.

"I'm just upset, that's all," she'd said. "You would be too."

"No, I wouldn't. You need to get over it. I'm tired of this, Benny. Yeah, so you didn't do so great first time out the gate. Lots of people don't. You could learn from what happened and move on but no, you're wallowing."

"Wallowing?" Benny had wanted to hit him.

"Yes, wallowing. We don't laugh any more, do you realize that? Tell me, when was the last time we laughed?"

"If you wanted fun, Kenny, you should have married a circus clown," Benny had been icy. "You knew how important this was to me, and now you want me to lighten up? Lighten up?" She been ready to spit.

"I'm just saying I don't know what to do. You're so miserable. You've got a great job in the best agency, your boss loves you – "

"My job is hell!" Benny had shouted at him. "Hell. I only wanted to do it while I worked on becoming a real artist. I hate it there, hate it. You know how horrible it is. Everybody thinks it's so great. Well, it's not. Hello, and welcome to my life. I work like twelve hours a day in a job I hate, then I paint all night and all weekend and that was my great hope, that was the light at the end of the tunnel, my art. And now I don't even have that. I have nothing, absolutely nothing."

"What about me?" Kenny had asked quietly.

"You and me are all about goals," she'd said, wanting to be as cruel as she could. "What are we, besides that? We fell in love at university because we were the hardest working people we knew. You, doing it for your parents, me doing it despite my parents who just wanted me to be happy whatever that was. They only wanted me to get a degree if I wanted one, just be happy Benny, that's all we want for you. But you and me, well, we knew we had to be successful, you for your Korean family and me because I hated where I came from." She'd fallen silent, feeling she might have gone too far.

"You're in a lot of pain," Kenny had observed, and that's when he'd called in Shay who started going on about life in nappies and telling Benny she was being selfish and neglecting Kenny.

"I'm so not neglecting him," Benny had said. "Sometimes I don't even know who he is, anymore. He's hardly home. He's got this horrible new friend who he just wants to play with – "

"Can you blame him?" Shay had shouted, and then she started crying. "Oh Benny, I'm sorry. I'm sorry about the art show, I am. I thought it was fantastic, I mean what do I know? But I thought it was really good and everybody else did too, except that bitch from *The Sydney Morning Herald* and they always give horrible reviews, you know that. What about *TimeOut*, who said it was a brave new voice, and your technique had interesting potential?"

"Polite way of saying it was crap." Benny wouldn't be consoled. "And it was crap. All that hard work and it was a load of crap. It was the best I could do and it was crap. And now everybody wants me to cheer up because I'm ruining things for them, I'm spoiling their good time."

Shay had looked at her. "Benny." Her voice was quiet. "You're ruining it for yourself. You've got the whole world at your feet and you're ruining it for yourself."

"Well, I can't stop ruining it then," Benny was ungracious. "Thanks for dropping by but honestly, I'd rather you all just left me alone. You go home and carry on planning your fancy big wedding, okay?"

Benny had no idea that *The Sydney Morning Herald* was far from done with dragging her life through the dirt. But now, seeing the graceful little old woman in her lime green dress, and recalling the conversation with her sister, Benny was grateful for her bus adventure. Nappies to nappies, at least she'd have this journey of endurance, something of her own to remember.

She wished she had known how great Kenora was. She would have planned to stop off there. She guessed she still could disembark and stay but she was too tired to start seeking accommodation and she had her hostel booked. She wasn't really sure if she did though. Did hostels kept reservations? She dearly hoped so – they were arriving at 10:30 p.m., which was no great hour to be looking for a room at the inn.

She had been on the bus for what felt like a lifetime. Her brain was a sodden dishcloth in her skull. Her socks were glued to her feet; she was convinced they'd have to be surgically removed.

She went to the washroom in the Kenora bus station and noticed an alarming smattering of red spots on her cheeks. One timbit in Wawa and she had acne. Or maybe it was the cigarettes and the couple of coffees she had sneaked in. All that acid had to go somewhere. But she was too shell-shocked and travel-exhausted to care much. She stared vaguely at her reflection, thinking that she looked a bit vacuous. Certainly her expression suggested she was dazed and confused, but other than that and the acne, it was not too bad, all things considered. She dug out her dark Audrey Hepburn sunglasses and it immediately improved.

OPIATE FIELDS OF COUGH MIXTURE BLISS

Benny got back on the bus, stoned on cough syrup. She hadn't meant to buy it in the first place or drink it either, but she was worried the hacking girl's germs might be contagious and she thought she should buy medicine, just in case. She had convinced the pharmacist to give her the good stuff with codeine, then she uncapped it to give it a small test, and next thing she knew, half the bottle was gone.

She leaned against her window, wondering if she'd remember Jack after they parted ways and thought probably not. He must have felt her thinking about him because he sidled over to the seat beside her.

"They should have biohazard waste signs all over our bus," he said, and he looked wild-eyed. "They should have firemen at the bus station, ready to hose us off. I've never felt this disgusting in my life."

"Ooh yes," Benny agreed, through her codeine buzz. "Firemen would be great. And water, so nice and cool. It's so hot. I think I must sleep again."

THE DEATH OF BERTHA GERTRUDE, THE PRUDE

When she woke, they were on the home stretch toward Winnipeg and she felt hungover and confused. Rather than numbing her, the cough mixture had brought to mind yet another unwelcome memory.

She'd been sitting in a hidden alcove at school, reading a book and waiting for Shay to come in from netball. Nestled in between the boys' and girls' changing rooms, Benny had heard a group of boys rush in, shouting nineteen to the dozen. These were the cool boys, two classes above Benny. She hadn't payed them any attention until she'd heard one of them mention her mum.

"I'll meet you guys at the tennis courts. I've got to get past that lion Mrs. Harton to get my backpack out of the classroom," one of the boys had said.

"Get past Ten Ton Tessie, the cleaning maid? You're a brave man, Stevo, trying to sneak past old thunder thighs."

Ten Ton Tessie? Cleaning maid? Benny hadn't been sure which insult hurt the most.

"Aren't you in the same class as thunder thigh's daughter? The one with the funny name?" the main boy had spoken again and a younger lad had answered, a voice Benny had recognized, a boy who'd teased her mercilessly.

"Yeah, you mean Bertha Gertrude, the Prude?"

The boys had all laughed. "Bertha Gertrude, the Prude, Bertha Gertrude, the Prude," they'd chanted, howling.

"Would you ever have a girlfriend called Bertie Gertie?" the first boy had added. "She's cursed for life. Poor Bertie Gertie. You know who is cute though, and she's definitely got a thing for me, is Cindy Mathews. My mum knows her mum, and my mum says she's going to organize it so that we all go to the mall and maybe even see a movie or something."

The conversation veered into a discussion of girls, malls, and movies. The privacy of Benny's alcove had become a tiny jail of pain. She sat quietly, thinking.

Ten Ton Tessie and her daughter, Bertie Gertie. Cursed for life.

"Mum," she'd said later, on the way home, interrupting Shay's talk of her sporting exploits, "why on earth did you call me Bertha Gertrude? They're horrible names."

"Ah pet, don't say that. They're lovely. You're named after each granny, that's what."

"I've got granny names." Benny had been horrified. "Well, Mum, we have to change them or I'll be cursed for life, that's all there is to it. I want a normal name, like Cindy or something."

"You mean like Cindy Mathews, too-cool-for-school," Shay had said. Even when she was young, Shay was sharp.

"No, not like Cindy Mathews, she's boring. I want an interesting name."

"Can't change your name, love," Mum had replied. "It's your name. Everybody hates their own name."

"I don't hate my name." Shay had said. "I like Shandy."

"It's Shandra," Mum had said.

"It's Shay," Benny had insisted.

"Shandra, Shay, even Shandy are better than Bertie Gertie," Benny had added.

"Bertie Gertie? Where did you get that?" Mum had asked.

"It's what you called me. And I hate it, it's horrible." Benny fell silent.

"Benny," she'd said, as they neared home. "You must all call me Benny. Like from *Benny and Joon,* only Joon was irritating." They had watched the movie the weekend before and Benny had fallen in love with fresh-faced Johnny Depp.

"You must all call me Benny, or I won't answer. I'm going to tell the teachers at school too. And Mum, you must tell the rest of the family, okay? I'm Benny now."

Her mother had protested, but loyal Shay had agreed. "Mum, Bertha Gertrude's a horrible name. It's not fair. I think Benny is nice. You must call her Benny."

Benny's mother had shrugged it off as a passing phase and indulged Benny and the name stuck. It stuck, while the other hated moniker was increasingly hidden. As she got older, Benny took great pains to hide student cards, driver's licenses, her passport. She became quite paranoid about it and the one and only thing she was grateful for, to *The Sydney Morning Herald,* was that they only ever knew her as Benny Harton Chau, an exotic name of which she was fond.

A few nights after the Ten Ton Tessie incident, Dad had come to tuck Benny in. Shay was asleep in the top bunk. Benny was sitting up, her tiny face crumpled in a concentrated scowl.

"What's worrying you, my sweet chickie chook?" Dad had asked, smoothing her hair. "I always know when you're not right as rain."

Benny had sat up. "Dad, I want to go to that school on the hill, the one that's for girls only."

Her father had laughed. "Bertha, I mean, Benny, we'd love you to go there too luv, but that's one of the most expensive schools in Sydney."

Benny had thought for a moment. "Can't Mum clean there?"

"No can do luv, Mum's stretched way too thin right now. I'm quite worried about her. Now, lie down, you've come untucked." He pulled her blanket up to her chin.

Benny had laid down.

"What's so bad about your school anyway? You've got Shay there, it's a good school."

"It's got boys," Benny had said and her father had laughed again.

The following day her dad went to his boss and asked him to sponsor his ambitious pint-sized daughter. His boss said he'd see if he could do it as a tax write-off and if he could, he would. And he did.

And so, Benny had gone to the school of her dreams where she'd mingled with pure-bred girls from another universe. The kind who emerged from the womb with perfect mani-pedis and thick, blow-dried hair. And she'd never felt inferior or second-hand in anyway because she knew she was going to be a famous artist, and they would be the ones talking about how they'd gone to school with her.

Benny decided she may as well finish the cough syrup.

MOSQUITOES THE SIZE OF BATS

If it was Wednesday, it was Winnipeg. Benny, in town for less than a day, loved The Peg on a thousand levels.

When the bus finally came to a halt, she was ready to run. She grunted in response to Jack's queries as to the locale of her hostel, fled out into the night and jumped into a cab. She arrived at the hostel at 11:00 p.m.

The hostel was in a tiny, old Victorian house. It had low ceilings, narrow corridors, and steep staircases. The dorm room slept four while in the real world it might have housed one small child with difficulty.

Despite the lateness of her arrival, Benny's roommates were all awake. A friendly American girl hinted at the possibility of their sightseeing together and a tall Scottish girl smiled vaguely while a German girl kept her attention fixed on her laptop. The German girl, seated on the only chair in the room, was surrounded by a network of equipment that most high-end offices would envy.

The room was hot and airless. As if the two bunk beds didn't take up enough of the tiny space, the German girl's portable office was laying siege to kilometers of precious acreage. In addition to all of this, an immense fan swung and rocked like a shuddering old palm tree, groaning and creaking. Every now and then it would bob and bow in Benny's direction, sighing mightily. She'd be blasted by a warm wind for a few seconds, which only added to the heat and did nothing to cool the air.

"The highest ever recorded temperature in Winnipeg, in May, was 37.8 degrees Celsius," the German girl reported over her laptop. "They say today it was 36. But I think it feels close to 40 in this room."

The others agreed.

Regardless of the heat, Benny managed to get some sleep during which vivid nightmares dragged her across the barbwire of being at school with the scornful boys who laughed at her art show, while Kenny stood transfixed by the pale and intriguing Andy Warhol – Malcolm Rockwood to his mum.

She woke drenched in sweat, not sure if it was due to the burn of the memories or the heat of the small Winnipeg room.

She got up, had a cool shower, and went outside for a cigarette to find it was equally hot outdoors, despite the earliness of the hour. She went back in and found a seat at the breakfast table, checking out age groups and watching the line up of people accessing their email off the quarter-coin Internet facility that resembled at ATM machine. She knew she too should be checking her email, but she couldn't generate the interest. She hoped her family had forgiven her and received Dad's gift that she had sent Express.

She watched a wrinkled crone in Mountain Equipment Co-Op gear fiercely chop an apple into equal-sized tiny pieces while her partner, a man about sixty, made porridge from raw whole grains.

Benny was still somewhat stunned by the distance she had traveled. Life felt surreal but in a good, chilled out sort of way, no blacktop face-grazing dementia here, thank you very much.

The room was a large one, half-dining area, half lounge. People sat around tables, studying maps and guidebooks while sunshine streamed in through the large open windows and life was clean and peaceful.

Benny pushed herself up from the table and went to get a large cup of coffee. Post-Kenora, she had taken to coffee in the same way she'd taken to nicotine: like a duck to water.

She finished her coffee and forced herself to go for a walk, still feeling more zombie than human.

She stopped off at The Bay for a dose of air con and the opportunity to layer herself in sunscreen and expensive sweet-smelling lotions. She lay back and enjoyed a complimentary makeover from the young Lancôme girl who banished the shadows from under her eyes and refreshed her Cleopatra eyeliner. She left The Bay to wander around town, hopping on and off the free intercity shuttle and getting the lay of the land, and finally heading down to the Forks. It seemed to Benny like there was no shortage of entertainment in Winnipeg.

Down on the banks of The Forks – which was, as its name suggested, the fork of two rivers where the fur traders conducted their trade eons ago – Benny sat on the grass and leaned against a large tree, a warm summer breeze playing with her hair. The river smelled of grasslands, swamps, and mud and there were ducks waddling along the rich thick wet edge. Soft reggae came from the café behind. Benny had her shoes off and was digging her bare feet into the thick spongy grass.

She saw a group of people line up for a splash boat cruise and the second time it left, she ran down to join the group.

Kent, the guide, was a laidback fellow with a deadpan delivery of the history of Winnipeg: tragedies the rivers had seen, bridges falling down, or refusing to open, basilicas blowing up due to a single dropped cigarette butt and countless floods through the ages.

The jaunty splash boat lived up to its name and Benny leaned out to be baptized by the big, muddy drops of river water.

Back on the river bank, once more admiring the view and leaning against her tree, Benny lit a cigarette and watched a couple of spry old ladies eating ice cream cones while the kids around them played with brightly colored, twisted sausage balloons. The mosquitoes were biting. The summer smell of a barbeque filled the air and it was good, even to a vegetarian nose. Soon, though, the air grew hot and heavy. Dark purple clouds filled the sky and a girl started drumming nearby. It began to rain and Benny was soaked in no time, the rain stopping as abruptly as it had begun. The mosquitoes bit with increasing enthusiasm. It was summertime, the livin' was easy, the mosquitoes were bitin', and the cotton was high. Benny watched the drumming girl; she'd attracted a crowd of small children who loved her playing and were jumping up and down with abandon.

Benny examined her feet with their many raised angry-red mosquito bites. She scratched viciously, bringing blood to the surface. She went into the market to buy some calamine lotion and smothered herself with it. Then she perused the vast selection of teas, chocolate, bread, exotic foods, souvenirs, clothes, and cotton candy. Benny, cautiously testing the waters of previously forbidden food, bought sticky pink cotton candy on a stick. She ate about a third of it and realized she didn't like it.

Leaving the market, she found a tourist info booth and investigated bus tours. The first one was set to depart the following morning at 8:30 a.m. For a person used to arriving at work at 6:30 or 7:00 a.m., 8:30 a.m. now seemed an ungodly hour to even have brushed her teeth. She said she'd have to think about it.

She got lost on her way back to the hostel and walked a thousand kilometers further than she'd intended. Mosquitoes continued to sink their teeth into her without mercy despite a thick layer of the newly purchased *Deep Off!* that she'd sprayed on top of her cala-mine. It rained on the walk home, in generously oversized drops. She walked past the Winnipeg Art Gallery, a great big triangle-at-one-end building. Despite her gallery phobia, she thought the WAG looked interesting.

She passed a beauty clinic offering a trim and a $6 perm. A perm? Did they still even make perm chemicals in this organically recycling day and age? And for $6?

She got back to the hostel and decided to check her email. This was a frustrating experience since the automated-teller Internet vending machine was designed with a sense of fair play in mind; no one person could be logged on for longer than ten minutes. Which was all good and well but the keyboard needed an almighty blow to activate each painstaking letter and thus it took nearly the entire ten minutes to type in a password alone. Benny got a message through to Shay but given her time constraints, she gave up using the space bar – her missive summary of Toronto to Winnipeg was one long word with no spaces in between, a couple of commas not really helping out. Benny would probably see Shay in person with photos, scrapbooks, and a decoded version of the trip long before Shay would be able to figure out the text:

Loveyouall,itsallgood,gladdadgotpressie,givelovetom+d.gottologoff.darncomputerxoxo

Benny felt a large headache brewing. She thought it must be due to sleeping in a bed, which now seemed like an anathema. She'd got more sleep on the bus than she'd had in years, and she'd been relatively headacheless to boot. But one night in a bed and her head was killing her. She wished she could mainline codeine into her jaw – anything to ease the ache. And did it ever feel hot. Her headache could be due to the sledgehammer of heat battering her forehead.

She took a cold shower, relishing the moment of relief, then went to see if the good-looking boy at the reception desk knew where she could score a giant salad. Turned out he was a fellow Aussie, also from Sydney, Cremorne Point specifically. His folks must have money. He told her the gas station on the corner had a good selection of fresh produce. However, he said, if she was interested in having a pizza with him, he got off at 10:00 p.m.

Pizza! They were nearly as toxic as doughnuts. Benny nearly laughed out loud. "Ta, thanks, mate. Maybe some other time."

Benny found the gas station and bought apples and plastic trays of pre-sliced raw carrots and broccoli, a priceless treasure.

She went back to the hostel and fell to chatting with some of the other fellow hosteliers. It started with them admiring her fresh produce. Apparently she was not alone in her struggle to find non-abused or non-deep-fried nutrients.

A short, bearded guy took the opportunity to read a restaurant review out loud. "An unusual dining experience that combines two very different options: Mongolian buffet and Canadian barbecue. Greek, Italian and Egyptian influences presented in contemporary Prairie style. Exceptional Athens shrimp. This cozy place does a fine job on mussels in tequila sauce and Italian sausage."

Benny made a terrible mistake in a very short time. She let down her conversational guard and to her horror, she found that her affable roommate – Jenna from Michigan – had attached herself with the speed and tenacity of a burr in a shag rug.

In her efforts to discourage the young bearded man who was show-ing interest in her, Benny had taken her eye off other potential social entanglements and in that tiny moment, the girl from Grand Rapids had rushed in.

Not sure how to extract herself without seeming terribly rude, Benny sat next to Jenna and faced her itinerary for the following morning, as whipped up by the big bossy young teacher. Their first stop was the art gallery, then a jaunt to the planetarium, then a free concert at lunch time. Jenna, resplendent with a generous overbite and an earnest expression, talked a million miles an hour, had everything mapped out for the morn-ing and turned her attention to their afternoon plans. Benny decided the best course of action was to take a back seat in the decision-making and simply allow herself to be led. She even thought it might be fun, being with someone so focused and organized. Be nice to just trundle along and do whatever she was told to do.

Benny told Jenna she was going outside for a cigarette. She sat on the rickety wooden front steps of the house smoking and scratching. Her one arm looked like she had two elbows; and that was only one of the bites.

THE PEG SLAYS THE FASHIONISTA

Benny was a fan of Abba. And the Bee Gees. And on this day, one of the Brother's Gibbs songs was stuck on repeat in her head. Well, a version thereof. "The New York Mining Disaster 1941" – Benny's brain was humming the same melody, but the lyrics had changed. Hers was: The Winnipeg Traveling Companion Disaster. And of course there were other themes and thoughts, like how on earth had she let herself get hooked up and entangled with an Amazonian bossy teacher-person machine thing and could she extricate herself without having to commit murder?

She tried to tell herself that Jenna wasn't a bad girl, not really. It's just that she was so bossy. Being with Jenna was like having to suffer a double math period on a Friday afternoon, followed by two hours of field hockey, a ridiculous sport Benny hated with all her might. Admittedly, the flashing danger signs had been there, warning bells ringing when Jenna had worked on their itinerary.

Jenna, The Amazing Wonder Woman is Leaping into Action, All Ye Beware, Beware!

Benny felt resentful. Look what happened when one tried to do normal social things. It certainly was the last time she'd try anything like that.

In the aftermath of the disaster, she made a mental note to inform Shay of her desired inscription for the gravestone of her future: *Never Ever Think It'll Be Okay.*

Benny had woken up at 6:00 a.m. to an insistent voice in her head telling her to make a speedy exit via the washroom window.

"Nonsense," said she to the voice. "It'll be okay. Nothing to worry about here."

Jenna, perhaps sensing Benny's thoughts of escape, sat up immediately, blinked for a moment, and leapt off the top bunk, gathering Benny and hurrying them off to the washroom so they wouldn't waste a minute of their day.

By 8:15 they were seated on a concrete picnic bench with Benny breakfasting on the last of her precious apples while Jenna chowed down on a truckload from McDonald's. Jenna explained at great length how cost-effective Mickey D's was. For example, just look at how much food she'd gotten for $1.99 in comparison to the high-priced, extremely low value-for-dollar cost of Benny's pint-sized meal. Benny agreed with her but wanted to point out that bigger is not always better – less of fast food was definitely more of what she wanted.

Benny, coming from a family where money was tight, was used to Mum whipping up tuna casseroles and macaroni seasoned with butter and black pepper; good, solid, cheap food that lined your gut. But she was still stunned by people thinking they got a good deal simply because they were scoring football-field sized meals for a toonie with change to spare. "Do you have any idea how unhealthy your $1.99 meal is?" she wanted to say but realized there was no point.

And besides, Jenna was a poster girl for fit and strong and healthy. She was close to five foot nine inches of muscled, double-cheeseburgered, unfailing, unflagging, unstoppable energy.

By 8:30, Benny was exhausted. And they'd only just begun.

It was inexplicably chilly outdoors. The temperature had plummeted to 16 degrees Celsius, which, compared to the 34 of the previous day, felt positively frigid. There was also a cutting windchill factor.

"I'd say with the windchill, it's like a high of maybe six degrees," Benny said, and Jenna nodded in agreement.

Benny had learned to calculate the weather like a real Canadian. Back in Australia there was one temperature, cut and dried.

"It's 20 degrees in fair Sydney," the radio announcer would say. Over and out. Ten four, roger that, have a nice day.

But in Canada, Benny found humidexes, windchills, UV indexes, BAR pressures, and humidity percentages. There were an endless number of complicated calculations just to get the real-life temperature on the ground. Benny could, therefore say, with certainty that six degrees Celsius was the high they were currently enjoying while sitting at their outdoor breakfast table discoursing on value for money, dollar for nutrient.

Given the speedy rush with which they'd left the hostel, plus the extreme heat of the previous day, Benny was ill-equipped and without any kind of suitable protective apparel. In other words, she was bloody well freezing to death. A large cup of coffee can only be hugged for so long before it loses its body-warming qualities.

"It's so cold," Jenna said in a tone that indicated this was not meeting her approval.

"Yeah, mate, you're so right, it is," Benny said, shivering. "What say we return to base camp to fetch reserve forces and backup – like a sweatshirt maybe?" She hugged her chest, her arms covered in goose bumps.

The idea of backtracking was met with zero tolerance.

"It WILL get hotter," Jenna said with grim determination. "Gosh, it's much earlier than I thought," she noted. "Sorry for rushing you like that."

"No problem. It's fine," Benny said, her teeth chattering. "So, what shall we do? The gallery won't be open yet."

"True. But the Legislative Building will," came back the firm reply.

"Ah. Right. The good old Legislative Building." Well, by Benny's calculations, at least they'd be warmer. "Sounds great," she said.

They set off at high speed. Benny thought the vigorous pace was to help them warm up, but later she realized it was simply Jenna's natural stride. Benny had to trot along to keep up.

Despite her initial lack of enthusiasm, her agreement fuelled only by a desire to find central heating, the Legislative Building was a delightful surprise.

Benny thought it was a place of charm and loveliness but finally, having explored every nook and cranny, it was time for them to leave that warm and protective embrace.

Back outside, it wasn't any warmer, despite Jenna's directives to the weather god. Benny was so cold she could hardly speak.

Propelled by the instinct to survive, she headed for the nearest clothing store. For once, Benny had Jenna in tow. She threw herself gratefully at the mercy of the closest comfort garment she could find, in much the same way a lonely man would throw himself into the soft scented cleavage of a woman. That the garment was cowl-necked, made of a rough, scratchy, hairy fabric, wool maybe, and as close to a macramé sweatshirt as she had ever seen. Whatever it was made of was irrelevant because it was warm. Oh dear God, it was warm.

Swaddled in coarse knit, she hugged it to her while Jenna watched with buck-toothed disapproval at Benny's cavalier spendthrift attitude.

"I'd never waste money like that," she said as they stepped back into the icy wind. "I'm going back to the hostel for a sweatshirt. You go straight to the art gallery, I'll meet you there." And off she strode.

Benny watched her, speechless with rage. Thanks to Jenna, she was a whole two packs of cigarettes poorer and her careful look – which had survived buses and sleepless nights and other countless obstacles – was in tatters. She had been deconstructed. She dug her nails hard into the palms of her hands and waited for the red haze to leave her vision. Then she turned and headed as instructed to the Winnipeg Art Gallery.

ROMANCE BLOOMS AT THE ROCKIN' RODEO

Inside the cool sanctuary of higher ground, she realized the beautiful power of art to soothe, her own horrific previous gallery experience notwithstanding. Her chest relaxed, the tension fell away from her as she closed her eyes and took a deep breath. Cool air, subdued lighting – it was like two kind hands had settled on her shoulders and caressed her briefly, rubbing her temples. Half an hour into her self-guided tour, the Benedictine attire incident had ceased to be important although she was still pissed off about the needless money spent.

Floating on a zen art high, she went down to the gift shop to meet Jenna who was inspecting the price tags of fridge magnets.

"Ridiculous," she said. "Did you have a look around? We have to leave now or we'll be late for our concert in the park but we can come back here tonight for Rooftop Jazz."

Benny hoped to find a way to ditch Jenna long before Rooftop Jazz but she nodded and followed the big blonde out.

"I must get something to eat on the way," Jenna said. "Come into Mickey D's with me, it won't kill you."

Benny's headache, a tiny nagging hinting pulse, began to thrust and pound at the base of her skull. The pain emanated from two pressure points; she could imagine their ruby red glare buried deep and working hard to expand their reach of inflamed pain.

She kept her sunglasses on inside the McDonald's but the vicious fluorescence lanced her eyeballs even through her dark shades. For want of anything better to do, she studied the menu, wondering if there was anything at all she could consider eating. She'd always found it odd how the girls at her school had loved McDonald's. They'd rush there en masse after sports practice. Benny, having skipped sports to do extra art, had never been part of that crowd anyway and the menu, therefore, was alien and unfamiliar.

"I guess I could try a fish burger," she said to Jenna. "I do try to eat some fish now and then. Although what the quality will be, God only knows."

"You can't believe those documentaries," Jenna said. "Like *Fast Food Nation*, and crap like that, where they say cows' intestines are mashed into the food and there's bacteria that'll kill you. I mean, who in their right mind would eat any kind of burger raw? It's not just McDonald's food either, it's all the fast food chains. They've all the same bacteria but only if you're an idiot and eat the stuff raw."

"Alrighty then," Benny said. The pain of her headache had blossomed like the mushroom cloud of an atom bomb.

She studied the menu. "I'll take an order of pancakes to go," she said, "and a coffee."

"Oh, I'm having mine here," Jenna said. She gathered up her order: a Big Mac, large fries, and a giant Coke, and threaded her way to a table in the middle of the crowded joint.

Benny waited for her pancakes and coffee and joined Jenna. She chewed on a couple of codeine and two Xanax, then dug into her food.

"Wow, these are delicious," she said, chewing slowly, her plastic utensils bending in unhelpful ways. "And this coffee, it's fantastic." A smooth fog was wrapping Benny in a cotton wool embrace, the barbwire pain was still there but buried. Meanwhile, mouthful after mouthful of buttered, syrupy heaven made its way into her mouth.

"I'm having such a great day," Benny said dreamily. "The Legislature Building. I loved it so much. It reminded me of school."

Jenna shuddered. "I hated school," she said. "Well, I hated everything but math and sports."

"I liked everything but math and sports," Benny said. "My sister's more like you."

She pushed her tray away from her. It was empty. Sticky and empty.

Jenna looked at her watch and jumped to her feet. "We are so late," she said, rushing out with Benny following clumsily, bumping into tables and apologizing.

They found The Exchange, a park hosting the concert, and sat under angry black clouds while the wind whipped around them and a band attacked their instruments onstage.

"What's this band called?" Benny asked Jenna who was studying a flyer. "Whoever they are, great guitar playing."

Jenna pursed her lips. Benny, her narcotic vision twisted, saw gigantic pink sausage balloons stretched tight over gigantic Chiclet gravestone teeth. She looked away.

"She's called Sister Dorothy and she's very socially aware," Jenna said.

"She's also very melodic," Benny said, closing her eyes.

Two local women sat down at their table. "This icy weather's very unusual," said the one, a middle-aged woman in a black polka-dotted dress. "Not the expected state of play at all. So, you two girls on holiday?"

Benny nodded while Jenna launched into a discussion with them about life, babies, careers and snow. It seemed to Benny, through her pill-induced sleepy haze, that the Winnipeggers were very proud of the regular minus 30 that punishes their city for most of the winter. And the floods. And the summer that only lasted two and a half months.

The women finished their lunch. "Well," said the one, brushing crumbs off her dress, "have fun, you two. Wish I could be free as a bird on a summer's day, even if the day's a freezing cold one. How long are you here for?"

"A week," Jenna said, while Benny opened one eye.

"I'm heading up to Churchill tomorrow," she said, having made a quick decision, knowing if she didn't leave, she might end up killing Jenna.

"What?" Jenna was dismayed. "But I can't come up with you tomorrow. I've got to wait for a friend to meet me here. Why don't you wait with me and we'll all go together, the three of us?"

"No can do, mate, I'm afraid I've got a schedule to keep."

"Churchill is wonderful," the woman in the black polka-dotted dress said. "Great bird watching. And you'll see the whales this time of year too. The train is something else though. Historic, let me tell you."

The other woman laughed and grabbed her friend by the elbow. "Don't let her get started on things historic. You girls will grow old for the hearing."

They waved goodbye and walked across the muddy grass. The wind was still icy, the clouds low and dark.

Benny, slumped in her chair, was reluctant to move, but Jenna was standing, waiting.

"The Planetarium," she said.

Benny opened the other eye and looked up at her.

"Oh, come on," Jenna said. "One last thing. You won't even be here tomorrow. You could have told me, you know."

Benny sighed and pushed herself up out of her chair. Her headache knocked about in the back of her skull, like an expensive car part about to do some major damage.

The Planetarium was great. From what Benny could recall. She was tiring in earnest, numb. She fell asleep, woke to find herself being shepherded down a tunnel, through an underground maze and then led into shop after shop. She stared blindly, mumbling. Back up into the street, she noticed they were repeatedly crossing the traffic against the 'Don't walk' signs.

"That's against the rules," Benny said, noticing with alarm that her drugs were wearing off. She lit a cigarette while Jenna scowled at her.

"I cannot believe you smoke," she said.

"Neither can I," Benny said, exhaling cheerfully and brushing ash off her hairy sweater.

She had decided that the garment was some sort of sack reincarnated; it might once have held horse food. Bran, oats or barley. It did smell sort of bran-like. It reminded her of being with Dad and she sniffed it, trotting after Jenna who veered into an antique store filled with junk.

Benny finished her cigarette and went in to find Jenna arguing with the owner about the price for a ship in a glass bottle. Benny had no idea why Jenna would even want the thing.

"You visiting?" she heard a voice close to her ear and she jumped. Then she did a double take and the man laughed.

"Yes, he's my twin," he said and pointed toward the fellow Jenna was still arguing with, although less heatedly and money was being exchanged. "That's Ed, I'm Archie. Mum thought she was having a boy and a girl and she was ready to call us Archie and Edith."

"Wouldn't that have been a bit odd?" Benny couldn't help asking.

"Well, you had to know Mum."

Ed looked up, left Jenna and joined Archie, sticking out his hand to Benny. Jenna, perplexed and abandoned, picked up her bottled ship and looked around, lost.

"We have like the worst snow storms, ever," Archie said to Benny. "You see that streetlight out there?"

Benny craned her neck obligingly.

"Well, the snow covered that."

"Wow," Benny said.

"We've lived here our whole lives," Archie said. "This store belonged to Mum. We live above it. You want to come up for supper later?"

"She can't, she's got plans," Jenna spoke. "Come on, Benny, time to leave. Places to go, things to do." She held onto her ship tightly.

Benny looked from Ed to Archie, and back again. Ed had a ponytail and an earring. Archie, a handlebar moustache and wild Einstein hair. But there was something familiar about him and Benny couldn't figure out what it was. Then she realized. He was wearing exactly the same macramé sweater as she was. They had identical top halves.

A great belly laugh bubbled up in Benny and exploded. The entire day came to a head and she laughed so hard she leaned on the counter. She was practically in tears. The other three looked at her. Jenna shrugged.

"We only met yesterday," she explained to the men. "Come on, Benny, you probably need to eat."

Benny, still howling, waved goodbye to the confused duo and followed Jenna. Outside, tears still streaming down her face, Benny doubled over and laughed until she could no more. Jenna, clutching her ship in a bottle, watched her, not amused, waiting.

They eventually set off down the street.

"So, let's go and get cleaned up," Jenna said, "then we'll get some supper, okay?"

"I'm not hungry," Benny said. Her headache had eased up slightly but she'd had enough of Jenna to last her a lifetime. "I need a drink," she said, spotting a pub. "You go on back to the hostel and find a place to have supper. I'm going to get a nice big gin and tonic at the Rockin' Rodeo across the street. Okay with you?"

"Great idea, I'll come with you," Jenna said, "I could do with a beer. Who knows, we could get something to eat there. My feet are killing me."

Benny sighed. There was no escape. "Fine," she said.

They pushed open the door to the pub and wound their way through the ruby velvet interior.

"Booth or bar?" Jenna asked.

"Bar," Benny said immediately, thinking that if she had to spend any more time alone with Jenna, she'd stab her with blunt cutlery.

She climbed on a barstool, looked at herself in the mirror, and started laughing again.

"I can't believe I bought this piece of crap," she said.

"Yeah, it was a waste," Jenna agreed.

Benny took a long slug of her gin and tonic. "Now, that's heaven," she said, closing her eyes.

"Pretty dingy place," Jenna said, looking around. She put her ship on the counter, one hand holding it tightly as if it were a prized object likely to be whisked away.

"Some partying's been done here, for sure," Benny said. "How much money would it take for you to walk barefoot across this carpet?"

"What are you talking about?"

"It's a game," Benny said. "My sister and I play it all the time. It's a dare, like how much to walk on crushed glass, or swim across a snake-infested pond. You know, stuff like that."

"That's just stupid, if you ask me –" Jenna started to say when the conversation was interrupted.

"Excuse me, ladies," a deep voice said, "but would it be too forward of me to ask if I could buy you a drink?"

An innocuous enough pickup line but even without looking, Benny's heart picked up the pace.

She sensed him before she even saw him, his voice echoing in her ear and she knew he'd be rough, raw, spicy. Just like the forbidden boy she'd kissed when she was thirteen, all those years ago.

She saw his hands first, long, elegant fingers tapping the counter, his dirty workman fingernails ragged. She worked her way up his sculpted forearms that were freckled and flecked with tiny scratches and sores. She watched his fingers pick absentmindedly at a small scab. Her gaze traveled up his muscled biceps, to his wide shoulders and finally to his boyish face, his shy smile, bad cap hair and downward glance.

"Yeah, mate, you can buy me a drink," she said. "Soon as I finish this one."

"British?" the man guessed.

"Nah, 'nother one of the colonies, Australia."

"Cool accent."

She heard Jenna snort beside her and clutch her ship to her chest.

The man looked at Benny and ignored Jenna. He was older than Benny had first thought. His eyes were strange and wild with dark blue edges and pale irises. His nose was upturned, his skin pockmarked, his cheekbones high. His mouth was fairly ordinary but when he twisted his lips in a sideways smile, Benny felt her gut lurch.

"Mickey," he said, his voice deep, gravelly, and slow, and he held out his hand. She took it, reacting to the electrical connection, almost jerking when they touched. She blushed and he laughed.

"You felt that too?" he said.

"Yes, I did," she said, and she kept hold of his hand.

"And I'm Jenna," the ship-bearer announced loudly.

Mickey nodded in Jenna's direction, his eyes never leaving Benny. "Come and join me and my friend," he said, pointing at a booth in the far corner.

"Okay," Benny said, sliding off the stool. Jenna, uncertain for a moment, followed.

"This is Frank," he introduced his friend who eyed Jenna with appreciation.

"I like your ship," he said, and Jenna melted into the seat beside him.

Benny slid into the booth, Mickey close beside her. He was drinking beer, chasing shooters on the side. Benny was mortified. Mickey was so cool and here she was, dressed like some kind of New Age hippie. But Mickey didn't seem to notice, or care.

"You're good for a drink?" He was solicitous, caring.

"Yeah, right as rain, no worries. So, what do you do for a living?" she asked him.

"I'm a landscaper," he said airily. "I do rich people's gardens, fountains, flower beds. There isn't a flower I don't know and love."

Frank, listening, one ear following Jenna's explanation of her ship, laughed at Mickey who flushed red. Benny, confused, looked from one to the other, but Frank turned back to Jenna and Mickey scowled into his drink.

"Are you from Winnipeg?" Benny wanted to recapture the moment between them.

Mickey brightened. "Nope, I'm from the east coast, Nova Scotia."

"Nova Scotia!" Benny was excited. "I love Nova Scotia. Where exactly are you from?"

"A place I bet you never even heard of," Mickey said, his good mood back in tow and they all proceeded to get drunk and rowdy. Benny couldn't remember when she'd had that much fun. It was great, from start to finish, even when some guy tried to provoke Mickey into a fight but Mickey held up his hands and shook his head.

"I'm not that guy," he told Benny, "I'm not the guy who fights. I could, you know, and knock him down too but I don't want to do that, not now, now that I've met you."

And she believed him, him with his chipped front tooth and his sideways smile. He smelled so good – spicy soap and male sweat.

Jenna, three sheets to the wind, was making out with Frank, her tongue deep down his throat. Benny had been surprised by the speed and precision with which Jenna had fallen upon Frank, but then again she hadn't suspected Jenna could drink like a sailor either.

Benny, disturbed by her longing to touch Mickey, battened down her desire.

"I'm leaving tomorrow, to go to Churchill," she told him.

"What for?"

"Because it's there. And the train is there. And I don't know, I just need to go. If you like, I can see you the week I get back. I'm only staying in Churchill for a week. You want me to come back down and see you?"

"Sweetheart, there's nothin' I want more in the whole world."

He held her hand and the current passed between them again and she couldn't help it, she kissed him like there was no tomorrow. She kissed him like she'd kissed the boy in the barn – without reserve.

Around them, the bar was emptying.

"Well, time to go anyways," Mickey sighed and got to his feet. "Frank, come on buddy, time to go."

Frank and Jenna, tongues still entwined, stood up. Jenna somehow had her ship under her arm.

"See you tomorrow," Mickey yelled after the departing couple and he laughed.

"What's the bet he throws her one right in the flowers over there. Real class act, those two."

Benny agreed, holding his big warm hand.

"Me and Frank, we share an apartment – he'd better not be takin' her back there. Where are you stayin'? I'll walk you home." He hummed a little tune and held her close. "See how we walk so well together, incognito," he said happily, and she thought he meant in synch or unison but she didn't say.

The night was starry and it had warmed up and all Benny's senses were tingling and alive.

When they got to the door of the hostel, Mickey kissed her long and hard and she put her hands up under his T-shirt, and caressed his tight abs. His upper arms were giant, cut, body-builder smooth.

"Take care of yourself on your crazy train ride," he said, his voice like brandy and hot chocolate in her belly. "And I'll see you when you get back. Hang on, got a pen?"

Benny dug a pen out of her bag. "Write it all down here," she said. "Cell phone, home phone, home address, email, everything."

He laughed. "My mum's phone too? The pub my uncle goes to, in case I'm there too?"

"Yes," she said, meaning it.

He wrote carefully, neatly. She studied his writing under the streetlight. "Wow, you're very neat."

"I write poetry in my spare time," he said, with his crooked smile, "I read everythin' I can find. I play the classical guitar. My brother died when he was 18, killed when he was drivin' drunk. I was 14. I want to share my whole life with you, all my hopes and dreams."

Benny, still well-inebriated, felt speechless with love and good fortune. She looked up at his thin dirty-blonde hair, his thick neck corded with muscle and she wanted to rescue him from his loneliness and his pain. His hardship pierced her heart and she put her arms around him and held him tight. His nipples were hard and his stomach felt like iron. He moved her hands down to his buttocks.

"Like steel," he said. "Feel." She did.

"Wow," she said.

"You can come and stay with me when you get down, if you like. Phone first, 'cuz I could be workin' overtime, I'm tryin' to make as much money as I can, so's I can pay off my debts and buy a house in the country, maybe get a piece of land and build somethin' myself. I'm also a stone mason, a carpenter, a builder. There isn't anythin' I can't build."

The door opened and the young guy from the front desk came out for a smoke.

"Hiya Bens," he said to Benny and she felt Mickey stiffen.

"Hey, Adam," Benny said vaguely, and she pulled Mickey closer and sighed. "I guess I'd better go in. I've still got to pack and get ready for the train."

Mickey took her by the shoulders and gazed into her eyes. "Benny, I ain't, haven't had much luck lately. Well, ever, really. The last girlfriend I had, well, that was two years ago, I come home and she's in bed with my best friend. I got to tell you, I seen that, it hurt so bad, I pulled him off of her, she said I tried to strangle her, but I don't remember, I just hurt so bad. The judge, he told me I could never talk to her again, but I didn't want to, the bitch. Then she had my best friend's baby, although I'm not his friend no more, nor him me. So you see, I've had bad luck and I want to ask you this, are you going to do that too, hurt me, lie, betray me? 'Cuz if you are, don't come back down, leave me alone instead. Because I know I only met you tonight, I know that, but I feel like this, us, has been here forever. Like you and me, have been forever. Can I trust you?"

"Oh yes," Benny said. "You can trust me, Mickey. I haven't had it easy either, Mickey, and I also feel like this is special."

He was distracted. "I wish I coulda bought you some flowers," he said. "Roses, like on a first date. You're the real deal Benny, you are. I feel bad. Like I let you down. I shoulda bought you roses on the way home."

He looked dismayed, saddened by his failure.

"No, no," Benny hastened to reassure him. "Please Mickey, I don't need flowers. Really, I don't. I'm so happy I met you, that's the universe's gift to me and all I need."

He grinned, boyish again. The young guy from the counter walked back inside, giving Benny a glance. Mickey glared after him.

"You got anythin' goin' with that guy?"

Benny told him no, no way. She laughed and he stiffened.

"You laughin' at me?"

"I'm not Mickey, I'm laughing at how totally absurd it is that you'd even think that I would like a guy like that. You're my type, not him. Anyway, he's an Aussie from a rich neighbourhood. Like I told you, not my cup of tea."

"You spoke to him?"

"Course I did silly, he works the front desk, he's a fellow Aussie and all that. He's a nice enough bloke, asked me out for a pizza, but nah, zero interest, mate. Seriously Mickey, he doesn't mean squat to me. Now, you on the other hand… C'mon mate, give me your other hand… Yeah, that's better."

He grinned again and relaxed. "Pardon me, Benny, it's been a ways since I had a girlfriend. So now listen, you go up to Churchill with a boyfriend in mind, 'kay? Me."

"Yes," she said kissing him again, then she smiled. "Okay then, good night." She pulled away from him and walked backwards through the door, smiling at him all the while. She blew him a kiss, went to the Internet ATM and wrote a quick message to Shay, Mum and Dad, using hyphens to replace the dead spacebar.

Having-the-most-fantastic-time-ever!-Going-up-north-tomorrow,-massive-twoday-train-ride,don't-worry-okay?-I-may-not-email-for-a-week,-lots-of-love-to-all,xoxo

Then she went to pack, set her alarm clock, took her pills, pulled the blankets over her head and fell into a dreamless sleep for the few hours she had before she had to leave.

She woke to the buzz of her alarm, feeling hungover but not catastrophically so. She had a shower and lugged her backpack to the door of the room, taking care to make as little noise as possible so as not to wake Jenna. She realized, half way out, that Jenna hadn't come home at all. Benny smiled and tried to remember what the friend had looked like or what his name was but all she could think about was Mickey – big hot electrical Mickey – the poet with a crooked smile and biceps made of steel.

She felt disloyal but she couldn't help but compare Mickey to Eli and while Eli was gentle, beautiful, and kind, Mickey just seemed so … alive, so astonishingly red-blooded, so high-octane male. She also acknowledged that Mickey was more dangerous than Eli, no doubt about that, which only added to the attraction.

Benny stopped at the front desk. "Can I book a bed for the night I come back?" she asked Adam. No way could she just arrive at Mickey's, luggage in hand.

"Sure can," Adam said, "hang on one sec, I just restarted the computer."

"You're always here," Benny teased him. "Don't you ever get any sleep?"

He laughed. "Sleep when I'm old," he said. "Okay, you're all booked in, have a good time up there, see you when you get back. Wait, I'll get you a cab."

Benny thanked him and went outside to wait. Daydreams of Mickey soon dominated her thoughts. She thought about his sadness, the loss of his brother, his poetry she wanted to read, his rough beauty, and how hard he worked. She couldn't believe her good luck at having met him when she'd been least expecting it. She hadn't thought it possible but Mickey excited her more than Eli ever had. To hell with Eli anyway. He'd left her all alone and all she had to show for her heartbreak was one email saying she was one of his fav memories. *Memories!* Memories didn't kiss you like there was no tomorrow or give you that hot-all-over feeling. She didn't owe Eli a thing. She didn't owe anybody anything.

OLD LADY TRAIN

On the way to the train station, Benny wondered how she'd let herself become so dictated to by Jenna. She vowed to never talk to anyone again lest a repeat ordeal befall her, but she also thought that were it not for Jenna, she'd never have met Mickey. Her benevolence to Jenna extended to a wedding invitation, perhaps even as special guest of honour.

She dragged her luggage through the architectural beauty of the train station in Winnipeg, scanning the crowd on the platform, taking in the chatty camaraderie around her and sorting out the demographic. Lots of bird-watching old folks and one young guy with a shaven head. He looked earnest, clean, Italian. He was sniffing in her direction like a bloodhound finally on the scent of something interesting. Benny ducked down – neediness steamed off him, even from a distance. She climbed up into the train and stowed her luggage, thinking the train ride would be a great opportunity to get some good sleep. Not that the chair was all that comfy mind you.

She closed her eyes and retraced her journey. Seemed like she'd crossed a universe since landing in St John's. The decadent party with Chris was light years in her past. Teenie, a distant fury in a business suit, then the post-Ottawa descent into depression, all the failures of her life flashing before her eyes. Followed by the endless ride west with Jack the GAP poster boy and his jiggly belly. And what about her newly acquired intense passion for nicotine and the pleasure that came with every cellophane gift-wrapped pack of sweet-smelling tobacco freshness. Benny had no idea how she had existed without that reassuring friendship. She also had no idea how she'd break the news of her new best friend to Dad who'd be likely to kill her. She pushed the thought of his disappointment from her mind, and wondered if she had time to jump off for a quick cigarette when the old steel lady answered by shaking her battered frame to life. Benny thought she knew what the sinking Titanic must have sounded like and she looked around at her fellow passengers. Was no one else concerned? It appeared not. They were all chatting happily and leaning on each other's seats.

Benny dug around her narrow seat for a safety belt. She found it but decided the seats were so tight she'd be tucked in safe and sound, no matter what. She had two empty seats facing her, as well as the one beside. She wondered if she could put her feet up on the seat in front but feared it might be disrespectful to Old Lady Train.

The train continued to shake and rattle, like an ancient rocket ship warming up and bracing for a launch.

Benny decided she couldn't wait any longer and she pulled out her camera. Three photos of her and Mickey taken at the pub. She looked drunk with happiness, wild-eyed, wanton. Hardly recognizable. Mickey was earnest and sincere, his head slightly cocked to one side as he gazed at the camera, his smile shy. Dimples, oh my God, his dimples. And those unworldly weird blue eyes – pale ice blue, startling.

And for a second, Benny wanted to run from the train and forget Churchill, run back to Mickey and throw her arms around him. As if sensing her thoughts, the train gave an almighty sneeze and lurched forward, there was no turning back now. Wheezing and protesting, they chugged out of the station, too late for Benny to change her mind.

They passed a sign for the Paris Café: Canadian food plus delicious Chinese cuisine.

CHUGGING UP TO CHURCHILL TAKES A WHILE

Late that afternoon, Benny's suspicions were confirmed: she was not a fan of rail travel. So much for the excellent sleep she had envisaged. She could only nap intermittently with her head twisted in a variety of unthinkable angles. She woke, tangled in pain, her limbs asleep and crushed. In her wakeful moments, she eavesdropped shamelessly and took stock of the players who had gathered to travel this long barren path to the north.

A middle-aged Newfoundland woman with brassy ringlets was holding court at high volume. Her white miniskirt parted to reveal white mini shorts. Benny had seen this item once before when paging through a Sears catalogue but she never figured she'd actually see anyone wearing it. 'It' was a skort – a DNA mix of a skirt and shorts. Hiked up high, the garment revealed long, tanned legs and Benny was reminded of a big blonde Hanoverian brood mare at the yard.

Ouch, bitch. She's probably a really nice person.

The guy across the aisle was fiftyish, with neatly trimmed sideburns and a full head of grey hair. His getup screamed academic. He was clearly a professor of some sort, and he hailed from Philadelphia. Benny figured contract law or mechanical engineering. Sitting in front of him, leaning over his seat and eyeing Benny with unabashed adoration, was the clean-shaven Italian with the beautiful bone structure and designer specs.

Both the Professor and Italiano made it clear they were interested in Benny but she avoided body language cues to engage and instead studied the plethora of purple, yellow, and white wildflowers growing alongside the tracks.

As night fell, she took two sleeping pills, crunched on a codeine, and washed it all down with a mini of Southern Comfort. And yet she still woke at 5:00 a.m. And, she woke ravenous.

It was often the case that the more drugs she took, the hungrier she woke. She had completely run out of food and the diner only opened at 7:00 a.m. – she had checked the night before.

Arms folded, foot tapping, she was first in line. She ordered porridge and was disappointed by the tiny serving. She ate it quickly and ordered another, this time with an order of fresh fruit on the side as well as toast and peanut butter.

Oh, Kenny, if you could see me now! Nada organic and, yes I know, all this sugar's been filtered through cow bones, but do I care? Couldn't give a damn.

She ate two small tubs of orange marmalade and polished off three mugs of coffee with milk and sugar.

She chatted with caution to her fellow tablemates, wary, on the lookout for another Jenna. One woman, sixtyish and stylish in lavender and white, and a gent from Arizona, were both staying at Benny's B&B in Churchill. The old fellow was stone deaf. Benny thought he must be pushing seventy; his face was inwardly sunken like a cadaver, his eyes made huge and bulbous by his specs. The woman had been into computers; she hailed from Atlanta, was in Winnipeg doing research and analysis on her family tree.

I don't want to know… Please, don't explain.

"Don't stay in Canada," Ms. Atlanta said firmly when she learned Benny was from Australia. "It's career suicide. I'm telling you now, go to the States."

Benny, listening with half an ear, focused on how peaceful it all was, while she watched the countryside slowly chug by. Chug very slowly by…

She wondered how many weeks it would take to get to Churchill at this rate. She tuned back to the conversation to hear Ms. Atlanta say that most of the folks on the train were bird-watchers and that apparently the bird life up in Churchill was out of this world.

Aha. Benny thought this might explain the bird-like portions of the food; it was a bird-related thing. She wondered what Mickey was doing and if he missed her.

She went back to her seat, settled down and checked what the others were doing. The Professor was dozing with his head tilted back, and his mouth open. His chins were a-doubling in accompaniment to his snorting breath. The Italian gazed westwards, craning back to look back at Benny every now and then.

A loud speaker announced they'd soon be making a brief stop in The Pas and Benny thought she'd be wise to stock up on food. The cuisine on the train, apart from being small in size, was most disproportionately expensive in price.

Her iPod was tuned in to Janis Joplin, the Doors and Jimi Hendrix; all courtesy of Eli who said retro was in, man. Well, Eli was retro now. Benny looked out the window and practiced saying Assiniboine just because she loved the word. Then she drank some water and thought she was riding the slowest train in the universe.

At 9:30 a.m., as scheduled, they stopped at The Pas and Benny leapt off the train and lit a smoke. She found a lot of good photo ops but had less luck with food. She caught sight of Italiano following her around but she ignored him.

Back on board, the playlist belted Axl Rose crashing and burning on a midnight train, never to return. Benny was ravenous. She dug through her bag, hoping to find a stray piece of gum but all she found was one bottle of Southern Comfort that she downed with a codeine pill to help pass the time. While onwards they lurched. Slowly. Benny slumped into a nap.

11:15 a.m. She woke feeling sick. Over-priced or not, it was time to admit defeat. She made her way to the diner-takeout counter where she bought a Kit Kat, a Seven Up Light and a three-metre egg salad sandwich. Back in her tall narrow blue seat, she relished her picnic and watched the landscape changing, wishing she could imprint it in her mind's eye forever. The view was like nothing she had ever seen before. Graphic and sculpted, stark and bleak. Benny was filled with a great and sudden love for the old train. She decided to savour every single second, make it all last, to which end the train was obligingly helpful.

Slow was her thing, although she had seemed to have hit a rhythm of sorts with a lurch and jerk routine.

Italiano and the Professor were dozing again. The rest of the avid birdwatcher flock was chattering away.

"When I was in rehab –" one ginger-haired biddy offered but shut up when she realized Benny was listening.

The train ground to a stop for no apparent reason except that they had pulled up alongside a marsh. The train seemed to do a fair bit of that – sudden and inexplicable stopping. Maybe there was a bird or a tree of note? Benny craned her neck and saw they were next to Cormorant Lake, tranquil and lovely with limestone rocks and a heron settling with careful precision and neatly folding wings. Tiny waves hurried to the pebbled shore. The skyline was endless. Thin, dead white ghost trees stood tall, giving way to tamaracks. Marshy water was abundant with bulrushes, reeds, and mirrored reflections on reddish streams and ponds. "No Trespassing" said the sign nailed to the wooden spike by the side of the tracks in the middle of nowhere. Hazy sky. Benny felt sleepy, dreamy, and her mind resumed its preoccupation with Mickey; it seemed he was never far from reach.

If Eli had been a course in *Romance and Doing The Crush 101*, then Mickey was her Master's thesis. Because despite being a drug dealer, Eli had been a good boy at heart – he'd meant well. Meanwhile Mickey had bad-boy written all over him like the yellow and black warning label on a tempting package of drugstore contraband.

Benny thought back to her thirteen-year-old self in the hay bales in the barn behind the stables. She had thought when she met Eli, that he was her adult version of that boy, but Eli had been too nice a guy and now it was Mickey who reminded her of her first secret pleasure; that harsh young lad destined for nothingness – his hands calloused, his walk arrogant, and his sideways twisted smile.

She chewed hard on her lip as the train moved north. It might be better to avoid Winnipeg entirely on the way back down. Avoid Mickey. Not see him. Just not go there at all. She took out her camera and studied his face – his chipped-tooth smile, his dimples, and his earnest gaze.

Boys like Mickey were the fork in the road her life could have taken all those years ago – and did she want to take it now? She felt as if her every suppressed appetite was fighting its way to the surface and it was getting harder and harder to keep them all shoved down.

She sighed, tired out. This was her holiday, enough already. Why did she have to overthink everything?

THE BIG OLD TRAIN THROWS A PARTY

4:10 p.m. Benny switched seats. She had watched a brilliant plan maneuvered the night before by a young girl who had since disembarked. She'd filled the space between the two facing twin seats with her luggage, and voila, she had a mini double-bed. Very mini but sheer luxury given the circumstances. Benny was also further back in the carriage and she could see more of the train curving ahead.

Earlier, during lunch, she'd sat next to the Professor while enjoying a delicious but unfortunately small omelet. Dining with them were two kindly Canadians. The Canadians, and Benny considered herself one too, politely refrained from sharing their thoughts when the Professor detailed his theories on how Canada should be run. Benny was mostly AWOL from the discussion anyway. She was thinking about Mickey and the amazingness of his kiss.

She had two good naps in the afternoon, and woke to relocate and watch the Professor moving up the carriage, talking to anyone too polite to tell him to buzz off. His North American rail pass had cost him $US606, and it allowed him to travel anywhere in the USA or Canada for a month.

Yeah, whatever mate, like who cares?

Benny had concerns of her own. According to the guidebook and surrounding conversations, the prognosis of the activity level in Churchill was not good and she wondered if she'd find enough things to keep her entertained for an entire week. If not, she'd take the earlier train back down; it left in three days.

The loudspeaker announced that the train would be taking a three-hour detour up to Thompson.

Incy wincy spider, climbing up the spout.

Benny listened to the idle chatter around her. Alaska was great. Start at the coast and go straight up. Skagway sounded interesting. Benny recalled Jenna saying there were buses from Whitehorse to Skagway and a ferry down to Vancouver via the Alaska Marine Highway – all of which sounded like they had potential.

Benny looked out the window at acres of Canadian Shield pink rock. The Professor headed toward her, his gambit to study the map on her lap, but Benny ignored him. She knew he wanted to use her trip as an opening line to monologue about his but she'd already heard the entire boring tale. More than once.

Eventually, after a lengthy period during which Benny was certain dinosaurs were birthed and died, the big old steel lady crawled into Thompson, which appeared to be little more than a big industrial town. She found a strip mall plaza of sorts and stocked up on enough supplies to last her until she reached Churchill.

She returned to the station platform and smoked while Italiano introduced himself. His name was Simone. He and Benny practiced pronunciation for about an hour but she couldn't get the accent in the right place.

"Simona," she said, stumbling over the last vowel over and over again.

"Benny, you keep saying hello to a girl," he laughed. "It is Simon-é," he said, gesturing like he was conducting an orchestra.

Benny thought he seemed nice but boring. She wanted to get back on the train, but it was being cleaned and then it had to turn. Benny watched the turning and thought it was like a battleship doing a three-point turn on a two-lane freeway. After the turn, a large carriage was added which was good news since the incoming human traffic was heavy, and, by all appearances, they weren't traveling light: suitcases, backpacks, carry-ons, plastic bags filled with Kentucky Fried Chicken, large taped-up boxes, babies, pushcarts, toys, pillows. There was even a disconcerted tabby cat meowing protests in a large cat box.

With the new arrivals jostling to get in, it took over an hour for Benny and Simone to board and another half an hour for them to find their seats in the now reversed train. Standing initially politely, at the fringe of the noisy crowd, Benny realized she would have to be more assertive if she were ever to be reunited with the interior of her cabin, and the faded fabric of her own personal seat.

She elbowed with determination, and eventually found her possessions, only to discover that a family of four had taken over her brilliant new sleeping arrangements. She grabbed her stuff out from under them and shot back to her original two seats that fortunately were still free.

The Professor and Simone had battled equally, fighting through the crowds of families, luggage, and fast food. Hours earlier the Professor, standing with Simone and Benny, was the first to recognize the potential danger of the crowded onslaught and the instant he'd sensed a problem, he'd abandoned both Simone and Benny with astounding speed, vanishing in a flurry of flailing and shoving. Benny turned to look at Simone, who raised his eyebrows and shrugged. Benny gave him a quick wave, farewell, good luck, and dived into the fray.

Once she settled down, she heaved a deep and heartfelt sigh of relief, and spotted the Professor, sleek and smug as a cat, unruffled, reading a book, oblivious to the chaos. He caught her eye and smiled. She nodded somewhat curtly and locked her earbuds into place.

Her heart was still pounding in response to the unanticipated adrenaline rush of having to fight her way back onto the train. She looked around. Her lovely old-world rocking-and-gently lurching train was now a porta-street party.

On a good note, she'd done well in Thompson: a half-jack of Southern Comfort, a bag of Cheddar smart popcorn, a couple of slabs of chocolate, an egg salad sandwich and a novel, *Forty Words for Sorrow*. She never had to move again.

The train was a moving social club. Card tables crowded the aisles, belting nickel and dime delight; and young boys in low-riding sweats and backset earphones strode up and down the carriages, stepping over the floor-seated festivities.

"Eeet's going to be a long night," Simone commented from across the aisle. He pulled out a fleece pillow and blanket, apologizing with his lopsided expression for his ordinariness and basic needs.

Benny closed her eyes and listened to Pat Benatar's "Heartbreaker," at high volume. She was now enthralled by the energy around her, and she wished she could somehow join in.

The train and her mixed bag of passengers scratched forward on the tracks, the old lady digging in deep with rusty nails and pulling herself forward on her belly.

At midnight, Benny put her book away and decided to give sleep a try. Not so easy when a millennium-sized party swirled around her head but she'd polished off most of the Southern Comfort while she read, and she figured her body had to admit defeat and sleep. Simone was quiet and still under his polar fleece. As far as she could tell, he hadn't moved a muscle since taking shelter under his soft and fluffy makeshift tent. His slender vulnerable ankle was the only visible part of him.

Benny woke at 3:30 a.m. in contorted agony. Her head was throbbing, her twisted limbs screaming in pain, nearly as noisily as the train, within which the party continued to rage. Benny did not disguise her admiration. She chewed another two codeine, finished the few swigs of Southern Comfort that were left over, and at last fell into an exhausted sleep at 5:30 a.m., reawakening to find that her right arm was dead. She waited until tingling returned, then fell into another nauseous doze.

THE END OF THE LINE

8:00 a.m. Benny dug out her guidebook. "Never did I such a miserable place see," was the comment on Churchill.

Never did I such a happy prognosis hear. Hmmm…

She looked out the window and all she saw was an endless expanse of desolate land. *Hey, hang on a moment, what happened to the trees?* Even the dead ghost twig trees were gone. There was nothing out there, nothing. Well, nothing except for the rain, the scrub, and the greyness, all of which abounded. *Wow.* Benny thought it was, without doubt, the bleakest possible scenario of all bleakly possible scenarios she'd ever seen.

It seemed cold out – why else would the train walls be heated? Benny pressed her hands to the train's warm sides and her chest filled with excitement. *We're nearing the end of the line! This train is the only way in and out.*

It was a thought that both delighted and terrified her. She'd overheard that one could be airlifted out of Churchill by chartering a small plane, but it would be so unthinkably expensive she'd have to spend the entire rest of her life paying it off.

So, she he turned her thoughts from escape hatches and backup exit routes to the unbridled excitement of the moment. She had covered 5,423 miles since the start of her trip. She was moving toward historic Hudson Bay. Her teeth were furry but the lineup to the washroom was like a feature attraction at Canada's Wonderland, and she wasn't even going to try braving it. Her hair cried out for shampoo and her clothes needed to socialize with bleach and scalding water. Yes, historic.

She fogged up the window looking for any signs of life outside but all she saw was quintessential desolation meeting more of itself. The train continued to crawl. Benny figured it was quite possible that she could crawl more speedily on her own hands and knees, but given the conditions out there, it might not be advisable. She strained to see anything other than the rain and spotted fuzzy, yellow moss lichen stuck to the rocks. Inch by inch, the train dragged forward, and then suddenly, with no warning at all, she came to a shuddering, shaking stop in Churchill, Manitoba. They'd arrived.

CHURCHILL, CANADA'S REAL WONDERLAND

"*The wind it was howling and the snow was outrageous.*" Thus spoke Bob Dylan and he was right. The wind it was howling indeed and the sleet was outrageous. The icy downfall, sidefall, get-under-your-raincoat-fall, was all that greeted the passengers as they fell down off the train into the mud.

Benny guessed she'd been expecting something more by way of reception. Like a parade with a marching band and a round of applause. Give it up for the courageous pioneer folk for having made it all the way to this desolate place of isolation.

But all they found by way of "Welcome to Churchill" was the relentless stinging gale and two feet of mud.

Weighed down by twenty-six pounds on her front, and thirty on her back, Benny listed dangerously on the narrow train steps. At the mercy of the heavy, uneven loads and the gusty wind, she stepped down with uncertainty into the slippery clay. She carefully hitched up her cargo and looked around. Not that she could see much; it was raining too hard.

The train station was closed for renovations. There were no cabs in sight. Benny walked past her equally-hapless fellow passengers who were also milling about, wondering what to do next. This chaotic, untended arrival was all somewhat unexpected.

A presence loomed beside her; it was Simone, looking fragile and lost, with quivering lips and wet lashes. His expression implored her to save him.

"Oh, come on then," she said brusquely. He seemed ready to collapse at her feet in a heap of wet and muddy relief, but she dragged him forward by the arm.

At Benny's insistence, they stopped at a bakery café to ask for directions. It smelled so good inside that Benny was tempted to offload and set up camp, but she didn't think the owners would accept her token of appreciation with the same enthusiasm with which it would be offered. They pointed the way to the B&B and ushered them out the door. Half an hour later, soaking wet and half-blinded, they found Bobbie's B&B.

"Come in," Bobbie said, as she opened the door. "Come in, I'll give you shelter from the storm."

Well, as everybody knows, it was the great Bob Dylan who said that. Clearly he must have walked this Manitoba road.

Bobbie herself was less embracing and certainly less communicative than the sultry welcomer of that song. Benny introduced Simone and said there was no way, mate, that Bobbie didn't have a bed of some kind for him. She stared Bobbie down in a way the battleship matron couldn't refuse.

"Well, I could find him a room all right, but then you'll have to share with Hirokio," Bobbie told Benny, her lips thin and tight. "And that's only if she doesn't mind. We'll have to see." She called up to Hirokio and Benny got the immediate impression that the bowing Hirokio, who'd been there for a month, could do no wrong in the eyes of The Bobbie, while she would never meet her approval.

Benny thanked the smiling Hirokio. "Sharing with me, you saved his life, mate," she said, pointing at Simone who was pestering Bobbie about polar bears. His momentary relief at having found lodging was undone by the Bobbie's update on the polar bear situation.

"Nooooo polaaar beeers???" Simone wailed in despair. "But I did ride the train all the way, for the polaaar beeers…"

Benny viewed his pain from a distance; she was bounding up the stairs behind Hirokio who'd been instructed to show Benny the ropes. She listened to Hirokio recite the list of do's and don'ts while she quickly unpacked and re-dressed in black leatherette trousers she'd found in a seedy fashion store near Regent Park. Who knew they'd turn out to be such perfect rain gear?

She went downstairs to find the distraught Italian had hardly moved. "Let's go for a walk," she said to Simone who, for a moment, had quite forgotten the beeerless state of his life. Clearly he liked Benny's outfit. A lot.

Out of the B&B and back into the eye of the storm, they set out to explore Churchill and the first thing they found was a mangy group of skinny sled dogs chained to the rocks crying mournfully. Not sure what to do about that, they continued on their way. They wandered around the town centre, admired the Arctic Ocean, and checked out the port and grain mill, the tour centers, the Churchill River, and the Hudson Bay.

"Noooo polaaaar beeers," Simone sighed, a lament on repeat.

"Hey, Simone, teach me to play pool," Benny said, inside the entertainment centre, trying to distract him once again from his situation of desolate beeerlessness.

She beat him three games to nothing. It seemed she had a natural aptitude for the game. Having vanquished Simone, she took on two legendary twelve-year-old champions and beat them too. The one lost more gracefully than the other. Benny did a lot of victory dances that did nothing to elevate the mood of the players around her.

"Let's come back tomorrow," she said to Simone, her smile wide, "and the day after that, okay?"

"No. Tomorrow is polaaar beeers," he insisted.

"Okay mate, whatever."

"Has anybody ever told you that you are a leetle strange?" Simone asked when Benny stopped to take a photograph of a rusting old staircase in the middle of a field.

She looked at him through the pouring rain. "And your point would be?" she asked.

They went over to the old grain mill, half of which was still in operation.

"There must be a way in," Benny said, frowning.

Simone, wiping rainwater off his glasses, pointed at the "No Trespassing" sign.

"They only put that there to make it more fun, mate," she said, finally finding a way inside. Once in, she found a lot of heavy machinery and orange flashing lights in the low musty corridors. She nearly made a clean getaway but a couple of none-too-friendly men in hardhats led her out, one of them holding her firmly by the arm.

"I tell her," Simone said to the men who glared at Benny and left.

"I got some good pics," Benny said cheerfully. "Listen, I'm hungry. Let's go back to that café – the one we got directions from."

Gypsy's Bakery and Café was no less a haven the second time around. Benny ordered a cream-filled doughnut and a latte and sat down at a table near the window.

"Good, huh?" she asked Simone, her mouth full.

He poked his Maple Dip with a cautious finger. "Too much sugar," he said dismissively.

"No such thing, mate," Benny said. "No such thing."

After Gypsy's, they went to check on the howling chained dogs and found a batch of puppies eating something that Benny thought looked like a human foot. She mentioned to this to Simone who went green.

"Only joking, mate, only joking."

Tired out, they went back to the B&B where Benny seconded the upstairs washroom for an hour. She had a bath and the absolute pleasure brought forth by the exquisitely hot water was indescribable. Not to mention the joy that came courtesy of the freshly laundered, fluffy, Tide-scented towels in the bathroom.

"Oh, Bobbie," Benny said, rubbing her clean, scented self dry, " how dearly I do love you."

She went downstairs to join the others in the common room just in time to hear Bobbie announce there would be French toast for breakfast the following morning. "Did you put your wet towels in the laundry basket?" she snapped at Benny who nodded meekly.

Benny sank into a wicker chair and closed her eyes. The common room was full. Hirokio was reading. Simone was paging through a brochure on fine dining in the area and Ambrose, the old dude with the sunken mouth, big ears, and gigantic fly eyes – Mr. Arizona 1929 – decided to engage Benny in a conversation.

Deaf as a post he was, apparently resisting hearing aids. "My wife died three years ago," he shouted at Benny, apropos of nothing, his eyes misting over. "Breast cancer. She died in my arms. She did. How old do you think I am?"

You're 103. "Uh ... sixty-five?" she said.

"Eighty-two."

"Wow."

He trumpeted his life story. Ambrose was Catholic, one of sixteen children raised on a farm. He was moving to Minnesota after the Churchill trip. He'd had open-heart surgery eleven years ago, been married for thirty years. He said he wouldn't mind marrying again and he looked at Benny meaningfully.

"Huh?" Benny jerked awake. Surely he wasn't thinking along the lines of her as a potential future bride?

"Good luck with that, mate," she said, thinking, *men, they're really something else.*

Ambrose finally trundled off to bed at 8:00 p.m. and the quiet was like a gift.

Simone went out into the storm to find a restaurant. He was sinking into deep mournfulness. Benny wanted to tell him she was sorry it wasn't working out for him but she didn't care about the bears, she was simply happy to be there. She was in love with the deserted playground of Churchill and thought she could wander around contentedly for days, playing pool and taking photographs of rusted objects sprawled in the sand. Churchill, Benny's own private Wonderland.

DEFINITELY NO POLAAAR BEEERS HERE

It was Sunday and Benny had suffered the lack of polaaar beeers incessantly pre-, during, and post-breakfast. Following Bobbie's delicious French toast, Benny made a hasty and solo escape to the shores of the Hudson Bay, agreeing to meet up with Ambrose later to go to the 10:30 a.m. Sunday mass. She loved churches of all denominations; they reminded her of life at the all-girls school, when things were orderly and filled with promise.

The beach was spectacular. Benny discovered a configuration of boulders – pale blue with soft curved edges that had been sculpted by ten thousand years of brutal weather. Alien in their magnificence and uniqueness. She just stood and stared. Maybe they were from some other planet and had dropped by for a visit.

She also found a dead bird, stripped of flesh with one clawed foot up near its remaining eye. She spent a fair bit of time trying to get the right shot of the symmetrically fanned-out feathers on the bleached bones but she eventually admitted defeat. The perfect death composition would not translate to her camera.

She arrived at the mass just in time. Ambrose waved her over wildly and she joined him, sitting back to listen: "If you do a job well, you will be given opportunities to express your potential. Be patient; travel light; give away possessions; and be ready for God's call."

Benny was perturbed. She didn't want to travel light. She wanted more possessions and nice ones too, and she certainly didn't want to be patient. She was all for the opportunities to express her potential but she'd like them served up with a sense of immediacy.

Hey God, time marches on, I've waited long enough, mate.

A mural behind the altar featured Jesus preaching atop those breathtaking boulders, amid snow and ice with a First Nations fisherman nearby and a dogsled heading off into the forest. *Forest? What forest?* The visual made no sense. Churchill was as flat as Benny's mood and about as forestless too.

"You want to come for a drive?" Ambrose invited her loudly after the service. He leaned toward her and bellowed before they'd even finished the part about going in peace to love and serve the Lord.

"I rented a truck!" he beamed toothlessly.

"Uh, no thanks, Ambrose. Places to go, dead things to see."

One of Benny's goals for the day was to escape her roomies. They'd been a family for so short a time, but she was already looking to avoid them with determination. They were all too needy. Well, apart from Hirokio.

She wandered around the quiet town for several hours, poking around to her heart's content. She found a community cultural centre showing a film on polar bears. Her timing was good and her feet were aching, so she settled down, happy to be entertained and, what do you know, quick as a flash, Simone plopped down beside her. The Italian fridge magnet stuck like glue. Benny sighed, accepted her fate, and dozed. She couldn't remember a single thing about the movie when she woke.

It had occurred to Benny that she was sleeping a lot more than usual, albeit intermittently. She'd always been so hyper, so driven, an insomniac. Now, given the opportunity to slow down, she appeared to be doing exactly that, to the point of snoozing whenever the opportunity arose. She had the half-formed thought that her sleepiness might be due to the increase in her meds, for surely she'd never taken this much daytime Xanax or codeine before, and never previously mixed them with alcohol either. But, she reasoned, she was on holiday. She deserved a rest, regardless of how it was achieved.

"Hey, Simone," she said after the movie ended. "Did you see the bikes outside Bobbie's? Do you think we could ride them?"

Simone replied that he had noticed them and had no interest in them. "I just want –" he began to wail.

"Polaaar beeers!" Benny finished for him. "Yeah, I know. Listen, I'm going to see if Bobbie will let me ride one of the bikes, see you later."

She realized she hadn't ridden a bike since she and Shay were kids, but she was suddenly overwhelmed by the urge to get back to the B&B and give it a whirl. She bade a hasty goodbye to the ever-wilting Simone and hotfooted it back to Bobbie's. After checking with the old turtle that it was okay to borrow a bike, Benny made her selection – a feisty purple number.

Kind of tricky, after not having done it for so long. She got ready to board while half of macho Manitoba hydro watched from elevated cherry pickers; they were tending to some emergency. Throwing caution to the wind, Benny climbed on and pedaled off – in none too shabby form either.

Enraptured, she pedaled up hill, down dale. She was unstoppable. Gravel, railway tracks, marshlands, tarmac, graveyards, rocks and grass, she barreled over them all. Not too bad for an out-of-practice city girl. By the end of the day, it seemed most of the locals knew her well by sight, leaning out of pickup trucks and waving or raising a hand from their verandahs as she shot by. Benny, grinning madly, waved back, one hand steering.

Late that evening, she swerved up to the bike rack, arriving home as darkness was falling. She pushed the bike into place and went inside to wallow in another bath. Exhausted by the day, still exhilarated, she descended to the common room and found it empty save for Bobbie's twelve-year-old grandson. He was covered in a painful looking rash, which was hardly surprising. Bobbie was so scary Benny thought that by the end of her week there, she might be covered in a rash too.

"Who're ya talking to?" Bobbie yelled from the kitchen.

The grandson was explaining the controls of his video game to Benny.

Bobbie knew he was talking to Benny since she'd walked past and seen them both.

"I'm talking to Jesus," her grandson yelled back. Benny could feel Bobbie's scowl through the wall.

"Let's play another game," she said to the grandson.

Benny wondered what happened to the woman from Atlanta. She'd never shown up. Simone had gone off in search of fine dining. Ambrose had gone to bed. Hirokio was upstairs, writing in her Hello Kitty diary. Benny, feeling fond of them all, hung out for a while with the grandson, admiring the cleanliness of the place – Bobbie, Super Dictator Grandma Cleaner.

CRUISING THE HUDSON BAY

1:00 a.m. Benny's alarm sounded with insistency. She'd hoped to catch the northern lights in action but they continued to evade her. She and Hirokio stared up at the sky where nothing was happening. Benny apologized to Hirokio for the inconvenience of the unforgivable hour and Hirokio was gracious and understanding. They commiserated about the absence of the lights for a while and went back to sleep.

She woke again at 6:00 a.m. and was on her bike half an hour later, pedaling furiously up the sandy road toward Cape Merry. Once upon a time the bike had boasted twelve gears; it was currently stuck in the lightest one, which was a good thing since Benny had no idea how to change gears. She cycled up to the lookout point and inhaled the sweet blue morning air, enjoying the breeze brushing her skin. The weather had been way more obliging since the day of their arrival, crisp, clear, and dry. She climbed back on her bike and freewheeled down the steep hill, with an angry tern swooping close and cackling warning cries about babies and nests.

Benny cycled her now familiar route around the town, through the graveyard and back down to Bobbie's for breakfast: blueberry pancakes and unlimited coffee.

"I'll see you on the boat at 1:00," she said to Simone who was leaning his head in his hands, elbows on the table.

Benny spent the morning on her bike, taking a break to lie on one of the ancient boulders, soaking up the sun, and daydreaming about Mickey. He was never far from her thoughts. She wondered if she should phone him but she was too afraid. What if he'd forgotten her? Much better to be in the vicinity when she made the call. And besides, Benny had never been a fan of the telephone while Shay, on the other hand, was umbilically connected. Benny would lie on the sofa, pretending to read, listening to Shay rabbit on. She couldn't fathom where Shay dredged up half the things she talked about. Even under threat of torture, Benny wouldn't have been able to carry on that level of crap for that length of time.

So, she was afraid to phone Mickey. She was afraid she'd blurt out her real thoughts: will you hurt me? Are you trustworthy? Why on earth am I so attracted to you?

Benny also had a tendency to daydream while on the phone, then she'd drag herself back to the conversation and say stupid things, obviously miles behind the latest topic. No ... it was better not to phone. But oh, dear god, let him have missed her.

She shaded her eyes with one hand while she stroked the rock with the other. *Come on rock, bring me good luck. Let Mickey want me like I want him. I'm afraid, rock, I am, but I can't help it, I want him so much. So, c'mon, help me out.*

She looked at her watch. She hopped off the rock and thought about making a stop at the library to check her emails but she couldn't be bothered so she cycled into the area of town filled with expensive crafts and souvenirs.

Shortly after noon, she went to get her pics of Mickey printed out and then she pulled up outside the boat tour office and was soon joined by Simone. Just before 1:00 p.m., they were herded onto a minibus and driven out to the boat.

Benny thought the tour was wonderful. She scanned the churned-up murky water for Beluga whales, spotting dozens of them breaching and diving. The boat turned out into the harbour and Benny, leaning over the side, made eye contact with a beautiful sea lion that was swimming right next to the boat.

The boat rounded a cove and amazingly, astoundingly – since the season was so absolutely categorically wrong – they saw a polar bear lumbering impassively on the opposite shore.

Benny turned to Simone, expecting to see delight but he was sitting down, looking sadly at his camera. "But, only ONE polaaar beeer we did see," he said.

She thought she might tip him overboard.

"You're a glass half full, mate," she said, shrugging, and turning back to look at the bear who was still gazing in the direction of the boat.

The next part of the tour didn't impress Benny. Back on land, they were marched off to stand guard among several million mosquitoes in an old fort built by the British in 1733. Benny thought the whole fort fascination must be part of the male gene thing because she couldn't summon a flicker of interest. Not that she had much time to listen to how the fort took forty years to build and was relinquished without a single shot being fired; she was too busy swatting mosquitoes that could chew through leather trousers.

The tale of the Brits and their fort took an hour and then the group was taught how to load a cannon which Benny thought would no doubt come in handy down the line.

They also heard about "Da Beeva" and priceless fur hats that lasted forever. The guide was passionate about his subject matter and thus endearing but Benny related more to the kids who were whining, scratching, and wanting to leave. She'd seen this island from the vantage point of her morning bike ride. She'd taken in the distant view of the cannon and the fort and shrugged. Men and their war games. Far more impressive, for her, were the not-of-this-planet blue stone boulders and the whales and the remoteness of the entire location.

Reunited with her bike, she bade the wilted Italian farewell and set off to do her circuit of the town. Back to the white crosses in the graveyard and down to the shacks alongside the Hudson River, every shanty complete with dilapidated sofa and failing old office chairs out front. Benny was intrigued. Did the owners sit and watch the sunsets in these saggy leftovers? Bones and bicycle parts and pieces of trash were scattered everywhere. Hub caps and antlers, number plates and car parts.

Beluga Motel read the sign on one.

Tied-up dogs guarded these deserted shanties. Benny pulled up on the purple bike, searching for clues as to who lived there, but finding none. She wondered if perhaps the dwellers were millionaire recluses but she left none the wiser.

Benny suddenly realized that she'd done Churchill – top-to-toe, inside out and upside down. All she wanted to do now was hurry that big old train down the tracks and find Mickey. She was filled with longing to see him, be held by him and touch him. Any reservations about the intensity of her attraction toward him had vanished, and the only thing she wanted was to be with him.

She took one last look across the Hudson Bay, waved farewell to the shacks and their secrets, and set off at high speed. Time to prepare her farewell night and pack for the long steel road back down.

BOBBIE DOES LAUNDRY

Back at the B&B, Benny told Bobbie she would be leaving the following day and Bobbie, delighted by this news, offered to do a load of laundry for a small fortune if Benny so required.

"Surely, at this point in time," she asked pointedly, "there is laundry to be done?"

Benny grinned. "Right you are, mate," she said mildly, thinking batty old bitch. She handed over her bundle, hoping that the scanty and frivolous nature of her underwear would cause the old duck some irritation.

She went into the immaculate living room to wait for her spinning laundry. She looked around and wondered, in a vague sort of way, whether she should steal something. Why? Just because Bobbie was so irritatingly Bobbie. Bobbie was the kind of relative who would drive you to drink, drugs, and teenage pregnancy just so you could be in her face with all that destruction. But what's the bet anyway, that, if one were to succeed in doing the worst possible thing, that Bobbie's only reaction would be a satisfied smirk – that she'd known all along that would be your end, and now look, she'd have to be the one to clean up the mess.

Benny decided against the option of revenge-theft. It was bad karma to take that which was not freely given, and she most definitely wouldn't let Bobbie win by goading her into behaving badly, tempting though it was. She sat in the easy chair that was so comfy she was in danger of snoozing. In an effort to keep awake she wondered if she'd left anything undone in Churchill the Great but she didn't think she had.

She wondered, eyes closed, half dozing, if she could ever live in Churchill, Manitoba. It was one of the farthest places from Sydney, Australia, not just geographically but in just about every way imaginable. But Benny liked it and since she was also using this trip as a reconnaissance mission to find a possible permanent abode, she had, as she'd made her rounds about the town, inquired about job opportunities at the library, the cultural centre, the grocery store, and even the video store. Seemed like there was always work if you wanted it, but you couldn't be too choosy. It might not be a regular gig and you had to be able to cope with the very long, dark and freezing winters.

She wondered if perhaps she could start a bakery coffee shop much like the one she and the wet, shell-shocked Simone had staggered into on that first cold morning. She was feeling unusually positive and believed she could embrace the idea with enthusiasm, but then realized she'd have to learn to bake, which, in itself, might present several challenges and take a good few years longer than she had left to live.

Benny was startled to find that she was considering a "job" sort of job, when her entire life had been focused on her artistic career.

Had she given up on her art entirely? She hadn't picked up a paintbrush since the horror of the art show. Her art, once the most precious thing to her, had fled the country of her mind. It was betrayed, in exile.

"Doesn't even matter," she muttered, and she realized she was slumped down and twisted in the chair. She sat up, and straightened her limbs.

There were worse things than living out her life in Churchill, Manitoba. It was even exotic in a way. People would ask, so what's up with Benny these days, and Dad would say, "Oh, she's up in Churchill, on the shores of the Hudson Bay; she became a baker."

Yeah, right. Benny gave a snort.

She wondered if any of the original train-folk would be coming down with her or if they were staying for the week. She had bumped into some of them in the over-priced tourist shops buying moccasins, fluffy toys, dream-catchers, and Aboriginal artwork. Turned out the woman from Atlanta had changed B&Bs but the Professor was nowhere to be seen. Benny figured he'd gone straight back down on the train, three minutes after seeing the inhospitable gale.

She considered the option of getting off at Thompson and taking the bus back down to Winnipeg, just for something different, but no, she wasn't going to abandon that old steel lady. They were going down south together.

Next thing she knew, Bobbie was shaking her awake, telling her to come and fold her laundry please.

GQ IS FORLORN ON FLORAL

Benny's last night in Churchill. She was bathed, laundered, packed, and ready at 8:30 p.m. She'd taken advantage of the washroom, doing a thorough cleanse in preparation for a journey she knew would be lacking in these amenities. She had exfoliated, face-masked, shampooed, conditioned, manicured, pedicured, moisturized, powder-dusted, deodorized. She would have been an excellent contender to win Ms. Shopper's Drug Mart Product-User of the Year.

She came out of the bathroom to see Simone sitting on his bed, staring forlornly into space. He was clearly flouting the very strict Bobbie policy that all bedroom doors must, at all times, remain closed because there were people of Both Sexes in The House. Oh, yes, he was flouting all right, and he was obviously a man on a mission. He was dressed up for a night on the town, all spiffy and natty. Benny couldn't help laughing at the juxtaposition – a GQ fashion moment sitting glumly on the floral bedcover of a Churchill B&B.

"You all right, mate?" she made the mistake of asking.

He looked up at her and sighed. "You will some fine-dining with me?"

"Nah, I'm going to read in bed, mate. Long day ahead tomorrow, may as well take advantage of the bed while I've got it."

"This holiday was not…" he floundered, "this was … I am a sad man," he concluded ruefully and shrugged.

"Can't help you, mate. Life's what you make it, you know. We all get knocks, yeah, it's how you take it on the chin. Well, have a good night."

She climbed into bed, clutching a Linwood Barclay she'd found in the living room. Hirokio was nowhere to be seen. She thought about what she'd said to Simone and laughed.

"Bit rich coming from me," she said out loud. "Me, Miss-The-World's-Done-Me-Wrong."

She lay down, the book on her chest and thought about all the things in her life that had gone wrong – her art show, her marriage. Her unspeakably grannyish-name, her parents' lack of wealth and absence of social standing. Benny always felt as if she'd been given the short end of the stick, that she'd had to be the one to make a silk purse out of a sow's ear but now, tucked up in Bobbie's fragrant linen, she thought maybe her life hadn't been all that bad.

Sure, Mum and Dad didn't have buckets of money to throw around but they loved her and were fantastic parents. Shay … well, you couldn't ask for a better sister. Loyal to the last, she never judged Benny, no matter what she said or did. And look how Dad's boss had sponsored her to go to that school.

Oh, the art show hurt. Yes, that still hurt. All those years of work, to end in such public humiliation. That debacle was still housed in her chest like a bitter stone.

And then there was Kenny … although she was surprised to find less of a jolt of hurt when she thought about him. So she tried again, tried to re-imagine her horror of that moment, when she saw the local newspaper, the lifestyle section with the giant headline: *Behind the*

Marriage Lies Another Man and a picture of Kenny and Malcolm the Rock holding hands. Kenny looking forlorn, with the caption saying he had no idea how to tell his family ... or his wife whom he loved with all his heart.

"I had to do it this way," he'd told Benny later when he finally came home to face the music. "*The Herald* wanted to do a story on how many gay men there are in heterosexual marriages and then, when Malc told them about us, they asked us if we'd do the story, because there're so many others out there, married to women but in love with other men. And I thought if I did it this way, there'd be no turning back, and I wanted there to be no turning back, don't you see? I just didn't think it would feel like this Ben, our marriage. It should feel like it does with Malc and me, and you'll see that one day too."

"I hate you, Kenny," she'd said, "I hate you. I curse you. And now, after my art show too."

"I know. I've never been as happy as I was that night, talking to Malc, and I watched your pain and I felt sick, just sick."

"*You* are sick," Benny had shouted. "Twisted. I hate you! I hate you!"

She'd shouted unspeakable things at him and he'd stood and taken it. She'd pummeled his chest, his thin chest, and she'd hit his skinny arms and he'd let her.

The memory of her viciousness shamed her. She sat up in bed. "Ah, Kenny," she said out loud to no one in particular. "I'm sorry, I really am. You must have been so unhappy all those years and I never knew. I thought you were like me, ambitious, but you were locked down."

It was astonishing to find, after so much time of harbouring such hate, that what she felt toward him now was sorrow. Tears filled her eyes at the thought of his bravery; how he took the hits she threw at him. She'd never even asked him how his family had reacted or what they'd said. She was too full of self-pity, refusing to speak to him, wishing he'd died, leaving her a respectable grieving widow instead.

Benny lay back down and opened the book. Yeah, maybe her life hadn't been that bad. Maybe she'd been the one living a glass half empty, never mind Simone.

She propped the pillows behind her head and cracked open the diet Dr. Pepper she'd sneaked past eagle-eyed Bobbie, along with a box of Glossette almonds. She snuggled down contentedly. There wasn't going to be too much by way of this level of comfort for the next couple of days, so she may as well make the most of it while she could.

She figured she really could live in Churchill if only she could learn how to bake. There was no doubt in her mind that Churchill, Manitoba, was surely one of God's – and her own – favourite places on earth.

COMING DOWN IS VERY SLOW WORK

Later, they were back on the train, heading south. "So where's your googly-eyed admirer?" asked Murtha, the woman from Atlanta.

Seemed a lot of the original crew going up had decided to come back down on the Tuesday train.

"Oh, he's around," Benny said and sure enough he was. Simone had tried to sit right next to her on the train, but she'd put a most impressive evasive-action technique into play and he ended up two rows in front of her, facing the other direction. He kept bopping up to look at her, but Benny avoided eye contact.

Back at the station, while they waited to board, he'd asked, "Can I take a photograph of you?"

"What for, mate?" Benny had responded, irritated. Then thinking she was being overly rude, she compensated, "Well, yeah, of course you can."

"It is so that one day when you are faymoose I can say that I did know you then," Simone explained and Benny burst out laughing.

"Oh, Simone," she said, "my days of faymooseness have long come and gone."

They were all headed back to the Peg. Ambrose, having decided at the last minute to come down, hadn't been able to get a sleeper so he was dozing across the aisle from Benny. Murtha was behind, playing cards.

Benny blew up a couple of air-pillows and wondered if sleep was possible. She got settled, thinking happy Churchill thoughts; both the pillows and the moment felt just fine.

Later she sat up and stretched. She could see Simone was still doing his jack-in-the-box routine to gaze at her.

Ambrose arrived for a chat. He said he'd found a way to upgrade to a sleeper.

"Want to see my room?" he yelled.

"No thanks, Ambrose," she yelled back.

"Want to take a shower?"

"No thanks, Ambrose." She did a quick armpit sniff; maybe he was trying to tell her something.

She was looking forward to being back at the hostel for a couple of nights. She was going to contact Mickey from there despite his earlier offer that she stay with him. Benny told herself she wasn't sure if she was even going to see him, and besides, one never knew, maybe he'd found a new girl in the interim. Part of her hoped he had, even though it would break her heart. But that would be a safer heartbreak than getting involved with him and risking worse.

She was suddenly restless. They'd been this way already. This was a road much traveled – she'd been here, done this set of tracks. She was eager to get back to Winnipeg, to Mickey, and whatever that might bring.

THE TRAIN OF THE LIVING DEAD

Night fell. The hours passed and the train, like some kind of horror-movie special-effect, transformed into an express ride from hell. Shake, rattle and roll; the skeletal old bones were convulsing, shrieking. The horn blew regularly, irregularly: short blasts, long hauls. Perfectly timed to shatter and destroy any kind of sleep activity. Cold air blasted up Benny's back. She took just about every pill she could, downing them with Southern Comfort but this only added to the hallucinatory horror of the night.

Suddenly, sometime in the darkest hours before dawn, the train ground to a halt and two creatures of the night appeared out of nowhere: two hugely obese, unnaturally pale men, who waddled slowly through the carriage, stopping to chat next to Benny, then disappearing. Benny checked her watch. A mere seven hours of the journey left but the train had stopped and wasn't going anywhere. A baby shrieked at the top of its lungs, awake in all its despair, determined to take the world with it.

Simone had changed position in his seat and now faced Benny, shrouded in a bright orange toweling bathrobe. Earlier he'd been reading a Danielle Steele novel from Bobbie's collection. Danielle Steele? Benny hoped he wouldn't be garnering any kind of misguided heroics from the square-jawed, comic-book males adorning the pages.

Benny, drugged and foggy, would have reached for more medicinal help but she knew there wasn't a drug that could help her now. The night was a black hole. This was ballet of the ghost passengers, on a train stalled in space and time.

By the next morning, when dawn finally broke, Benny was shattered. At mid-morning, when the train crawled into Winnipeg, the passengers collected their belongings and readied themselves to disembark. That there was still a world out there at all was nearly incomprehensible to Benny.

She shook off the dismally clutching Simone and grabbed her bag. "Good luck, mate," she said briskly. "Hope the rest of your vacation's a good one, yeah?" Then she strode away, as quickly as she could, found a cab, and went back to the hostel.

THE ELECTRIC CONNECTION

"Hey, where's Adam?" Benny asked the girl behind the counter, a multi-pierced gothic lass with ragged nail-scissored chopped hair and a good few inches of smooth pale belly showing between her T-shirt and the waistband of her jeans.

"He got beat up last week," the girl said, chewing a half-painted fingernail. "Real bad too. Broke three ribs, his teeth got cracked, his nose broke. He's in a coma. You're in the same room as before, same bed."

Benny thanked her, horrified to hear about Adam. "Do they know what happened?" she asked. "Adam's like the nicest guy on the planet. Who'd do a thing like that?"

The girl shrugged. "I dunno. I got a phone call at like three in the morning and they wanted me to come in because there's supposed to be someone at the desk round the clock, which is ridiculous if you ask me. And they didn't take his money or nothing, I don't get it. They think he went outside for a smoke and got laid into. God only knows why."

"Let me know if you hear anything about how he's doing, okay?"

The girl said she would and Benny lugged her bag to her room.

She had a shower and scrubbed at her travel dirt, her heart pounding like a mad thing at the thought of seeing Mickey again. She got dressed, and looked at her watch. It was only lunchtime. Mickey would still be at work. She tried his cell phone, hardly able to breathe. Her heart was so loud and strong in her throat that she felt sick.

He picked up on the second ring.

"Hi Mickey, it's Benny, you know, from the pub the other night. Her armpits felt slick with sweat and her breath was caught in her chest.

"Hey, you," he said, his voice all deep and slow, "I been waitin' for you. Where're you at?"

She told him and he sounded surprised, hurt.

"Why didn't you come here, like I told you, stay with me?"

"Ah Mickey," she said, giddy to be talking to him, "I don't even know you mate, not really. Not yet. I can't just land at a guy I don't even know. And anyway I thought Frank was there with you?"

"He went," Mickey said shortly. "He's gone over to stay with his sister. Only me here now. So listen up, I gotta finish work here but I'll tell them guys I gotta go early today. I'll be with you at 2:00, okay?"

He hung up and Benny put the phone back in the receiver, feeling equal parts ecstatic and idiotic. She wandered out into the garden to wait for him, lighting up a smoke and sitting in the shade of a big tree.

An hour later, a big truck pulled up and Mickey jumped out.

He ran over to Benny and gathered her up and she clung to him, her arms around his thick neck, sinking into him.

He put her down and looked at her. "You got no idea how happy I am to see you," he said and his smile was shy. "So where's your stuff? Come on sweetheart, you're comin' home with me, I won't hear otherwise, okay."

As if she could argue. She beamed.

He grabbed her backpack from the room and stopped at the front desk on their way out.

"Can she have her money back?" he asked the crop-haired girl, politely.

"No way, José," the girl said. She was snapping gum and reading a book and she hardly looked at him. "She booked the bed, she's got to pay for it."

"But she isn't going to use it and she didn't know that," Mickey persisted.

"Ah, it doesn't matter," Benny said. "She's right and it's only twenty dollars, it's okay."

"Twenty dollars is twenty dollars," Mickey was stubborn. "Every cent counts."

The girl ignored him and Benny pulled him away. "Come on," she said, "I want to see where you live, I want to have fun with you. Forget the money."

Mickey glared at the girl who ignored him and followed Benny out to the truck.

"This SUV is so cool," Benny was impressed. "Whose is it?"

"Mine," Mickey started the engine. "Well, from work anyways. Them guys there, they got it for me. That's why Frank moved out. He got all pissed off 'cuz they promoted me and he said he wouldn't work on my team, so they transferred him to another unit."

"How childish of him," Benny said. "I know I only met him once but I would have thought he'd be more mature than that." Her words sounded stiff and formal to her ears. She felt self-conscious, and wished she could be more nonchalant.

Mickey shrugged and revved the engine. He grinned at her. "Hear that sound, eh? Power!" He pulled out into the street. "Gonna take you on a tour."

He drove her around Winnipeg, showing her this sight and that. Benny smiled when she saw the Legislative Building and she told him about Jenna and the macramé hair shirt and he laughed.

"So what happened to Jenna?" she asked him. "Last time I saw her, she had her tongue three feet deep down Frank's throat."

Mickey shook his head, "No idea, could care less. I don't even remember what she looked like. I only had eyes for you." He broke into song and Benny laughed and moved closer to him.

"The only problem with this cab is that it's too darn big," she said, "I can't sit right on top of you."

He turned to look at her. "Oh, you'll get your chance," he said casually and it seemed to Benny that she stopped breathing.

"So, that's Winny-the-peg," he said. "And now, here we are." He turned into a parking lot. "That's *mi casa* up there. I rent from the guy who owns the Hakims under. There's a pub there too. You can't see it from the back here. Now, I'm tellin' you, the apartment's a mess, don't think I don't know that, but I been working so hard I didn't have time to un-pack my stuff. I been waitin' for the winter slump to do that. Although them guys says there's work if you want it, even through winter and I'm gonna take it for sure. Frank says he likes being a seasonal worker 'cuz he can sit and watch *The Simpsons* and get stoned but I want to work, I'm tryin' to save up, build a life. Them guys, like Frank, only live for now, don't have long-term dreams."

He grinned at her and led her up a set of narrow, dark stairs. "Careful now," he said, "let me go first okay. Owner should of put a light in. He's such a loser though, I bet he'll never do it." He turned to her at the top of the stairs and dug in his pocket.

"I got you some keys made," he said and grinned. "The key chain's a flashlight, look, so you'll be able to find the lock." He turned the flashlight on, and was disappointed when it didn't work. "Piece of shit," he said, shaking his head. "I'm sorry. I'll get you a new one tomorrow, okay?"

He pushed the door open to reveal a single small room with one window on the far side. An oval, old-fashioned basin was in the corner, with an open closet along the one wall and a tiny toilet and shower washroom adjoining to the left. The door to the washroom was broken, hanging drunkenly by a couple of nails. The room had a sloping ceiling and outside a large Molson sign flickered on and off. A kingsized air mattress lay in the middle of the floor, and was piled with rumpled sheets, a dirty flattened pillow, and a crocheted blanket that had seen better days. The remaining space was filled with over-flowing broken cardboard boxes and torn black plastic garbage bags, all spilling their contents.

Benny was dismayed. "Wow. Yeah, really needs some work. How on earth did you and Frank both fit in here? And does the door to that washroom not close?" She wished she hadn't given up her room at the hostel and suddenly felt afraid.

"Sweetheart, I know what you're thinkin' and I don't blame you for a minute." Mickey put his arms around her and she buried her head in his chest, not wanting to look at the anarchy of the broken room. And yet strangely, she acknowledged, she was also excited by the squalor, excited by the homelessness of just the two of them being there, amid chaos and dereliction.

"Benny, sweetheart, I know it don't look like much but I'll fix it for you, this weekend. I haven't had time till now but you'll see. Give me this weekend, that's all I'm askin'. I never had a reason, before you. I'll put a door on the closet, build you a bookshelf along here, where you can put your stuff, an' I'll unpack my boxes, fix the door to the washroom and I'll get you a blackout curtain so's the light don't bug you from that sign. Okay?"

"You can do all that in one weekend?" Benny asked, watching him navigate the mess of the room, pointing out all the things he'd do.

"Sweetheart, you ain't seen nothin'." He smiled that crooked smile. "Wait till you see me with a power drill. I'm quick-hand Luke, baby. And, let me show you something more. You're gonna like this, I give you my word." He led her over to the window and pushed up the sash. He climbed out on the ledge and held out his hand. Benny crawled out onto the asphalt rooftop and her breath caught as she looked around.

They were way up high, with flashing car lights flying by below, music coming from the nearby pub, and cars honking their horns. Benny peered over the edge of the wall, turned to face Mickey and beamed.

He stood behind her, smiling his crooked smile, proud. "That's why I got it," he said, flicking a match against his boot and firing up a smoke. "Cool, eh? We'll have ourselves picnics up here at night, lie on a blanket in a world all of our own." He was excited, happy. "Sweetheart, I know the room's not so great now but that's why the landlord gives it to me cheap, an' I said I'd fix it for him. And now you're here, I got every reason." He pulled her close. "You're my dream come true," he said and his voice broke with emotion. "You got no idea how long I been waitin' for you."

Benny hugged him. She was suddenly exhausted. The train ride had been a long one she had been filled with equal amounts of longing and fear. Would he still be there? Would he want to see her? Then the drive around Winnipeg, the arrival at the upside-down room – she was overcome with tiredness.

"Mickey," she said, and yawned before she could stop herself, "I'm a bit shattered. Can we lie down? I don't want to waste a minute of our time together but I'm knackered. The train and all that you know."

"Don't you worry," Mickey was gentle. "C'mon. I should of thought of that. How could I not have thought of that?"

He led her back into the apartment and straightened out the sheets and the blanket and fluffed out the stained pillow.

"I only got the one pillow," he said. "Here, you use it, I'll roll up my winter jacket and on the weekend, we'll go shopping and make this place a home, okay?"

Benny thought she should at least brush her teeth but she couldn't summon the energy. She was too tired to even dig out her sleeping meds. She pulled off her trousers and climbed into bed in her panties and T-shirt. Mickey gently pulled the covers over her.

"I'm goin' out for a smoke," he said. "You just sleep now."

The air mattress bed was surprisingly comfortable and Benny fell fast asleep, oblivious to the on-off of the Molson sign that lit up the room in blue and red.

WALKING ON SUNSHINE

When she woke in the morning, Mickey was gone. Benny sat up and looked around the room, wondering what she had let herself in for. The room was like a vagrant's shelter, a temporary stop for a drifter.

But, Benny argued with herself, Mickey had explained all that. He had explained why it was such a mess, and he had good reason. She tried to imagine both Mickey and Frank in the room but failed. She got out of bed and padded the few steps to the tiny washroom with a dirty toilet and filthy shower. Benny thought it would take more than bleach and a steel brush to eradicate the squalor and, looking at the stains, she knew she had to leave.

She pulled on her clothes, planning on grabbing her backpack, heading for the bus station and not looking back. But at that moment a phone rang and Benny jumped, startled, trying to see where the ringing was coming from. There was a cell phone next to the bed. She hadn't noticed it when she got up. She reached for it, wondering whether she should answer it. "Hello?" she said cautiously.

"Hey, baby, you're awake! I wasn't sure if I should phone before now or later. You were so wiped out, I couldn't believe how you were sleepin'."

Benny, listening to the wonderful sound of Mickey's laugh, felt all the tension drain from her body. "Yeah," she said. "I just woke up, I was going to take a shower but the washroom – "

"Ah, now listen, babes, don't you be upset about the place okay? I know it's not so great but it'll be our home okay? I promise you, I'll fix it this weekend, you'll see. Them guys here said I can borrow any tools I like and I am goin' buy some lumber on the way home and you'll see. You go and get a nice breakfast and have a nice day, okay? And I'll bring stuff to clean the washroom. I'm sorry about that babe, I should of cleaned it. My bad, okay?"

Benny felt relieved. "Yes," she said reassured. "I'll go for a walk, do something, get something to eat."

She hung up and brushed her teeth in the basin that she figured doubled as a kitchen sink. She went out, locking the door carefully behind her. She took stock of where she was and walked around, enjoying the sights and sounds. Mickey's apartment was close to the hostel, right in the middle of downtown and she recognized a few familiar spots. She made note of the Internet café next to the Hakims, and she went back upstairs, wondering if there was any way she could brave the shower. She opened the door and the phone was ringing. She answered it.

"Where were you?" Mickey sounded annoyed. "I been phonin' you for hours."

"I went for a walk and forgot to take the phone, I'm not used to having a phone again, sorry."

"No, babes," he sounded abashed. "I just worried is all. What're you going to do now?"

"Have a shower, although the washroom's filthy. Don't forget to bring home bleach, rubber gloves, and a steel brush."

"I can do that. Listen I won't be home late okay? What do you want for supper? Pizza?"

"That's fine," Benny said, thinking what the hell, pizza was the last of her worries. "As long as it's vegetarian. Although where we'll eat, I've got no idea." She looked around.

"We'll get a small table, or TV dinner trays," Mickey said confidently. "Trust me, sweetheart, trust me. And listen, if you go out again, take the phone with you, will you please? For me?"

She told him she would. Then she braved the shower, thinking that a new shower curtain needed to be added to the shopping list. She decided to stop by the Internet café and tell Shay she'd made it back down okay, and she strapped on her money belt. She had buried her travel cash inside a pair of socks deep in the bottom of her backpack.

Despite her misgivings about the apartment, Benny was happier than she'd ever been, happier even, than she'd been with Eli. She hummed *Walking on Sunshine* as she entered the dark café that housed more rowdy game boys than hostel travelers.

She sat down next to a boy playing a very noisy war game. She logged on and found emails from Dad, Shay and Teenie.

Teenie said,

> Hey chickie! Where are you now? There's an opening for a senior web designer at a good agency I know – you interested?

Benny wrote back to Teenie first,

> In Winnipeg, still en route to the great west, Thanks T, not ready to come back yet – still have to dip my toe in the Pacific. Also, I like print more than web but thanks for thinking of me!

Then she wrote to her family, nondescript messages saying everything was fine but she was tired, might stay in Winnipeg for a week or so and catch her breath. No mention of Mickey.

Then she logged off. It was only 3:00 p.m., and a long while before Mickey would be home. She wandered into a mall and bought a book, *Body* by Harry Crews, a bargain for $2.

Then she went back to the apartment, blew up her air pillows and had a nap. She woke to the fragrant smell of pizza and the feel of Mickey's big warm body close to her.

"Hello," she said, sleepily. "I'm much more tired than I realized."

"Sweetheart, no wonder. We'll get an early night. I can't be late for work again, them guys is getting a bit pissed with me. I got you some beer too and I hope you don't mind but I gotta get this doobie inside me before I do anything else."

Benny helped herself to a slice of pizza. "Ooh, this is fantastic," she said and Mickey laughed. He finished the joint and pushed the food aside.

"Eat later," he said, his voice husky. "I gotta take care of my girl now. That all right with you?"

More than all right.

The next day Benny woke at noon. She stretched out, wondering what to do. She ate a leftover piece of pizza while she got dressed, then went for a walk and sat down to read *Body* in a small park nearby. She got lost in the book, checked the time, and was amazed to find it was close to 5:00 p.m. She got up, stretched, and ambled back to the apartment, finding to her surprise that the door was half open and there was the sound of hammering coming from inside. She pushed the door open and gave a cry of surprise. The room was transformed. Two big garbage bags stood in the middle of the floor; the mess had all been cleared. The closet sported brand new white doors and Mickey was putting the final nail into a new shelf that ran alongside the wall. The bed was made and decked out with a new pillow and two new pillow cases, and a thick black curtain hung over the window; it was tacked up and pulled to one side with a bulldog clip. There was a little trolley next to the sink with a dish rack, a set of wire grocery shelves on wheels and a kettle beside that. And the washroom door was properly attached.

Mickey looked up at her and grinned in triumph. "A bit better eh?" he said in his deep voice and he flipped the hammer around his finger – Wild West style.

Benny burst out laughing. "Yeah, you could say that," she said.

He came over and hugged her tight; he was covered in sweat and dirt. "I explained to them guys that I needed to leave at lunch today, had to do this or my girl could leave me. I know there are still some things we need here but it's a start, eh?"

"Ah, Mickey, it's a brilliant start, brilliant." Benny was happy. She entwined his dirty fingers in hers.

"Let me get all cleaned up," he said, running his fingers through his hair, his eyes shining, and his grin triumphant. "You explore. You can unpack your things in the closet. Later tonight I'll hook up my stereo, okay? But let me go and get cleaned up."

Benny lay down on the bed and snuggled her face into the brand new pillow. She listened to Mickey showering, and wished she were in the hot soapy water with him. She fell asleep and next thing he was lying next to her, smelling of shampoo and some kind of spicy aftershave. She rolled sleepily toward him and he kissed her long and deep, his breath sweet. She ran her hands over his body, his incredibly firm and beautiful body.

"You take my breath away," she murmured and he laughed.

"No, baby, that's what you do to me," he said and he lifted her T-shirt over her head.

The Molson sign flickered on and off and Benny felt like they were spinning across the universe in their own tiny spaceship, the room sailing through a galaxy of stars and light.

When she woke, he was gone and she sat up in fright. It was completely dark out, only the neon lighting up the room. She saw that the window was open and she leaned outside.

"Havin' a smoke," Mickey said easily, "Come on out and bring the comforter with you, I don't want you to get cold out here. Wait, let me help you."

He grabbed the comforter from her and helped her out the window.

"We should get some Muskoka chairs for up here," he said. "Sit and watch our view."

She laughed and settled down next to him, her back against the wall. Mickey was smoking a joint and he offered it to her. She took a drag and immediately felt the hit.

"Wow, that's strong," she said and he laughed.

"It's who you know," he said. He reached for her hand. "Are you happy?"

"Happier than I've ever been," she said.

The answer satisfied him. "Come sit here, between my legs, lean up on me." He pulled her closer to him.

"Benny," he said, "I know I told you about my brother gettin' killed and that, and I'll be the first one to tell you I ain't always played it straight. I got into trouble more than once. Like that judge, he sent me for anger management but I didn't finish the program. I know I should of, but I'm not so good at finishing crap. Then I ran up all my credit cards, couldn't pay them, that's why I left Nova Scotia. I'm tryin' to save up enough money here to pay everything back 'cuz my family's there and I miss them even though they're not what you'd call the best support. My dad, he drinks more than he should, and so we never had money. Like I could of been NHL for sure. I skate backwards faster than forwards but we never had no money for skates or nothin' and I always had secondhand crap that never worked. And then, when Jimmy died, you'd think my dad would clean it up, right? But he didn't. He drank more. Alcoholism runs in our family. I remember tellin' my granny my troubles and askin' her why we're the way we are. I told her, it's not fair."

She could feel him getting maudlin and she turned to face him, stroking his face. The marijuana had her feeling dizzy, spaced out.

"I'm with you now," she said softly. "Everything'll be different. We're together now, right? It's all going to be different. Hey, can we get a new shower curtain?"

He laughed. "Sweetheart, we can get anythin' you like. Any colour you like. And a mirror for the bathroom and let's get a TV, just a little TV. I can afford that, we can go down to the pawn shops, and see what they got. And maybe a DVD player, they're cheap these days. We can lie in bed together and watch movies. What do you think of that idea?"

"I love it," she said, kissing his neck. "Love it."

"Well, we'll go back to sleep for a bit and then when we wake up, we'll go shopping. So, not bad for a day's work eh, what I did with the room?"

Benny told him he was incredible.

THE TIME OF HER LIFE

The weekend was one of the best ever. Benny and Mickey drove around in the big truck; sightseeing, shopping, bartering with pawn dealers, picking up groceries and movies. He was like a rock star, mesmerizing in the way he walked, the way he talked. She watched people respond to his energy, his power, and she felt so proud to be his girl.

Saturday night they lay in bed, watching old Kung Fu movies, and drinking beer with Southern Comfort chasers, and Mickey smoked a few joints. Benny told him she couldn't handle his pot and he laughed. "I'll get you some easy hash instead," he said, "You'll like it better."

They woke up late on Sunday, and went out for a walk. In the afternoon they sat on the banks of the Forks and watched the Red River swirling past. Mickey leaned against a tree while Benny photographed him.

"You're so beautiful," she said, "like James Dean only with lighter hair."

He looked happy at that but then he sighed heavily. Benny lowered her camera. "What's the matter?" she asked.

"Monday," he said, depressed, flicking his butt into the mud.

"I always liked Mondays," Benny said, "I always liked going back to work, being at my desk. I like the routine, makes me feel safe."

"Well, sure a desk job is fine but me, I dig and work with wood and stone and cement and my hands get all cut up and the foreman, he's an asshole. I'm the leader of my crew right but the one brother who owns the company, he's such an asshole. The other brother, Bruce, he likes me all right, he's the one who got me the truck and my own crew. But Jerry, the asshole, he's always visitin' me onsite, checkin' up on me."

His face was dark. "Like in the morning, right, I get a bag of dough-nuts for the guys on my crew. You can get a whole bag of yesterday's doughnuts from Second Cup for two dollars – a whole bag. I sit with my guys in the front of the truck and we drink coffee and eat dough-nuts but Jerry, he says we're wastin' time, right. He always comes and checks up on me."

"But you're team-building," Benny objected. "That's good communica-tion if you ask me – mentoring. How come he doesn't see that?"

"He sees what he wants to see," Mickey said, his voice low and hurt. "And he watches every piece of lumber I use, every frickin plant and shrub. Like I'm some kind of baby or somethin'. I know my stuff and I'm faster than any one I know, and I can pour concrete like nobody I know. And he says we all got to be in the yard for quarter to seven in the morning. It's hard for me to be there then, and if I get there even fifteen minutes late, he gets all pissed off."

"I wish I had a job to go to tomorrow," Benny said, wistful. "Then our life would be perfect. I would do a nine-to-five, and we could come home and make supper together and go for a walk and be like everybody else."

"Hey!" Mickey sat up. "I'm goin' to ask them guys if you can join my crew."

Benny laughed nervously. "Mickey, I don't know the first thing about gardening and landscaping."

"Ah, now sweetheart, it's not complicated. You'd mostly be puttin' plants into flower beds. I think you'd like it and we'd be together the whole time!" He was excited, happy again. "I'll talk to them guys tomorrow. What's the bet Jerry says no, but Bruce says okay. Well, Bruce's the one who runs the show, so what he says goes, no matter what Jerry wants. Bruce likes me and so does his ma. She does the accounts and she pays me in cash. So I get my unemployment money and I get paid in cash. I tell you Benny, I'm richer than I ever been! I been approved for a new line of credit the other day, seein' as this is another province."

Benny wondered if Bruce and Jerry would agree to her working with him. She wasn't sure she wanted to. It seemed somewhat unprofessional to her but she was trying to be less uptight about things, and maybe that kind of thing was done here in Winnipeg. In a way she hoped they would say yes. The prospect of being employed, even in something so new to her, was exciting.

"I'm goin' to make you a vegetable crockpot for supper," Mickey was saying. "I know spices like the back of my hand and if you let it all sit there for a couple of hours, it's the best thing in the whole world. You'll love it. Let's go by the market and get us a bunch of vegetables."

They got up and strolled inside the market, picking out vegetables. On the way home, Mickey sang and danced as he walked beside her.

"I'll play you guitar later," he promised, "serenade my lady."

She swung the grocery bag while she walked and snuggled under his arm. "Oh," she said, "I think you already did that."

THEM GUYS TOOK MY TRUCK

The next morning, she lay in bed, half asleep, listening to Mickey cursing as he stumbled into his work boots. The night before, he'd finished off the better part of a six pack, the rest of the Southern Comfort, and a couple of joints. He was clearly not in good shape.

"See you later," he growled, "and keep the phone with you." He hacked deep and spat into the sink. Benny wished he'd leave so she could go back to sleep.

He slammed the door and she heard his footsteps marching heavy down the stairs.

She stretched out under the covers, sighing happily and wondering what to do with her day. She thought she'd start off with a long hot shower. She still wore her flip-flops in the shower since that filthy old grout refused to get clean no matter how much bleach she poured on it. She made a note to buy a shower mat from the dollar store.

She dried off her hair, thinking that Mickey did like to party hard but to be fair, it was the weekend, no harm there.

She sat down on the bed to brush her hair and noticed the cell phone signaling a missed call. She picked it up and as she did, it rang.

It was Mickey, irritated. "Where you been, Ben? I told you to keep the phone with you."

"I was in the shower Mickey. Take it easy."

His mood turned airy, delighted. "Hey, guess what? Bruce, the owner, he said you can work here, isn't that somethin'!"

Benny felt nervous. "Should I buy some trousers?" she asked. "Tan ones maybe? All my clothes are black. What kind of shoes must I wear?"

"Babes, don't worry, just wear your oldest stuff. You'll be fine. Just wear stuff that can get dirty, okay? I'll help you tonight. So what you up to, the rest of the day?"

Benny felt irritated. "Don't know. Maybe get another book, go down to the Forks, read."

"Well, I'll let you go. I gotta get back to them guys anyways. Don't let no one chat you up, okay? You're my girl, remember?"

She laughed. "Don't you worry, Mickey."

Outside the day was windy and Benny chose the comfort of a coffee shop instead of going down to the river. She sat in an armchair reading the newspaper, watching passersby holding tightly onto their handbags and coats as pieces of paper whipped by on the sidewalk.

She found a secondhand bookstore on the way back to the apartment and bought a copy of *The Girl With the Dragon Tattoo*. She walked back to the apartment, surprised to find the day had flown. She was sitting outside under the window ledge, protected from the wind, nearly a third of the way into her book when she heard the door open and Mickey come in. She checked at her watch. It was nearly 6:00. She got up, dusted off the seat of her trousers and leaned inside the window.

"Hey," she called out happily to Mickey who was scowling, his face like thunder, sucking on his thumb. Her heart sank. She climbed inside. "What's the matter?" she asked.

He didn't reply, sat down on the bed and rolled a joint. He took a long drag and cracked open a bottle of beer. He looked at her, his eyes eerie and otherworldly. His body slowly relaxed and he exhaled.

"That asshole Jerry. He took my truck away. He said I used up too much personal mileage over the weekend."

Benny didn't know what to say.

"I told him and Bruce I was only gettin' you acquainted with the city but no, the asshole takes away my truck."

His eyes filled with tears. "And they put another guy in charge of my crew. They said I still need to learn some ropes." He was crying openly now.

Benny was embarrassed for him, mortified by his shame. She went over to him and put her arm around him. "It'll be okay," she said. "You'll get your crew back, and you'll get the truck back. You didn't know. They didn't tell you not to use it, it's not fair. They didn't tell you. Come here." She hugged him while he sobbed.

"I thought things was gettin' better," he said, his face streaked with dirt and tears. "Hey, I got you something." He reached into his pocket and pulled out a chunk of hash wrapped in plastic wrap.

"Oooh, it smells nice," Benny said, sniffing it. "This is how Morocco would smell, I think. It makes me think of camels and of exotic places."

Mickey smiled, his mood lifting at her happiness. "You'll like how it makes you feel too," he said. "Here, I'll show you how to roll it. I got you some papers too." He held his lighter to the chunk and crumbled off tiny bits. "I like it straight up but you'll like it better with tobacco." He broke a cigarette into pieces, rolled the hash with the tobacco, and handed the joint to her.

Benny lit up and immediately made a new friend.

"Very, very nice," she said, a lovely warmth filling her body.

He grinned at her and for a moment she felt like every single puzzle piece was fitting together perfectly.

BENNY GETS HER HANDS DIRTY

The next morning, Benny nudged Mickey. "Time to get up," she said. By her calculations, they needed to get up at 5:30 a.m. to be at work before a quarter to seven. Mickey grunted in response and Benny climbed over him.

"Mickey," she said sharply. "Come on, get up. You can't hope to impress Bruce and Jerry and get your crew and your truck back, if you don't get to work on time. Get up, okay?"

He grunted and sat up, his thin hair sticking up in all directions. Benny looked at him critically. "We must get you some hair gel," she said. "Your hair totally defies being controlled."

"Hair gel's for pussies," Mickey said and he hacked into the sink. He growled and studied his bloodshot eyes in the mirror. He splashed his face with water and brushed his teeth with vicious anger, delighted by the blood on the toothbrush.

"Need to get a tooth pulled," he muttered. "Okay, I'm ready. Let's get this show on the road."

Benny was nervous and excited. They waited at the bus stop and she glanced around her, at the other workers off to do their day. It felt good to be part of the working world again. Mickey sat on a low wall, kicking at it with his boot. He was sullen and angry about the loss of his truck. Benny was in a good mood; this was an adventure.

The bus ride took nearly an hour. "Where's the yard?" Benny asked, looking around her when they climbed down from the bus.

"Fifteen minute walk," Mickey said, surly. Benny looked at her watch. "Oh, we'll be late," she said, hurrying Mickey to walk faster. They rounded the corner of the yard on the dot of a quarter to seven. The guys were all waiting in a large group, and when they saw Mickey, they gave a rousing cheer. Apparently, there was a betting pool that Mickey would be late and one guy was coining the winnings, much to the amusement of the rest of them. Mickey did not find any of it funny. He led Benny up to the office and introduced her to Bruce, Jerry, and their ma, Vera, who did the accounts.

"I've never done this kind of stuff before," Benny told Jerry, feeling nervous. Despite all the descriptions and warnings Mickey had given her, she liked Jerry. She sensed in him a fellow worker.

"Nah, don't worry," he told her, "I've put you with George's crew. He'll show you the ropes. You do look a bit fancy dressed though." But he said it kindly.

"I didn't have anything else," Benny apologized.

"I thought she was coming with me," Mickey protested.

Jerry regarded at him calmly. "Well, she's not. Come on, Benny, I'll introduce you to George."

Benny shrugged at the furious Mickey and followed Jerry who introduced her to a weathered old man about sixty and was missing most of his teeth. He flashed her a gummy grin. She smiled back.

"Time to go," he said, and she had some difficulty understanding him. "You ride with me, missy, up in the cab. Come on boys, let's go."

Benny noticed one other female in the yard, a stocky short girl with dark hair. She was smoking a cigarette and eyeing Benny with disdain. To her surprise, Benny saw Frank too. He was whispering something to the girl, and both of them watched her as she climbed into the cab, next to George. Benny was about to wave at Frank but he dropped his gaze and turned away.

George was silent on the way to the job, except to hum a little now and then and suck on his gums. Benny was happy to look out the window. The back of the truck was loaded with tiny flowering plants. They arrived at the jobsite and were joined by the two other guys, teenagers, enjoying the summer with an easy job.

"Time to unload the truck," George announced and Benny rushed at it. George and the boys laughed. She stopped and looked at them.

"Gonna burn herself out real quick," George commented. "Hey, young 'un, take a moment. Look around you, orientate. Take a few breaths of the air now. Have a smoke, if you smoke. Seems I'll have to teach you about how to take it easy."

Benny blushed. "Never been one to take it easy," she said.

"Now's a good a time as any to learn," George said, breaking the filter of his cigarette in a way that reminded her of Dad.

They stood around and one of the boys handed her a Tim's coffee.

"Got a spare on the way," he said, blushing. "Got a double-double, generally works okay for girls."

Benny thanked him and took a chocolate doughnut from the box he was holding.

"Okay then," George announced, fifteen minutes later, "time to unload. Now, missy, take it easy, okay? Watch us fellows for pace."

They unloaded the truck and Benny did think she could have done it four times as fast.

Then they all sat around while one of the boys went to get mid-morning tea.

"Now, we put the plants into their places," George pointed, his mouth full of blueberry muffin. "We follow the design what Bruce did. That, missy, is Step Two."

Benny nodded. She was vigorously slapping on sunscreen, much to the amusement of the others.

"Factor 60," she said, holding it out, glad she had remembered her sun hat.

"You're gonna be real sticky come end of day," George observed. "Anybody next to you on the bus gonna get stuck to you like crazy glue."

This cracked them up and they all howled, Tim and Kyle nearly rolling on the ground.

"Back at it," George said, and he got up and dusted off his pants. "Come on, missy. I'll show you what flowers is what. These boys already been educated by me."

Benny had a wonderful day. On the way home in the truck she found a radio station with hits from the '80s and she sang along loudly.

"See you tomorra?" George asked as they swung into the yard. "We didn't scare you none?"

"George! I had such fun! Yes, see you tomorrow and thank you."

"Remember to go and see Vera and collect your pay. You get paid by the day, eh."

Benny thanked him and headed toward the office. She wondered where Mickey was. She saw Jerry standing with the crew that Mickey'd been out with. She collected her pay from Vera: $70 in cash.

"Wow," Benny thanked her. "I had no idea it paid this well. Excellent, thanks Vera. See you tomorrow."

"George said you did a good job," Vera said. "He phoned into Jerry. He always phones and updates. He said we better pay you good 'cause you use up a lot of sun protection creams and we don't want you to get sunburn or nothing." She cackled and turned back to her balance sheets, all neatly penned in blue ink on ledger paper.

Benny laughed and went out to find Mickey. Jerry saw her looking around.

"He's round back with the other stoners," he said. "They think I don't know but I do. So, Miss Australia, I hear you did good. You coming back tomorrow, George said."

Benny was enthusiastic with her confirmation. She saw Mickey appear from behind the building and she said a quick goodbye to Jerry and rushed over.

Mickey's eyes were red and his gaze unfocused. She grabbed his hand, chattering to him about the day. He wiped his nose with his free hand and gave a large sniff. Then he seemed to rally his thoughts.

"Bus'll take forever," he said. "Can't wait to get home and get clean. I hate being dirty like this all the time. Never can get my finger nails clean."

He grouched his way to the bus stop while Benny carried on telling him about her day. They got on the crowded bus and swayed against each other, Mickey absentmindedly stroking Benny's hair. She fell silent, contented and suddenly tired out from the day.

They got home and Mickey sank down onto the edge of the bed. "I'll just get this doobie in me while you shower," he said and Benny didn't argue. She stood under the hot water, wondering whether she'd feel stiff the next day from all the physical activity. She came out of the washroom to find that Mickey's mood had improved. He was howling with laughter at *King of the Hill*, wiping tears from his eyes.

He turned to look at her and she saw that his neck was thick and red with buried boils. His eyes were a matching blood-red and his thin hair had a bowl-shaped dent from his baseball cap. For a moment, she felt strangely distant from him, removed, and judgmental.

"I wish we had a fridge," she grumbled, rolling herself a joint. "I'm craving an ice cold diet Coke. We never have anything cold here."

Mickey jumped to his feet. "I'm gonna go get you some, babes," he said. "Anything else? Ice cream? Milk? Whatever you need, my baby, I'll get you."

Benny lay down on the bed, lit up and inhaled deeply. "A diet Coke would be great," she said. "Thanks, Mickey. I guess I'm not used to being out in the sun all day, never mind working so hard too."

He laughed. "Yeah, it takes some getting used to. Never you mind, babydoll, I'll be right back. Hey you want me to get you a veggie burger or somethin' from the Bishop downstairs?"

That sounded like heaven. "Oh yes, I'm starving," she said. "Oh Mickey, thank you."

The Fox and Bishop was the pub underneath them, next to the Hakim's. Mickey collected his keys and left. "Be back before you can say who's your daddy," he said and vanished.

MICKEY GETS SOBER

Benny finished her joint and fell asleep. She woke up and the room was quiet. She sat up, feeling like something was wrong but she didn't know what it was. She looked at the lit up alarm clock that she and Mickey had gotten at the pawnshop. It was close to midnight. She wondered where he was. She grabbed her cell phone and called him.

He answered and she could hear he was in a pub.

"Hey, Benny!" he said, and he sounded delighted to hear from her. "I'm down at The Bishop. Come and join me, I've met a group of buddies here. We're having a party."

"No thanks Mickey. I thought you were getting me supper? I'm starving."

"I got waylaid, babydoll, I got waylaid. I'm real sorry, I am. C'mon down and have supper here."

"No way," Benny was icy. "I'll make a plan."

She hung up and wondered what to do. She was ravenous. She pulled on her black trousers and hoodie sweatshirt. She locked the door and navigated down the stairs, wishing the stairwell was better lit and that Mickey had replaced the flashlight that never worked.

No way was she joining a drunken Mickey at The Bishop. She spotted the Tim Horton's on the corner. 24-hour. That'd do just fine. She headed across the street.

"Bowl of vegetable soup, a honey and whole wheat bagel, and a coffee," she said. She collected her food and sat down at a table, watching the street and the nightlife outside, dunking pieces of her bagel into the soup.

She finished her food and sat drinking her coffee, watching the entrance to The Bishop. It was busy, seemed people didn't stop coming in or out, not even at this late hour, on a Tuesday night. She corrected herself, Wednesday morning. As she watched, Mickey spilled out with a drunken group. She watched them all stand in a circle, smoking, and then she watched them drift apart and go their separate ways. She saw Mickey stare up at their apartment and she was chilled by the anger in his face.

She sat stiffly in the uncomfortable plastic chair, watching Mickey staring upwards. Then he walked toward the dark and narrow stairwell. Benny didn't want to go back. But she realized she didn't trust him any more and she shot to her feet and hurried across the street. Her cash was stashed in her backpack, along with her expensive camera.

She rushed inside the apartment and found Mickey standing lost in the middle of the room, gazing around. He turned to her and his face, so furious only moments before, crumpled into tears.

"I thought you'd left me," he cried. "I would of deserved for you to leave me. I'm real sorry Benny, please forgive me. I'll clean up my act, you'll see. I'll go to AA from tomorrow, I promise I will. I don't blame you for being angry with me. I done you wrong." He wiped his nose on his sleeve. "I'm so sorry."

"It's okay," Benny said, wondering how she could have thought he'd be rooting through her stuff. She hated herself for the thoughts she'd had. He was a damaged, hurt boy, her damaged hurt boy.

"Come to bed and sleep," she said, holding out her arms. "You can shower in the morning okay? But listen, Mickey, don't be in a bad mood in the morning, okay? I'm telling you now, any crap from you and I'm outta here." She didn't mean it but she wanted to scare him. "If you really mean what you say, about wanting to be with me and cleaning up your life, then it starts tomorrow. No being late for work, no hanging out with the stoners. Jerry knows all about that. That's why they took away your truck and your crew. You've got to show him and the rest of the world you mean what you say."

Mickey nodded, flooded with remorse. She helped him undress and they climbed into bed.

"Where did you go?" he asked, his voice shaky.

She told him she went to Tim's for soup and coffee but he didn't seem to believe her. "You meet anybody there?" he asked. She swatted his arm.

"Get a grip, Mickey," she said. "I'm not the unfaithful kind, okay. But I am the hard-working kind, so get that into your head."

"I will," he promised her and he held her close. "Come here, babydoll, I don't ever want to let you go."

She stroked his head until he fell asleep then she quietly dug out her sleeping meds and swallowed them dry.

The next morning it was as if he had been waiting for the alarm to go off because he leapt out of bed and rushed into the shower. Benny was dressed and waiting when he got out, and he brushed his teeth and smoothed down his wet hair. He was subdued.

He was silent the entire bus ride, and quiet when they got to the yard. Benny waved goodbye and headed over to George.

"Stiff and sore today?" he asked. She did a few bends to check and groaned.

"You bet," she told him and he laughed.

"Today we lay sod," he told her and Benny looked confused. "Grass," he said, "green grass, girlie. You gonna hurt tomorrow." He chuckled and they climbed up into the truck.

Benny caught sight of Mickey's pale thoughtful face as she left. He was sitting in the cab of Jerry's truck, staring into space. She noticed George was watching her, but he was silent.

Laying sod was hard work. Benny was glad George was pacing her.

"I'm going to need a series of massages after this," she told George who found that very funny. "All my money's going on spa therapy, I'm telling you now!"

"Better that than the bottle like your boy does," George said, immediately clamping his toothless gums shut, sorry he had said anything.

"Ah now, George," Benny said, "Mickey's trying. He wants to be sober; it's not easy. His family's to blame. His dad's an alcoholic, his brother died driving drunk, so he's had it hard." She felt as though she was making excuses for Mickey and George was unconvinced.

"Everybody's had it hard in life," he said. "One way or the other. And take me, I likes to drink as good as the rest of them but I gets myself to work on time. I holds down a job. Been with Bruce and Jerry since their dad was the foreman."

"What happened to him?" Benny was curious.

"Heart attack. 57. Young he was. Lucky he had trained Bruce and Jerry. Bruce is the creative one you know. He makes the designs and such. Jerry is the business one, and Vera, their ma, she's one tough lady. I'll tell you a secret." He laughed. "Well, it's not a real secret 'cuz everybody knows, but I got a thing for Vera. I asked her out a few times but no, she tells me she's still married, waiting to meet him on the other side. I always liked her, even when Big Jerry was still alive. And he knew it too. I told Vera that time and again. Vera, I says, Big Jerry, he knew, and he wants me to be taking care of you while you have time left on this earth – he wants you to be happy. But she's a stubborn old mule that Vera."

Benny laughed. "Don't give up," she said. "That's my motto. Don't ever give up on anything, and that includes people."

George gave her a shrewd look. "Some things, some people, is worth giving up on," he said, turning back to his work.

MICKEY SINKS INTO GLOOM

Mid-afternoon, George called in a progress report and Jerry told them to come back in. They pulled into the yard the same time as Mickey, who was still pale, subdued, and distracted.

He climbed down from the cab, waved a hand goodbye to his crew, and looked over at Benny, unsure what to do, his back to the stoners behind the shed. She ran over to him.

"Let me get my money from Vera and we'll go home," she said.

On the bus on the way home, she tried to get him to tell her about his day but he was quiet. Benny fell silent and by the time they got home, all she wanted was a hot shower and a night with *The Girl with the Dragon Tattoo*. They stopped at a Swiss Chalet and got a big bag of takeout.

"We need a fridge," Benny told Mickey and he nodded. "We're wasting so much money, shopping like this. We'd save money with a fridge." He nodded again. He had picked up two litres of diet Coke from Macs and poured himself a beer-glass full. They ate in silence as soon as they got home, watching the weather channel on the tiny TV, and sitting on the bed. Benny showered and read her book in bed while Mickey played his guitar, picking mournfully at sad melodies.

"You're doing really well," Benny offered support, but Mickey didn't say anything, just tightened a string on his guitar and listened to the tuning, one ear cocked.

Benny shrugged and went back to her book. She wished she could have a joint but knew it was out of the question. Whatever it took, she'd help Mickey sober up.

Benny acknowledged that, with regard to matters of sobriety, not only was she taking more pills than ever, she'd also added cigarettes, hash and lots of alcohol to the mix. She rationalized that she deserved to let loose a little after all the hard work she'd done over the years. Mickey, on the other hand, was clearly substance-addicted in a real way that was screwing up his life and she had to help him.

Later, in bed, Mickey turned his back to her and lay motionless. Benny quietly swallowed her sleeping meds and stroked his shoulder, trying to comfort him and before she knew it, she fell asleep.

The next morning, when the alarm went off, Mickey leapt out of bed. It was Thursday. He was focused on getting sober with grim determination. He leaned on the sink, hacking deeply and scowling, and he moved slowly, in pain. He wouldn't look at Benny but concentrated on slicking his wayward thin hair with water, brushing his teeth and doing up the laces of his work boots. He stared into space over Benny's shoulder on the way to work.

Benny was relieved when they arrived at work so she could be with George.

"You feel the sod?" George asked her and she laughed.

"Aching all over. But in a good way." She looked across the yard at Mickey who was standing apart from the rest of the men. He was smoking morosely and frowning deeply.

George followed Benny's gaze.

"I'm really proud of him," she said. "He's working hard at getting sober but he's having a hard time of it."

George shrugged. "Men like Mickey always have a hard time of it," he said. "One way or another. I shouldn't say this missy, it's none of my business eh, but you're too good for him. And watch your money because when he falls off the wagon, which he's aiming to do big time, he'll sell you and his mother to get what he needs."

"Ah, George," Benny admonished him but she did worry about her hidden cash.

Much to Benny's relief, they were back to planting flowers and George didn't have to tell her to take it slow; her body wouldn't have moved fast if she'd tried.

"Don't know why I never gardened before," she said to George over lunch. They were sitting under a large tree, eating sandwiches that George had made. "I love it. The earth smells so good."

"Well, them things," George pointed at the flower bed. "Them's like putting flowers in a vase for rich folk who wants a pretty garden for the summer. Don't last. What I likes is the perennials. You make a garden that lives by the seasons, what grows and every year digs deeper into the earth. I like trees the best. A tree makes for a friend."

"Wherever I end up, I'm going to garden," Benny said.

"So where're you headed, missy? What's your story anyways? And how'd you end up with your boy?"

"Just lucky, I guess," Benny laughed but George looked at her grimly.

"I don't know for sure, George," she said, serious. "This whole trip is kind of weird in a way because it's like nothing I've ever done before. I worked so hard all my life, you know – school, jobs, trying to make something of myself, get all nice and shiny and famous and then things didn't quite work out like I planned."

"They never do," George observed. "Didn't mean to interrupt. Here's another cheese one, you want to split it down the middle?"

"Love to. Anyway, I don't really know what this trip is but that's okay, I'm just going with it. My plan was to get to the end of the map, get to Vancouver, and then think about what to do next. But now I met Mickey and he's like no one I've been with, he makes me so happy. Once he gets sober and gets all the toxins out of his system, things will get back to what they were and we'll have fun again."

"Yeah, well, time to get back at it, missy, and my piece of advice to you is to be careful. I've met too many men like Mickey in my time, and I ain't aiming to upset you but he's trouble."

"He's never had anyone to love him before – " Benny objected, but George had gone to wash his hands.

Later that evening, when she and Mickey got home and he was in the shower, she transferred her money from her backpack to her camera bag and she headed for the door.

"Going to the Internet café," she called out to Mickey who was toweling himself off and didn't seem to notice her or care. She hailed a cab, went to the bus station, secured a locker, and she stashed her camera bag, only carrying her earnings for the day.

She found she was dragging her feet, unwilling to return to the tiny apartment. She sighed. A sober Mickey was turning out to be much less fun than she had anticipated.

DOLLAR STORE DIAMONDS

But in all fairness, Benny figured, Mickey was detoxing and that couldn't be easy. And considering how much he imbibed, he had to be going through an intense withdrawal. She pushed the door of the apartment open and found him staring blankly at the TV, watching Martha Stewart.

"You want to grab something to eat?" she asked and Mickey shrugged. Benny sighed. "I'm going to get takeout from Tim's," she said. "You want to come, or you want me to get you something?"

He got to his feet silently and stood beside the front door, waiting, his head hanging low, his gaze on the floor.

"Oh, for God's sake, Mickey," she said. "You're being a total loser."

His eyes filled with tears. "I can't do this," he said and he started crying.

Her heart melted. "Oh Mickey, baby, you can." She hugged him. "You've just got to get through this and it'll all be better. It will, I promise. I know how hard it is, I really do. But you don't want an addict's life, Mickey, living from hand to mouth, always in debt, never knowing if you've got a job or if there's money coming in. Look what a great job you did with this apartment, look how talented you are."

He shook his head, his face covered in tears. "I can't," he said, and he wiped his nose on his sleeve. "Tomorrow's Friday night and all's I want is to go and get drunk and smoke some pot. What's so bad in that? I'm entitled to have some fun. I can't do this."

"Yes, you can," she said. "C'mon, let's go and get some food. You need to get some food. Come on."

She led him down the stairs and to the Tim Horton's. Mickey stared longingly out the window at his old haunt, The Bishop, across the street, listlessly spooning soup.

"It'll get better," Benny said but her words sounded hollow. "Tomorrow night, let's you and me go and see a movie. We need to do more fun stuff at night in general. You need something to look forward to at the end of the day, not just coming home, getting clean, having supper, going to bed. That's why you feel miserable. We need to get out more." She was struck by sudden inspiration. "You should use this experience of getting sober, to write some poems, what do you think? We'll stop at the dollar store on the way home and buy you a notebook."

At that, Mickey's spirit's seemed to lift a little and he gave her a small smile. They finished eating and went to the dollar store.

"I got no money," he said, subdued again.

"Don't worry, I'll cover this. I love dollar stores. I'm going to get a notebook too and some new pens."

She was paging through the notebooks when Mickey popped up at her side, grinning, holding a stuffed toy monkey. At the sight of his smile, the tension drained from Benny's body; she hadn't realized how tightly she'd been holding it all together.

"I want to buy this for you," Mickey said, "I'll pay you back. Monkey-man wants to thank Benny the princess for saving him, for loving him, for believing in him when no one else did."

He bounced the monkey on her shoulder and nuzzled it into her neck. "I found this stuff too, babes," he said, showing her his finds: two trays, some colourful napkins and an empty sparkling mosaic picture frame with a glittering heart at the top. "We'll get a photo of you and me all blown up," he said and Benny smiled at him.

"Did you get a notebook?" she asked and he dug into his basket.

"Yes ma'am, I did. And some pens and crayons and markers too. Look," he said, sounding shy, "I found this too. I know I don't got the money to buy it for you but if you get it now, I'll pay you back, soon as I get paid." He held out a necklace in a clear plastic packet, with white cardboard backing. It was a large silver heart studded with sparkling stones, with a silver chain. Benny thought it was beautiful.

"Oh, Mickey, thank you." He smiled at her and looked wistful.

"Only wish it could have been the real thing for you, my baby."

Benny paid for the lot, and they headed back to the apartment. Mickey put the necklace on her carefully and Benny sat reading in bed, hugging her monkey, while Mickey, next to her, chewed on a pen and scratched words into his notebook.

"That was a fun night," he said later, turning to her, twisting the pen in his beautiful, long fingers. "You're right, it doesn't have to be gettin' high is the best thing." He pushed his notebook and pen aside and lay down on his elbow next to her. "Come here, my baby, let me show you how much I love you. You do know I love you, don't you? You do know you mean everythin' to me. I'll go to my grave in love with you, Benny."

Benny put her book down. "Ah now, Mickey, and you mean everything to me. All that matters is you and me and our world."

The next morning he was still in good spirits. Benny spent the day planting with George and was relieved to see Mickey smiling when his team pulled into the yard.

"Come on, babes," he said, putting his arm around her. "What say we get a bunch of scary movies and spend the night in bed? We can get some Ho Lee Chow take-out?"

She grinned at him. "I can't think of anything nicer," she said.

The next morning was Saturday and Benny took them to McDonald's for breakfast and Mickey scribbled in his notebook, staring into space, dashing words across the page, crossing them out, and scratching them back in. "You know," she said to Mickey, pouring syrup over her pancakes, "it's funny. Most of my life, I wouldn't be seen dead in a McDonald's. Now its like a daily event."

Mickey's expression told her he couldn't see anything remotely amusing about it, shrugged and went back to his scribbling.

Benny decided to ignore him and enjoy her breakfast. She thought, for a brief second, what Kenny's reaction would be to her questionable nutritional lifestyle but realized she didn't care.

That night she took them to a movie and they held hands in the dark and Mickey kissed her, and they made out like a couple of teenagers.

"I got no idea what that movie was about," Mickey said, grinning as they left the theatre. "But I sure did have a good time. And you, my baby?"

She linked her arm through his. "The best ever."

On Sunday they went for a long walk along the edge of the river and discussed their hopes for the future.

"I tell you Benny, we could get ourselves a piece of land back home for next to nothing and I could build us a house, lay some timber; we could live rent free."

They walked past an old Cadillac for sale for a thousand dollars.

"Cheap for a car," Benny said, peering in the window. "Needs some work. I just love old cars."

"Buy it," Mickey was expansive. "I'll fix it up for you. I'm great with cars, babes, I can make anything run. Buy it! I can see us in it, cruising along, having fun in the back seat."

"Where would we park it? And I don't even have a Canadian driver's licence…"

Mickey shrugged. "You could get one. It's easy. Anyways, you could transfer over your Australian one."

"Where would we park this thing? And what about insurance?"

Mickey shrugged again, disappointed, perplexed by her lack of enthusiasm.

"Anyway, it's not like I've got a thousand dollars lying around to drop on an old car," she laughed, trying to restore his former good cheer but he was sinking into gloom.

"I'd buy it if I could but I got all those debts to pay, so's I can go back home." He was angry about the money he owed, as if he had inherited someone else's debt.

"What do you want for supper?" Benny tried to cheer him up. "Hey, how about we go and get a curry at that place down the street from us?"

"Hate curry. Listen my baby, can I borrow twenty dollars off of you? I need to get some smokes. I'm outta of cash. I'll pay you back as soon as I get paid. That asshole Jerry, man, he holds my money like it's his."

Benny gave him a twenty, wondering what she could suggest they do, to salvage the weekend. Then she sighed.

"You're like a kid, Mickey," she said. "I can't think of anything for us to do tonight. Let's get some Swiss Chalet. It's the easiest."

"I could do you a crockpot," Mickey straightened up and smiled.

"Bad idea, last time you made such a mess and I had to clean it up. Took me forever to get the carrot peels out the basin. And washing that big pot in that small basin doesn't work either. Let's just get takeout. I want to have a nice shower and read my book in bed. I'm worn out,

Mickey. I'm not used to all this physical labour and we did a lot of stuff this weekend. I just want a peaceful night, okay?"

He smacked himself on the forehead. "I'm sorry my baby, I shoulda thought. Listen, why don't we get that takeout from the Indian place like you said? You wanted that? I can try some, maybe I do like it. We'll get a whole bunch of stuff okay, and try it all? We can eat off of our new trays, get some candles, have a romantic dinner with our new napkins."

He danced around her, grinning with manic glee. "Come on, sweetheart, I know, I know – I'm a lot of work, but I love you and you'll see, I'll make you happier than you've ever been."

Benny looked at him, his high cheekbones, rockstar eyes, and she nodded, sure, Indian takeout, why not?

At the Indian place, Mickey was convinced the young guy behind the counter was flirting with Benny, and he kept glaring at him.

"Don't tell me you didn't see it," he hissed at Benny outside.

"I really didn't. And Mickey, he was a teenager for God's sake. Here, take a bag. We got enough food to last a week." She held out a bag, thinking that while his irrational possessiveness could be irritating at times, it was also endearing. He cared, in ways no one else had before.

Mickey threw an angry glance over his shoulder and took a bag.

Turned out he loved Indian food and ate most of it. Benny picked at her plate.

"It's good stuff," she said. "I'm just so tired."

"I'll play the guitar for you my baby, help you go to sleep. Here, I'll clean up too. You have a shower and get into bed, okay?" He rushed around, whistling, throwing things into a big garbage bag. Benny, exhausted, fell asleep to the sound of him playing the guitar while he watched an old episode of *C.S.I.*

A POETIC HIGH IS NOT ENOUGH

Monday morning saw Mickey's good cheer still in place. He whistled in the shower, seemed even jaunty.

"We had a great weekend," Benny reported to George. "How was yours?"

"I got Vera to have supper with me on Saturday night," he said and Benny gave him a high five.

"Way to go, George," she said. "I'm telling you, happy-ever-afters, here we come!"

"I'll get us coffees," George said and he grinned. "Yeehaw, missy, weren't for you, I mighta given up."

That night though, Mickey's mood sank and Benny couldn't think of a single thing to cheer him up.

"Them guys was all getting high behind the shed," he said on the way home on the bus and he stared off into space, withdrawn. He ignored Benny and scribbled into his torn, bent notebook, the spiral spine twisted out of shape. She was almost sorry she had suggested he write; she had lost him to that now, instead of to beer and drugs. She surreptitiously chewed a couple of codeine and half a sleeping pill while he was in the washroom.

The next morning he was cold, quiet and sullen, and no better that night.

Benny read and took more drugs to sleep, adding a full sleeping pill to the mix. She woke to find Mickey staring at her accusingly; he was propped up on one elbow, watching her sleep.

"How come you sleep so well?" he asked, his tone icy. "Must be nice, eh." He got up stiffly and ignored her on the way to work.

By Thursday morning, Benny was at the end of her rope. Mickey wouldn't talk to her; his anger was a wall. Benny sat in the truck waiting for George and as soon as they left the yard, she broke down, crying wretchedly.

George patted her shoulder. "Ya kiddo, he's a bad one. I seen it coming. I told Jerry I wouldn't work with him, first day he came. He's bad news girly, you deserve so much better than that."

Benny cried harder and George pulled over at a Tim's. "Gonna get you an extra large coffee and a box of Timbits. Be right back."

His kindness made Benny cry even harder. But by the time he got back, she'd calmed down.

"He's worse when he is sober," she told George.

"That's 'cuz he ain't really sober. An' he's punishing you for making him stop drinking. Being this unhappy, he's proving to himself that he was right all along – that being sober is hell, that it's no way to live. That drunk is better. Next thing he'll tell you he chooses to drink, that he needs to drink. Come on missy, we got ourselves a nice job today."

Benny drank her coffee in large swallows, the burn soothing. At lunch George handed Benny the sandwich he'd made her.

"Tell you what I think," he said, after they'd eaten. "You should get back on that bus, missy, the one going west. There's good life out there and it's waiting for you. Get on the bus, he's a no good son-of-a-gun. He'll only bring you hurt and trouble. But enough of that, it's not my business but I like you and I had to say it. Let's go and plant us some more of them flowers. This was a bigger job than Jerry thought. I hope we finish up in time."

They carried on planting and George called in an update to Jerry. Benny, listening, realized they had a way to go. George cupped his hand over the phone. "You okay to work a bit later?" he asked, "Jerry says he'll give you time and a half."

"Sure, no worries," Benny said. "Will you ask Jerry to tell Mickey I'll meet him at home?"

George relayed the message into the phone, listened and nodded. "Okay, yeah," he said, snapping the phone shut. "Away we go."

Benny grinned at him. "We're the A-team my friend. Bring it on."

George laughed. "You got that right."

By the time they finished, it was nearly 7:00 p.m. The light was still strong, the flowerbeds beautiful, and Benny and George were bone-tired.

They clambered into the truck and went back to the yard that was deserted apart from Jerry, Bruce, and Vera. Benny and George sat down and waited for Vera to make up her envelope.

"You care for a wee drink for the road?" Bruce held up a bottle of Macallan's scotch.

Benny's eyes lit up. "You got the good stuff, I see," she said, and then her face fell. "Uh, no, I guess I'd better get home to Mickey."

The others exchanged a look. "Ah, here's the thing, Benny," Jerry said, pouring a small shot and handing it to her. "Mickey didn't come back to work after lunch. He came back to Ma here instead, said he needed all his paycheck, that he was feeling sick. Then he went home. But if you ask me, he's set for a bender."

Benny took a sip of her whiskey.

"We know you tried to help him," Bruce said. "We did too. He could be a great guy, he really could but there's nothing for it, and you can't help somebody who doesn't want to be helped."

Benny's eyes filled with tears. She knew he was right. Mickey was out there somewhere, getting drunk, and there was nothing she could do. She raised her glass. "Well, here's to you guys," she said. "I guess the odds are I'll be getting back on the bus and moving on. If he's drinking again, I don't have much choice, do I?"

"Be the best thing you could do, missy," George said. "But I tell you this, eh, you're one helluva worker."

Bruce and Jerry agreed and Benny grinned.

Vera started packing up and the others got to their feet. "We'll give you a ride to the bus stop," Jerry said. They dropped her off and George got out and gave her a hug. "See you tomorra," he said, "but if I don't eh, I'd be happier, you know what I mean?"

"Yes, George," she said and her throat closed with tears. "Thank you."

She watched them drive off and she waited for the bus in the darkening blue of the late evening sky.

It took forever for her to get home. She had no idea if they were right, that Mickey wouldn't be there, that he was out drinking. Or if he was there, that he'd be manic drunk, firing up joints and chasing them down with one beer after another, trying to get as punishingly drunk as fast as he could.

She climbed the narrow stairs cautiously and tried the door, which was locked. She took out her key, unlocked the door and pushed it open. She looked inside, and stopped breathing for a moment, her hand flying to her throat.

The room was completely empty. Absolutely empty.

THE SIXTEEN-DAY SPECIAL

The room had been stripped, except for her backpack in one corner and her few clothes in the closet. The bed was gone, all Mickey's possessions were gone – the tiny TV, his guitar, every box and bag he owned. She had no idea how he'd managed to pack it up so fast but she could imagine him, fuelled by savage anger and hatred, throwing things together, dismantling their life.

She stood, leaning against the wall, feeling as if she'd been cruelly violated and punched in the gut. She slid down until she was sitting, with her hands around her knees. It was still hard to breathe. The neon Molson sign flickered on and off. She saw that he'd left the empty picture frame, the one with the sparkling heart. It lay in the opposite corner, abandoned. Apart from that, and her backpack, he had taken every single thing.

He was punishing her for trying to make him change. "But you said you wanted to change," she said to the empty room. "You said it, not me."

The words echoed. She realized how dirty the room was – how dingy. She couldn't seem to bring herself to move but sat, in the darkness, smoking one cigarette after another.

"Well, it was fun while it lasted I guess," she said out loud but her heart was bleeding and torn. At last, out of smokes, she realized she had to leave. She couldn't stay there. The room was ugly and bereft. She picked up her backpack and looked at the empty picture frame in the corner, blue and red light reflecting off the sparkling stones.

"I loved you," she said out loud to the dirty empty room. "Even when I knew deep down that I shouldn't. I knew I shouldn't have, but I loved you anyway."

She put her backpack down, not willing to leave. "I've been on this trip forty-two days. I've traveled over six thousand miles. I met you twenty-three days ago and we lived together for sixteen. Sixteen days.

That's not a lot in the bigger scheme of things. It shouldn't hurt this badly."

She took a cab to the nearest Holiday Inn. She checked in and let herself into her room. It was freezing and she turned off the air con. She sat down on the edge of the bed and wondered what to do with herself. Wondered where Mickey was. She sat there for a while, not thinking, not doing anything. It was too late to order any food, so she took a bottle of wine from the mini bar and cracked it open. She unpacked her backpack and spread everything out on the floor. It was time to regroup and take stock of the damage.

She felt something hard wrapped inside one of her T-shirts; it was the cell phone. She hadn't even thought about what might have happened to it but there it was. She stared at it. No missed calls. But Mickey must have put it there because when last she'd seen it, it was next to the bed.

Her spirits lifted – he had a way to contact her. And then just as suddenly, she was filled with anger and irritation. All this was nothing more than a dramatic play on his part to force her hand, to force her to let him do whatever he wanted – get drunk, get high, lose jobs, live a filthy chaotic life. She sat staring at the phone, taking large swallows of the wine. She wanted to be like Mickey, get ragingly drunk and forget all her pain.

She ran a bath, using the small free shampoo as bubble bath. She got undressed and examined herself in the mirror. She was covered in dirt and scratches, with a few bruises here and there. All hard-earned from her gardening labours. She thought about George and was glad she'd met him. She studied her expression in the mirror. Her face looked old, hard and cold. She held the sparkling cheap necklace that had made her so happy. Even now she couldn't bear to take it off.

So happy to spend my money. I bought this heart, I did.
But he found it and he loves me. It's not his fault he's got no money.
Oh yes it is … He's a loser, a con man…

She grabbed a couple of mini bottles from the bar and climbed into the scalding bath, adding more hot water. The bubbles quickly lost their fizz but the bath felt wonderful, and she lay back, drinking and trying not to think. A part of her missed Mickey but most of her was just furious with him.

She was exhausted from the long day of planting but her mind was buzzing. She knew that his leaving was for the best but she missed him. She missed his manic high energy and his broken beauty.

She lay in the bath drinking until her body was wrinkled. She felt tipsy and horribly awake.

"You knew this was going to happen," she said, getting out of the bath. "So why does it hurt so much? You knew, you even took your stuff to the bus station. And thank God for that." She started singing.

"All by myself... Don't wanna be all by myself anymore ... great. Here's to all of us looking for the happy-ever-after, all of us failing miserably."

She realized she was beginning to feel nauseous but still not the least bit sleepy. She staggered over to her backpack, crunched down two codeine, crawled to the bed, climbed under the crisp sheets and pulled the pillows close.

"All by myself," she mumbled quietly and fell asleep with the lights still on.

She woke up at 3:00 a.m., rushed to the washroom and was violently sick. Sitting on the cold tiled floor and hugging the toilet, she felt wretched, shivering and icy. She ran another hot bath and tried to get warm, needing to get out quickly to throw up again. Her stomach felt like she'd been drinking battery acid. She raided the mini bar for all the carb snacks she could lay her hands on and wolfed them down, hoping to settle the horrible sickness. Then she went back to bed and woke up 10:00 a.m. It was Friday and she had a hangover.

LOVE HURTS

It was also time to get moving. She got dressed, opened her map and inked in the red path to and from Churchill. She phoned the Greyhound terminal to see what time the next westbound bus left town. She put her dirty clothes into a plastic bag, thinking she'd make do until her next stop.

She double-checked she hadn't left anything in the room but it was neat and tidy. She checked at her watch. Four hours before the bus left. She dug out the phone and stared at it, wondering what she'd do if he called, knowing she'd forgive all and rush back into his arms.

Her eyes filled with tears. She tried to remember Mickey when he was ugly – the boils on his neck, his hair thin and squashed by his baseball cap, his eyes red and unfocussed – but all she could see was his crooked grin, that electrical sparkle, his animal energy.

She left her backpack with the concierge and went for a walk, taking the phone with her, just in case. She headed down to the river, stopping to listen to some steel drums at an outdoor concert in a small park along the way. She sat down under a tree, wishing she wasn't hungover and wishing the bus left earlier. She was listlessly picking at a patch of grass when a shadow fell across her. She looked up, hoping it was Mickey; he'd found her, he was sorry, everything was going to be fine but of course it wasn't him and despite her delight at who it was, her heart sank for a second. It was Adam, the young guy from the hostel, the one who had been so badly beaten up while she was in Churchill. Benny suddenly remembered with a sick flash of guilt that she'd never followed up on him; she'd fallen down the rabbit hole with Mickey, to the exclusion of all else.

"Hiya! Adam. How are you, mate? I heard you got beaten up and were in a coma. I meant to come and see you in hospital, then things got really crazy. I'm so glad you're okay. When did you get out of hospital? You want to sit down? You don't look so good."

Adam lowered himself carefully; it was clearly painful for him to move. His face was still bruised and covered in stitches and there was a large shaved area on his head.

He talked with difficulty. "Re … remember the … uh … ah, sore…"

"Take your time," Benny said, "we're in no hurry here."

"The guy," he managed to say, "that guy you were with…" His tongue struggled to form the words, "that night, you remember?"

"Yeah, Mickey," Benny said, "tall guy with kind of weird blue eyes?"

Adam nodded. "Him. He hit me. Was waiting outside a couple days after you left. Said I must leave you 'lone when you got back. I said there's nothing between us but he didn't believe me."

His eyes filled with tears. "I told him. I begged, leave me 'lone, I tole him I don' even know you really. But he hit me an' hit me."

Benny was aghast. "Mickey did this to you? Mickey put you into a coma? Oh my God." Her hand flew to her mouth, her eyes wide. "I had no idea Adam, no idea. Oh my God. I'm so sorry. Well, I don't know where he is now. You want to press charges? Do you want me to go to the police with you?"

Adam shook his head slowly. "No. No point. Jus' wanted to tell you."

"I'm so sorry," Benny said, again, "I'm so sorry." It made sense, given what she knew about Mickey now. "He left me anyway. I don't know where he's gone." She had a thought. "But you know what, he did phone me. He left a message on my cell, the police could trace him…"

Adam shook his head and winced. "Don't want to," he said thickly. "Me, I'm going to get better, s'all that counts. Bye now. Good luck." He got to his feet slowly, his face a grimace of pain, one hand pressed to his ribs. Benny watched him go.

She wondered if she should contact the police, give them the phone, have them track Mickey down, but she didn't think any good would come of it, not if Adam wasn't willing to press charges. She was horrified and suddenly terrified that Mickey knew where she was but she figured he was still out partying. Nevertheless she decided to go to the bus station early. She tried to remember if she had ever told him of her planned route but she didn't think she had. She'd be surrounded by people in the bus station – she'd be safe. She dusted the grass and dirt off her trousers and went back to the Holiday Inn, keeping an eye out for Mickey. She grabbed her bag and got into one of the cabs lined up outside.

"The bus station," she said, her voice shaking.

"And which bus would be taking you where?" The driver was chatty, but Benny had no interest in idle conversation.

"Nowhere of any interest to you, mate," she said sharply, biting her lip. The driver looked at her in the rearview mirror.

"Just being polite, sunshine," he said, his tone calling her a bitch. But Benny didn't hear him. She was still trying to process everything that had happened in the past sixteen days. Only sixteen days.

She was relieved to get to the bus station and made straight for the counter.

"I've got a season ticket," she said, "and I want to go to Moose Jaw."

She grabbed her camera bag out the storage locker and sat outside chain smoking, picking at her nail polish, chewing gum and tapping her foot nervously. When the bus pulled up, she was the first to board. She secured a window seat near the back and exhaled a huge sigh of relief. She closed her eyes, happy to be on the bus, heading away from him. And to think she'd thought his possessiveness was endearing. She'd been so blind.

She plugged in her iPod, and as soon as the bus pulled out, she turned up the volume. She flicked the playlist to an old *Kill Bill* soundtrack and tapped her fingers in time to the beat while the bus drove past muffler stores, print shops – the detritus of dwindling city limits.

Yeah, that had been some experience. And despite everything she now knew about him, she missed him terribly, and her heart felt utterly broken.

TOO TIRED FOR REINCARNATION

The bus left Winnipeg and headed for Moose Jaw. It was going to take eleven hours and thirty-five minutes to do four hundred and four miles. Benny thought the length of time was disproportionate to the mileage but figured it would make sense once she got going. She was slumped in her seat, craving motion, peace and quiet. She pulled her sparkling heart necklace out from under her shirt and held it in her hand, her eyes closed.

It didn't take long for her to realize that this wasn't the bus of peace and quiet. This was the bus of B-grade movies with the volume pumped up super-high.

"The volume's broken," the coach conductor announced, having to shout to make himself heard above the DVD. "It's this, the loudest, or nothing."

Benny would happily and instantly have voted for "nothing," but not so with the rest of the full-to-capacity bus, who shrieked with laughter at every Hugh Grant utterance; ironically the movie was *Mickey Blue Eyes*.

Benny was in a less-than-ecstatic mood and, to add to the woes of all the bad movie-watching she was being forced to do, the bus was a less spacious and older model than the ones coming out from the east. The worn grey velveteen seats were small and closely packed. Benny could smell the menthol chewing gum of the woman behind her.

She leaned against the window and stared at the passing scenery, not really seeing any of it. She was trying to understand why she missed Mickey so much when she knew what a loser he'd turned out to be. She reminded herself that not only was he a loser, he was dangerous – look what he'd done to Adam. But, she argued with herself, he'd had a tough upbringing, he'd lost his brother early in his life, his parents sounded useless. He was an addict – he had a disease – she should have been more supportive, she should have helped him. She missed their room, she missed being with him, missed his dimpled, chipped-tooth grin when he did something cute. He knew what he had, and he worked it. Benny would have given anything to be back in his arms.

But he'd left her, hadn't he? He'd left the room empty, a heartless move intended to cut her deep. He'd left wanting to hurt her – he'd placed their sparkling picture frame in the corner; a conscious gesture – look, you mean nothing to me. To open the room and find it empty, well, it was the last thing Benny had expected. The very last thing in the world.

You'd think I'd be used to these kind of shocks by now. You'd think I'd be used to it by now.

She began to cry, not caring if the menthol-chewing woman behind heard her, and thinking the terribly loud movie would drown out any audio of her sorrow anyway.

She buried her face in her hoodie and cried without reserve until her eyes were swollen like golf balls and she had no more tears left. She blew her nose loudly, and wiped her face. Her eyes stung from the heat of her tears and she couldn't breathe through her nose. Her head throbbed with unbearable agony; she'd worsened her hangover — no mean feat.

She blew her nose again and dug into her cross-Canada guidebook, looking for a motel in Moose Jaw. Given they'd only arrive after midnight, it would be wise to book a room at the next stop.

She turned up the volume on her iPod, chewed a codeine and fell into a nightmarish doze in which Mickey was standing at the bus terminal, waiting for her.

"Hey, sweetheart, I missed you." He held out her arms and smiled a shy smile. Benny woke in a sweat, her heart pounding hard. The chatter on the bus was loud, *Mickey Blue Eyes* had vanished, *Shrek* was now filling the TV screens.

A few hours later Benny's mood barometer dropped even further. It seemed they were back, yet again, for a stop in Portage La Prairie. This was now her third visit to the picturesque little town. Groundhog Ville La Prairie. THREE visits? Her level of misery was off the Richter scale of measurements. Was there no other route? Apparently not. This accounted for the mileage to time discrepancy; they were inexplicably traveling in circles.

She changed the playlist to a New Age steel band with flute accents, hoping it would ease her jangled nerves but it screeched hard in her ears, and she admitted defeat and turned her iPod off.

Her face still felt puffy, tender. She looked around. There was an assorted lot on the bus: a trendy, pierced-mod-rock-Goth young couple who were fast asleep, a big, buxom, blonde German woman who was the strapping outdoor enthusiast-type, some lilac-haired biddies, and an ultra-seedy, middle-aged dude in bad plaid with slicked-back, greasy hair; he smelled of stale smoke even from where Benny sat.

They made yet another stop in Brandon, Manitoba, at Charlie's Diner. The retro décor diner was filled with warm afternoon sunshine, and the jukebox was playing. Benny leaned against the wall outside and lit a cigarette. She watched the setting sun light up a green and gold magical prairie sunset and she hugged her arms to her chest, wishing she didn't feel so sick and miserable.

Later, back on the bus, a red moon hung low in the sky. It was so large it could have been the sun. Benny's heart felt lacerated by jagged glass but she did feel the smallest sense of creeping peace.

A beautiful boy boarded the bus at Brandon, his bare feet black with grime and dust, his trouser-ends ragged, a tattered black hoodie pulled close to his delicate face. Benny caught herself hoping it was Mickey but that was impossible and stupid besides. She reminded herself once again about Adam and how Mickey had broken him, and she called to mind Adam's battered and bloody face and she told herself she was lucky to have escaped Mickey. But she still loved him just the same.

Onwards they journeyed. Benny watched a mother and daughter scramble onboard – Mennonites maybe; they sat prim and neat with their matching long pink-blonde braids and their gold framed specs. Later they huddled together under a nubbly old pink blanket and rested their heads on shabby satin pillows. When they woke, they pulled out delicate knitting, their needles long and remarkably thin.

The bus was also populated by a cheerful band of good-looking backpacker boys who scurried on and off for the smoke breaks. They lit up, and kicked a football back and forth, balancing it on the sides of their feet, almost dancing.

Back on the bus, Benny watched the prim and proper mother knit gray-mauve wool, her needles creating tiny stitches, her fingers rhythmic and gymnastic. Benny closed her eyes. *I really hope reincarnation's a myth. I'm too bloody tired to do this life more than once.*

She brushed her teeth at the bus station in Virden, and combed her hair, but she was feeling a bit fuzzy all round. Having a smoke outside, she saw that an indoor rodeo was scheduled for later that night and she wondered if she should get off the bus, find a motel and check out the rodeo but she decided to stick it out to Moose Jaw instead.

Turned out the buxom German woman was a friendly South African. Too friendly for Benny's comfort. She longed to be in her motel room, alone.

REMORSE AND MENTAL REHAB

It was 5:00 p.m. Well, 4:00 p.m. Saskatchewan time. The bus stopped in Whitewood for a leg stretch and snacks. The strong, tanned, bouncy South African woman bought a box of chocolate chip cookies and offered them around. Benny took a couple, envying the woman her happiness. Benny was achy, gritty, grumpy, and furious because everybody had voted for the video again except for her. This time it was *Meet the Parents* and the volume was still at maximum.

She dug into her bag and took out a small bottle of Southern Comfort to wash down the cookies. She figured at the rate she was drinking, it'd be better to buy a bottle and a hip flask. Not only would it be cheaper, but she could drink more. Her stash of meds was still holding out well although she figured she'd stock up with more codeine soon.

The only good thing in Benny's life was the scenery – acres of emerald green dotted with huge golden hay bales, railway lines, barns and farms.

The bus driver changed. The new gal was a spunky, chunky, blonde chick who thought life was a NASCAR racetrack. The bus took the corners with two wheels aloft and the countryside flying by.

In addition to being a speed freak, the bus driver was also a chain smoker, which meant a lot of rest stops. Good news for Benny, who jumped off with the other nicotine cravers and lit up with enthusiasm.

They pulled over in Indian Head, stopping next to a traditional heritage grain silo. Heavy purple clouds hung low; a storm had vented its wrath and was now in retreat. Honey gold fields stretched for miles, all freshly rain-washed. The gravel and sand roads glittered underfoot and there was a silver sparkle in the air, glancing off the stones with a brilliance that was startling. The sun burst through the clouds to fan perfect biblical rays.

Watching the backpacker boys grind their cigarettes into the dirt, Benny recalled how Mickey could flick a butt spinning, using his forefinger and his thumb. It was like he knew every bad boy trick in the book.

Back on the bus and racing once more down the highway, Benny heard her phone ring. She grabbed it out of her pocket and looked at it, her hands shaking. Yes, it was Mickey, it was his phone number on caller ID.

"Answer the frickin' phone," one of the boys yelled from the back of the bus. "Trying to watch a movie here, eh."

Benny shot up in her seat. "You shut up," she screamed. "I never wanted the movies, I've sat through hours of them. So you SHUT UP. And if I don't want to answer my phone, I don't have to, okay?"

In one fluid movement, all the boys at the back of the bus stood. Seems Benny wasn't the only traveler with illegal alcohol onboard.

In an equally fluid movement, the big blonde South African woman also stood up. "Sit down boys, now. You catch my drift?" She eyed them back into a seated position. "That's better. Now, you leave my girl here alone, you hear me? Trust me, you *skelms* do not want to take me on."

"What's a skellum?" asked the unwashed man who smelled of smoke.

"A retrobate," the woman said shortly. "And don't think this an op-portunity to chat me up, boytjie. You're not my type."

"I think you mean a reprobate," the man said. "And don't flatter yourself lady, you're not the all-that you think you are."

The Mennonite mother and daughter sank down into their knee rug.

The bus driver, sensing a problem, pulled over and turned off the engine. She stood up. "Prairie madness got you all already? C'mon, everybody off, get some air, take it easy, have a laugh. We've got a ways to go yet. And I'll tell you this, anybody who tries to get back on the bus with attitude will be left behind and I've got the power to do that, so don't tempt me. Everybody off now. C'mon, take a walk."

Benny missed most of the goings on. After she shouted, she stared at the phone, the bus argument a dim chorus in the back of her mind.

She couldn't answer the phone. She just couldn't. She wanted to hear what he had to say first, if indeed he had anything to say. She couldn't see a way for him to put this right. He'd left her with nothing. He had promised to love her to the grave and then he packed up and left because he wanted to get drunk instead.

She watched the light flash on the phone while the message was being recorded and she felt herself being herded off the bus by the big blonde woman who had given her cookies.

"C'mon *liefie*, come and get some air." She was kind and Benny stepped down, clutching the phone, not wanting to access her voicemail too soon in case she interrupted the process and lost the message.

The blonde woman lit a smoke and passed it over to Benny who inhaled deeply. She dialed the voice mail number.

"You have one unheard message. To listen to this message, dial one now." Benny dialed one with infinite care.

And there it was, Mickey's deep easy voice filling her ears. She closed her eyes, manna from heaven. He was sorrowful, remorseful.

"Hey, sweetheart, how're you doing? Listen, I was wrong to do the things I done. I'm a jealous loser that deserves a whore for a wife. I've treated all my girls as if they had to prove their love and I'm wrong for that and more besides. I trust you're okay? I'm not so much. I left, you figured that right? I lost all my stuff, I don't even know where, went on a bender, lost it all. So now I'm going to mental rehab. I need it. My rollercoaster has run off the tracks. I know you don't want to hear this, Benny and I don't even know where you are but I love you. I love you Benny. I'm sorry for what I done. Anyways, wherever you are, take care. I'll try to call you again, okay?"

Benny saved the message carefully and cradled the phone. She was overwhelmed with relief. He wasn't lost to her. She felt exhausted but in a peaceful, contented way. He was getting help. He was sorry. He loved her. She knew she'd have her world back before too long; she'd have her home again, with him. This life of a homeless traveler was for the birds; all she wanted was her little room with Mickey, with the flickering neon light and the big bed where nothing else mattered.

They got back on the bus, everyone calm again. Benny leaned her head against the window and fell fast asleep.

She woke later as they pulled into Regina, memorable for having a funeral home as its opening visual act. Benny saw that the Ramada Inn was saluting epilepsy.

She called her motel in Moose Jaw and booked two nights. Her hangover was history but she was exhausted. When they arrived in Moose Jaw, she fell from the bus into a cab, so exhausted she was nearly hallucinating by the time she got to the motel.

MONKEY MAN MAKES IT TO MOOSE JAW

The motel room was a shoebox done up in pink and blue décor, with cigarette burns on the striped worn plaid carpet, and burnt-orange lampshades. Faux wood wall panels added a rustic element to the ensemble. But the interior design was rendered insignificant by the clean, soft sheets and the double bed that was as welcoming as a long-awaited hug from a friend.

Benny lay in bed and wondered what to do about calling Mickey. She was beyond exhaustion, beyond sleep. She felt unpleasantly wired, on edge. She decided not to think about things, but rather go back to Stieg Larsen's world, *The Girl with the Dragon Tattoo*. She couldn't remember where she'd put the book and she emptied out her entire backpack, still not finding it.

Must be here somewhere. I'm sure I had it when I left.

She found a zippered compartment she'd forgotten about and she ripped it open; it had to be there. It wasn't, but something else was. The stuffed toy, Monkey Man, the one Mickey had "bought" for her at the dollar store, bought with her money. He was shoved down deep. She pulled him out and saw that he had a piece of paper around his middle, with an elastic band holding it in place.

Benny sat down on the floor. She was afraid to open the paper. She leaned back against the bed, holding Monkey Man. When she couldn't wait any longer, she snapped off the rubber band and unfolded the piece of paper. It was a poem. A long one, more like bits and pieces gathered in a hurry.

Tell the lazy loser
gotta go down

gotta go down fast!
if he don't
I'll never get out of here

Sweetheart,
you might be sorry
you might get what you wish for
wished you hadn't met a sinner
like me
a dreamer, like me
You are my love
because I found you
call to me
call out my name
maybe I'm a loser
burdened, feel so old
but I've always dreamed
of someone to hold

The coldest of breeze
is an icy bite
I am the icy love
you should
watch your step

Oh lonely bottle
help! I'm down again
help me find my place
take this sadness and replace
replace this empty hole
take my soul
set me free.

Benny didn't know what to think. She left the piece of paper on the floor and climbed into bed, holding Monkey Man. She lay curled up on her side, perfectly still, with hot tears running down her face and her pillow was soon soggy and uncomfortable. But she didn't move, she just lay there and cried herself to sleep.

MARCIA, QUEEN OF MASSAGE THERAPY

In the morning Benny woke, feeling full of flu. Her eyes were swollen shut, and she had a cold sore on her lip from all the angst.

Because she didn't know what else to do with her pain, she walked Moose Jaw from top to bottom, walking until she could no longer. Shaking with tiredness, she sat down on a bench outside a tourist shop filled with souvenirs. She lit a cigarette and wondered what to do with the rest of the day. She didn't even have a book to read. She figured Mickey had taken it, heaven knows why. To leave space for Monkey Man, she supposed. Just then she heard a familiar friendly voice behind her – the South African woman, her arms full of Moose Jaw souvenirs.

"Hello *liefie*, good to see you, man! Ag, listen, don't you look sad. Tell you what hey, come let me buy you a cup of tea and you can tell auntie all about it. What do you think?"

Before she could stop herself, Benny was crying again. The woman sat down next to her and hugged Benny tight.

"It's a man, right? Bloody men. Can't live with them, can't live without them. Actually, I can live very happily without them, I'm Marcia and I'm gay, so at least I don't have to worry about men screwing up my life. Although, let me tell you, *liefie*, being with a woman isn't that easy either. Women are as crazy as men, just in different ways. Why do you think I'm on the bus? My wife was driving me nuts back home. So I said to her, listen, Amanda, I need a break, I've got to get away from you, no offense intended. I need to get out of this place before you drive me bonkers. I need to think about you and me, and a whole lot of stuff."

"How long have you been married?" Benny blew her nose into a large Kleenex that Marcia offered her.

"Only a year. But we've been together for ten. Who knows, maybe the marriage aspect was a bad idea because it's all gone south since then. And I haven't got a clue why. You'd think the opposite would happen but all of a sardine, Amanda is convinced I'm going to cheat on her and why would I do a crazy thing like that? I love her, for God's sake. But she checks up on me like a crazy person. She even had me followed by a private detective, can you believe that?"

"Why did you come to Canada, of all places?" Marcia's cheerful stream of consciousness was lifting Benny's spirits, and she dried her face on another Kleenex.

"We got married in Toronto. Amanda's got some cousins there, so we thought hey, why not. We had our honeymoon in Niagara, and it was the best time of my life. Anyway, so I thought I'd come back and do some traveling across Canada. There sure is a lot of land here, this place is huge. And I'm a freelance accountant so I can do this, my clients understood, they were like *ja*, great, we wish we could come with you."

"How long have you been traveling?"

"Nearly a month. From here I go to Vancouver, then I'm taking a little cruise down to Seattle and then I fly home from there. Back to Johannesburg. And let me tell you, one peep of nonsense out of Amanda and I'm gone. She says she'll be on good behaviour from now on – apparently she got some therapy while I was gone, which is a good thing I tell you. She needed her head read, or shrunk or whatever it is they do."

Benny laughed.

Marcia adjusted her shopping bags. "Listen *liefie*, I know what you need. Tell me this, when do you leave Moose Jaw?"

"Tomorrow on the morning bus."

"Excellent. Okay, so come with me, don't argue, just come."

She pulled Benny to her feet. "This way." She led her down the street and around a corner and rang the doorbell under an elegant sign: The Namaste Spa Clinic.

Benny opened her mouth to object, but Marcia put a finger to her lips. "Be quiet my friend. Trust me, Marciatjie knows what you need."

She introduced Benny to the spa manager, rattling off a series of treatments she wanted for Benny.

"Toodle-oo *liefie*. Now lie back and enjoy, okay?" She waggled her fingers at Benny who was led away and instructed to get undressed and wrap herself in a fresh waffle robe handed to her by the woman.

Next thing, Benny was lying in a darkened room with candles flickering, aromatherapy oils burning and soft music playing. The bed was soft and supportive and she nearly fell asleep.

"Can I offer you a heat wrap?" a quiet voice asked and Benny jumped in fright.

"Didn't mean to startle you. Do you want a heat pad on your legs? It'll help relax you."

Benny thought a heat wrap sounded wonderful. "Yeah, for sure, heat would be fantastic."

The woman covered her with hot, scented cloths and Benny thought she might cry again, from the sheer kindness of the moment.

"Are you allergic to anything? Oils or face masks or anything?"

"Nah, it's all good." Benny felt dreamy, half asleep.

The woman smoothed on a face mask on that smelled like fresh oranges and she gave Benny a scalp massage that felt so good Benny's brain tingled.

The luxurious spa therapy went on for hours. Benny's body was massaged, then exfoliated then massaged again. Not one but two face masks were applied. The day ended with a mani pedi and Benny, her feet immersed in swirling water, blessed Marcia with every good intention she could think of.

When it was finally time for her to leave, she waited at the manager's desk, hoping to see Marcia.

"Your friend left long ago," the manager said, "but she left you this envelope." She handed Benny a thick creamy envelope embossed with the spa logo. "She also, uh, paid for everything, tip included, so you don't have to worry about anything."

Benny thanked her and allowed the woman to guide her to the front door. "Before I go, could I get a brochure?" Benny asked. "With a full list of the treatments I got here today?" Something about the manager was making Benny feel very gauche.

The woman smiled. "My dear, we don't have anything like that. You either know about us, or you don't. But I'll tell you this, the package you got today was $500."

"Are you serious? For a spa day?" Benny was incredulous. "Well, I have to admit, I do feel amazing."

The woman laughed. "She's a good friend, that's for sure."

Benny ripped open the envelope outside the elegant ivy-covered door.

Hey liefie, hope you had fun! Listen, try not to let the bastards drag you down, okay? Easier said than done I know! Be strong, I know you are! Whoever he is, he's not good enough for you. Trust me. Stay in touch! Come and visit!

Benny smiled. "Thank you, Marcia, guardian angel." She tucked the note, with Marcia's email address, into her camera bag.

She looked at her watch – it was close to 6:00 p.m. She was feeling a bit weird but attributed it to post-massage fogginess; to be expected after all that aromatherapy she was sure. She ducked into a bookstore she had seen earlier and replaced her copy of the book Mickey had taken, stopped to get a pizza with double mozzarella and artichokes, and headed back to the motel. She showered and washed the oils out of her hair and climbed into bed with her book, her supper, and Monkey Man.

"Well, I'm glad to have you with me anyway," she said to him, "regardless of how you got here or why."

Still feeling out of sorts, she read until she fell into a deep dreamless sleep and woke in the nick of time to gather her belongings and get back on the bus.

THE ENERGIZER BUNNY STUMBLES AND FALLS

Onwards to Calgary. The bus left at 8:00 a.m., the trip was nine hours and twenty-five minutes and this time the ratio made sense to Benny. Passing through the village of Chaplin, she dabbed cold sore medicine on her lip, paged through her guidebook, and wondered where to go after Calgary. Monkey Man sat on her lap. Benny thought she should feel limber, given the ministrations of the previous day. Her body should have felt revived and energized but she felt drained – all the life sucked out of her.

She figured she might stay in Calgary for a night or two, then head out to Banff/Jasper/Lake Louise during the day to take maximum advantage of the view from her bus window. She had thought of staying over in Jasper for a night, but the cheapest accommodation she could find was $299 a night, which was exorbitant.

Benny looked around. The bus was full. Benny had an empty seat next to her but was in danger of losing it; a lilac-haired biddy boarded and Benny could tell she was a bossy one. No relaxed old grandma, this. She was standing there at the front of the bus in a candy-striped skirt and old-fashioned cat's eye specs, looking stern.

"Who's going to share?" The bus driver demanded, hitching up his ill-fitting grey uniform.

Glum faces stared back at him. Boys slid down behind baseball caps. Benny dived into her carry-on as if it held the meaning of life. A woman near the back raised her hand.

"There's an empty seat here, next to me."

Benny missed Marcia and the racecar bus driver. The energy on this coach wasn't the same.

They drove past a giant cobalt-blue swimming pool in the middle of a grassy airfield – children splashing with fat sun-browned mothers standing by. Then into strip-mining fields of what looked like dusty chalky limestone.

This bus driver was obviously not a smoker; not much stopping allowed. Pity, Benny was parched. A diet Coke would be great about now. Benny eavesdropped on the couple behind her, who were talking about the underground tunnels back in Moose Jaw. Illegal Chinese immigrants were brought out to take care of the dirty laundry of the men building the railroad. The Brit, whose brilliant idea this was, would have been fined a whopping $100 back in the day, had he been caught. To avoid any potential fines, he'd decided to bury the evidence, condemning the

Chinese to live underground and sleep in four-foot long by three-feet high bunk beds with nothing more than two shared buckets for toilets, emptied twice a week. No escape.

Benny shuddered. And there she'd been, thinking Moose Jaw was spa haven. And it was, but it certainly had a shady past.

The couple behind Benny moved on to chatting about Al Capone, who came to Moose Jaw to mix his brew during prohibition, building himself a new hideout.

Benny lost interest in their discussion and continued planning her journey. At the next leg stretch she phoned the Calgary hostel to book a bed, only to be told she couldn't book one in advance, but that it should be okay. Should? Benny hated depending on the currency of "should."

They pulled into Medicine Hat and had an hour to explore, but Benny was feeling too lethargic to move. She was the energizer bunny felled by a tranquilizer dart intended for an elephant. She flopped down in her window seat and stared blankly at a church spire.

Why am I so tired? Maybe I'm detoxing from all that massaging and aromatherapy. I've heard that happens.

She looked out the window to see a powder blue Cadillac drive past with "Just Married" on the rear windshield, cans and streamers dragging behind. Benny wondered what day it was. She had lost track of time. Then she sat up straight in her seat, rudely dislodging Monkey Man and her guidebook onto the floor. She stared ahead – a terrible thought had occurred to her.

"Here you go, dear," the stern biddy in the candy-striped dress with cat's eye glasses picked Benny's belongings up off the floor.

Benny thanked her vaguely.

Am I pregnant? She was horrorstruck and immediately convinced that it was true. She clutched her stomach and felt as though she'd go crazy unless she knew one way or the other. She felt sick as a dog on about a thousand levels and it wasn't detoxing from too much massage.

She tried to clear her mind and do the math but she couldn't even remember when she'd had her last period. She tried to remember if it was up in Churchill. She'd kept such careful track of the times and miles, how could she have let this get away from her?

If I can just think. C'mon, think, think, think.

She was so anxious that she chewed down two Valiums, apologizing to the baby if there was one.

I'm panicking big time. I need to calm down. It's fine, it's fine, it's fine.

She fell into a drugged sleep.

WHERE'S THE BEEF, MAN?

When she woke, they were in Alberta. She sat up, dying of thirst, disoriented. Was she pregnant? She wasn't going to think about it, that's all there was to it. She looked around. Much the same crew on the bus. She'd sell her soul for a drink of water.

At that moment, like an answer to a prayer, the bus pulled into a Greyhound terminal and Benny leapt off, bought two diet Cokes, a bottle of water and a large bar of chocolate.

She downed the water in one gulp, crammed the chocolate into her mouth and bought a couple of Kit Kats for the bus ride coming up. Then she lit a smoke and wished she had done more justice to Medicine Hat just because it had such a cool name.

Back on the bus, Benny rearranged her belongings and watched the green pastures of Saskatchewan vanish, along with the lovely yellow daisies. Alberta seemed more arid and brown. The asphalt fell away behind them and Benny felt as though she had landed on the moon; it was that pale and dusty, very flat and very brown. Wasn't there supposed to be famous beef out here? Where was all the famous beef?

She did see a lot of horse trailers and Stetsons, which made her think about Dad and she felt guilty. She hadn't emailed in the longest of times; she'd have to take care of that in Calgary.

Along the way the bus loaded up with more passengers and Benny wondered how everyone could fit. She also wondered if they were all headed for her hostel, the one where she wasn't able to book a bed. Would she lose the bed she did not yet have?

"Would you please stop bumping my seat like that?" she asked the boy behind who shrugged an apology he clearly didn't mean.

Benny looked out at the endless brownness and knew in her achingly weary bones that this was going to be a long stretch and not the easiest one at that. There was no escaping the fact that she felt more than a little green around the gills. Everything felt weird and her head and knees ached painfully while nausea continued to swim through her blood.

This couldn't be pregnancy, although the thought continued to haunt her – this had to be the flu.

While Benny loved a narcotic, she had no use for speed or drugs that made her hyper. She was born hyper, thank you very much.

Benny, unbeknownst to her family, and even Kenny, had been quietly imbibing feel-good chemicals for years. She was a teenager when a school friend introduced her to Valium appropriated from the friend's mother's stash. And after that, Benny had found drugs relatively easy to come by, given the rarefied environment of highly-strung girls with even more highly-strung mothers. In addition to which, she'd learned early that doctors will give you anything you want – it was simply a matter of manipulating the conversation, faking the symptoms and the right expressions. And, following the Disaster of Epic proportions, that is, Kenny's relocation to the other team, Benny never had to worry again. And as for acquiring codeine, although it wasn't that easy, it was never problematically inaccessible.

So, Benny had no use for flu meds. They made her feel jumpy, restless and anxious, her nerves all shot to hell. And there she was, experienced drugstore cowgirl, right in the heart of Stetson land without so much as an appropriate pill to ease her pain. Talk about the ironies of life.

She tried to cool her forehead against the window and stared at the world outside. She'd never seen land like this. There was not a shrub, rock, barn, discarded car, tractor, sheep, house or postbox. Nothing, nada, zero. Brown flatness. And more flat brown flatness. No daisies, no ponds, no hay bales. Wow. She inspected further and concluded that there was a kind of greyness to some of the brown. The sky was pale, the sun icy and shrouded, but piercing, nonetheless. Benny looked into the sun and immediately saw black spots dancing in front of her eyes.

Several hours later, she admitted that the barrenness had a certain empty appeal. Flat brown met more flat brown. Empty land touched empty sky. They were on the Trans Canada Highway heading west, which was super cool bananas in BennyLand. She wondered if her scrambled mental ramblings were due to flu, fever, Prairie Madness or possible impending pregnancy.

Shortly after sunset they stopped somewhere nameless and faceless. Half the population of Canada clambered onboard, all of them immediately putting their seats into maximum recline. And the bus was still the smaller gray velveteen version; the bigger, airier ones were ancient history. Oh, for the luxury-liners of the east. Outside the bus, the scenery was getting slightly less flat. Inside the bus there were changes also. The seats were full, with people having to stand at the back. A girl in front of Benny lost her seat by visiting the washroom despite having left her possessions as a marker. This bus took no prisoners. Benny resolved not to move a muscle or drink any more liquids.

I feel so sick. And it's a long, long way to Tipperary. Oops-a-daisy, I mean Calgary. Maybe this is what they mean by the stampede?

She bundled her hoodie into a pillow, clutched Monkey Man to her chest, and tried to doze.

THIS AIN'T THE RITZ CARLTON

When Benny finally rocked into Calgary with a busload of Satan's Frat Boys, it was the middle of the night. The bus had become increasingly rowdier as even more delinquents fought to board. It was a moving undergrad party with loud tales exchanged of who got drunker when and how. Benny was forced to listen to stories of parole officers and proud disturbances of the peace.

"You mean like now," she muttered. The Frats tumbled over each other to get outside to smoke and then they fought their way back in. Benny, aching all over, felt like she was a hundred years old, and she didn't even have the energy to get off the bus to smoke.

They made it to Calgary amid hoots, yells, and applause. Benny found a cab, got to the hostel and joined the long line of bed-hunters all coming in to roost from all directions.

The man at the front desk was a clear fan of the Marquis de Sade, relishing his small moment of power.

"Have you made a reservation?" he asked each person, in response to which came the same dispirited broken reply, "No, because we were told reservations weren't allowed."

Benny wanted to hit the man. She took in his pale narrow face, his old-fashioned wire rimmed glasses, and his combed-over greasy hair, and she knew this was a man she could not afford to antagonize. She knew that he was just waiting for an excuse to pick a fight and deny a bed and she didn't want to be the person at the receiving end of his grudge against life. She answered his questions, showed him her passport and filled out enough paperwork for the Ritz Carlton. And finally, oh finally, she had a room, with a bed.

YO' BED IS READY, MIZ DAISY

Armed with bed sheets, Benny climbed the narrow flight of stairs to her room, every step an Everest. She punched in the keycard but the door failed to open. She stared at the door thinking she would have to go back downstairs to change the key, but she was immobile. Unable to summon the energy to move, she pondered why it was that keys and doors hated her so much – it had to be some karmic mistake she'd made in another life – clearly she'd been a door-offender of note.

She dropped her backpack to the floor and leaned her forehead on the door, willing it to open. Which it did, suddenly, and Benny crashed into the arms of an extraordinarily beautiful black girl who caught her before they both sank to the ground, Benny lying on top.

"Whoa there, darlin'," the girl said and she laughed. She had a deep, throaty laugh. "Way to make an entrance."

"I'm SO sorry," Benny said, and she rolled off the girl, but felt too weak to get to her feet. "I think I've got the flu. I hope I didn't infect you. I just got into town. Which is bed number four?"

"You are a wreck," the girl said, cheerfully. "Were you having problems with the door, by the way? Fucker sticks like crazy. I keep telling Anton-the-peanut head to fix it but you think he does anything about it? Nah, not a thing. I tell him, Anton, I could pull a new door out my ass before you'll fix this one."

"Bed number four?" Benny asked weakly and the girl pointed.

"Bottom one there, across from mine." The girl's bed was like some kind of Sultan's tent, hung with sequined shawls and layers of pillows.

"Nice bed," Benny said. "You here for a while?" She was still lying on the floor.

The girl shrugged. "Long story. I'll tell you about it sometime. First things first. I'm Chrystal Ashworth, and you are?"

"Benny, good to meet you." Benny noticed the girl was wearing thin black gloves to her elbows. She wanted to ask about them but she felt too sick. She crawled out into the hallway, grabbed her bag and crawled back in. Then she hoisted her camera bag onto the bed and climbed on.

"Uh, yeah, well you're making strides, girlfriend, but you forgot to actually make the bed," Chrystal said.

Benny groaned. "Don't care."

"Whoa nellie, you really aren't well. Haul yo' ass outta there, you can't sleep on that mattress, I'll do it for you."

Benny rolled back down on the floor, clutching Monkey Man. "The floor is nice and cool. Why's it so hot in here? Or is it just me? And what's that smell?" The room was thick with the odour of newly applied wood varnish and over-spiced raw meat. It was difficult to breathe.

"That's the debugging stuff they applied to the walls yesterday. Don't ask me what bugs because I ain't going there. I didn't ask Anton and he didn't say. And girl, this is the hottest hostel this side of the sun. I swear we could fry eggs on our foreheads at night. I was on my way to tell Anton I need a fan in here when you made your fabulous entrance. Good one by the way. Okay, haul your ass back up here, yo' bed is ready, Miz Daisy."

Benny laughed. "Chrystal, you're too funny."

"Yeah, so I been told, so I been told. So, how long you been feeling sick?"

"Uh, let's see, um, three days, I think. Thereabouts … three days – "

"Aches, cough, fever, what? Details girl, details."

"Aches, hot all over, sore throat, headache, no energy, feel very weak."

"Did you take anything for it?"

"No, I just thought I had a bad massage – "

Chrystal let loose a loud honking laugh. "A bad massage? Girl, I don't even want to know. Your private life is your private life."

"Oh God, I'm going to be sick," Benny shot to her feet, hand pressed to her mouth. "Washroom?"

Chrystal jumped up and led Benny down the hall.

Benny rushed toward the toilet, slammed the door closed but it swung open. Benny, retching violently, tried to close it with her foot, but gave up.

Chrystal vanished for a moment, reappeared and handed Benny a wet face cloth. Benny was hugging the toilet bowl, groaning.

"There's nothing left to throw up," Benny said miserably. "Why doesn't my stomach know that?"

Her stomach heaved again and she groaned.

"Wipe your face, girl, it'll make you feel better."

Benny did as instructed. "Oh yeah, that's nice."

They sat there for a while, Chrystal refreshing the cloth, hunkering down and patting Benny's back.

"I think I can take a chance of going back to the room," Benny said.

They walked slowly back to the room and Benny lay down.

"Thanks again for making the bed," she said.

"No problem. Okay, girl, let mama help you out. Hmmm." Chrystal dug into the depths of her Arabic tent and emerged with a satchel. "Are you allergic to any over-the-counter drugs?"

Benny laughed. "No. I'm down with them." Her throat was raw. "But I'm afraid to take anything, in case it comes back up again."

"Yeah, you got a point there. Well, I'll leave some Gravol next to your bed, good for nausea, also helps you sleep. For aches, pains and general flu-related symptoms, here're a couple of NeoCitran nighttime. Dear God, I sound like an infomercial. And here's a bottle of water, and some Fisherman's Friends for your throat and failing that, some Cepacol. How many nights did you book yourself in for? 'Cuz you gonna need some rest, girl. My sister's a nurse and I figure you got a virus, but they take ten days to get outta your system, so I suggest you take it easy, okay?"

"Four nights," Benny said, hoarsely.

"Good. Alrighty, now you close your eyes, get some rest. I'm going to go and nag Anton just for the hell of it. And I'll try to get us a fan. You try to get some sleep."

Benny didn't need to be told twice. Despite the stink and the heat, she fell into a dreamless sleep.

WHAT'S WITH THE GLOVES?

When Benny woke, it was 2:00 p.m., the following day. She groaned and raised herself up on one elbow to see Chrystal watching her from the opposite bed, over the top of a big laptop.

"Welcome back," Chrystal said and she pushed her laptop to the side. "I thought you was dead, girlfriend. Never seen nobody sleep like that. You feel any better?"

"I think so. Hard to say."

"I got you some orange juice," Chrystal pointed, and Benny nearly fell out of bed in her eagerness to grab it. She chugged the entire bottle before pausing for breath.

"I guess that was a hit," Chrystal said. "I gotta go out soon anyway, an interview. I'll get you more juice on the way back. An' I'll try to get you some toast or something."

"Chrystal, you are the best thing that ever happened to me in my whole life."

"Nice, calling me a thing! A pleasure, girlfriend. Shit happens in life, gotta look out for each other. 'Kay, gotta get into my little power suit, get all executive."

She pulled on a tight pinstripe skirt and a crisp linen blouse.

"How do you keep it all so well laundered?" Benny asked.

"Dry cleaners, girlfriend. A modern wonder of the world, they can do amazing things. You should give them a try."

Benny laughed. "My stomach hurts, don't make me laugh. So, what's the interview?"

"Long story," Chrystal said vaguely, "I'll tell you sometime. But for now, I gotta dash." She grabbed her suit jacket and her laptop bag. She was still wearing the gloves, and Benny wanted to ask her about them but Chrystal was out the door too fast.

"See you later girlfriend, wish me luck!"

"You don't need luck," Benny called out, "because you rock, Chrystal. You go get 'em."

She heard Chrystal laughing as her high heels clicked down the hall.

Benny thought about reading but she fell asleep instead, and the next time she woke it was midnight. Chrystal was fast asleep in her Arabian nights fantasy bed, snoring slightly. Benny leaned out of her bed, hoping Chrystal had replenished the orange juice and she had. There was also a paper sandwich bag with four pieces of buttered toast, long cold. Benny chewed on her midnight feast, thinking she'd never tasted anything so delicious in her life. She drank the orange juice, pacing herself better than she had on the first bottle. She needed the washroom, and she was dying to have a shower, but she didn't want to wake Chrystal by unpacking all her stuff.

She eased herself off the bed, thinking she'd need to wedge the door to remain open since it was unlikely her keycard would suddenly work. She was glad the room was so brightly lit by the streetlights, it made it easier to navigate. She tiptoed to the door, wedged it open with the pillow, and was relieved to see it still in place when she got back from the washroom. She made her way noiselessly to her bed and sat on the edge, eating another piece of toast.

She admired Chrystal's fantastic bed adornments; everything matched, even Chrystal's aqua eye mask was decorated with silver beads and sequins – an imitation of a masked ball design. Something told her Teenie and Chrystal might get on well.

Suddenly Benny started, what the…? She leaned forward, closer.

Chrystal's hands, one tucked under her cheek and the other holding the bed sheet, were a strange pinky white, as if she had dipped her hands in a powerful bleach to just above her wrists.

Benny's breath caught. So that was the story with the gloves.

Feeling ashamed of herself for some reason, Benny lay back on her bed and stared at the bunk bed above her. She had seen people on the subway with skin markings like that, but she'd had no idea what they were. She wondered if Chrystal had been born with the condition and if she'd worn gloves her whole life. She was glad she hadn't said anything about the gloves.

She felt wide awake. The aches seemed to have left her and despite feeling weak, she felt better. She rolled onto her side, holding Monkey Man, and wondered if she could get her showering gear out of her bag without waking up Chrystal. She also wanted to check her phone, to see if Mickey had called.

She unzipped her camera bag quietly and dug out her phone. Yes, there it was, one missed call. Mickey's number. She stepped out into the hallway and dialed up her voicemail.

"Benny?" he sounded drunk. "Where are you? Oh shit – dropped – burnt my – ah shit – listen Benny, I, where are you?" Followed by the sounds of the phone being dropped, some scrambling, incoherent muttering and hang-up.

Benny saved the message carefully. Just in case she was tempted to call him. It was a great reminder of Mickey when he was drunk.

She crawled over to her bag and quietly extracted her toiletries bag and towel. Wedging the door again, she eased her way out and indulged in a long, hot shower, shampooing twice and letting the hot water run over her face and down her back.

She combed through her hair, looking in the mirror, thinking she was a bit pale but not too bad, all things considered. Her heart necklace sparkled and she held it tight for a moment.

Oh Mickey, you stupid loser.

Digging through her toiletry bag, she found the chunk of tightly wrapped hash, She sniffed it, wondering if she could risk rolling a joint in the hostel garden, thinking not. That pleasure would have to wait.

She got into her pajamas and went back to the room, collected her wallet, her book, Monkey Man, and the key card. Then she closed the door quietly, tested the key card and tiptoed downstairs.

"This doesn't work," she said to Anton who was reading *Hustler*. He jumped, shoved the magazine under a desk calendar and looked at her.

"You're only telling me now?" he said.

Benny shrugged. "Chrystal helped me out until now. Can I have a new one?"

He handed over a keycard and smiled, a ferrety sharp smile. "You need anyone to show you the sights of Calgary?"

"Rather have root canal, thanks mate," she nearly said but didn't. "Ta, mate, I'll bear that in mind."

She wandered into the common room and stretched out on the scratchy sofa. She read for a while then raided the vending machine for a Mars Bar and a diet Coke. She read until 3:00 a.m., went back to bed, yawning, quietly pushing the door open and climbing into her bed. And woke to hear Chrystal swearing quietly.

THE GLOVES ARE OFF

"Fuck, fuck, fuck, fuck, fuck."

"What's wrong?" Benny eased up on one elbow and checked the time. It was 11:00 a.m. Her sleeping patterns were completely out of whack.

"I didn't get the job that I really, really, really wanted. Fuck, fuck, fuck. Sorry girl, did I wake you? How're you feeling?"

"I'm fine, much better. I can't thank you enough for taking care of me. What was the job?"

"Events Organizer at a place I really wanted. Oh fuck. Oh SHIT."

This last proclamation came when Chrystal realized she wasn't wearing her gloves. She stared at her hands in horror, then over at Benny. Chrystal's hands shot up to cover her face and she burst into tears.

Benny decided the best strategy was upfront honesty. "Hey, Chrystal, mate, if it's your hands you're worried about me seeing, don't, okay?"

"Oh fuck," Chrystal said, from behind her hands. She sounded utterly defeated.

Benny went over to her and sat down. She took one of Chrystal's hands in hers. Chrystal jumped and tried to pull away.

"No you don't, mate. We're friends right?" She stroked Chrystal's hand. "You have beautiful hands, Chrystal."

"Don't fucking lie to me girl, I look like a fucking freak. You want hands like this?"

"What is it?" Benny held her tight.

"Called vitiligo. People of 'colour' get it. Michael Jackson apparently had it, but he had it evenly all over his body, go figure. I only got it like two years ago, came outta nowhere. Now I think, fuck, what if I get it on my face, what then?" Chrystal was crying hard.

Benny put her arms around her. "Oh mate, I can't even imagine."

She held Chrystal until she cried herself out.

"I'm done, girl. Thanks. I needed that. Too much shit built up inside me. Ah, fuck."

"Hey, I know what we should do," Benny said, looking at her watch. "It's lunchtime, what say we go out for lunch, my treat. Somewhere fantastic, with white linen napkins, silver cutlery, a wine list of note. What do you say?"

"Yeah, right, with me swollen like the Goodyear blimp on a crying jag."

"I will not take no for an answer," Benny insisted.

"Girlfriend, I've got hands like a freak, I just lost the job I wanted and you want me to go out in public? I'm gonna stay right here and carry on crying, thank you very much."

"You can't carry on crying," Benny said, "because there's no way you, or anyone, could have tears left. You've got to give your weeping ducts time to replenish and it may as well be while you're at lunch with me."

Chrystal gave a shaky laugh. "Yeah, well alrighty then. But I got nothing to celebrate."

"Wrong, wrong, wrong. Haven't you heard of 'acting as if'? We both need to act as if life is fantastic and it will be. Trust me, I need a break too."

"You're telling me your life isn't fantastic? Why?"

"I'll tell you over lunch," Benny said, "Up you get, we need to get dressed. Where are we going by the way? You pick, I'm new in town. The only room I know, apart from this one, is the washroom."

"And we sure as hell ain't going there. How about the Calgary Tower? I heard the restaurant is great, I was going to treat myself to a meal there once I landed myself this job I just lost."

"Sounds perfect. Okay then, the Tower it is. Let's get ready."

GETTING INTO THE CLOSET

"So, listen," Benny said. They were up at the revolving top of the Calgary tower, watching the Rockies turn in the distance. White linen tablecloths, silver cutlery, a delicious Sauvignon Blanc – it was very civilized.

"My husband, well, my ex actually … he used to lock me in the closets – "

"Sick fuck," Chrystal said, breaking a bread roll and spreading it with butter.

"No, I asked him to. Thing is, a therapist told me I should. I had bad claustrophobia and this guy I went to see, one of the top guys in Sydney, he said the only way to cure your fears is to face them. He put me in the closet in his office, when I went to see him."

Chrystal looked at her, bread roll half way to her mouth. "Girlfriend, you let him? I would never have let him."

"Well, I wanted to get better. I was tired of being such a slave to my fears. Like I couldn't go in any elevators, I couldn't even go in those revolving doors. I had to drug myself to the gills just to fly, not that I ever mind drugs, I admit, but it was interfering with my ability to have a normal life."

"That sounds like a shrink-quote verbatim, girl," Chrystal said, scattering crumbs, chewing enthusiastically.

"Yes, but it's true. This shrink, he'd been bitten by a dog, his worst fear – so he made himself run that route every day and go past the very dog that bit him, and I made Kenny put me in the closet and I got over my fears."

"Yeah, well, I know what you're getting round to, girlfriend and no way am I confronting my hands. Bad enough I gotta live with them."

"All I'm saying is that they are such a torment to you, but they don't have to be, and if you practice baring them in public, then slowly but surely, you'll see its fine and you won't care and you won't have to wear gloves the whole time."

"Gloves is my fashion statement, girlfriend. They're my latest accessory. I'm starting a trend here. I'm gonna make my fortune in this, I tell you, turn everybody on to gloves and rake in the money. It's another Patent Pending Chrystal Ashworth Scathingly Brilliant Idea. Of which I have many, let me tell you. And, just one of them gotta fall into place and I'll have won the lottery, girlfriend. I borrowed the saying from that movie, *The Trouble with Angels*. You seen it?"

"I have not," Benny said.

"Girlfriend, you should, Hayley Mills is brilliant…"

"Hmm. Well, scathingly brilliant idea or not, all I'm saying is that your whole life would change if you could accept your hands, and stop trying to hide them. No one hates them except you."

Chrystal shook her head. "Enough about the hands, girlfriend. I know what you're saying but I hate them and I don't care what anybody thinks, I hate them. But let's raise a glass to you and me and the fabulous success of our future lives. Hell girl, lets raise a whole bottle. Oh look, this one's nearly empty, I'm getting us another one and I'm splitting this lunch with you, this ain't no lightweight bill."

They got pleasantly drunk and ate up a feast of fine dining. It was evening by the time they fell into a cab and went back to the hostel.

The next morning Benny woke early, left Chrystal a note, and went sightseeing. Her head was aching and her stomach felt like she'd been swilling anti-freeze but other than that, she felt fine.

It was the dawn of a perfect summer's day. Benny walked around the early, quiet downtown, taking photographs and wondering if she could live in Calgary. Then she wondered if she was pregnant; that ever-present fear was still dogging her – a horrible thought she tried to push to the back of her mind. If she didn't think about it, it might not be there.

She stopped for buttered toast and orange juice to settle her stomach. She sat on a park bench, eating her breakfast, watching the executives bustle into their offices while a homeless man slept on a bench across from her, oblivious to the world.

She found an Internet café and logged on to find a series of worried emails from Shay. Benny wrote back, explaining about her flu and telling Shay in detail about her new friend Chrystal who had taken care of her, about how fabulous Chrystal was, with her plethora of scathingly brilliant ideas and how Benny had finally made a real friend.

Then she wrote to Dad, also telling him about Chrystal and describing their lunch and the fun she'd had.

Am only going to stay in Calgary another day, then must carry on. The rest of the West awaits! Love you Dad, look after yourself.

Back at the hostel, Benny flopped down onto her bed. Chrystal looked over at her. "Good day?"

"Fabulous," Benny yawned. "I'm going to head out tomorrow. You want to get all dressed up and hit the town for a fare-thee-well drink?"

"Thought you'd never ask," Chrystal slammed the laptop shut. "Come on, girlfriend, I've had it with this day."

They went to a chi-chi drinks lounge and drank twelve dollar martinis, finally cabbing it back to the hostel at midnight and falling fully clothed into bed, with Chrystal soon snoring loudly.

When Benny woke, Chrystal's bed was empty except for a note:

Gone for a run, hate goodbyes. Stay in touch girlfriend. And I MEAN that. Or I'll hunt you down and well, you know the rest … xoxo

Benny put Monkey Man on Chrystal's pillow and left her a note too:

> Look after him till I see you again. Butterscotch martinis are
> his fav. I'll miss you, will email soon as I can.

She gave Monkey Man a farewell pat on the head and left.

NOT NOW, BABY. PERIOD.

Benny left the hostel feeling slightly hungover and arrived at the terminal
to find the designated driver for the morning was a bad-tempered, jittery
individual. His pale sausage fingers shook when he checked tickets, his
belly shuddering. Benny made the mistake of sitting directly behind
him; she'd thought it would be the perfect place to admire the view
that she knew was going to be spectacular, but the driver's shaking and
sweating distracted her.

Two hours into their departure he made a call.

"It's me, baby," he said. "I'm driving really badly today."

Benny silently agreed and tried to ignore him. The Rockies were jaw-
droppingly, breathtakingly incredible, with mountain goats grazing by
the roadside.

While the bus driver grated the gears and grappled with the bus, Benny
was in awe at the beauty.

The bus was close to empty, and Benny was going wherever it took her.
The sign on the front said "Kelowna," and Benny had no idea what, if
anything, was there. She'd picked the Kelowna bus only because it had
seemed like it was heading in the right direction, that is, the Rockies.
Benny's plan of action was to hang around the area for a couple of days
and imbibe mountains from her economical bus window seat.

They were currently heading into Golden. They had been through
Banff and Lake Louise in all their rich majesty.

Benny felt good, with only one nagging worry: the horrible phantom
pregnancy issue. She was glad to find that thoughts of Mickey were

beginning to hurt less. She still couldn't bear to take off his necklace and she checked the cell phone regularly but there were no new missed calls.

The bus stopped for thirty minutes in historic Revelstoke to change drivers. Benny wasn't sure if the sweating shaking fellow had thrown in the towel or if it was a scheduled change. Either way she didn't care but she was hoping for a better replacement. *C'mon universe, give me someone easy on the eye.*

She staggered off the bus, blinded by the brilliant sunshine, and wandered back and forth in search of the washroom. She couldn't help but notice, during the course of her confused perambulations, a vision of a man sitting casually on a bench, his legs stretched out in front of him. He was like a cat in the sun.

She found the washroom and checked herself in the mirror. Then she went into a cubicle and discovered to her immeasurable relief and joy, that she was not pregnant. Benny, former agnostic, dropped her face into her hands and prayed.

Oh God, thank you. Seriously, thank you.

What a gigantic relief. She'd never been so happy to get her period in her life.

Beautiful colour palette of Cadmium Red, Primary Magenta and Transparent Pyrrole Orange on a canvas of cheap raw toilet paper. Sheer perfection.

She was surprised to find herself thinking in such painterly terms but she didn't care about anything except for the fact that she wasn't pregnant. She hummed to herself as she washed her hands and dried them on rough paper towel.

Then she wandered back out, whistling *Free Bird* and smiling. She dug out Mickey's phone and looked at it.

Time to say goodbye. She searched for a good-sized stone, and found a rusty old iron rod instead. She knelt on the ground and smashed the phone, taking pleasure in damaging it as much as she could. Then she dropped the remains in the trashcan and checked her watch.

With some time to kill, she bought a stash of junk food from the convenience store, then she went behind the shed near the bus and fired up a joint she'd rolled in preparation for such an opportunity.

She inhaled deeply. Well, she had one thing to thank Mickey for. Without him, she might never have discovered hash. And did she ever love it.

Suffused in relaxation, she strolled back to the bus, where it turned out the universe had been listening to her because the sun-cat leg-stretching wonder of nature and genetics was the new bus driver.

Benny, blissful with non-pregnancy and hash, thought he could drive her bus anytime. His embroidered nametag declared him Antonio, and he climbed onboard, cleaning up the garbage that had been left by his predecessor. He flipped switches, pulled levers, took the gear-stick in hand and smoothly pulled them back out onto the road.

Benny looked out the window to admire yet another emerald glacial lake, but she switched back to hear Antonio say, "…and if you have any questions, feel free to come up and ask me."

She would have to find a question to ask him. She watched him clean the windshield, admiring his range of motion, and thinking it was a pity about the wedding band. *You lucky dog, Mrs. Antonio.*

Benny thanked God again for her non-pregnancy and dug into her bag of treats for a Joe Louis. She wondered how she'd managed to survive her previous incarnation of health food obsession. She bit into the soft chocolate-covered pastry and thought about Kenny. She suddenly wanted to phone him, and decided that she would, at the next stop.

KENNY'S HAPPY-EVER-AFTER

"Wurley's Fudge – thirty different flavours" said the sign in Sicamous as they drove through.

There was no end to the entertainment on board as offered by Antonio; Benny watched him masterfully swat and kill a bee with a single blow.

Onwards into Salmon Arm, which Benny thought was a really weird name. As in the Arm of the Salmon? Fish don't have arms. She had the odd vision of a genetically mutated fish standing upright, pointing west with a big fat human arm.

They pulled over in Kelowna and Benny tried to calculate the time in Australia. They were something like twelve or sixteen hours ahead, she couldn't quite remember. Time was irrelevant when emailing, and she hardly ever phoned.

It was 4:45 p.m. She wondered what that would make it in Sydney... either 2:00 a.m. or 6:00 a.m.?

She bought a phone card and paged through her little notebook. There it was, Kenny's number, at Malc the Rock. She dialed the phone card numbers carefully, her heart pounding, fingers shaking a little.

The phone rang in Australia, and Benny clutched the receiver with both hands, wondering if this was a good idea.

"Hello?" It was Malc. Benny would have recognized his voice anywhere.

"Uh, Malc, hi, this is Benny, did I wake you? I'm in Canada, lost track of time, but I wanted to phone – "

"No worries, it's 10:45, Saturday morning, good time to call." Malcolm didn't seem surprised to hear from her. "You want me to get Ken?"

"Yeah, thanks."

Benny waited, her hands sweaty. She wiped her top lip and forehead and leaned her head against the wall next to the phone booth.

"Benny? Are you alright?" Kenny sounded surprised. And wary.

"I'm fine. I'm on holiday actually – "

"Yeah, Dad, I mean your dad, told me. Sounds great. We're all really envious."

"Yeah, it's being something alright. One day I'll show you the photos. Listen Kenny, I don't want to keep you, I just wanted to say ... I guess I really wanted to say ... Well, I'm so sorry. I'm sorry I was such a bitch when you told me. I know ... I know it must have been so hard for you and I only thought about me. So I wanted to say sorry and that I wish you and Malc all the best, I really do. I know it's taken me a while, I know that."

She heard Kenny sigh down the line. "Ah Benny," he said. "I loved you so much. You were my best friend, the fighter I couldn't be. You were the one who made me do stuff and I loved being with you. You're so passionate about everything and I thought I could make you happy, make us happy. I thought that we could have a life that was fine. And I never realized it wasn't fine, until Malc. The last thing I ever wanted to do was hurt you, so I'm sorry too."

"It's okay, Kenny, it really is. Listen, when I get back, maybe we can have dinner or something, with Malc even. I don't hate him, you know, I just want him to make you happy."

Kenny laughed. "He does, Ben, he does. I've never been this happy, all my life. And I'm so glad you phoned. Because the only thing I hated, about all of this, was how I hurt you and I miss you – I miss you so much."

"Yeah, I miss you too. I never thought I'd say this but us not being together, well, I've had some great adventures I wouldn't otherwise have had. What did your mum and dad say, about Malc?"

"They weren't surprised. I was surprised when they weren't and then they just said they love me and all they want is for me to be happy. I thought they were so cool. It's weird how your parents can surprise you. You think you know what they're thinking and then you've got no idea. So you're traveling across Canada? That's amazing!"

"Oh, Kenny, this country, it's incredible. It's so beautiful, it takes my breath away. I might stay, try to build a life here. I don't feel like I have a life back home anymore, you know what I mean? I mean I've got Dad and Mum and Shay and little Harry and all that but a life – my life… Well, who knows? I'm trying not to think too much, just let it play out."

"Wow, that's not the Benny I know," Kenny said, and he laughed. "You used to plan what time to brush your teeth and exactly how much toothpaste to use. I'm impressed."

"Well," Benny sounded apologetic, "I must tell you, I'm not nearly so health-conscious as I was either … I've discovered that I like pizza and doughnuts, Kenny, even although I'm sure you won't approve."

"Oh my God," he said, "doesn't brush her teeth on schedule, eats doughnuts. Who would have thought?" He laughed again. "Benny, have fun. I am. Enjoy life, I am. We were so uptight, you and me. We didn't mean to be, but we were. Enjoy it all, I say, okay?"

Benny smiled. "Yeah, I can do that. Listen, I gotta get back on my bus but it was great to talk to you. I'm glad I didn't wake you up. So, I'll see you when I get back then?"

"That will be wonderful," Kenny said, and he sounded like he really meant it. "Take care of yourself out there Benny and I'm very glad you phoned."

She could hear she'd made him happy and she fought the urge to skip her way back to the bus. But she did have a grin from ear to ear.

THE STD CAPITAL OF B.C.

Still in a great mood, Benny stood in line to board for Kamloops, drinking a diet Dr. Pepper and trying to work out the schedules of arrivals and departures, none of which made the least bit of sense. Getting around by bus was a mathematical science, a Sudoku brain teaser. Unless you were simply going from one town to another in an uncomplicated and linear direction, you had to buy several linking tickets and carefully piece the route together.

Benny turned to the pillow-clutching, bear-hugging young lass behind her and asked her advice.

"I got no idea 'bout any of that," the girl said immediately, "but I hate traveling alone too. We'll get seats next to each other and try to figure it out."

Her name was Julie and she was nineteen. She'd been in Kelowna for a week, taking time-out from her trailer life in Salmon Arm to party wildly and peruse potential study options. She was smart as a whip and by the time Benny left her waiting for her mom, they both ached from laughing.

"Look out for the Billabong Pub in Sorrento," Julie said, by way of farewell. "It's my favorite hangout. And don't pick up any boys in Enderberry; it's the STD capital of B.C. I hope my dad doesn't come to get me. I'm wearing his favourite sweatshirt, he'll have a whole bunch of puppies, I'll tell you. I can't wait to sleep in my own bed," she continued, "I've been gone a whole week and I totally miss my mom and my sister."

Empowered by knowledge of the Enderby boys, Benny waved goodbye to Julie who was resplendent in a Maple Leaf sweatshirt, still clutching her pillow.

The bus filled up. Benny got stuck next to an eleven-year-old boy who regarded her with suspicious alarm and sat as far away from her as he could on the edge of his seat.

Benny glared at him. She wasn't that scary-looking. Then she tried to snooze – it was too dark out to be scenery spotting.

It was close to 11:00 p.m. when they pulled into Kamloops and she was nearly too tired to find the hostel, and thinking she might cab it to the nearest motel instead. But, rallying her energies, she found a cab and made it to the hostel, a magnificent old Victorian mansion that used to be the Courthouse.

She found her bed – the standard bottom half of a hard pine bunk with three inches of foam mattress and stiff cotton sheets – and sank down, chewing on a couple of codeine for good measure and falling fast asleep. The room had three bunk beds, with Benny the only occupant.

She woke up and went to the washroom, wondering why the magnificent old building wasn't a heritage site or museum. She got dressed and went down the majestic staircase complete with stained glass window. She read a brochure at the front desk: the Shuswap Indians got to Kamloops first, this was the true west and there was a lot to do both in summer and winter. P.S., this was cowboy country.

She walked down the main drag and thought this really might be it. She could come back here; she could live here, in Kamloops.

She strolled around, photographing, and returned to the hostel to read *The Girl Who Played With Fire*, wondering all the while if this could be her next home. Kamloops was scenic, hilly and quite brown and the local job centre had lots of opportunities. She stayed for two days and then she decided it was time to continue.

The next day, with a hefty joint inside her as well as three cups of coffee with milk and sugar, she was feeling no pain and she was ready to float her way to Edmonton.

EDMONTON AND THE WORLD'S LARGEST MALL

Waiting to board the bus to Edmonton, Benny tried very hard not to, but found herself talking to a retired music teacher, Maureen, who said Benny was her omen, her sign to travel and explore, not shrivel up and die. She said Benny had great courage and Benny thanked her.

On the bus Maureen tried to match-make Benny with every available man. "Talk to the fellow beside you," she hissed at Benny during a leg-stretch stop.

"Why would I want to talk to him?" Benny said. "And he should cover up that wound. It's not hygienic."

A big, blonde, Swiss fellow had got on at Jasper, his knee gushing blood. Benny was surprised she didn't throw up, so raw was his wound. He was dressed like a hiking guide circa 1920, and he was in his late thirties, early forties. He seemed to expect some sort of repartee from Benny and was disgruntled when she turned up the volume on her iPod and stared out the window.

And him with such a bloody great opening line too.

Later, he forgave Benny enough to brush his big naked hairy thigh up against hers. She swaddled herself in lap rugs and kept as much distance from him as she could.

The sunset landscape from Jasper to Edmonton was stark and beautiful, mountainous with rivers, lakes and shores. Blue, shaded and sparkling. Off the scale of great art and design. Benny thanked the Great *He She They It* of the Heavens and told them they were none too shabby with the paintbrush.

They arrived in Edmonton close to midnight and Benny immediately characterized it as a glitteringly big town of small skyscrapers and sprawling suburbs. She shared a cab to the hostel with Maureen who was following Benny everywhere, unwilling to let go of the good omen that was going to save her from shriveling up and dying. That Maureen had to sleep in another dorm due to the hostel being close to full, was another reason for Benny to thank the Godly Beings.

She woke at 8:00 a.m. and lay in bed listening to the others talk about their day ahead. They were about to leave and Benny sat up, as much as her bed would allow, and inquired generally about the World's Largest Mall.

"Oh, we're going there now if you'd like to come with us," a pixie-like Brit offered.

Benny thought about it for a moment.

"Yeah, sure, be fun." She dressed quickly and joined the group.

Their first stop at the Mall was the food court and Benny treated herself to Mongolian vegetables for breakfast, followed by a candied apple and cookie dough ice cream. It seemed to her, wandering around, that the mall didn't have anything specifically Edmontonian about it, except for the fact that it was like six malls in one.

Later, back at the hostel, Benny took a long hot shower and did a load of laundry. While the dryer spun, she attempted, yet again, to work out possible travel routes and combinations of time, money, and connections. The ferry from Alaska to Vancouver was ringing in at a whopping $US500. Cancel that idea. But Yellowknife was intriguing and Whitehorse was a must.

She dropped her laundry off on her bed and went for a walk in the blue evening light, looking for the Fringe Festival, which turned out to be a replica of the food court at the Mall, only this one was in tents and booths. Mini-doughnuts, pizza slices, roasted corn, ice cream, curries, smoothies, cookies, elephant ears, fairy floss, and marshmallows dipped in chocolate.

Benny chugged a litre of diet Coke out of a plastic green bottle shaped like an alien and she wondered where the art stuff was.

She found some crafty jewelry, a stand with tie-dyed skirts, and she saw several of her fellow hostellers banging on drums, climbing out of boxes, mooing in cow suits, cycling and juggling. She went into the retro Princess Theatre to watch *A Clockwork Orange*, having never seen it. Some guy had come in with his wife; he was confused and loudly embarrassed. He'd thought this was going to be a live Fringe act. He expressed his confusion throughout the entire movie, and even after the film ended, he continued, "But I read a review in the newspaper…"

She walked around Old Strathcona, hub of fashion and art; okay, so the fringe stuff was only fringe, the regular real merch was fab. It was all priced way beyond her wildest daydreams. Benny nodded at the obliging sales folk and hoped she didn't look as poor as she felt.

She got back to the hostel close to midnight and got chatting to Tom from Detroit who tried to convince her to stay for the week. He'd been drilling up in Yellowknife, the very place Benny had decided to head for. He said it was dangerous up there, it wasn't what one expected; she'd be disappointed if she went. But if she were to stay, he could assure her that disappointed was the very last thing she would be…

"Yeah, thanks but no thanks, mate." He helped her stock up on her hash, then she wished him goodnight and went to bed.

It was time to forge on. She just hoped she wouldn't find Maureen on the Yellowknife bus.

A GRITTY TURN

The bus left Edmonton in a steady downpour of rain. Benny was nearly blinded by a migraine and was oblivious to the weather. The bus left at midnight and the barbaric departure hour only added to her woes. She'd smoked a quick joint before leaving the hostel and chewed on two codeine tablets, but nothing seemed to relieve the pain.

Eleven hours later, they stopped in High Level, a muddy swamp with no instantly apparent moments of grace. Benny, her head still tender, saw that *The Shades* were playing at the Stardust Motel, and loads of families got off the bus, so the town must have something to offer. Onwards, the road was as bumpy as any in the Outback and Benny felt right at home. It felt good to be moving again, trucking northwards into permafrost one more time.

Yellaknife, the locals seemed to say – although Benny realized she still didn't have the inflection quite right – did sound challenging. They would be getting into town at midnight. Tom from Detroit gave her the names of some people she could stay with if she got stuck. She explained she hated doing that, imposing on strangers, to which Tom replied that just going there and trying to find a room would be hard to do, as well as very expensive. Besides, he added, it would be the middle of the night and it wasn't exactly the safest place on the planet. Benny tried not to reflect on his words of warning.

The road to Yellowknife was like a rock-hard washboard. And the bus had devolved yet again. This latest model was more like a yellow school bus with picture windows front to back, the most basic of seating and a linoleum floor. There wasn't a whole lot of seat padding, velveteen or otherwise.

And it was noisy too. It shook, rattled, and jolted in a way similar to the old Churchill train except that this bus moved at high speed; it hurtled across the terrain. Let no man or moose step into its path, this projectile would not be easily stopped. Despite the somewhat crude simplicity of the interior, there was still the inevitable TV and old fashioned video machine and Benny watched classic Keanu Reeves in *The Replacements*, gliding onto the football field in slow-mo, his hair bouncing and falling like a shampoo commercial. She wondered how many times she'd seen that scene on planes and bad late night TV.

They stopped for supper at 4:00 p.m. Benny enjoyed a bowl of delicious French onion soup in Winnie's Café in the middle of nowhere. A local girl was describing how she had frostbite. She explained in detail how she very nearly had to have her foot removed. Benny silently thanked her for oversharing and tried to focus on other things. A bouncy Swedish girl invited Benny over to her table.

"Uh, no thanks, I'm happy as a clam right here."

Benny chatted with a Yellowknife woman, a petite, polite, reserved woman originally from Delhi. The woman said she knew a small print firm up there that needed somebody, and that Benny should look it up, you know, business cards and what-not. But work had become remote and far less appealing than it once was.

The petite Delhi woman was chic in big Gucci sunglasses and a designer outfit. Benny thanked her for the chat and snuck back outside into the grey mud for some feel-good hash.

She wasn't getting that same lovely, laid-back and kindly Churchill, Manitoba, feeling going up this road up north. This was different. The terrain looked familiar but the attitude was different. The people seemed edgy, grittier, as if Benny had strayed onto a construction site and thrown down a picnic blanket. Churchill was visited by bird-watchers and peaceful folk looking for a holiday, while this gang was coming for quick money the hard-laboring way.

Benny went back inside to buy some gum. The wallpaper in the café was peeling, the dirty cream walls were bare except for a single large dream-catcher; the lino floor was dirty, and the lighting dim.

Ms. Delhi said people were bad-tempered in Yellowknife.

"Too much politicking," she said, shaking her neatly coiffed head. It was time for her to move on she said to Benny. Life was too short. Outside, it was raining again and a single gas pump stood in a sea of mud. Mosquitoes floated around inside the diner, cruising for contented just-fed blood. The Swedish girl was phoning B&Bs in Yellowknife, without much success, it seemed. Benny watched a fat mosquito try to exit via the screen window and she bet the sucker was full of her blood. She discovered they were in a town called Enterprise, as in the starship, only not.

SHELDON WHITE SEEMS HELPFUL

Crossing The Great Slave Lake by ferry, Benny once again let herself experience full-throttled, unrestrained joy at the wondrous almost gleeful moment. They passed through a national park and spotted three herds of buffalo. Benny was in love with the tundra, boreal forests, swamps, and boulders.

The bus continued to rocket forward. The driver took no prisoners. He sat casually hunched over at the big wheel, his brow furrowed, seeming distracted but his hands guiding the bus like a father absentmindedly shepherding his son by the shoulder. Benny watched his body anticipate each bump and jolt, his accelerator foot remaining unchanged throughout, pedal to the metal. Benny lost all sense of time, and of her surroundings. They traveled for hours, and a heavy rain started to fall. The bus eventually came up close to a supersized, white, neon-illuminated cross set on top of a church.

"Yellowknife city limits," Ms Delhi Chic told Benny who thought the glowing icon was a good omen, but directly thereafter they hit Shoppers Drug Mart, cheap clothing stores, high-rise buildings and the city metropolis of Yellowknife.

Off the bus and straight into Joe's Pizza – *Eat In or Take Out*. Flashback to the Churchill arrival; similar pouring rain and sloshy, ankle-deep muddy glue. The café was filled with truculent teenagers smoking up a storm. Benny dropped her bags at a table in the back. She sat down, put her head in her hands and groaned. Her entire body was jolted and shaken from the ride. It felt good to rest her forehead on the comfort of her folded arms. Fearing she might fall asleep, she sighed, sat up and saw that Sean Connery was watching her. She blinked a few times and the hallucination cleared enough to reveal a Sean Connery look-alike – well, Sean some twenty years back. He was eating a generous double cheeseburger and fries with an order of lasagna on the side. Benny was impressed. He waved her over to join him.

"What are you doing in this godforsaken neck of the woods?" he asked. His accent, without Scottish inflection, surprised her. She reminded herself that he wasn't really Sean Connery. He just resembled him closely. Turned out he was an archeologist who'd been up in the area for months.

"Not a lot of places to stay up here," he said, sounding much like Tom from Detroit, "and they're all expensive and not very safe either. You're very welcome to share my tent, but I've got to tell you it's not the driest place in the world."

Outside, the rain was pelting down hard and Benny had a dismal vision of herself, wet and shivering, out in the middle of a field in heaven knows where, with water pouring in from all sides and piles of rock samples for company. Oh, and Sean. There was that upside to be considered. However, while it was very kind of him to offer, and she truly did think he was being genuinely kind with no ulterior motives, camping had never been her thing.

"Very nice of you to offer," she said. They talked while Sean continued to eat and it was pleasant to engage in the general chatter of nothingness, up there in that Yellowknife café at midnight with the sound of the rain outside and air filled with the thick fog of teenage cigarette smoke.

"So what are you going to do?" Sean asked. "The bus you just came up on is the only one out of here for the next three days and it leaves in a couple of hours."

Benny started to say she had no idea when the chair next to Sean was scraped aside and a man in a dirty white chef's apron sat down noisily and drew himself up to the table.

"Well, hello there," the newcomer said and Benny felt Sean stiffen. She looked up to see a blonde jock-god smiling at her with all the force and focus of a quarterback doing a Pepsi commercial. His green eyes glowed and his dimples cut deep. Benny felt the vortex suck of his power and extended her hand.

"Benny," she said. He took her hand in his big paw and she felt dismayed. She had been expecting a Mickey-like jolt of electricity but all she thought was that his hand felt unexpectedly doughy. She wanted to snatch her hand back but he was holding on tight.

"Sheldon White at your service," he said. "Ex-jock, now chef of Joe's Midnight Café in Yellowknife. Welcome."

Benny thought she heard Sean Connery making a snorting sound but she was mesmerized, locked in the lava lamp glow of Sheldon's green eyes and that flashing grin.

"Where are you staying?" Sheldon asked.

Benny shrugged. "I've got absolutely less than no idea," she admitted. "Any suggestions?"

He looked at his watch. It was getting close to 2:00 a.m. "I get off at 4:00," he said, "soon as the bus leaves. You're quite welcome to come and crash at my place, no strings attached. It's no castle, I'll tell you that much but it's clean and dry. Your honour will be respected madam, I'm a gentleman and a man of my word, isn't that right, Johnny?"

Benny looked at Sean Connery who was staring into his coffee. He gave Sheldon a half-glance, leaned over and shook Benny's hand and got to his feet. "His place will be drier than mine, that's for sure," he said, donning an Indiana Jones hat and tipping it at Benny. "Put supper on my tab, Shel. See you tomorrow night and try to have something new on the menu, won't you?"

He threaded through the thinning tables, the teenagers yawning and straggling out into the wet night. Sheldon watched him go. "He's just sore because he wanted you for himself," he said casually and Benny felt flattered that Sheldon wanted her.

"So how about it?" he asked. "You want to crash with me?"

Benny was exhausted. It seemed like it was his place or get right back on the bus. "Yes, please, that would be lovely."

He told her she had a couple of hours to wait, to help herself to the magazines and newspapers, that the cafe owner wouldn't notice. "And if he does, I'll tell him it was for a buddy of mine. It'll be copasetic. Come to the counter, I'll fill up your coffee."

Benny passed the two hours of waiting by falling into a numb jet-lagged timeless zone. She read up on all the latest celebrity cellulite disasters and their marital catastrophes while outside it continued to rain. Sheldon finally started to close up the cafe, moving through what was clearly a familiar routine of packing and cleaning up. She watched him work, admiring his focus, his neatness. She got up and went over to him.

"You're very neat and tidy," she said.

"I was taught that at chef school," he said. "*Mise en place.* 'Everything has its place'. It's a motto I live by. The other motto I live by is one my dad taught me. He said a man without his word is nothing; 'be a man of your word, my son.' And so I am. I'm a man of my word." He wiped and cleaned. She noticed he had an earring in each ear and a large tattoo on the back of his neck. He also had a Toronto Maple Leaf tattoo on the back of his calf and more tattoos peeking out from his sleeves. He was a big man, linebacker solid, not trim. He moved as if he were in pain – his knee she guessed.

"Enjoying the view?" he asked and she blushed.

"Sure, why not?" she countered and he grinned.

"I think we'll have ourselves some fun, you and me," he said, closing the last of the cabinet doors, "if we ever get around to it." He took a look around. It was pristine. "Okay," he said, "you wait here, I'll bring the truck around. Wait by the front door."

HASH SUNDOWNER IN A YELLOWKNIFE DAWN

She stood under a small awning, feeling drugged by her need for sleep, glad the rain was easing up. The dripping eaves were lit by a bare light bulb that hung outside the café and dark blue of the night sky held a glow, heralding the sunrise that was minutes away. Sheldon pulled up in a dark green battered GMC van that had seen better days. He leapt out, grabbed her bag, and threw it in the back. She was glad she hadn't let him touch her camera bag, what with a throwing arm like that. She climbed into the truck that smelled strongly of hash. Her feet were buried in a pool of CDs. She looked down.

"Oh, don't worry about those," he said. "Listen, I just have to make a stop-off, okay? It won't take long then I'll get you home to bed. You look exhausted."

"I am," Benny admitted. It was nearly 5:00 a.m., and they drove in silence for a while.

"You like Pearl Jam?" he asked.

"Sure," she said and he popped the CD in. They swung into a used car lot filled with rusting cars piled at random. A large Alsatian barked and pulled at a chain, its teeth bared.

"Wait here," Sheldon said and he hopped out of the car. The rain had stopped but the mud was intense, and Benny had no desire to get out. She watched Sheldon greet a wiry man in a dirty white undershirt, who came out to see what the dog was barking at. There was a lot of hand slapping back and forth, and then Sheldon returned to the truck.

"Hate this mud," he said, "but what can you do?" He started the engine and backed out of the car lot. He rolled a hash joint with one hand while he drove, and Benny knew she was looking at a one-trick pony strut-its-stuff, but she was impressed anyway. He lit it and offered it to her.

"Oh, this is good," Benny said, closing her eyes.

He laughed. "I get the best," he said, "This is the end of my working day, this is my sundowner. It's upside down, like so many things here in Yellowknife. So, how old are you anyways?"

"Twenty-five," she said, losing track of who she had told what to. "You?"

"Thirty-five, going on thirty-six soon. Too old to be up here, doing what I do but hey, it could be worse. I was a Marlie you know, all set to be a Leaf. I'm not shitting you, it's the truth. But one season with the AHL and I blew my knee out. Never came back. So my grannie, she loaned me some money. She said, boy, you always liked to cook, now go and learn how to do it right. So I did. I worked in some good restaurants in Toronto. But then the travel bug bit." He looked over at her. "I'm sure you know how that is," he said and she nodded. "So I got as far as here and then I got offered a job doing the night shift at Joe's and I've been here for three years now. I like it. I guess one day I'll move on, go back to Toronto, I dunno."

"What about a girlfriend?" Benny asked and he laughed.

"I was wondering when we'd get to that. I had a girlfriend," he said. "She was psycho. Left me and ran off with a bush pilot, thank God."

"How long ago was that?"

"What are you, the girlfriend police?" He sounded irritated. "I dunno, say, two years ago, maybe less, maybe more." They pulled up at a block of apartment buildings, once cream-coloured, now gray and weathered. "You'll be glad to know I'm in the basement," he said and he led her down the stairs. "Much better for sleeping in summer. I'm lucky, the guy who owns the building lets me stay rent free. I cook for him and his wife sometimes and I take care of him, if you know what I mean." He opened a door and pushed his way inside. It was dark and Benny blinked, letting her eyes adjust. The place was a mess. So much for *"mise-en-place!"* He turned on a couple of lights and Benny saw a large La-Z-Boy chair facing a big screen TV and an old wooden desk in the corner with a computer. The desk was covered with papers and junk. He guided her through a living room of sorts to a tiny bedroom. A double bed filled the room with bookcases lining two of the walls, their shelves packed tight with blankets, rolled-up posters, girlie magazines and all kinds of knick-knacks including a pair of praying white hands. The bed was covered with a pristine homemade knitted Toronto Maple Leaf blanket. Sheldon took it off the bed and folded it neatly before laying it on the top of the bookcase.

"My mom made it for me," he said. "Here, let me show you the washroom."

Given the mess of the outer rooms, Benny was surprised by the immaculate perfection of the washroom. Gleaming shaving equipment was laid out on a face cloth, all precisely lined up. The entire washroom was scrubbed and polished.

"Wow," she said. "You do keep this clean."

Sheldon shrugged. "So listen, you want to bath, shower, sleep, what? There's a kitchenette. We walked through it on our way in but I don't have any food in there. Why would I, I eat at the café for free. What do you want to do?"

"Sleep," Benny said immediately, "sleep, sleep, sleep."

He laughed. "Okay, well, don't mind me, I'm going to wind down, watch some TV. I'm back on shift at 7:00 tonight, I usually go to bed around noon, so if you want to walk around or anything do whatever you want. You can't walk to the café from here and this area isn't the greatest, so be careful." He dug into one of the desk drawers and handed her a set of keys. "For the apartment. Welcome to my humble abode."

"Fantastic, thanks. Right now, all I want is bed," Benny gave a jaw splitting yawn. "If I wake up and you're sleeping, I hope I won't disturb you."

He grinned at her, that flashy all-star grin. "Sweetheart, when I'm sleeping, wild buffalo couldn't wake me." He climbed onto his La-Z-Boy and pointed a remote at the TV, reaching for his hash next to him. Benny went into the bedroom and pulled on her pajamas. She had no idea what she was doing in this apartment in the middle of nowhere with a guy she had just met, but she didn't care. Her need for sleep was overwhelming and besides, Sheldon was a hunk, not to mention charming. She climbed under the blankets and found the mattress thin but comfortable. The pillows were equally thin and she was surprised. Somehow she'd imagined Sheldon to have a more luxurious bed. She soon fell fast asleep, waking briefly to voices arguing loudly in the other room; it sounded like a man and a woman were arguing, with Sheldon shouting back. When she woke again, the TV was belting out what she thought sounded like an orgy of people grunting and thrusting. She was vaguely aware of Sheldon climbing into bed, and she was woken up several hours later by his loud snoring.

She lay there for a while, knowing there was no way she'd get back to sleep. She climbed over him gently but he had been right, he was oblivious. She grabbed her backpack and pulled it into the bathroom. She closed the door and ran a deep hot bath, laying all her toiletries and shampoos out on the shelf beside the basin. She took her time in the bath, refilling it twice with hot water, soaping and scrubbing. She finally got out and pulled on a new set of clothes, stuffing her dirty ones into a plastic bag. She figured she'd find a laundromat. She checked her watch, surprised to see it was 3:00 p.m. She gathered her camera bag and her dirty laundry and left Sheldon a note, setting out to explore.

She was immediately disappointed. There wasn't much by way of tourist attractions. The area around Sheldon's apartment was a dreary wasteland of welfare housing.

She found a laundromat. The yellow and brown walls were lined with signs forbidding the patrons to do an array of activities. She filled up a washload and went for a walk, hoping to find a used bookstore along the way. She found a man selling Goodwill trinkets on the sidewalk, blue plastic necklaces and unreadable old paperbacks, alongside drawings that he'd coloured in badly. She wondered if he was trying to make a living the sober way, and if so, felt she should be supportive but when she examined the necklaces and the crayoned ducks, she had to walk away.

Benny found a dollar store and asked the owner if there was a bookstore nearby. He waved her down the street. She finally came to an antiquated store, its windows gray with dust. Inside she held out slim hope for a treasure; the shelves were primarily stocked with the usual

Danielle Steeles and Dean Koontz. In the end Benny picked out *The Drifters* by James Michener, feeling it suited her mood. She went out into the sunshine of the late afternoon, thinking it would be a good idea to pick up some food for later. She found a Chinese takeout and ordered a vegetarian stir-fry with noodles.

She went into the convenience store for a bar of chocolate and a diet Coke and grabbed a box of Kellogg's Special K and a litre of skim milk. Then she went back to see how her laundry was doing. She put her clothes in the dryer and sat reading *The Drifters* and eating her chocolate until the cycle finished. When she walked back to the apartment, the shadows had lengthened but the light was still strong. She walked fast, laden with laundry, food and her camera bag, leery of the gangsta boys who seemed genuinely unfriendly and dangerous. No hip hop MTV kids here. She got back to the apartment just as Sheldon was about to leave. He looked at her in a rather cool way, she thought.

HELP YOURSELF TO MY PORN

"Everything okay?" she asked.

"You left the bathroom in a mess," he said. "But it's not your fault, I never explained. You need to clean up after yourself." He pointed to the kitchen counter and Benny looked over at a roll of paper towel and a line-up of various cleaning products: Vim, Windex, anti-bacterial wipes.

"I'm sorry," she said, laying down her bags.

He flashed her a spectacular grin. "Don't worry," he said, his mood switching back. "So, listen, I'm going to head out. I'll be back around 5:00 a.m., and if you like I'll pick you up and take you for a drive okay? Show you the scenery, the greenery, such as it is. Here, let me show you how to use the TV controls. I watch a lotta porn; you're welcome to watch some if you like. Some chicks are into that, some not. I always think if you are not, what are you hiding? And hey, if you want to use the computer, feel free too. That girlfriend of mine though, she read all my emails. Don't read my emails okay?"

"I would never do that," Benny was shocked. "What kind of person would do that?"

He laughed. "More than you would know. So look, here are all the controls, okay?" He showed her the various TV channels, including his vast array of porn. "I also got a bunch of DVDs," he said, showing her a box next to the La-Z-Boy.

"You know, it's a good thing I work shifts because we can share the chair." He laughed. "Have a good night, make yourself at home. There's no password on my computer, just turn it on. That girlfriend I had, she was psycho, man, she would look at my histories of what I was looking at on the Internet and then, she'd get mad at me for surfing porn without her. Weirdo. She broke all that." He pointed to a panel of kitchen cabinets without their doors. "The landlord was pissed, I'll tell you. Tried to get me to pay for it. I told him to go and find her."

"I'd never spy on you like she did," Benny told him again, wanting him to know she wasn't like his ex-girlfriend. He shrugged as if to say you will, you won't, who cares. Then he left. Benny flicked through the box of DVDs. There was a collection of Bruce Willis movies, along with a bunch featuring big-busted blondes with long red fingernails cupping generous cleavage, all of the women pouting at the camera through a soft-filtered lens. Benny turned on the TV, and scrolled through until she found the channel with *C.S.I.* and *Criminal Minds,* and she ate her vegetables and noodles that were really tasty. She watched TV until midnight and then she cleaned the bathroom, scrubbing and polishing. She felt she understood Sheldon's need for bleach and cleanliness and she wanted to show him that she was a kindred spirit. She wished she had been more aware of the mess she'd made.

After she cleaned, she climbed into bed, propped herself up against the wall with the thin pillows and read. She was too wide-awake to sleep – she felt as if she'd been with Sheldon in Yellowknife for weeks, but in fact, it hadn't even been twenty-four hours. It was only Friday night, and she still had all of Saturday and Sunday before the next bus left at 4:00 a.m., on Monday morning. She had to admit she was a little disappointed in how things were working out with Sheldon and she wished she had gone camping with Sean Connery instead.

But Sheldon was fine. He was just moody and in future, she'd clean up better.

She pulled out her maps and studied them, wondering if she could cut across to Hay River and then go up to the Arctic Circle from there. She thought she'd do some online research and she turned on Sheldon's computer. She launched the Internet browser and found the Greyhound bus site. Seemed she was out of luck, there was no direct connection across to Hay River; she'd have to go the whole way back down. She sighed. She surfed the net and found some celebrity gossip sites but it seemed not much was happening in their worlds either. Then, unable to stop herself, she checked Sheldon's history, peeking quickly at the pull-down menu at the top. Whoa. Hardcore porn for sure. Benny felt dismayed. She suddenly wished she could leave his apartment but go where? She had no idea where the centre of town was or, for that matter, where she was.

She poked around the cluttered desk for a bill, trying to find an address, and she found a letter with the address on the envelope. She wondered if she should call a cab and leave. But where would she go? And besides, there was no phone. Sheldon only seemed to have his cell phone. She told herself it was only two more nights and two more days and then she would go to the café with him and wait the nine hours for the bus to leave.

She was dog-tired but viciously awake. She decided she had to do whatever it took to sleep and she reached into her backpack and got out her meds and was sound asleep in no time.

She woke to find Sheldon staring at her sourly. "What drugs are you on?" he asked. "It's like close to 10:00 a.m. I thought we were going driving. I thought we had a date."

Benny sat up, groggy. "I'm so sorry," she began to explain but he left the bedroom and went to his La-Z-Boy where he flicked on a noisy porn channel, his golden face sullen.

Benny sighed and got up. She used the washroom and wondered what she was going to do with herself for the day.

"Where's the main town from here?" she asked, and he ignored her. Great.

"And another thing," he said, turning to her while a bunch of people were doing it all kinds of ways onscreen with the volume blaring, "you lied."

"What?" Benny asked, feeling cold with fear. "What did you say?"

'SHROOMS, COKE AND HASH

"I beg your pardon?" she asked him again but he had gone silent and was focused on a woman with big yellow hair who was sucking hard on an enormous penis. Benny went back to the bedroom and sat down, feeling isolated and trapped.

Sheldon gave a loud sigh and got up. He turned off the TV and unbuttoned his shirt, revealing a torso of Celtic tattoos and a colourful sleeve of snakes and roses. He turned and lumbered out the room and she saw a gigantic crucifix running down his spine and across his shoulder blades. An intricate Jesus was carefully inked, his face sad, head hanging down. The words *et tu* were in big letters across the back of Sheldon's neck, written above Jesus' head.

He came back into the room, pulling on a T-shirt. "Well, I gotta go out anyways now. Come if you want," he said.

Benny figured anything was better than being left alone in his dingy apartment. He rolled a joint in the truck and they drove through streets lined with gray buildings. Sheldon was sullen, silent. He drove for about half an hour and then turned into the driveway of a rundown house. Benny looked around at the long line of row houses and silently followed him up rickety wooden stairs to a brick porch with a sagging old sofa. A tired old dog with a milky eye and a white muzzle raised his head, and then went back to sleep.

Sheldon rapped on the door and waited. A tall man with a thick black handlebar moustache opened it and greeted Sheldon.

"This her?" he asked and Sheldon nodded. The man turned and led them through the narrow hall that stank of cat pee and damp walls. They walked into a kitchen where a woman was feeding a baby in a high chair. The kitchen smelled of sour milk, burnt soup and fatty fried meat. Benny tried to breathe through her mouth.

Sheldon pulled up a chair at the messy table and sat down. Benny, uncertain, followed suit. The woman greeted Sheldon and ignored Benny. The man sat down and held his hand out to Sheldon who reached into his pocket while holding out his other hand. They did an exchange, with Sheldon taking a wad of small bills from the man.

The man grinned. "Party time," he said and he got Sheldon a beer, offering one to Benny who accepted, not knowing what else to do. The man rolled a large joint and offered it around. Benny took a cautious hit and tried not to inhale too deeply, thinking she needed to keep her wits about her.

"What else you got?" the man asked Sheldon who laughed.

"I got mushrooms. You interested?"

"Hell, yes," the man said.

"And me," the woman said. "I'm gonna put this baby to bed. Don't start without me."

"Too late, Angie baby," Sheldon said, swallowing the mushrooms theatrically. He offered some to Benny who shook her head. Sheldon laughed.

The woman came back and sat on Sheldon's lap. He put more mushrooms in his mouth and fed them to her with a kiss.

"You want me to give you some of that?" the man asked Benny.

"I don't even know your name," she said to him.

"You can call me Jack," the man said generously.

Sheldon laughed. "His name is Richard," he said, "Ree-shard, like the French say. Because he's French, man."

The woman was still sitting on Sheldon's lap, facing him, with her arms around his neck and Benny saw an ornate scrolled tattoo that covered her lower back.

"Let's go watch some TV," Richard said and they filed into the living room where the thick dirty green curtains were closed against the sunlight, and the floor was covered with baby toys, a large playpen in the centre. Richard kicked it to one side and hunted for the remote control. Benny was afraid she was going to be subjected to more porn but Richard flicked on *The Hangover* instead. Benny felt her shoulders relax. Next to her, Sheldon ran a finger up her leg.

"Worried, were you?" he laughed and his green eyes shone like a wild cat.

"Shut up and watch," Richard said.

"Like you haven't seen this a hundred times," Angie said, and he swatted her.

They watched the movie for about half an hour. "We need more drugs to enjoy this better," Richard said. "Come on, Sheldon, share, man, you know it's rude to hold out on your buddies."

"What we need is some coke," Angie said, sitting upright. "That's what we need."

"Sweetheart," Sheldon said patiently, "you don't have any money for coke."

Angie looked like a kid denied Santa.

Sheldon got up. "You owe me," he said, pointing a thick stubby finger at Richard. "Come on Benny, we're going for a drive to get Angie her candy."

"I want to come too," Angie said, but Sheldon shoved her down on the sofa.

"No way José," he said. "You went mental last time. You wait here."

They left, with Angie's complaining voice trailing out behind them.

"They're not good people," Sheldon said. "You see how they take care of that baby? I would never do drugs in a house with a baby. And that Angie, she's psycho, man."

Benny thought of reminding him that not only had he done drugs with them, he'd supplied them. But she kept quiet.

"So, what you want to do now?" he asked her.

She was startled. "I thought we were going to buy stuff for Angie?"

He laughed. "No way. She's got no money. That was just an excuse to get us out of that house. Did you see how dirty it was? So, what do you want to do?"

"What's the time?" Benny asked. It was only midday.

Sheldon suddenly swung the car around, and headed back in the direction they had come.

"I've made an executive decision to give myself a good time," he announced. "Angie's right, some cocaine's exactly what I need now. We'll go visit this guy I know, then we'll do whatever you like."

Benny's heart sank. "Okay," she said, wondering how on earth she was going to extricate herself from this mess, thinking at least Sheldon had a good capacity for chemicals – either that or he was used to driving wasted.

Sheldon drove them down a new series of unremarkable gray streets and pulled up at a ramshackle detached house with boarded up windows and a porch heaped high with junk. The house was right next to a grimy strip mall and Benny figured it would be a good excuse for her to not go into the house.

"I need to go in there," she pointed to convenience store, "but how long will you be?" She also didn't want to let Sheldon out of her sight in case he went back to the apartment without her.

Sheldon was irritated. "I dunno. Not long. It's not like I'm going to stay here long, I'm just going to hook up, that's all. Okay, well, go and do your girly shopping but be back in twenty minutes, okay?"

Benny looked at her watch and nodded. She had no real intention of leaving the truck. She strolled off in the direction of the store, watching Sheldon knock on the door and go inside. Then she stopped and sat down outside, making sure she was out of sight but could see the front door.

"Oh my word," she said out loud, "oh dear heavens, what have I done? I thought Mickey was hardcore but this – this is ugly. How on earth did I end up here? And how on earth am I going to get out of this? He's a pig, an utter pig."

She kept an eye on the front door, her arms around her knees, which were drawn up to her chest. Finally, well over an hour later, Sheldon emerged, swaying against the doorframe. He staggered to the truck. She didn't want to get in and drive with him but she didn't know what else to do.

"A bit fucked up," he slurred. "Let's go home, 'kay?"

She got in and buckled her seatbelt.

Sheldon drove slowly, his hands gripping the steering wheel. He was careful not to go over the speed limit and they made it home, with Benny never happier to arrive at a destination.

They went inside and Sheldon flopped down into his chair and flicked on the TV.

"I'm going to the shops," Benny said and she turned to leave. "You want anything?" She figured he would have left for work by the time she got back.

"Nah," he slurred. "Wait, yes, get me some Chinese food, anything I don't care. Go to the guy on the corner okay? Tell him to take care of his buddy, Sheldon, give me the works."

He dug in his pocket and pulled out some money.

"I thought you ate at work," Benny said, unwilling to have to face an entire night with him.

"Nah, got a couple of days off," he said, "I was way overdue. Get me some pop too, not the diet crap either. Two litres of Coke, okay?"

"Okay," Benny said and she left, closing the door quietly behind her.

She looked at her watch. It was only early afternoon. She still had to get through the night and do the following day, and then wait for the bus in the café. She sighed. What a mess.

She got the takeout and his Coke and she made note of a cab's telephone number on the wall of the takeout place.

She walked slowly back to the apartment, hoping he'd passed out. But he was awake, smoking a joint and lying back on his La-Z-Boy. If anything, he seemed more alert than when she'd left. She handed him his food and the change from his money.

"You didn't get any for you," he sounded hurt. "You were supposed to get some for you too."

"Not hungry," Benny said, and it was true. She sat down on the floor.

"No, wait," he said and he got off the chair. "You sit on the chair. Must be a gentleman. No, wait, I've got a better idea."

He pushed the chair into the kitchenette and dragged the mattress in from the bedroom, shoving it in front of the TV. He lay down and propped himself up on one elbow attacking his food with gusto.

"Come on, let's watch a movie," he said.

"I'm not watching any porn," Benny said.

"We can watch anything you like," he said. "Come on, come here. Lie down next to me."

They started on Sheldon's Bruce Willis collection, and Benny smoked too much of Sheldon's strong raw hash. She vaguely recalled him handing her a couple of pills.

"Here," he said. "You'll like these."

Benny stared at the pills. She was slumped down. "What are they?"

"Percs," Sheldon said. "Like the codeine you're so in love with, only way much better."

Benny shrugged and swallowed the pills with Sheldon's leftover Coke.

A MAN WITHOUT HIS WORD...

She woke to find Sheldon grinning at her. "Wakey, wakey, sleeping beauty. It's nearly 2:00 p.m. I was beginning to think I'd be needing to take you to emerg, passing out on me like that."

Benny eased herself up. She felt cocooned in a marshmallow of foggy obliqueness. She unstuck her tongue from her mouth with difficulty.

"What happened?" she asked thickly.

Sheldon shrugged. "We watched some movies, took some drugs. You don't remember?"

She shook her head. "I'm so thirsty," she said and Sheldon grinned his gummy little smile.

"I take good care of you, I told you." He opened a plastic bag and handed her a can of diet Seven-Up. She grabbed it from his hand and downed it in one mouthful.

"Ow," she said. "My head hurts. In fact, all of me hurts."

"I got you some Chinese noodles," Sheldon said.

"Oh, I'm so not hungry," Benny replied, wondering why she felt so bruised and sore. Even her ribs felt crushed.

"Suit yourself," he shrugged and opened up a bag of food. "So, tell me," he said, conversationally, grease on his chin, his back against the wall, "are you enjoying yourself, Bertha Gertrude?" He said her name slowly with relish, watching her expression.

She sat up in shock. "Have you been going through my things?"

He shrugged. "You're in my house. And by the way, that's not the only lie you told. First off, there's no Benny, there is only Bertha Gertrude, who is you." He pointed a chopstick in her direction. "And what's more, you are not twenty-five, you are TWENTY-NINE!" He shouted the last two words.

She was frightened. "So what?" she asked. "So what if I call myself by a name I prefer and so what if I lie about my age a bit? What's the harm?"

"The harm, Bertha Gertrude, is that you lied. A man without his word is nothing. Haven't you heard that? Don't you know? You lied to me. I opened my home to you and you lied to me. Liar. Liar."

Benny sighed. "I don't like my name," she said, "I don't like my age. I can do whatever I want." Her head was throbbing badly and she couldn't understand why her ribs hurt.

"Nope," he said. "You can't. You must tell the truth. You must tell me the truth."

"Why? I don't owe you anything?" She felt as if she was talking to a madman.

He got up, pushed his food aside and lit a joint. "Bertha Gertrude, you twenty-nine-year-old lying bitch. Yes, you heard me. Why are you so ashamed of who you are?" he asked. "Why?"

Benny rubbed her neck, which also seemed sore and tender. "I never wanted the life I was born to, okay? And no one says I had to, either. Not you, not anyone. It's my life and I can make of it anything I want to. So I made Benny out of Bertha Gertrude – I made me."

"Well, I beg to differ," he said. "And don't think I don't get it, I'm not stupid. You're not the perfect princess you wanted to be. I bet your parents don't have money; they're not up to your standard either. You choose to let that shit matter. Success, what's success? Success is being who you are. Being true to yourself."

"As if you do that," she blurted out. "You sold drugs to those people, and you took drugs with them, with that baby in the house, then you said they were wrong, so you lied about what you did."

"No, I did not. It's not my baby. It's not my house. They're fucked up. I just am who I am."

She realized there was nothing left to say.

"Anyways," Sheldon said, looking crafty, "you think you're in control but you're not. You think you remember everything that you say and do, but you don't."

Benny was baffled. "What on earth are you going on about now?"

He cocked an eyebrow. "Last night," he said. "Tell me what you remember 'bout last night."

Benny thought. "You know I don't remember," she said. "I already told you. Why are you being so difficult?"

"Just tell me what you remember," he spoke slowly, as though she were an idiot child.

"We watched movies and smoked hash. There, are you happy?"

"Yeah, we did that. And then?"

"And then nothing. What's with you? I've had enough of your stupid games." She got up to go. "I'm going to read and leave you to bond with your computer like I know you like to do. A couple of wankers, the both of you."

He looked at her through a thick haze of smoke. "You enjoyed last night," he said slowly and she stopped, her back to him. "You enjoyed every minute. You were making all the right noises, and now you tell me you don't even remember?"

Benny felt sick. A man without his word is nothing. She turned back to him. "Are you telling me we had sex last night? We didn't. I would remember that, I would know that."

"You think so? Let me tell you something, Miss I-don't-really-take-drugs – you were right out of it."

"So you like making love to a corpse then. That's your idea of fun then?" Benny was shocked, sickened, cold.

"Oh, you were moaning all right. You enjoyed it from what I could tell. How was I to know you wouldn't remember?"

"What specifically and exactly did we do? And I'd like to know it all okay?"

He told her.

She stared at him for what felt like a long time. Then she grabbed her smokes. "I'm going out," she said and he shrugged.

"Not my fault if you can't handle your drugs," he said. "I'm only telling you to be helpful. You lie to yourself all the time. I'm only trying to help."

"Yeah, by raping me and throwing it in my face," she wanted to say but she couldn't speak.

She walked out into the afternoon, not caring where she was going. She found the park, sat on a bench and lit a cigarette. She hugged her arms around herself with her knees up to her chest. She heard a keening sound and realized it was coming from her.

Oh God, I'm so sorry. I don't remember, I don't remember. How could I let him do that to me and not even remember?

She hated herself. She should have taken better care of herself. How naïve, how arrogant she'd been. She'd thought she was in control always. She'd always been scornful about people who got into trouble, thinking she'd never do that. And now she had. She opened the door and let a dirty man violate her.

She sat, chain-smoking with her thoughts whirling in circles of self-blame and doubt. Then, anger at herself, rage.

Time, given the long day, was warped and twisted and Benny felt utterly adrift. She still felt strangely drugged, hungover, weird. She dozed on and off, lying on the bench, and hoped it was safe for her to sleep, but regardless, she was unable to stay awake.

A couple of young mothers were there with their babies, and Benny told them she'd had a rough night, and she asked them to look out for her if they were going to stick around. They gave her cigarettes and told her not to worry. Once, when she woke, one of the women handed her a coffee. It was lukewarm, milky and sweet and Benny gulped it down. The next morning Benny woke to find the park deserted. She sat up, shook her head gently. It was clear, the fog and pain had gone. She walked back to the apartment with reluctance. Sheldon was splayed out on the mattress on the floor. He was naked, out cold and snoring like a pig.

She packed her bags. She was dying to have a shower but loathe to use his washroom. But better to use it, than have to carry his filth.

She took a deep breath and grabbed her toiletries. She locked the bathroom, undressed and examined at her body. She was covered in bruises on her neck, her breasts, her arms and her stomach. Love bites and teeth marks patterned her skin and even the tender flesh on the insides of her thighs was bruised. She stood for a long time, seeing her body in a way she never had before. It was her body, hers, and it was precious.

She had a long hot shower and she was gentle, apologizing as she soaped and cleaned. She wiped the steamy mirror clean with a towel and looked at herself.

Winnebago of my soul, you're my motorhome, baby. I won't let you down again.

She dried off and got dressed in fresh clothes, the softest in her backpack. Then she went out and grabbed her stuff.

Sheldon was awake, raised up on one elbow, watching her. "Going so soon?" he asked sarcastically and she nodded.

He sat up and rubbed his bullet-shaped scalp hard, his thick, blunt fingers raking his short hair. He cleaned out the corners of his eyes, yawned and got to his feet.

"I'll take you to the bus stop," he said.

"I'll catch a cab," she said, icy.

"Oh princess, stop with that crap. A cab won't even find this place and I can tell you're in a hurry to leave."

He pulled on some shorts and a T-shirt and yawned again. Then he lit half a joint he found.

"So, take me to the bus already," she said, exhausted.

"Keep your little panties on, I'm coming," he said.

Benny couldn't think of anything to say on the drive to the bus.

When they pulled up to the café, Sheldon held out his hand, his fist closed. "Hold out your hand," he said and when she did, he dropped a large chunk of hash into it.

She couldn't help herself. She took it and closed her fingers around it.

"Let it never be said I didn't take good care of you," he said and grinned, his teeth tiny yellow Chicklets, his smile gummy.

"Yeah, let it never be said," Benny said, and she got out the truck. "So long, Sheldon." She wanted to tell him to rot in hell but didn't want to give him the pleasure. She hauled her backpack down and then she turned her back on him, heard him drive away and she headed for the café.

PLAN B AND A SILVER-THREADED SCARF

Once inside the café, Benny asked the short-order cook if she could leave her backpack behind the counter and he agreed. He stared at her with open curiosity.

"Aren't you Sheldon's new girlfriend, the one that came in on the bus a couple of days ago?"

"I guess I am," Benny said, making sure her locks were in place.

"He was bragging about you like crazy," the young guy said. He had a face full of fierce acne and he was chewing on a toothpick. "He said you were a real class act and he needed a couple of days off to show you the town. Joe was pissed off with him for that. Sheldon's always missing work."

"So, my backpack is safe there?" Benny had no desire to discuss Sheldon.

"Yup, safe as houses. Don't you worry. My name's Alvin and I'll take care of everything."

"I'm going for a walk," Benny said. "My bus leaves in twelve hours, I guess I've got some time."

Alvin laughed. "I won't be here all that time but Joe will, and he's the boss."

Benny left the café and walked down the street. She was looking for a drugstore. She went into a badly lit plaza with a McDonald's, a convenience store, a Chinese takeout, a dry cleaner, a purse and accessories store, and a pharmacy. Of these, only the McDonald's, the pharmacy, and the convenience store were open.

Benny went into the small, old-fashioned pharmacy. The shelves were low and white-painted metal, the aisles narrow and dark.

Benny pressed a silver bell on the pharmacist's counter.

"I'll be with you in a minute," the voice called out. Benny leaned over the counter and saw a tall woman with dark curly hair counting pills. From her accent, Benny thought she must be from the Middle East.

Benny sat on the cracked brown visitor's chair and waited.

"So," the woman said, coming over to Benny and standing with her hands in the pockets of her white coat, "what can I do for you?"

The woman's photo I.D. had her name, *Sima*, below the picture.

Benny hesitated. "I very foolishly had unprotected sex last night. I'm hoping you can give me that pill, the morning after one."

"Plan B," the woman said. She looked at Benny closely. "Are you all right?"

Benny nodded but her eyes filled with tears. "I'm totally fine," she said, "fine. Really. I just need to take care of this."

"I understand," the woman said. "But you know the pill won't protect you against any diseases?"

"Yes, I know," Benny said. "And you don't have to tell me how stupid it was, to have sex like that. I know."

"I would never call you stupid." The woman gave a sort of a smile. "I'm only trying to give you the information you need."

Benny got up. "Well, I'm good. Just need the pill."

"And may I say, a scarf perhaps? Or maybe you'd like to see someone..." The woman was trying to be diplomatic.

Benny had forgotten about her bruises. "Oh, right. No, I'm fine. Well, sort of. This was all my fault anyway. I got drunk, I let this happen." She didn't want tell the woman about the drugs.

"It's never your fault," the woman said. "Even not knowing a single thing about what went on, it's never your fault. Be angry with him, not yourself."

"But I put myself in the situation," Benny argued.

The woman shrugged. "I had a husband who hit me for twenty years. I thought he loved me. I thought I loved him."

"The thing is," Benny hesitated. "I was so drunk I don't even know how I got these bruises. I mean, he told me all the stuff he did but I don't remember. How can I not remember? I'm so angry with myself for that."

"Sometimes," the woman said, "not remembering can be a gift." She placed her hands gently on the counter. "He did the terrible things to you, he is the one to blame. My advice: take your gift of not remembering, and walk away."

Benny sat down again. "But if I do that, then I'm giving up responsibility for my role in the whole thing."

"No," the woman said. "You are making a choice." She shrugged. "Let me tell you something. Where I come from, a lot of bad things happen to a lot of women. It's not their fault. And what do they do? They get on with their lives. If you don't want to bring this man to justice that's fine, but don't torture yourself with the punishment he deserves."

Benny took a deep breath. "I don't want to waste any more time in my life on him, that's for sure," she said. "So can I get the pill? I'd rather be safe."

The woman got the package ready for her and Benny paid.

Another customer came up to the counter as Sima was explaining the side effects to Benny, and she waved him away, telling him to come back in a few moments. The man looked at Benny's neck and left.

"You're right, I wish I had a scarf," Benny said. "I hate this."

"Wait here for a moment," the woman said. She disappeared around a corner and came back with a scarf.

"Not your style exactly," she said, smiling, "but in a moment of crisis…"

"In a moment of crisis, I'm very grateful," Benny said. "Listen, do you have a business card or anything? I'd like to be able to thank you when I get home, whenever and wherever that might be."

The woman waved her off. "Sometimes my dear, it's permissible to simply accept a gift from another. You don't have to thank me."

"Well, then I thank you now," Benny said, wrapping the scarf gently around her neck. "It's beautiful." The scarf was long and crimson and sewn with silver thread.

Benny left the pharmacy just as the man was coming back. He stared pointedly at her scarf.

Benny went to the McDonald's and got a coffee. Then she swallowed her pill.

HOW MUCH IS TOO MUCH?

Ten hours later Benny was back on the bus. She was the first to board, viciously elbowing the gangsta boys out of the way and grabbing the back seat. She was looking forward to twelve hours of shut-eye and would let no one challenge her for that. The bus driver, same dude who looked like MacGyver, grunted a "Hello" at her and picked his teeth.

Benny arranged herself at the back of the bus as if she had her own private room at the Frontenac. She made herself a comfortable nest and lay there for a while, thinking. That Sheldon was rotten and wormy to the core, there was no doubt and she wasn't going to torture herself with self-hatred or blame. She'd just take better care of herself in the future. Which led her to a question – did she really do too many drugs? How many was too many?

It had all started way back in school, so way back that she didn't even know if she could stop. Did that mean she was an addict? How could she know? She layered on another sweatshirt; she couldn't seem to get warm. She tried to calculate how many pills she took daily and lost count.

She leaned into her bag and sniffed the chunk of hash he'd given her. It was so delicious. Rich, aromatic and dark. She thought about how the first step in any program is the acknowledgement of that problem. But first she needed to assess whether she had a problem or not. No point in acknowledging something that didn't exist. Therefore step one was to evaluate the situation. Carry on as normal and simply be aware. She pulled out a scrap of paper and a pen, while the bus bounced along. She downed her usual mix and made a note.

Two codeine, one sleeping pill, one mini Southern Comfort: nighttime sleep mix. She looked at her watch. It was 6:00 a.m. She packed the piece of paper away and snuggled down.

One thing was for sure. No men for a while.

She selected a soothing playlist, pulled on her sleeping mask, and fell into a coma, aided by her meds.

BEAUTIFUL BROKEN LITHIUM BOY

She woke as they were crossing The Great Slave Lake. *The Replacements* was on one more time. Benny went back to sleep. And thus she made her way back down south.

She decided to detour to Grand Prairie and do an overnighter there instead of going the whole way down to Edmonton. Her legs were aching and the inside of her mouth felt like she'd been chewing on a wet fluffy toy. She felt like she'd escaped from a wild animal, a feral encounter. She thought Sheldon made Mickey look like a boy scout, and she repeated to herself that she was not going to hook up with any men unless she was one hundred percent sure they were solid.

She had to change buses to get to Grand Prairie. Of course she did. What was more surprising was that she didn't have to do more than the one change. While she waited, she smoked a cigarette, aware that her love affair with nicotine was now fuelled more by boredom than lustful craving. She flicked the half-smoked cigarette away and joined the lineup for the bus.

She was aware, boarding at Valleyview, that she was joining a crew who'd been together for a while and she counted herself lucky to find a two-seater of her own. She sat down and regrouped. She had a monster headache brewing from a multitude of directions. She decided the only course of action was to mix medications with a cavalier hand; come at it from all angles.

She took her meds and looked around the bus, stopping at a vision of a boy draped across the seat next to her. He was vampirically pale and gothic, with bleached white hair; he was as delicate and elegant as a butterfly. He had matching bracelet tattoos on each pale slender arm, with blue-green veins visible beneath his milky skin. Benny counted eight rings piercing his right brow alone and she knew she was staring but she didn't care.

After Mickey's determined chaos and filth, Sheldon's brutish heaviness, this boy seemed a wonder bleached clean from sin and darkness. Benny reminded herself of her vow: no men, or boys, and she thought it would be easy to stick to because it was highly unlikely the boy would even notice her.

She watched him wake from his slumber and uncoil as gracefully as a snake. Awake, he was nervous, jumpy, and restless. He tore open a bag of red licorice and lowered a piece into his mouth like a carnival trick. He ate a couple more pieces, tapping his foot, shifting and constantly rearranging his position. He finished his candy meal, dug a pair of rectangular blue sunglasses out of his bag, and fell asleep again at a neck-breaking angle. Benny was mesmerized.

They arrived in Grand Prairie at 8:30 a.m., a decent hour for once. Since it wasn't an obscene time of the night, Benny stood uncertainly, unsure where to go, caught unawares. She heard somebody cough politely behind her. She turned around to see the boy.

"You'll like this," he said to her by way of introduction, handing her a CD. "It's been a long time since I saw a girl in a Static-X shirt."

Ah, the *Wisconsin Death Trip* sweatshirt scores. Benny had absolutely no idea who the bands were, that she so freely promoted: Misfits, Papa Roach, Static-X. Like who cared anyway? She was all about the sweatshirt design – the visual part of this equation.

She thanked him.

"Tell you the truth, I've got no idea who these guys are," she said. "I like the graphics."

The boy laughed. "I'm Ryan," he said. "I would shake your hand but I don't like to touch people."

"I'm Benny. Why don't you like to be touched?"

He shrugged. "Dunno. Just don't. Hey, where are you staying? I'm hanging out at my aunt's place. She's not there. You're welcome to come and crash if you like."

"You know, I'd love to," Benny said, forgetting her vow in a split second. "Although I don't know if I'll be great company. I've just come down from a brutal encounter in Yellowknife and I need to emotionally detox."

The boy pulled a thin yellow and red book out of his pocket. It had an Indian mystic on the cover: *Scientific Healing Affirmations*.

"Here," he said. "This will help. Keep it. Let's grab a cab."

Benny pocketed the book and followed Ryan out of the tiny bus terminal.

His aunt's house was a low bungalow of yellow brick with a paved walkway leading up to a brown door with yellow glass panels. The grass on either side of the path was withered and dying. Ryan picked up a lonesome garden gnome and shook out a key. He opened the door and stepped inside.

"Phew, could use some airing," he said.

This was an understatement. The house was crammed thick with hot dead air.

Ryan pulled back the thick floral curtains and opened the windows. Benny looked around.

"She likes floral, yeah?"

Ryan laughed. "She does. She'll be back in a week, so stay as long as you like. Let me show you to the guest room."

He led her down the narrow carpeted hallway that was lined with pictures in dark frames. The pictures were oil reproductions of dogs with forlorn faces. Benny wished she had gone to a motel instead.

"Here you go," Ryan said, and he pushed a door open and stood aside. The room was a shrine to a sporting legend, the walls glittering with polished trophies of all kinds.

"Wow," Benny said, looking around at the sparkling array. "Whose are these?"

"My cousin. He was killed in a drunk-driving accident when he was twenty-three. He was good at all kinds of sports stuff. My aunt never got over it. And then there's me, fuckup supreme." He smiled in a self-deprecating and yet appreciative kind of way, as if the level of mess he'd achieved was a badge of honour.

254   LISA DE NIKOLITS

Benny wanted to probe him for details of his own personal disaster, but she was distracted by the room.

"I don't mean to be difficult, mate," she said, "but I can't stay here. I'd be too worried I'd mess it up and it's like there's the spirit of a dead guy in here."

Ryan was perplexed. "It's only to sleep," he said. "He's dead, he won't care. Why are you so sensitive? I can't let you sleep in my aunt's room. She'll notice, so you'll have to take the sofa."

"But then where will you sleep?"

"I sleep outside, under the stars," Ryan said. "I like to be free of earthly pain. My last doctors, they wanted me to take lithium but I said no way, man, I can transcend this shit. It's all in that book I gave you."

"What do you mean?" Benny wished they would leave the boy superhero's room. It gave her the creeps. It was all locked up and dead. She saw a large framed picture of the boy. He had a thick neck, small eyes of an indeterminate colour, sandy hair and a smattering of acne across his bulldog cheeks.

Ryan laughed softly. "What I mean is the book. The book is how I'm going to transcend it all. I've got it committed to memory. That's why I must sleep in the garden." He brushed past her lightly, taking care to hold his body away from her. "Let me show you the rest of the house."

IT WAS OBSERVATION

"This is the washroom," he said, showing her a wine-coloured bathroom with floral towels and china fixtures. There were even yellow and blue flowers on the taps. "Make sure to clean up after yourself. My aunt is particular."

Benny looked around. "Sure, no problem. If there's one thing I've learned, it's how to clean a bathroom. So, listen, why did they want you to take lithium?"

"Anger," Ryan said vaguely. "Are you hungry? I am. I'm always hungry.

I like being hungry. I hate being satiated. Being hungry keeps you closer to God, you know."

Benny wondered if she could tell him how beautiful she thought he was. But there was something odd about Ryan so she decided to stay silent with the compliments.

"So, listen," Ryan said, "you want some tea or something? My aunt has lots of alcohol here. I don't drink, ever, but you can."

Suddenly all Benny wanted was a drink. "You know, I think a drink would be lovely."

She inspected Ryan's aunt's supply and found an expensive bottle of Kentucky bourbon. It was half empty.

"Stellar," she said, filling a glass with ice cubes and rich bourbon. She took a generous mouthful. "Can we sit on the sofa?"

"I sit on the floor but you can take the sofa." Benny had noticed that Ryan was prim rather than graceful – contained rather than elegant. He was also much younger than she'd first thought.

"How old are you?" she asked, sitting down on a rock-solid shiny floral settee. "Actually, I think the floor will be more comfortable." She slid off the settee onto the plush beige carpet and laughed.

"That was like a fun fair slide," she said.

"Just don't spill anything," Ryan said. "My aunt will kill me." He smiled beatifically and gazed up at the ceiling. "I'm nineteen."

"That's awfully young to have been in rehab or whatever," Benny said, "although I guess there is no age limit."

Ryan looked at her through half-closed eyes, his bleached hair falling across his forehead. "It was observation," he said, "not rehab. I'm trying to make dreadlocks but my hair won't co-operate." He shook with silent laughter and hugged his arms to his skinny chest. He was covered with a fine downy hair. He was silent for a while and she thought he'd fallen asleep but he opened his eyes.

"Read the book," he said. "You'll see. It will free you." He yawned.

"We're good that I sleep in here, right?" Benny asked. "That room, it freaks me out. Or I can sleep in the garden with you."

"I don't have intercourse with anyone," Ryan looked at her in an accusing sort of way and Benny laughed.

"Listen," she said, "Sure, you're beautiful but not every woman wants to sleep with you, me included. I guess the house gets super hot, that's all and if there is karmic enlightenment to be achieved from sleeping on the lawn, well, I'm all for it."

Ryan smiled. "Do whatever you like," he said politely.

Benny wondered why he'd invited her to stay. Perhaps it was on the merits of her Static-X shirt, and he was regretting it. "Are you sorry you asked me over?" she said. "I can easily go to a motel you know. We can get me a cab."

Ryan's eyes flew open. "Of course not," he said. "Why? Are you sorry you came? Am I a bad host?" His eyes filled with tears. "I'm so stupid with social things, aren't I?"

"Not in the least," Benny rushed to reassure him, "I was feeling stupid, that's why I asked. I thought maybe you thought who is this socially inept idiot you brought home. I thought you were regretting it and I wanted to give you a way out."

Ryan smiled, relieved. He closed his eyes. "Well, that's alright then," he said.

Benny drank her bourbon like it was diet Coke. She got up and refilled the glass.

"If you drink so much that you throw up, don't make a mess," Ryan called out, his eyes still closed.

Benny laughed. "Don't you worry about me, mate." She sat down on the carpet and looked around. Half the furniture was covered in plastic and one of the table lamps was an ornate gold cupid balancing on crystal blocks and reaching a plump little arm up to the gold-fringed shade. All the plants and flowers in the room were perfect and it took a moment for Benny to realize they were fake. Plastic floor runners protected the carpet and a pine coffee table held an unused thick glass ashtray. Everything was shiny and pristine, except for the La-Z-Boy in the corner. It was chocolate brown, worn and well used.

"Who sits in the La-Z-Boy?" she asked.

"My uncle used to but he's dead. He gassed himself in the car after my cousin died."

Benny was shocked. "My God, there's a lot of tragedy in your family."

Ryan laughed and opened his eyes. He put his hands together, prayer position and rested his chin on the tips of his fingers. "You have no idea," he said. "We are one fucked-up gene pool."

"But your cousin, he wasn't a genetic tragedy. He was the all-sports star."

"Yes, he was our salvation, our one hope for normalcy. But he couldn't stay because we aren't allowed. He was too good for us, we all knew it. I mean take my family. My mother remarried this complete fuckup…"

"But what happened to your dad?" Benny interrupted Ryan and he seemed irritated.

"He left. Anyway," he said pointedly, "my mother remarried, my stepfather hates me, so I left to live on the street. I was homeless, sleeping on benches and stuff. Then I had to go in for observation and now I've come here."

The details were frustratingly vague to Benny but she realized that was all she was going to get.

Ryan looked at her. "You wanna watch TV or something?"

"I'd love a nice hot bath," she said, and Ryan leapt to his feet.

"Water," he exclaimed, "heals everything." He led Benny down the hallway and pulled two large towels out of a closet. "Take as long as you need. Meditate on the healing power of the water. Let it cleanse you."

Benny closed the door with relief and told herself she had to stop accepting these weird offers of accommodation.

ART COMES HOME

Benny soaked in the bath, luxuriating in the hot stinging water and she nearly fell asleep. Suddenly, out of nowhere, she was filled with the craving to paint, a longing so strong she felt it physically in her gut.

She jumped out the bath and pulled on her clothes, still half wet.

"Ryan," she called, zipping up her black leather trousers that were quite shapeless by now, "is there an art store nearby and will it still be open?" She was exhilarated by the revival of the desire she had thought was quite dead.

She rushed out into the hallway and nearly bumped into Ryan who backed off at high speed.

"A what?" he asked, bemused.

"An art store." Benny couldn't get the words out fast enough. "A proper art store."

"Yeah, sure," Ryan said, "At the big mall. I think they're open 'till 10:30 p.m. We'll just make it. You want me to call a cab?"

"Immediately, if not sooner," Benny cried out, she felt ecstatic and Ryan, wary of the manic mood swing, took a step back.

Benny laughed. "Don't you worry, I haven't lost the plot of sanity here. All I need are a couple of canvases, some acrylics and some brushes. I haven't gone loony-tunes on you, trust me."

Ryan called a cab, his long fingers dialing with careful precision. Benny found his childlike slowness infuriating and she wanted to hurry him along.

"You're all speeded up," Ryan chided her. "The bath was supposed to slow you down." He shook his head. "Well, at least in the mall there is this great Ayurvedic takeout place. We can get supper from there. It's all very cleansing and pure."

"Sounds fantastic," Benny said, her mind on a colour palette of purple, gold, lilac, pink, orange – all the colours of the sunsets she loved.

Inside the mall, Benny gave Ryan money to buy food, and then she rushed into the art store. She stood for moment, inhaling deeply. *Home…* She grabbed a basket and started plucking from the shelves with precision.

"Do you need any help?" a scornful teenager appeared.

"Nope, I'm good thanks," Benny beamed at the girl who looked startled.

Benny paid for her stash and found Ryan sitting near the food court, gazing up at the skylights.

"Food courts are so disgusting." He wrinkled his nose. "Troughs of swill. Look at all the people, filling up on crap, filling their bodies, polluting themselves."

"Yes, come on, we must go," Benny wanted to pull him to his feet but she recalled his aversion to being touched. "Let's go, I'm dying to paint."

"You're very strange, you know," Ryan commented, but he was smiling. "But you seem happier. It was the water, it helped you, I'm glad. You're going to love this nan bread, it's very – "

"Pure." Benny interrupted him. "Yes, I know. Hey, Ryan, while we're here, at the mall, is there anything you want?"

"Yes, please. A *Men's Health* magazine," he said, without even having to pause for thought.

Benny burst out laughing. "Well, I never," she said, "I would have thought you'd want a copy of Yoga Life or something."

"More practical tips in *Men's Health*," Ryan said, seriously.

Back in the suburban bungalow island, in the middle of the sea of dying brown sunburnt grass, Benny set up her studio in the kitchen while Ryan lay on the floor of the living room and read aloud to her from *Men's Health*.

Benny was nervous for an instant, then she picked up a brush and dipped it into a glistening swirl of paint, delighted by the old familiar action.

Cerulean Blue Chromium infused with late summer evening Phthalo Blue, a horizon of Cerulean Blue Deep for undersea aqua. Don't forget the egg yolk of Primary Yellow for setting sun backlight and then negotiate Yellow Iron Oxide and darker tones of Nickel Azo Yellow. Change to a big brush for Titanium White and mix in echoes of a dawn to come, carrying the ghosts of the day.

When she looked up again, Ryan was fast asleep on the floor, his one arm outstretched, his magazine beside him. It was 4:00 a.m. Benny gave a great sigh and turned back at her work. She had started two canvases, working on one while the other dried. She had absolutely no idea if they were any good at all. She didn't care a jot either. Her fingers were covered in paint and she hoped she hadn't made too much of a mess. She poured herself a large bourbon and took a swig, pulling at the nan bread, which was delicious. She stood at the counter, eating cold vegetarian curry and nan bread, drinking bourbon, and looking at her art.

DAWSON CREEK CALLING

She woke later that morning with a stiff neck. The sun was streaming down on her, and she dreamt she was under a tanning lamp, sharing bad decorating tips with a bunch of strangers.

"Floral," one woman had insisted. "You can't go wrong with floral."

Benny sat up slowly, and looked around for Ryan who was watching her from the kitchen counter. He waved, a leftover piece of nan in his hand. "This food is good for breakfast too," he said, his mouth full. "Hey, I like your paintings. They're totally fucked but in a good way."

Benny laughed and eased herself up off the floor. She wandered over. "They're very unfinished and rough. What time is it?"

"Nearly one o clock," Ryan said, gathering crumbs with his spidery fingers. "What do you want to do today?"

"Dunno," Benny was still half asleep. She sensed Ryan was keen to help her on her way. "What time does the bus leave for Dawson Creek?"

"I'll phone and ask them." He dialed carefully. "Okay, thanks. It leaves at 3:00 p.m.," he told Benny.

"I'll clean up all my mess and head out, if you don't mind," she said.

"Of course I don't mind," Ryan said, "it's been wonderful having you as a guest. It's been enlightening." He gave a small bow. He had a fine growth of pale fluffy stubble on his face.

"What do you want to do with these?" he asked, pointing at her two paintings, while she piled the empty paint tubes into a bag.

She glanced up. "I've no idea. Good point." She stood up.

Ryan examined his nails. "I could buy them off you. I mean I don't have any money right now, but I will one day and I'll pay you then."

"You want them?" Benny was surprised.

"I love them!" Ryan burst out. "I love them."

"Ryan, if I could, I'd hug you." He looked alarmed and she grinned. "But I know you're not into that so I won't but honestly, it makes me very happy that you want them. You can have them, a thank-you prezzy from me to you. Wait, I'm going to take a photograph of them, for a keepsake."

Ryan followed her as she went to get her camera bag. "Are you sure?" he asked, "I don't want to intrude or put you in an awkward position where you can't say no."

"Ryan, it's hard to explain but painting them was the gift for me, not keeping them. I really want you to have them." She took a few photographs, cleaned up the rest of her mess and gathered her things.

"Don't forget to sign them," Ryan said. "You're going to be famous one day and these will be worth a fortune but I'll never sell them, ever."

Benny laughed. "I wouldn't bank on the fame part if I were you, but I'm glad you like them anyway."

She gave her paintings one last glance, thanked Ryan again, and went out to the cab.

Benny, collector and cataloguer of every doodle since she was a child, left her art without a backward glance.

HANG THE BROKEN HEART HIGH

She made it to the bus and got stuck next to a guy sleeping ugly. His mouth was open and he was making a strange snuffling noise. She closed her eyes and relived the brush strokes of her paintings. Her art was back. Nothing else mattered. She buried her face in Sima's scarf, which still held hints of her exotic fragrance. Benny wore the scarf constantly. Her bruises were turning virulent yellow and green and she knew this meant she was healing but she looked worse than ever.

They drove north to Dawson Creek, heading toward the Alaska Highway and the landscape was majestic with giant wonders. They rolled into Mile Zero at 6:00 p.m., and Benny had an hour to explore. As always, she found great photo opportunities, and a sign that said: "Dawson Creek. Zero Mile and the Official Starting Point of the Great Alaska Highway." And, in case you missed that one due to subtlety, it added, as a big P.S. in large engraved type: "You Are Now Entering the World Famous Alaska Highway."

Benny strolled the environs and spotted a '48 Studebaker for sale for $7,500. Oh, how she wished she could. And one day she would, with a better partner riding shotgun than Mickey. She admired the car through the wire mesh fence and reached for her necklace. She undid the clasp and noticed that a couple of the sparkle stones were missing. She fastened the necklace to the fence and took a photograph of it.

"Sayonara, Mickey-O," she said. "And for the record, I did fall in love with you. Wherever you are, I hope you try to fly straight."

Then she rushed back to the bus, just in time to join the fight to board. Benny elbowed her way to a prime spot and got a double seater all to herself right up front, with a massive uninterrupted picture window.

Her plan had been to bus to Anchorage, Fairbanks, Skagway and Juneau, but she felt that route was overly ambitious. And while Alaska would no doubt be incredible, this trip was all about Canada.

She organized her bag and settled down, daydreaming back along the route she had travelled. The Yellowknife leg hadn't been a total disaster. She'd never forget Fort Providence and joining the little kids to buy ice cream in the tiny wooden store that was more like a shanty. Outside the air was so clear Benny wanted to drink it. The evening light shone low beneath purple clouds, glinting off puddles, and sparkling on the gravel. Wooden houses, so distinctly Canadian, with clean electrical lines geometrically etched against the darkening sky.

Benny snapped awake, realizing she had dozed off. They were stopped in Nampa – a town filled with farmer's wives, children, dogs, pickup trucks, a thousand muffler stores closing soon, and cowboys with Western shirts untucked over expansive stomachs.

"Have fun on your trip, Suzy," yelled three little boys. Benny looked out the window at petite bespectacled mom holding hands with two boys, a toddler standing in front of her. Suzy boarded shyly, clutching a peach-colored pillow. She was an awkward mixture of pre-adolescent independence and old fashioned family ties.

"Lunch today will be at 11:00 a.m. and supper will be at 5:00 p.m. We'll get to Whitehorse at 4:30 a.m. in the morning." The bus driver spoke into the microphone after he hacked up something that he then had to mop up from between his legs. Benny realized there might be drawbacks to her chosen seating arrangements.

9:15 a.m. The bus stopped in Port St John. Benny wondered if she should leave the bus for the delights of the Northern Pacific Gas or perhaps for the vacuum store next to the auto glass across the street. Not looking like a whole lot of photo ops out there. Well, maybe the Bowling Lanes building offered something of a roadside attraction.

She decided to get off the bus to use the washroom in the terminal and returned to find a number of folk apologetically waiting to board. She immediately dashed back to guard her prized spot. She simply could not go all the way up the world famous Alaska Highway, until 4:30 a.m., with a person crowding her. Not possible.

LORETTA LYNN RIDES THE RANGE

People continued to board. A woman hovered over Benny and asked if she would care to share.

"Uh, thank you, but you know what, if at all possible, I'd rather not," Benny said but she knew the woman would return. The woman's get up was thorough: cowboy hat, stiffly curled and hair-sprayed blonde locks, country-style denim-clad and silver buckles on everything. Benny spied her moving down the bus and stopping at two empty seats but she turned and came back to Benny. Benny reluctantly shifted her camera bag to the floor.

The bus started its engine; all systems go. Benny felt sleepy even although air con was on maximum blast, super-freeze. Loretta Lynn, sitting primly next to Benny, had her hands carefully folded in her lap, a back-support pillow wedged firmly in place.

Benny was worried she was getting the flu again, and she was quaffing cough mixture in generous swigs. While Loretta chatted to the bus driver, Benny admired the scenery and saw a lone wolf standing against a clear sky. Also, she was seeing llamas everywhere, but that couldn't be right, best she slow down on the cough syrup. She made a note to check her guidebook for llamas in a more sober moment. She also wished she'd see a moose.

3:00 p.m. They stopped in Fort Nelson for a leg stretch. A sign said: "We make your business our business." Benny figured she could always end up a business card designer at the Fine Signs and Stationery store but she thought it unlikely she'd end up in Fort Nelson despite the allure of the thriving business card design industry.

She dozed off and woke up convinced she was ill again. She tried to tell herself that the gritty-eyed feeling was due to lack of sound sleep, and her aching knees were the result of too much bus travel. She also felt horribly jumpy, startling at the slightest sound. Her hands were shaking and her mouth felt dry. Her brain was like a shrunken pea that had rolled under the kitchen counter – desiccated, wrinkled and green. She dug into her bag for a chocolate and gave a quick glance at the woman beside her who was now asleep. Benny thought she looked more like Sissy Spacek than Loretta Lynn. Or were they the same person? She couldn't remember. She decided there was something creepy about Sissy Loretta, what with her ringletted, hairdoed perfection, her unflinching happy-with-life half-smile, her perfectly clasped hands and her poised serenity as if she were sitting in a sunlit church. At that moment, Spacey Loretta opened her eyes.

"So, where're you from?" she asked.

"Uh," Benny reached for the simplest answer. "Toronto."

"You don't sound Canadian."

"Technically I'm from Sydney, Australia."

"Ah, I thought so! Have you been to Canada before?"

"I've lived here for the past year." Benny glanced down at the reading material in Sissy's lap; it was enthusiastic Christian literature. Benny dug out a trashy tabloid magazine and hoped Sissy would realize she wasn't a kindred spirit.

"And are you married?"

"No, my husband left me for another man."

Sissy's hand shot to her mouth. "Oh, you poor, poor thing. I'm so sorry I asked, forgive me."

Benny waved at her. "It's fine, really. He's happier now. So am I. I'm an artist and I'm planning a collection of works on my interpretation of the Canadian sky." She pointed out the window. "See the colours? They're fantastic. I've never seen colours like this."

"This is God's country," Sissy said, self-righteously.

"And thank God we can share it," Benny said.

Sissy shot her a look and asked, "Do you pray, dear?"

"I do, yes. It's called painting." Benny decided she had enough of Sissy.

Just before they neared Fort Nelson, Sissy started to pack up. At that same moment Benny saw a moose. Her first ever. Big fellow, he was crumpled and dead by the side of the road. It made her very sad so she turned to Sissy, thinking a chat would at least be a good distraction from the poor big dead moose.

"Where're you headed?" Benny asked.

Sissy told her she was on her way to join her hiker guide husband for ten days of trail clearing in the Rockies. It would take an hour by helicopter and four hours by horse to reach her destination. Following that, home to her ranch.

"Nice," Benny said, wondering how the hair would survive all that.

Sissy got off minutes later and once again Benny had the seats to herself. She relished the peace of non-Spaceness. Sissy had felt like quite the vortex of negative energy despite sitting quietly and not dishing out enthusiastic Christian commentary.

Benny decided that the scenery was so good she might just stay on the bus until her bus pass ran out, repeatedly going up and down the world famous Alaska Highway. It was that beautiful.

HE SHE THEY IT

6:00 p.m. The bus pulled into The Toad River Café. A smiling toad invited you in for a meal. What the jolly little chap didn't tell you, but what you soon discovered, was that his hospitality didn't come cheaply.

The menu was a high-priced one.

Benny ordered a fish burger and thanked her lucky stars she wasn't in the same leaky financial boat as the guy next to her who had counted out his quarters and couldn't afford the $4.50 soup – the cheapest thing on the menu.

Benny wanted to buy it for him, but she couldn't figure out a way to do it without being insulting and when she looked around again, he'd disappeared.

She finished her burger and went outside for a joint. She leaned against a tree, knocked sideways by the drop-dead-gorgeousness of the mountains and rivers around her. She flicked her lighter, ready to inhale deeply when she heard a voice.

"You don't need that."

She swung around but there was no one there. "Hello?" she asked, cautiously. "Hello? Anybody there?"

"You don't need that." The voice said it again and this time Benny knew there was no one there.

"God? Goddess? Universe? Hello? What don't I need?" But she knew the answer.

"You take too many drugs," the voice said.

"Uh, wait just a minute," Benny protested, but the air had gone silent and Benny knew the discussion, such as it was, was over. She put her lighter and the joint away, shaken.

Admittedly her drug intake had increased on the journey, by no small amount if you counted hash and cigarettes. She had been smoking much less though and her daily codeine and Valium intake was down due to the generous influx of hash. There was the breakfast joint, the mid-morning joint, lunchtime, mid-afternoon, evening and possibly, the before-bed-joint.

Yes, if she thought about it, it probably wasn't that great to be smoking so much of it. It would explain why she was so jumpy; she was startled out of her skin by the slightest noise.

She went inside to grab a tea for the journey. The soupless guy was staring at the chocolates, his hands in his pocket. "Listen, mate," Benny said, "can I buy you a coffee? Traveller's treat and all that?"

"Wouldn't say no," the man said, smiling to reveal missing teeth. "Been a bit down on my luck lately."

"Happens to the best of us," Benny agreed and ordered him a coffee, sandwich to go and chocolate bar for dessert.

"You shouldn't encourage people like him," a woman behind Benny said, after she'd given the meal to the grateful man.

"Never been in trouble, have you?" Benny asked the woman who snorted.

Benny got back on the bus, wanting to think about God and the chat by the creekside. It was hard to think though, because the bus was a stinking sewer of a place and that strong and damning description was perhaps an understatement. The latrine, the washroom, call it what you will the toilet's cup had runneth over onto the floor of the tiny enclosed space and right out onto the floor of the seating area. The bus driver said he was sorry about that, there was nothing he could do folks, but he did open his window.

The soupless guy, now looking more cheerful, poured his aftershave into the toilet bowl and the action did improve matters for about five minutes. That the addition of his cheap cologne was a step up gave some hint of the level of the disaster.

Benny sprayed a dash of her diminishing Gaultier into her facecloth, lay back and covered her face. She was keenly aware that she should have phoned ahead for accommodation in Whitehorse, but she had been too busy conversing with an admonishing God Goddess Universal Spirit. Although, to be fair, *He She They It* hadn't been admonishing, more kindly, like they really cared. Benny sighed. She realized she had been pumping her body with all kinds of crap: cigarettes, cough syrup, hash, sleeping pills, Valiums, Xanax, codeine, not to mention copius amounts of alcohol.

She refreshed her Gaultier facecloth and lay back to rest. She was grateful to be as far from the latrine as it was possible to be without riding the rest of journey on the rooftop of the bus; enter Priscilla, never mind *Queen of the Desert*, but *Escaping Queen of the Killer Latrine*. She could just see herself on top of the bus, her arms stretched wide, holding her facecloth out to the breeze.

DUE SOUTH, GOD OR JUST SOME WEIRD DUDE?

They got in to Whitehorse on schedule at 4:30 a.m., which Benny thought was a sick and disturbed hour. They staggered off the bus, which, for the sake of national health security, was yet another public transit vehicle needing to be set alight and the ashes buried. The terminal seemed closed.

"I close at 6:00 a.m. and open again at noon," the Greyhound Terminal guy announced when he finally appeared.

Benny looked around her, into the shadows. Where to start?

"It's not promising, is it?" A voice asked from behind her.

Benny jumped, thinking it was God again, but this time she got Paul Gross instead. A very young Paul Gross right out of *Due South*, only he wasn't wearing his uniform.

Benny and Shay had loved *Due South* as kids.

"Fraser?" Benny asked, peering closely at the man. "I think I'm hallucinating," she said. "I'm sorry I took all those drugs, God. I really am."

The man laughed. "I think you've got me confused with someone else. I came in on the porta-potty with you, remember? I sat across from you?"

Benny blinked. Right. She had noticed him earlier when the toilet disaster first took hold and he'd joined forces to fight the stench. She laughed. "Right. Sorry, I'm a bit tired. Overtired."

"Perfectly understandable."

Laptop, briefcase, designer specs, Prada shoes, great dimples, a bit on the short side and close-cropped preppy hair. But, despite being so clearly logo-marked for success, the man just wasn't Benny's cup of tea. He was too clean, too fiscal and too sanitized.

But at 4:30 a.m., as she stood there motionless, aware of the clock ticking its way firmly toward the 6:00 a.m. terminal shutdown time, she was not unhappy to see Mr. Due South.

"Call me Doc," he said and offered her his hand.

"A medical doctor?" she asked.

"No," he said, not caring to elaborate.

"We used to watch *Due South* in Australia," Benny blurted out.

Doc looked at her. "Yeah, I get that a lot," he said. "Listen, how's this for a plan. We'll go via my hotel and get me checked in. Then we'll find you a hostel and get you settled."

"I dunno so much," Benny said, "I haven't booked a room at the hostel. I should get there early, because if they do have a bed, I might miss out on it."

"Earth to Miss Australia, it isn't even 5:00 a.m., no one's stealing your bed. Come on."

Benny felt too fragmented to argue.

Doc got the bus terminal guy to order them a taxi and they got to the hotel, a very luxurious place. Doc was graciously and efficiently checked in while Benny was filled with envy at the quality of his abode. She audaciously priced a room only to be crushed. It was an entire week of her budget. So that settled that.

"Great," she said, once they had dumped his gear in the elegant room. "So, let's go and find the hostel." She was already heading to the door, when Doc pulled her back.

"Hang on a second," he said. "I want to unpack my stuff, I'll be speedy."

"Okay," she said, with clear reluctance, "I'm worried though."

"Relax," Doc said. "Chill."

Benny longed to lie down on one of Doc's satiny quilted double beds, but this didn't seem like the polite thing to do, so she perched on the edge of an uncomfortable armchair and waited it out while he showed her every piece of his Dolce and Gabbana Fall menswear collection.

"Lovely," she said repeatedly. "Wow. Yes, that's great." "Those shoes are awesome." "That tie is epic." "My God, what is that fabric?" "I can't believe the cut of that shirt."

As soon as he had finished unpacking and parading Whitehorse Fashion Week before his exhausted and trying-to-be-appreciative audience of one, she leapt to her feet.

"But wait!" he said, "I'm going to have the quickest of showers."

Why she didn't bolt out the door, was beyond her. It wasn't because she was feeling well-mannered, more likely it was immobility by exhaustion.

Eventually Benny and her fashionista maybe-angel headed outside. It was by now 6:30 a.m. Doc insisted on shouldering the load of Benny's backpack and she smiled a little when he staggered under the weight.

They finally made it to the hostel.

"But we're full," the owner said, taking an age to respond to their insistent knocking. "The last few beds went early this morning when the bus got in."

Benny thought she might kill Doc, bury the remains and take possession of his room. This was now all his fault. Whose bright idea was it to do the runway strut and have a nice shower?

Benny couldn't think what to do, so she just passively refused to leave.

The hostel owner sensed he had a problem. "Well, okay, so there might be one bed left," he said.

Ah. There usually was. Benny sat down in the living room while he disappeared to check it out. Doc made his excuses, bowed, and vanished.

SYPHILIS IN THE YUKON, GET TESTED!

"Who was that man?" asked Heinrich, the hostel owner, when he reappeared with good news that she did indeed have a bed, "and why was he carrying your luggage? Where did he go? And why was he so well-dressed so early in the morning?"

These were questions to which Benny had no answers.

Heinrich ground coffee beans and brewed a fresh pot and the entire world was instantly a more hospitable place. Then he seated her on the comfiest of sofas, said he was returning to his bed to snooze and that he would be down at 9:00 a.m. to sort out her bed – but not to worry, she did have one.

Benny sat on the sofa, cradling her mug of coffee and watching the world wake up. Lots of very active German hikers marched past on their way to conquer terrain. The hostel was impeccable. Heinrich had explained in painstaking detail what could be eaten from the fridge; free food was clearly labeled as such. Everything in the hostel, from the living room to the interior of the fridge was arranged by geometry. Benny could tell she would have to make her bed very neatly and properly before she could lie in it. None of that approximate sheet positioning here.

She watched more Germans popping up to greet the day, chatting, waving maps and strapping on ankle bandages. A lot of ankle strapping was undertaken by one very serious couple who wound and unwound until they got it exactly right, and then they buckled on backpacks, money belts, and cameras.

At 9:00 a.m., Benny was given her very own bed and a key to the front door. She lay down immediately, delighted to be stretched out and horizontal.

The bus from Dawson Creek to Whitehorse had taken one day and eleven hours. According to the math, Benny had now traveled a total of 9,621 miles but she decided to subtract the flying miles, more interested in the numbers on the ground. Which left her having covered 7,460 miles or 11,936 kilometres on this, the 64th Day of her Grand Canadian Adventure. Her money was holding out okay. Apart from a few T-shirts and a few fridge magnets, she'd been frugal and it was sad but true to say that the nutritional junk food detour had helped her funds enormously.

Facedown in the pillow, all she wanted to do was to sleep, but her exploring instincts kicked in strongly and she dragged her unwilling body outdoors. But the day had turned into an unwelcoming one. Gale force winds were blowing strongly; it was cold and the rain was an unforgiving downpour.

Benny, protected in her Churchill waterproof leatherette, did her by-now usual exploring, photographing, doughnut-eating discovery of the town's highs and lows. She had realized that she could create a routine under just about any circumstances.

She also found one of her most favourite street posters ever. It floated toward her, carried like a gift on the gusty wind.

Syphilis Outbreak in Yukon! Get tested! Use condoms!

Benny put it carefully under her waterproof jacket until it could be added to her collected treasures of found art.

She loved Whitehorse. It was everything she had hoped Yellowknife would be.

At 3:00 p.m. she crawled home, sank down into her neatly-made German bed and slept for three hours straight. Then she went back out into the extreme weather to seek fresh produce, following which she headed back to the communal kitchen to exchange stories with a girl called Michelle who was studying forestry in Ontario. It was her second career. She had been a nurse and she wasn't sure if she'd made the right choice with the tree saving thing.

"Who knows, maybe I'm not cut out to be a tree hugger, man. Hey, your food looks so nice and healthy."

Benny was chopping up a gigantic salad.

"I'm trying to connect with my former healthy self," Benny said. "I've been on a bit of a junk food binge, you could say. It's been darn delicious but it's time for some of the good old greens."

"Looks great," the girl was envious. "It's just that it's so expensive."

"Couldn't agree more," Benny said. "Here, you can have some, if you like."

CLEANING UP HER ACT

Benny tried to heed the word of *He She They It* and take fewer drugs. The hash joint she'd been about to light up at The Toad River Café, when the Godly Beings stopped by for a chat, was one of the last in her stash and she ditched it into the Yukon, along with the marble-sized piece of hash she had left. She stopped the daytime self-meds and alcohol, and made a deal with the Universal Spirit to halve her sleeping pills and nighttime codeine until her life got back to normal.

Once she had a real job, a place to live, a life to call her own, she'd work at eradicating them entirely. Cigarettes had been easier to give up than hash. Benny realized she didn't miss the inside of her mouth tasting disgusting and feeling furry, she loved her fingers not smelling of nicotine, and her clothes and hair not reeking of smoke. She'd hardly been smoking much anyway, just using what she needed for her joints.

She did miss her hash, oh yes, she did, but somehow, what with the Message of the Ancient Spirit reassuring her, she knew she didn't need the drugs. And she was still disconcerted by what had happened with Sheldon, and she realized that looking out for herself in the future was better done sober.

She suddenly realized, with utter horror that she'd lost count of the days since she'd been on a computer. She had no idea what was going on in the real world and with her family.

After supper, she found the hostel's small computer room, which was housed in a former broom closet. While she waited for the computer to access its brain, she perused the posters on the corkboard wall: canoe trips, a bus service down to Skagway, helicopter rides. All sorts of adventure activities – all of them expensive.

She logged on to her email to find two dozen messages. A bunch were from her family, increasing in frenzied concern until she read one entitled "Kenny phoned, all good." Apparently Kenny had phoned Dad, to share the good news of Benny's call and they knew from that, that she was fine, just on the bus. Benny felt bad for not having thought about them sooner. She had fallen into another world where things were different. She sent them a long update and apologized for having been out of touch.

There were a number of emails from Teenie, Chrystal, and even a few from the doeful Colin; job offers from Teenie, scathingly brilliant ideas from Chrystal, and Colin saying that Benny's successor had failed dismally – that he'd do anything if only Benny would come back. Benny spent hours replying and it was close to midnight by the time she got to bed and she fell into a twisted sleep, with all the people in her life engaged in an operatic dance and her future uncertain.

The next day saw another perusal of museums, art stores, and churches. Benny sat for a long time on the banks of the Yukon River that sparkled and bubbled over large polished pebbles. Later, she bought a dog tag with Whitehorse engraved on it and hung it around her neck with a piece of chain she bought at the hardware store. She thought about the necklace it replaced, the damaged heart she'd left behind on the wire mesh fence in Dawson Creek.

She came across an affable guy playing the guitar and she gave his hat a donation. Then she met another real sexy fellow, who gave her directions back to her hostel, she, having lost her way. He invited her to a jazz session later that night, but jazz had never been her thing and she'd seriously decided to give up on men for a while.

She came across two stretch limousines parked side by side, facing opposite directions. The one limo was black, the other white – both had inscrutable mirrored windows. They were parked in the middle of a vast parking lot that seemed, inconceivably, to double as a sports arena of some kind, with bleachers set off to the side. Benny wanted to get closer to the limos but there was something slightly ominous about the scenario. She zoomed in with her camera lens and walked away only to bump into Doc who was climbing down from the bleachers.

"Howdy," he said. "How's the hostel working out for you?"

She eyed him warily. "It's good. What've you been up to?"

"A little bit of this, a little bit of that, you know how it goes." He brushed imaginary dirt off his trousers and grinned at her, a flashy smile, with sharp teeth.

"You want to have dinner with me tonight?" he asked.

"No thanks, I'm sorted for entertainment. In fact, I gotta run, I made a date to meet someone." She backed away, her hand raised in farewell. Doc gave her a mock salute and a bow, walked over to the white limo and rapped on the door. The window lowered and when Benny left, Doc was standing next to the stretch, talking into the black window, his trousers whipping in the wind.

Benny wondered if she could live in Whitehorse. She sat down again next to the river, thinking and studying the sky, examining the colours.

SKAGWAY, NO ELK CARCASS THIS

Two days later Benny was sitting in the warm comfort of Mabel's Espresso Café in Skagway, Alaska, eating a cranberry and orange muffin, and drinking half a liter of Raven's Brew Coffee, *The Last Legal High*. She was thinking about her journey down and getting her facts and figures up to date.

Her last day in Whitehorse had seen her wakened at 9:00 a.m. by Heinrich, who was perhaps concerned that she did indeed like Whitehorse enough to be staying indefinitely.

Benny had forced herself to leave the comfort of her bed, got organized and headed out to breakfast on her farewell-to-Whitehorse doughnut.

Post-doughnut, she set off to locate the bus pick-up spot. The route to Skagway wasn't covered by Greyhound, and separate funding had been required.

She'd booked a ticket on the mini-bus taxi service to Skagway, operated and manned by one Andrew David Moore, a gruff, military type of fellow in an extremely bad mood. Apparently there were two no-shows for the day's run and Andrew wanted to wait for them.

"They're simply running late," he growled, positioned like a big army Ken Doll, his legs braced, arms crossed and biceps bulging.

Andrew was engaged in a standoff with an uptight, stressed-out fellow who was insisting ad nauseam that they depart immediately, as he needed to be in Skagway by 2:00 p.m. for the ferry. The man was fiftyish, an oil executive engineer-looking sort, with precision-trimmed grey facial hair, and he panicked out loud while Andrew busied himself trying to track down his AWOLs. At US$75 a pop, Andrew didn't want to leave anyone behind.

The ferry seeker, Alan, tapped his foot, studied his watch and broadcast his angst loudly. Andrew frowned and prowled the street for his missing cargo. Benny put the opportunity to good use and popped into Aroma Borealis, the store next door, to smother herself in free body-lotions.

She was sadly reminded that the northern lights had evaded her and she had yet to see a live moose.

She got back on the mini bus, moisturized and sweet-smelling, to find things had not improved. Alan was practically swinging from the roof in anxiety, while Andrew was an immovable stone monolith. Behind, the two Germans, a husband and wife team – the enthusiastic ankle bandagers from the hostel – sat quietly, uninvolved.

Alan told Andrew that they had to leave, that they were now officially late. Andrew said they were going to wait. He said they would make up the time.

"But I want to watch the scenery, not fly through like a rocket," Benny spoke up.

Andrew eyed her. "You're free to find alternate transportation any time, young lady."

"No, no," Benny said. "Never mind me. It's all good," and she sat down quietly.

Andrew finally admitted defeat. Not too graciously, it might be added. He accelerated out of Whitehorse in a cloud of dust and Benny set her camera for high speed and pressed her face to the window taking shots of the flying-by scenery. Andrew began to make quick stops.

"We must let the young lady take her pictures," he said, in a surprising change of mood.

Benny could tell Alan wanted to throttle her. He kept repeating, "I have a ferry to catch at 2:00 p.m.," until Benny thought she was going to throttle him. There were a lot of throttling desires swirling within the close confines of that hurtling little minivan.

"Alan," Benny said amicably enough, through gritted teeth. "Mate, let's be clear here, we've all noticed you've a ferry to catch. You can stop saying it now."

Then Andrew started taking pictures of Benny taking pictures, which incensed Alan even more. He sank into a furious, seething silence.

They passed a tiny desert en route, the Carcross Desert, affectionately known, said the sign, as the smallest desert in the world. Originally a glacier lake, it added.

They dropped the ankle-strapped German couple off shortly thereafter;

they were going hiking and camping in the mountains. As the pair set off, leaning forward at a steep angle, facing directly into the icy wind and stinging rain, Benny wondered if their vacation was turning out to be what they had imagined. They hadn't spoken much at all, and despite their wedding bands, they never touched. The only time Benny had seen them converse was when they were leaning over a map; he'd uttered two words in a question and she'd answered with one.

They drove through a spectacular landscape of emerald-green lakes with rocks, boulders, glaciers, rivers, streams, greens, blues, mists, yellow moss, red and purple wildflowers. Benny told *He She It They* that they'd chosen a most pleasing and magical blend of powerful paints and textures.

Andrew spent a good amount of time arranging Benny properly for one final photograph. It was the *Welcome to Alaska* sign at the border.

"We must get this one perfect," he said seriously and Alan snorted loudly.

They arrived at the Skagway, Alaska ferry stop at 1:45 p.m. and Alan flew from the bus like a wild animal.

"Delighted to have met you. It's been a real pleasure," Andrew said and he took Benny's hand in his immense one. "You do have my business card?"

"Yes I do, and thank you, that was good fun," Benny waved goodbye and strolled off to find a place to stay.

There were no hostels in Skagway and she opted for the Gold Rush Motel and its offer of free fruit for breakfast, all day tea and coffee, and a souvenir pen.

Skagway was a beautiful gem of a place and a tourist haven, the currency of which was in terrifying US dollars. Benny saw a fabulous coat for a mere US$7,000. She ventured into the stores with extreme caution just in case money disappeared from her credit card by her simply being there.

Country-sized cruise ships sailed majestically into town and off-loaded their overfed guests, letting them loose into souvenir city with sacks of money to burn. Benny watched them, noisy turkeys, with money fluttering around them like confetti at a wedding. She saw their age-spotted jewel-encrusted hands reaching for anything and everything, while she, jobless and poorer by the day, realized to her surprise, that she didn't want what they had, not in the least. She wouldn't trade her Whitehorse dog tag necklace for all the rubies in India, or her hostel beds for the goose-downy duvets of the cruise ship cabins. But it would be nice, she thought, to be able to treat her parents to a cruise one day, have them swan about in the lap of luxury and enjoy being waited on for a change.

Yes, Skagway was Mecca indeed for the bored travel tourista looking for expensive goodies to lug back home.

Meanwhile, Mabel's Café, tucked around the corner of a side street, escaped the attentions of the fur-coated spendthrifts, and was visited instead by scores of local shop owners who stopped by for their morning cuppa brew. They all said it was a good season but that they were getting weary. The local girls waited tables, chattering about love life gossip and nail polish.

Benny, watching from her checkered-cloth table, felt right at home in the tiny sheltered port, safe from the tourist-driven storm raging on the main street. She wondered idly what to do next. Mabel's was so nice that she thought she might stay for the day, drinking coffee and doing not much of anything. Jeanie, the proprietor of Mabel's, had it stocked full of wondrous soaps, candles, cards, and knick-knacks, and the music selection was so great it made it hard to leave. Benny had found a box of watercolour pencils in a hidden stash of art supplies as well as a pad of good art paper, which cost nearly as much as the coat she'd seen, but art was always worth the money and besides, she wasn't buying cigarettes any more.

A sexy lad in his mid-twenties dropped by for an espresso and he smiled at Benny. He stood around inside, lingering. Then he wandered back outside and looked in at her through the open loop of Mabel's "a". He smiled, gave her a half-wave, looked hopelessly down at his hands, smiled again and disappeared.

Benny watched him leave, grabbed a takeout coffee and went down to the harbour to try out her pencils. She was spellbound by the misty and scenic prettiness of Skagway surrounded by glacier-covered mountains.

It was a precious gem of artistry in the jewelry box of the world's natural beauty. And who knew? With a name like Skagway. It had sounded about as inspiring as the carcass of a dead elk since no history buff on the Gold Rush was Benny.

Sitting cross-legged on the wooden dock and looking around, she paused mid-sketch, realizing that she'd lost her driving fascination with things old, abandoned and destroyed. She'd spotted a good number of ruined houses and sheds in Skagway that her former self would have delighted in, but here she sat, content to wallow in the splendor of her natural surrounds.

She laughed out loud, causing a group of passing tourists to look at her oddly. They were all clutching bulging bags and she wanted to say to them, "stop shopping, look around, see where you are."

"But don't you wish you had somebody?" Loretta Sissy Space Cadet had asked, her parting shot before she got off the bus. "I mean, not all the time for sure but sometimes?"

Benny, drawing furiously with her new pencils, thought about Sissy's question. No doubt it would be nice to have someone to share this incredible moment with, but there were times when being your own best friend wasn't such a chore either.

THE MAGNA CUM LAUDE CHEERLEADER BLONDETTE

Early the next morning, Benny was waiting for her boat ride down to Juneau. She had scouted out the various ways of getting down to Prince Rupert and decided to splurge on a little tour boat and go via the Inside Passage, the mere utterance of which gave her goose bumps of excitement.

Sailing the Inside Passage to Juneau, Alaska. She could hardly stop herself from jumping up and down and screaming with joy and unrestrained excitement.

She was sitting on the dock of the Skagway Bay, watching the tide roll in and wash back out. She was quiet in the unearthly stillness, appreciating the rare moment of other-worldly beauty. The most hurried movement was the slow floating of the early morning fog as it drifted by.

Her peace was disturbed by the noisy arrival of a chaotic flailing woman who stumbled down the steep ramp, her bags threatening to topple her. Benny had watched the unsteady descent with some concern. The woman looked to be in danger of snowballing at any moment and Benny was directly in her path. She made it safely to the bottom and stood next to Benny, heaving in great gulping breaths of air.

"So, where're you from?" the woman asked, before she'd even unloaded her heavy unevenly yoked shoulder bag.

"Toronto," Benny said, hoping that would be the end of it and knowing it wouldn't.

The woman frowned. "You don't sound Canadian. Where are you from originally?"

Sigh. Benny was trapped on a beautiful dock with yet another relentless interrogator. She gave the abridged version on autopilot.

"I'm Susan, a nurse from Whitehorse," the woman said, unasked, "traveling down to see my friend in Juneau. I'm delighted to meet you."

"Likewise, I'm sure," Benny said.

"So, what do you do for a living?" Susan asked. "It's just that I'm envious, mind you. I'd love to travel, be a free spirit, and not have a care in the world."

Fortunately Benny's ship chose that moment to sail in and she was saved from having to converse further. She just didn't want to waste the beauty of the moment in idle chatter. She climbed onboard the boat, and muttered a "Hello" in response to the deckhand's "Hi, I'm Julie!" Benny immediately saw Julie's future – a suburban housewife feeding on Xanax, and sobbing hysterically when she wasn't rictus grinning. Julie was such an eager-beaver super-keen cheerleader type that Benny immediately wanted to throw her overboard.

Benny spotted a load of fresh blueberry muffins on a tray and her happiness level shot upwards off the barometer. She found a seat at the front of the boat and stowed her belongings. Then she got a mug of bad coffee just to warm up. While the temperatures weren't cold by Canadian terms, it wasn't exactly summer at the beach either. Benny waited for the muffins. She was ready already. Bring on the muffins.

They set sail and glided on down, on the lookout for bald eagles. Miracles of nature elbowed each other for attention: glaciers, seals, gravity-defying, crystal clear waterfalls set higher in the mountains than one would think it possible, boulders, mists, mirror-still-reflecting waters – all this stunning stuff and how about those muffins, please Princess Julie, Homecoming Queen?

They arrived in scenic Haines, where they acquired more passengers and set off again. Yet more glaciers, seals, eagles. And still, no muffins. Benny was about to weep with hunger and desire when she spotted a couple of bird-watchers brushing crumbs off their laps.

"Could I please have a muffin?" she asked Julie humbly.

"When I get to that side of the boat," the cheerleader answered smartly, bending over to serve in her very brief, very white shorts, and she turned away from Benny to shine her super-white smile in the direction of a smitten liver-spotted old dude.

"Huh?" Benny had been standing right next to her. But, not wanting to rock the boat in any way literal or otherwise, she went back to her designated starboard side. Half an hour later she got her muffin and cherry-flavored fruit juice although Julie did try to forget her again.

But Benny didn't care about the bouncy Miss Julie. She was sailing in one of the most beautiful places in the entire world with a freshly-baked muffin in her hand. She could count on one hand the times in her life when she had been that level of happy.

Replete, they moved on to whale spotting. Julie was so excited by the appearance of the whales that she nearly threw herself overboard, saving Benny the trouble. She was so excited that the passengers stopped watching the whales and watched her instead.

Benny spotted at least two dozen humpback whales frolicking and spitting into the air. She knew there was a more accurate term than spitting, but she couldn't remember what it was and she certainly wasn't going to ask Julie.

The only less-than-spectacular part of the boat trip was that it ended too soon. Benny could have stayed onboard for weeks. Even with the magna cum laude cheerleader blondette.

BARE-CHESTED BOYS STIR HOT FUDGE

Benny got off at Juneau feeling strangely panicked. Three seconds after her feet touched solid ground, she could tell that Juneau was not the same friendly little pond that Skagway had been. Big fish swam in these waters and Benny was not financially equipped to be a big fish.

And, as always, she was correct when she sensed there was an oncoming reason for concern – it cost her US$30 to get to the hostel by cab. She nearly wept in pain. When she got to the hostel, she found it closed; a daily occurrence, since the sign on the door said they were closed between 10:00 a.m. and 5:00 p.m. Everybody had to exit the hostel during that time; no dwellers were allowed to remain inside, everyone had to return later.

The sign also said – it was a long and detailed sign – that it was permissible to store stuff in the shed around the back. This seemed a little too trusting for Benny, but she investigated and yes, others had put their faith down on the ground, so she too lowered her luggage.

She had no idea if in fact she even had a bed although she had phoned this time, having learned the hard way from the Whitehorse near-calamity.

Given her financial concerns, the next thing she did was go to the Alaska Marine Highway offices to check when she could leave. It was Tuesday, and the soonest the Kennicott left for Prince Rupert was Thursday. She was going to have to be frugal to the max.

Too exhausted to do any more walking, she joined a $10 tour bus, content instead to sit back and watch it all go by. She got chatting with a mother and daughter choral duo from Kamloops. Passionate travelers, contented companions, they had toured Australia some time back and were in Juneau for this year's vacation on one of the super-sized cruiseliners that boasted sixteen restaurants, ten bars, and endless buffet spreads. Benny told them how she'd loved Kamloops and they beamed.

The tour was headed to the Mendenhall Glacier and its legendary mile-wide face.

Standing at the foot of the glacier, Benny could see why it was legendary; it was inscrutable and magnificent – a big old elephant, sleeping anciently, oblivious to the fleeting poking human curiosity.

Benny eavesdropped on conversations of things to be on the lookout for and apparently the salmon were spawning. Benny felt that while perhaps she should be interested in checking it out, watching salmon spawn had never been high on her bucket list. And anyway, didn't spawning simply mean that the unlucky fish had reached their final destination, that it was time for one last hurrah followed by sudden death? Who wanted to watch that?

She climbed back on the little tour bus and went back to Juneau. She explored the Old West-styled stores along the boardwalk and lingered for a while at the Fudge Factory which had the added bonus of bare-chested boys positioned outside, stirring huge vats of hot caramel. It smelled so good that passersby couldn't help but stop and exclaim in wonder. Benny thought it endearing how the aroma of melting caramel magically transformed both old and young into beaming happy innocents, regardless of financial status or social power. Then she did the responsible thing and ate a meal of good food, choosing the Armadillo Café, a trendy place filled with locals, where she ordered a halibut burger and watched the shoppers scurrying by. While she was enjoying eating healthily again, she vowed she was never going to let the fanaticism of her dietary past dictate her menus again.

She thought she was doing well on the pill front, too, and true to her word to *He She They It*, she was still only taking her nighttime meds. But, oh, she had to admit, she did miss her hash. The crumbly texture, the sweet spicy smell, and the feeling of beautiful warmth that flooded her body with that first deep hit.

Yeah, God or Whoever, she thought. *I get that I don't* need *hash but want it? Mmm, it was so nice.*

She congratulated herself for making the responsible choices in life and took a large bite out of her mouth-wateringly delicious halibut burger, thinking that a fudge dessert was imminent.

HOUSE RULES AND CONDITIONS: PLEASE PAY ATTENTION!

4:00 p.m. Benny crawled up the vertical hill to the hostel, thinking Juneau certainly had some steep inclines.

4:15 p.m. She stared down a group of Germans who arrived at high speed, breathless as they came to a stop and looked at the door in hopeful expectation.

4:50 p.m. A Japanese fellow dashed up as though half the world were chasing him and flung himself down on the porch.

4:57 p.m. The hostel owner arrived and instructed the crowd to wait three minutes. The Germans tried to get in immediately despite the three-minute warning.

"Three minutes, just like everybody else," the implacable hostel owner said and he closed the door against a pressing German hand.

Benny couldn't help laughing. "We're like rabid beasts," she said out loud, but no one shared her humour. She shrugged.

5:00 p.m. The sign swung from closed to glorious open. Benny was ready for the starting gun to be fired and she sprinted to the lead and inquired meekly about a bed. She had learned to read the body language of the hostel owners and this one wanted meekness and a bit of begging.

"…and you'll have to do kitchen chores at 10:00 a.m. tomorrow," the owner concluded after briefing her on "The House Rules and Conditions" that came with an allocated bed.

"Okay, that sounds fantastic!" Benny said with great enthusiasm. At that point she would have agreed to bear the dour hosteller's children.

She found her way to her tiny piece of bunked bed real estate, and got nicely disorganized on the surrounding floor space. Then she headed down to the common room where a South African told her she had an odd accent.

Benny wanted to tell the girl she had an odd haircut and a strange sense of style but she just shrugged.

"Listen, is there any way I can do my chores now?" she asked the stern hostel owner. "Thing is, I want to go sightseeing nice and early and all that."

The hostel owner was not happy by this change of plan, but he said that Benny could clean and dust the common room. She rushed around, spraying, wiping, cleaning and dusting, thereby entertaining her idly-reading and lounging fellow hostellers who seemed very amused by her willingness to actually pitch in. Benny sensed they'd lied to the level where they refused to do any chores at all, once they'd landed their beds.

She finished her housework and took a shower. It took half an hour to read the small print in the washroom, but she followed the instructions carefully: turn on the fan, then the light, adjust the shower mat according to steps one to three, complete the shower and wipe it all down as per instructions four to seven. All that, just to get clean. She thought she might have to take a few days' vacation from showering, given the logistics.

She got back to the common room and settled down to plan the next day. Lots to do for sure. She checked her email and Teenie had another job offer for her and this one even sounded interesting. She gnawed on a finger, put together a letter of application and sent it off, with a note of thanks to Teenie. She couldn't help but laugh – Teenie, never mind Betty Boop, was like a pitbull terrier – determined to have Benny settle close to her.

Chrystal had sent an email too but she sounded glum, not her usual scathingly brilliant self. Seemed her plans to relocate out west weren't working out and her leave-of-absence hourglass was running out of sand.

Benny sent her a long note, telling her to keep her chin up and asking her if it was the worst thing for her to go back to Toronto? And hey, how's this for a scathingly brilliant idea, maybe they could even share an apartment … she stared at what she'd written. No, it was too much of a commitment, she couldn't offer that. She wasn't even sure she was going back to Toronto despite the job application she had just sent off. She erased the bit about them staying together and sent Chrystal a note of general good cheer, assuring her friend that things would be fine, they really would.

Then she admired pictures of Shay's growing baby, Harry, and sent them a long update.

With a growing lineup of frowning people wanting to use the computer, she logged off and sank into the sofa, thinking about the Fudge Factory and how wonderful it had smelled. She looked around, feeling right at home among the other hostel dwellers, all of them pouring over maps, guidebooks and journals.

"Anyone game to hike up Mount Roberts tomorrow?" The question came from the girl who had told Benny her accent was odd – the one Benny had thought was South African but who turned out to be British instead.

In the spirit of the moment, they vowed to do it; all for one and one for all and Benny went to bed, tired out and happy.

JOLLY LITTLE BRITS TAKE OVER THE WORLD

Benny woke to the sound of pouring rain.

"It's much too wet to climb the mountain," one girl observed from under her cozy bedclothes, with only the smallest bit of her face peeking out. Benny remembered her from the night before for the vast quantities of Kraft Dinner she had consumed. Benny couldn't understand the North American love affair with Kraft Dinner, which, to her, tasted like badly-cooked macaroni with sawdust. But then again, North Americans seemed equally underwhelmed by Vegemite.

"Totally too wet!" Benny agreed, similarly happy under the covers.

"Yes, way too wet," chimed in another girl, part two of the Kraft duet.

"Nonsense, it's perfectly lovely," the little Brit insisted.

"But it's really, really wet," the warmly-tucked up, safely-dry bedfellows said. "Take a look out there; it's pouring with rain."

"Oh, nonsense! It's lovely," the little Brit said again. "Come on, let's go. Get dressed. We have to leave the hostel anyway. You know the rules."

Benny figured this was how the Brits conquered the world, with incessant jolly-hockey sticks and bullying good cheer. She pulled on her socks – she was the only sucker willing to follow the trim little British bottom up the rain-drenched, fiercely vertical mountain.

Less than two hours later, they had ascended a sheer 1,000 feet.

"That was incredible!" Benny said, soaking wet from sweat and the tropical torrential downpour. She was particularly proud of herself for not having fallen off the sheer slippery jungle face that was Mount Roberts. That alone had taken a series of skills she wasn't even aware she had. Some might call it the desire to remain alive. She had also been inadequately attired for hiking; PVC leatherette was great for being stylish and waterproof, but it was not the fabric most highly recommended by The North Face as good hiking gear.

Great rivers of sweat were running down the insides of her trousered legs and she was waterlogged both inside and out. Mud covered her shoes, her hair was plastered to her skull, and she'd never felt more alive.

"Well, we just hiked four and a half miles to the summit, 3,819 vertical feet, and we're now at the 1,760-foot level," the little Brit said.

"I'm very glad I didn't know that," Benny said, "because I wouldn't have made it. Wow, doesn't the air smell great? All woody, wet and earthy."

The little Brit, whose name was Phoebe, laughed. "Yeah, well it would, wouldn't it?"

Benny and Phoebe went into the cash-cow entertainment centre around which the gondolas circled, dropping off tourists with a desire to spend indiscriminately. It was also a good place for the weary to dozily watch a National Geographic movie and rest. Benny suggested to Phoebe that they do just that, and for the life of her she had no idea what they watched. It could have been global warming, or bears killing spawning salmon or bald eagles nesting. Her hike had tired her out.

They investigated the souvenir shop and nearly fainted at the price ranges. Insanity. But, contrary to all sense and sensibility there it was – the line-up for the checkout counter, reaching right out the door.

They took the Mount Roberts Tramway down, passing impassive bald eagles on the way. They went into the Red Dog Saloon and drank diet Cokes while admiring the décor, authentic old style West. But try as she might, Benny just couldn't get excited about the gold rush part of it all. Granted gold had been birth-mother to many of these northern-hemisphere towns but she thought the beauty of the land far outshone the dusty sparkle of the tales of greed.

Hungry from their exertions, they stopped in at the Armadillo where Benny introduced Phoebe to the halibut burger, which was met with enthusiastic approval. Content, they checked out The Brass Pic, estab-lished 1898, House of Negotiable Affection, and strolled by a popcorn wagon selling reindeer sausage.

"Surely that must be a joke," Phoebe said, frowning. "I can't see them really selling reindeer meat? Do reindeers even exist?"

"Maybe moose are reindeer?" Benny offered.

Pondering the matter, they walked over to the impressive three-storied State Museum and stayed for hours. Benny was entranced to discover that a bald eagle's nest was the size of a pickup truck – both truck and nest were suspended from the ceiling, side by side.

They saw all manner of wondrous things, not the least of which the snow and ice-wear fashioned hundreds of years ago. Benny saw the original creative for a thousand mega-cool contemporary brands – in particular, a pair of eye shield protectors carved from bone, putting Ray-Ban to shame. Not to mention the outerwear – stylish to the max.

"And handmade, too," Benny marveled, "with the crudest of tools. Nothing shabby on the fashion runways of the ice caps, I'll tell you that." Phoebe laughed.

Following that, they jumped on the $10 tour bus because Benny wanted to show Phoebe the glacier, which was no less impressive the second time around. Then they went to the post office to write post-cards. Unstoppable, they toured the town one more time, popping in and out of the Fudge Factory. They found an organic health food store where they stocked up on fresh produce and hiked back up the hill to their home.

They were back at the hostel at 5:00 p.m. on the dot. They traipsed in and smiled nicely at the hostel owner. He might be a tad old-fashioned in his ways, but his ship was neat as a pin and homely.

Benny packed up to leave. She had to be up at 4:00 a.m to catch a ferry with the Alaskan Marine Highway. She went to prepare dinner and met Phoebe.

"That was such a perfect day," she said to Phoebe who was slicing tomatoes, "of mountains, museums, walking, photographing, exploring, discovering."

"Don't forget shopping," Phoebe said. "Although I do wish we could have done more of that. Juneau is so expensive."

"Terrifying," Benny agreed.

THE CRUISE SHIP LOTTERY

3:30 a.m. "Benny? Benny?" Benny was woken by an insistent voice and someone shaking her. It was Phoebe. "Can I come with you? I must get out of Juneau immediately. And can you lend me $13?"

"Sure, no worries. Of course you can come and of course I'll lend you the money."

4:00 a.m. They stood on the side of the hilltop waiting for their bus ride, which was a mere $6. When Benny thought back to her $30 cab ride, she felt quite ill.

Phoebe and Benny thought they were lugging big backpacks, but they were accompanied by a sweet Norwegian girl who was practically carrying a house. Benny and Phoebe were in awe.

5:30 a.m. They boarded the ferry.

"Wow!" Benny said, overwhelmed by surprise and good fortune, "This ferry's a cruise ship!"

She'd been imagining they'd be on something akin to the tugboat ferries that populated the Sydney harbor. Sweet as they were, they were tiny by comparison and would hardly have rated as lifeboats on this ship. Their very own cruise liner, at a hundredth of the price!

"Yeah, it's very cool," Phoebe said. "Let's see where we can leave our stuff."

The captain was helpful and pointed them to a covered deck lounge where they could sleep on the floor. They staked out a spot and settled down.

"What is it about a ship," Benny said, "that makes one feel so unfettered by life's burdens? The freedom of being on water? That it's like an island haven afloat far from the shores of the real world?"

Phoebe laughed. "All of the above."

Their explorations completed, Benny sat down to read *The Shadow of the Wind*, a book that she'd found at the hostel. She sat facing the wake, with her feet up on the railing. They were back in their sleeping saloon with large surrounding windows, protecting them from the drizzle and the damp but granting them full accord of the natural magnificence that surrounded them. They watched whales and porpoises in the green glacial water.

"Planetary perfection," Benny said, grinning. "Poetry in motion."

4:00 p.m. They passed Petersburg. For some unknown reason, Phoebe was growing restless while Benny was happy to be doing so much with so little effort. What she was seeing was so unforgettable, so totally awesome that she could hardly take it all in, and the only thing she had to do was sit back and keep her eyes open. This was her kind of wonderful. Her feet were grateful too, as was her brain – no map consulting, budget checking or hostel accessing. Just sitting in the lap of luxury, humming along.

Later she roused herself, for the sake of the increasingly discontented Phoebe, to go up to the entertainment lounge where there was a talk on whales and what their teeth were made of. Benny tried to memorize the facts of this natural wonder but she could only summon up a vague image of interwoven palm fronds.

"Krill? No," she said to Phoebe who couldn't remember either. "That's what they ate, but what did they eat the krill with?" They both lost interest in finding the answer to this question.

After the talk, they hung out in the lounge where there were too many people for Benny's liking, none of them appreciative of the awesome surrounds. Who on the planet could be playing cards when they were in a place of such amazement? A good many folk, it seemed.

They got talking to a fifty-year-old guy named Steve who was an international English Second Language teacher. "Oh, how I wish I were twenty years younger and had more hair," he said to Benny.

He seemed generally discontented with life and a touch bitter at how it had all panned out. Benny was getting grumpy with all the conversation. She wanted to get back to her book and her view of the Inside Passage, aka *The Mega Wonder Nature Show*.

She left before she could get outright snippy.

Later that night, she lay on her bed on the floor, wedged up against the warm carpeted side panel of the ship. She was surrounded by resting bodies. One industrious privacy-seeking couple had even pitched a tent of sorts.

Benny wondered what her future held, and she thought about the raven who accompanies people on their journeys, seen or unseen. The raven, the trickster who made it all happen, this world as it is.

"Have courage," the Tlingit people tell their children.

"When? And for what?" Benny wanted to know but she guessed the answer was for everything, for life.

She wished *He She They It* would pop up again and give her a life map with nicely drawn directions and instructions enclosed, so she could know exactly what it was she was supposed to be doing, and where she was supposed to be.

"Have courage always. For everything," the hum of the ship's engines seemed to murmur and Benny gave a mock salute of acknowledgement. Wasn't that the truth? Everything worthwhile took courage.

In four months, she'd be thirty years old. It was a big one, a milestone.

She'd thought it would be so easy, leaving her homeland and coming to Canada and it had been. She'd been blessed by Colin's generosity, and she felt that the very land had embraced and welcomed her. It was as if the ancient spirits wanted her to take root; the elders wanted her to paint their skies. But, as her trip end grew closer, she was faced with the decision: stay in Canada and try to build a life, or go back to Australia and be with her family.

She felt torn by the decision, recognizing, perhaps for the first time in her life, that her actions affected her family too. She'd always rushed blindly toward what she wanted, without apology or thought, beyond thinking that she was right to do the things she wanted. But she realized it wasn't a matter of right or wrong – it was a matter of love and kindness.

She turned over, getting closer to the warm side of the ship. She sensed Phoebe was awake beside her. She didn't think the little Brit was having such a good time, but she couldn't help her out there.

Life, Benny thought, drawing her fleecy wrap tightly around her, is a treasure hunt. And if you get it right, the true beauty is the opportunity of the quest – not the currency or consequence. And sometimes, when you least expect it, just when you think you're in for a tugboat ride, you land a cruise ship instead. So, I'm sorry, Phoebe, but this trip is what you make it.

BACK ON THE BUS AT RUPERT

The guidebook said Prince Rupert was unremarkable. The guidebook couldn't have been more wrong.

"This," Benny said to Phoebe, "might, in fact, be the most beautiful place on the entire planet."

Phoebe nodded, seemingly not as impressed.

Benny gazed out the bus window in reverence and wonder. It seemed like she'd spent a lot of her journey gazing in awe but this was perhaps the most inspiring yet. Mossy cliffs and sheer mountains. Dense slender rainforests. A million shades of green. Spruce forests and islands set in glassy lakes, water sparkling and dancing off the rivers alongside. More waterfalls cascading into emerald lakes. Wisps of mist weaving on majestic rock face. A narrow winding road lined with wildflowers at the foot of the solemn mountains. She could only look at the beauty of the breathtaking magnificence and thank *He She They It* with all her heart.

Thank you for bringing me here, thank you.

She couldn't wait to get started on her sky series.

"Unremarkable?" she said, "I'm burning the book. It simply couldn't get more remarkable than this."

Phoebe, eyes closed, pretended to be asleep.

They traveled through beauty from Prince Rupert to Prince George and then went on to Vancouver. Benny was approaching her final destination.

INTO THE WEST SHE CAME

Well, she'd made it. They rolled into Vancouver at the decent hour of noon and Benny sat back in triumph and gave herself a congratulatory self-hug as she crossed the finish line.

It was the 72nd Day of her Grand Canadian Adventure. She had traveled over ten thousand miles by bus, train and ferry, and a total of 11,998 miles including flights. She had started her trip on the 15th of June and it was the 25th of August.

She had thought of adding Victoria to the trip, so she'd have the total east to west of Canada covered, but since Vancouver had always been the goal, she stuck to that.

She and Phoebe got off the bus, stiff-legged and stiff-necked, and hailed a cab. They checked into their hostel, feeling somewhat disoriented. While Phoebe wasn't happy with their accommodation, Benny was cheerful, having seen and stayed at much worse. She was delighted to have a bed, any bed. She lay down on the hard, unforgiving foam mattress, thinking she'd died and gone to heaven. She slept for four hours and woke to find Phoebe propped up on one elbow, flicking through an old magazine.

"Tell you what," Benny said, yawning. "Let's have a shower and go and have a spiffy dinner. What do you say? Up the top of the tower?" She wished Chrystal were with her instead, daring, delightful Chrystal with her sack full of scathingly brilliant ideas.

Phoebe grunted at the idea. Benny had no idea why Phoebe was even doing this trip or what had happened to the happy little Brit she'd first met. "Well, whatever, Phoebe. I'm going to get myself a great meal, and celebrate the grand finale of this incredible journey. But first, I'm going to shower."

She grabbed her towel and went to the washroom, where, standing under the steady stream of deliciously steamy hot water, she suddenly remembered something.

Eli.

She stopped, one hand soaping her armpit. *Eli.* The reason for this trip in the first place.

Benny started to laugh. She slid down until she was sitting on the shower floor, oblivious to the grout, the fungus and all the other things that had worried her across the thousands of miles she had traveled. She laughed until hot tears mixed with the water coursing down her face.

Dear sweet Eli. What had she been thinking? A gentle and lovely boy who'd saved her from loneliness and wakened her to life. It was him she had to thank for this trip and yes, he was Prince Charming to her Sleeping Beauty when she needed him the most, but like the fairytale lover, he had no place in the real world. He'd revived her with soft kisses and the scratch of his scraggly goatee. He was a fantasy lover when it was all she could manage and he'd asked no more from her than she could give. But he was a boy, an innocent, on a different path in life, certainly not her happy-ever-after, whoever that might be.

She dried herself and brushed her hair, realizing she was in need of a dye job.

"Your mousy roots are showing, Bertha Gertrude," she told her reflection in the mirror and found this hilarious.

"I think I'm a bit giddy," she said to Phoebe when she got back to their room.

Phoebe was lying on her stomach, reading a guidebook and she rolled over.

"Bus fever," she said. "Like cabin fever, only bus fever might be incurable. It says so right here in this book. If person succumbs to bus fever, you must drown said person, just like you would a litter of unwanted puppies." She waved the book at Benny. "Actually, it says there's lots for us to do here, I don't even know where to start."

"Well, I know I said dinner but I've got something I've got to do first, okay? Can you wait for a bit?"

"Take your time, I might go back to sleep or go and grab a McDonald's. I tell you, if I never see a bus again in my life, it'll be too soon."

Benny laughed and pulled on her shoes. "See you later," she said.

SUPERWOMAN GRANNYHERO

Benny stopped at a convenience store and bought a $20 calling card. Then she phoned home.

A beeping filled her ears and she wondered if she had got the numbers right. Then she heard her mother's voice.

"Hello?" Mum sounded asleep, confused.

"Mum? It's me, Benny. I'm sorry Mum, I've got no idea of the time. Did I wake you?"

"Benny, luv!" Her mother's delight resounded down the phone. "Harry, listen to this luv, it's Benny. Wake up luv, hurry up and get on the extension. She's calling long distance."

"It's okay Mum, I got a phone card. We've got lots of time. Listen, did I wake you?"

"Ah, no worries anyway luv. We'd always rather hear from you than sleep, you know! Besides, it's Sunday, and your Dad's got the day off, so we're going to go and do a bit of shopping and whatnot. Harry? Harry? Are you there? Did you pick up yet?"

"Yes, Cath, I'm here, no need to shout, luv, I can hear you. Benny my girl, how are you?"

"Yes, Benny luv, how are you?" They both spoke at the same time, Mum's gravelly voice and Dad's tobacco-rich timbre.

Benny laughed and tears filled her eyes. "I'm fine, really I am. Listen, how are you two? Are you both still working so hard?"

They both started to answer at the same time and Benny laughed again.

"Ah, you know," she said. "I missed you so much." Her voice choked up. "I missed you so much." She hiccupped, and her sobs escalated until she was crying full force.

"Benny, you all right luv? What's wrong?" Mum was concerned.

"Leave her a bit Cath, she's tired, that's all. Been on a bloody bus for ages, the girl's tired that's all."

"Yes, I know she's been on a bus, Harry, you don't need to tell me that, I only want to know if something else's going on. A mother's got a right to ask, you know."

They chattered back and forth while Benny cried loudly. She leaned against the glass booth with her head down, her nose running, sobbing her heart out.

"Should we phone her back, Cath?" Dad was worried. "What's the number? What if we get cut off? Cath, have you got the number, luv?"

"Of course I haven't got the number, Harry. She's calling from a tickey phone, she said she's got a card. Benny luv, should we phone you back?"

Benny tried to swallow, slow down and regulate her breathing. "No," she managed, "lots of time left. Listen, let me blow my nose okay? Don't go anywhere, and don't worry, I'm fine. I just miss you so much, that's all, I miss you so much."

Which threatened to set her off again, her crying jag seeming endless. Somehow odd memories were assaulting her from nowhere: Mum baking lopsided Rice Crispie treats late into the night for a bake sale, with Benny watching anxiously from her spot on the linoleum floor – Benny, worried the squares would fail, that no one would buy them, and everybody would laugh at Mum. She had wanted to tell Mum not to worry, she'd just say that Mum had been too busy to bake, that it didn't matter. And then, worrying all day that no one would buy Mum's treats – her wonky-looking, soft-in-the-middle squares.

Or Mum, coming home from a long day of cleaning to sew Benny's name into her school uniform, her hands swollen from bleach. Or the way Mum's knee-highs always seemed to have a ladder down to her right ankle. Why it was always the right ankle, Benny never understood. And the way Mum unfailingly put three pink curlers into the back of her hair the very minute she got home – to give her head some height, she said. And the seahorse necklace she always wore, with a tiny emerald eye, the gold plate wearing off the seahorse's body from Mum grasping it whenever she heard some gossip or when she was worried about something.

Standing in the phone booth, her head down and her face wet, Benny remembered being six years old, in her green dragon pajamas, and she and Shay were colouring-in at the kitchen table while Mum did the dishes and Dad watched TV in the living room. Then Mum dropped a dish – it shattered across the floor and Mum leaned on the counter and cried much like Benny was crying now. And Benny remembered that while she'd sat immobile, watching Mum with dispassionate perplexity, Shay had rushed over to hug Mum and Dad came running in.

"What's wrong with Mum?" Benny had wanted to know and both Shay and Dad shouted "nothing," while Mum carried on crying.

Benny, yellow crayon frozen in mid-air, watched Dad and Shay lead Mum out. And then she'd carried on colouring-in, trying to stay in between the lines.

She couldn't say any of the things she was thinking, so she blew her nose loudly and cleared her throat. "So, listen, I've got a grip now. You guys talk to me, what's going on?"

"Cath, you go first," Benny's father said. "Go on."

"Well, not much news from me dear, I got the contract to clean more offices and I've hired even more people! The business is doing quite well, I must say."

"Yeah, your mum's a right entrepreneur now," Dad chipped in. "Business is growing by the day."

"Well, Bens, luv," her mum sounded excited, "I do have the chance to grow it even more but you know, what with Little Harry, I'm so happy to be a granny, to tell you the truth. I do wish you could convince Dad to leave work though. We can afford it now and it's high time he stopped working so hard. You tell him Benny, he always listened to you."

"Ah, Mum, Dad," Benny was crying again, with silent big fat tears stinging her cheeks, "listen, I need to say... I really want you to know, well, I'm sorry, I'm sorry I had to leave. I'm sorry about how I was, after it all happened with my art show and then with Kenny. I'm sorry I was so horrible to both of you. Like it was your fault. You're the best parents in the world, I couldn't wish for any better. And I was so bloody rude, I'm so sorry."

"Bens luv, you were terribly hurt, we knew that," Mum said. "We understood luv, we did, and we would have done anything to make it better, anything. We hated to see you so hurt. You've got nothing to be sorry for."

"But I do, Mum, I do. Even more than just how I was about the art show and about Kenny, I'm sorry for being so stuck-up all these years. I was such a know-it-all, I'm surprised you didn't hate me."

She heard her father laugh. "Benny," he said, "you were only a kid, and you were born to see the finer things, the things we don't. And don't you know how proud we've always been of you? I never stop bragging about you, how fantastic you are. You've got ambition luv, you had it right from the moment you came into this world, yelling like the hospital was on fire. You knew right from the start what you wanted from life, what's wrong with that?"

"Ah, Dad, I was a bitch more often than not and you know it," she said. "And I'm sorry. And I'm so proud of you two, I always have been, I hope you know that." And even if that hadn't been the truth before, it was true now. "And Mum, you too, okay? I love you both with all my heart."

"Benny?" Mum spoke. "Are you okay, luv? I mean it's awfully good of you to phone and say all this but are you okay?"

"I'm fine Mum, better than ever. It's been so interesting, this trip, and you know, I like Canada so much. I don't know why but I feel like I fit in here. But I wish it wasn't so far away from both of you. I mean what's left in Australia for me, except you and Dad and Shay and Harry? So, I don't know if I want to come back home but if I don't, when will I see you again? I feel like for the first time in my life, I don't know what to do."

"Listen, luv," Benny's father spoke, "all we want is for you to live your life to the fullest, whatever that means for you. And wherever you need that to happen is where it must happen. If you stay in Canada, well, hells bells, we'll come and visit you. We got ourselves a book on Canada – a big thick thing and we looked up everywhere you've gone, and I have to say my girl, what a trip, what an adventure! You should be proud as punch. And Mum and I need to travel a bit too you know, get out of Australia and Canada looks fantastic. So, you do what feels right for you, luv."

Benny could hardly speak. "Ah, Dad," she managed. "Dad, thank you."

"Yes, I want to go to Quebec," Mum piped up, "and Prince Edward Island. I always loved *Anne of Green Gables*. I don't think I ever told you that. I used to read you fairytales about the north, you probably don't remember? Stories about how the beautiful snow was like goose feathers being shaken from heaven. Why didn't you go to Prince Edward Island, luv?"

"Couldn't go everywhere, Mum," Benny smiled and wiped her nose on the bottom of her T-shirt. "But hey, we could go there together. That would be something to look forward to."

"Yeah, so you think about it luv. If you want to stay, we'll make it work fine," Mum said. "And now, let me tell you about little Harry," she continued, "I know everybody says this but he is the cleverest baby in the whole world. Although you were very clever too. But little Harry, well…"

And Mum was off, talking nineteen to the dozen about Harry and his antics. Benny, keeping an eye on the time, listened, laughing, not saying much at all until she interrupted her mother with a few minutes left on the card.

"Mum, the card's going to run out soon and I don't want us to get cut off, so let's say our goodbyes now, okay? And I'll phone more often, and I'll figure out the right time. Is Dad still there?"

Mum lowered her voice. "I think he nodded off, luv."

"What time is it there anyway?" Benny asked.

"Just after 7:00 a.m.," Mum said. "My goodness, it's well after 8:00 now. Now, don't you worry about a thing, okay? Oh my Lord above, I nearly forgot to tell you, and I'd better be quick. That woman from the gallery phoned, what – must be about a week ago, we meant to email you about it. Anyway luv, she sold four of your pieces. Four!"

"But Mum, I told her to take them down and that was ages ago."

"Yeah, well, she said something about having a collective exhibit and she couldn't get hold of you, not that she tried very hard mind you, since she got hold of us just fine, but anyway, she put four of your pieces up and they all sold!"

"How much did she sell them for?"

Mum laughed. "$1,500 each! How's that?"

"It's incredible, Mum! I forgot to say, I started painting again on the trip and I've got a whole new collection figured out. It's going to be the Canadian sky series…"

Just then the automated voice broke in, telling them they had one minute left.

"Mum, we must hurry, make sure to give my love to Shay, tell Dad I'll phone at a better time next time, and Mum, you're my SuperWoman GrannyHero, you know that, right? Curlers and all? Knee-highs and all?"

Benny heard her mother laugh and they rang off before the dead air could cut off their happiness.

Benny replaced the receiver. She felt light as a helium balloon but as she stepped out into the busy world, she felt awkwardly alone and out of place.

The trip was over. She knew that. But what came next?

A SCATHINGLY BRILLIANT IDEA

Benny checked the time. It was after 3:00 p.m., and she was ravenous. She grabbed a tea and a sandwich and headed down Hastings Street, looking for somewhere to sit and think. She found a spot on a low stone wall under a tree, and was soon lost in thought.

"'Scuse me, Miss," a woman's broken voice said, startling her. "Can you spare me some change for a cuppa joe? Really need a coffee, you know how it goes."

Benny was startled to see that the woman was hardly more than a girl, but she looked middle-aged, with sunken cheeks, cracked windburned skin and missing teeth. Her hair was filthy bottle blonde with long black roots.

Benny dug out a toonie. "It's all I got, mate," she said, knowing that whatever she gave would never be enough. She watched the girl amble off and stop to share a joke with a skinny bearded fellow dressed in army castoffs.

The girl moved on to cajole a cigarette off a scowling older woman who was lugging a large paper sack and Benny thought how easy it was to take a wrong turn in life – a turn where one thing led to another, and another, until one day you woke up and the face in the mirror belonged to no one you knew, no one you ever thought you'd know.

Benny tried to imagine the girl's day – the endless exhausting scrounging for whatever she could find, driven by her need to get high.

Then she thought about her trip, and how lucky she was to have escaped any real disaster.

She thought back to Eli and how her life had started a slow spin away from normalcy the moment she'd met him. She'd given up her job, and her apartment, and all kinds of stability, lured by the taste of the counter-culture life that she'd seen he subscribed to.

She thought about Mickey and his movie star grin and how he could flick the butt of a cigarette spinning between his forefinger and thumb – she'd thought everything he did was so cool. He had taken her one step closer to loosening her hold on all the things she'd previously held so dear. She thought about their tiny room, lit by the flickering Molson sign, and about them getting high and sleeping on the air mattress, caring about nothing but the immediacy of the moment's pleasures.

Then, with a knot in her stomach, she forced herself to think about Sheldon. She wondered why she hadn't left his apartment and taken a cab to a hotel the moment she'd realized who he really was – it was as if some kind of strange inertia had seized her brain and frozen the natural instincts she'd thought she could always rely on. Sheldon, her brush with malignant darkness.

Benny heard arguing and she saw the girl shouting at an older man with a large balding spot and a long greasy ponytail. One wrong turn too many, and Benny could have been that girl.

She straightened her back against the tree and considered. She realized, with a small measure of pride, that the trip had taught her a couple of things, not the least of which was that she was a survivor. She could have fallen apart after Mickey or Sheldon, but she didn't. She'd gathered herself and carried on.

"I did," she said, out loud. "I carried on. And Sheldon was the sick fucker, not me. I didn't do anything wrong. And Mickey, well, he was electric."

She finished her sandwich, stood and brushed off her trousers.

She walked up the girl and dug out ten dollars from her purse.

"Here you go," she said, and the girl's face lit up. "You have a good day, okay?"

"Oh yeah! Right on, thanks, man, you're an angel, man, an angel!"

Benny knew she wasn't doing a good thing by enabling the girl's addiction but hey, if it helped her have one easier day on the street, then that was okay too.

Benny walked around Gastown, envying the bickering tourist couples who couldn't decide where to go next. She eavesdropped the easy familiarity of their complaints about one or the other walking too fast or too slowly, about who wanted to eat or window shop or stop or not.

Then she made her way to the Prada-paved walls of the Sinclair centre where she bought a half-price Juicy Couture sweatshirt, thinking it was time to retire "Papa"; he'd done his job and done it well. Time to change her clothes and become part of the real world again.

She stopped at an Internet cafe to check her email. She logged on, feeling somewhat vacuous in general and found a job offer from the Toronto agency that Teenie had put her in touch with. A whole job offer with a job description, a great salary, everything. As well as a note to say that they understood Benny was on the move, and not to worry about not replying immediately. She checked the date and saw that the email had only been sent three days previously. She printed out the documents and read her other emails. Shay was happy, things were good, there were lots of out-dated emails from Dad, as well as a note from Teenie and a short, recent note from Chrystal who sounded deeply depressed – she had no idea what to do with her life, her *joie de vivre* had flown the coop, she said. She felt flat as a pancake and wanted nothing more from life than a cave in which to lick her wounds. Did Benny know of any caves? And P.S., she'd ditched the gloves, got bored of the hassle. She was enjoying flaunting her hands and watching people's reactions.

Benny laughed at that. "I've got to go back to Toronto in a week," Chrystal wrote.

> My leave of absence is over, I've got to go back or I'll lose my job. Glum glum glum. Anyways, girlfriend, if you come back to the Greater Toronto Area and don't look me up, well, let me tell you, your life won't be worth a damn! xo Chrystal (who WILL bounce back, just not having a great day … xoxo)

Benny sat for a while, staring at the screen, thinking, chewing her lip and frowning. She logged off, and went for a walk in Chinatown where she bought an ink drawing of a fat little wise owl with one eye shut. It would be the first thing she'd hang in her new home. Then she bought another phone card and dug out her little book.

She dialed the numbers, concentrating carefully.

The cell phone was picked up on the second ring.

"Hello?"

"Chrystal, my dear," Benny said. "This is your best friend, Benny. Now, with regards to getting back your *joie de vivre*, I've just had the most scathingly brilliant idea…"

ACKNOWLEDGEMENTS

Most importantly, endless thanks to my editor at Inanna Publications, Luciana Ricciutelli, because, as my friend Danila Botha says, printed words on a piece of paper are just not the same as a book. And, with Luciana's guidance, the words in this book are now sculpted and finely honed in a way I could never have achieved without her. Thank you, Dear Luciana and everybody at Inanna for this cherished book.

Thank you to Bradford Dunlop for the beautiful cover artwork. Visit www.bradforddunlop.com for more of Brad's lovely images.

Thank you to the following wonderful women for endorsing *West of Wawa*: Laurie Grassi, Book Editor of *Chatelaine*, Ava Homa, author of *Echoes from The Other Land*, Nikki Rosen, author of *In The Eye of Deception*, Amy Lance (Wondrous Women Worldwide) and Danila Botha, author of *Got No Secrets*.

Many thanks to my dear friends: Sandra Gayle, inimitably creative and fabulous, thanks to Nancy Ceneviva and Andrea McBride, thanks to authors Ava Homa, Dawn Promislow, and Danila Botha for encouragement, feedback and other crucial writer stuff. Thanks to Kristin Jenkins, Jennifer Brown, and Jennifer Schramm for being good friends and quite simply for being who they are.

Thanks for my YouTube book trailer to Bonnie Staring (for the words and for her great sense of humour and writing-angst camaraderie).

Thanks to all my friends who listened to me chatting about Benny and her exploits over dinners and emails – while they were discussing real life issues, I was telling them about my imaginary friends.

Thanks to my family for unfailing love and support: to my sister for having such a great sense of humour and for being so Mont Blanc in her approach to life, to my Dad for always believing in me as a writer, and to my Mom for her love, and from whom I have inherited creativity and stalwart determination in the face of challenging times.

I thank my husband, my lovely Bradford, for his patience and his creative insights into my work – Benny is largely who she is because we "found" her together – with discussions on roadtrips, over dinners, and even on our honeymoon.

And I dedicate this book to Snowflake Chrystal Candy, my superb, magnificent cat who lost her mind. Snowflake sat on my lap while I wrote the very first draft of *West of Wawa*, some seven years ago, and she ate my Timbits and got in the way of the keyboard. And I miss her every day.

Originally from South Africa, Lisa de Nikolits has been a Canadian citizen for eight years and has lived in Canada for eleven. She has also lived and worked in the United States, Australia, and Britain. She has a Bachelor of Arts in English Literature and Philosophy from the University of the Witwatersrand in Johannesburg. As an art director, her magazine credits include *marie claire*, *Vogue*, *Vogue Living*, *Cosmopolitan*, *SHE* and *Longevity*. Her first novel, *The Hungry Mirror*, was published by Inanna Publications in 2010 and was awarded the IPPY Gold Medal for literature on women's issues in 2011, as well as long-listed for the 2011 ReLit Awards. She currently lives and works in Toronto.